THE APPLE KING

A Novel

BARBARA ANNE KING

Book Cover Design by Jenny Q, Historical Fiction Book Covers

Disclaimer

To the Croatian colony in Watsonville, California, and my children—Alexander, Natalie, and Jared.

AUTHOR'S NOTE

The concept for The Apple King was the result of serendipity. It happened in June 2019 during my book signing for *The California Immigrant* at Kelly's Books in Watsonville. A woman approached me and asked if I was familiar with *Blossoms into Gold*, a history of Croatians in Pajaro Valley. Since I was not, she retrieved it from the shelf and took me through a few pages. Then she disappeared before I learned her name, leaving the book on the table. At the end of my event, the book was still there. Rather than return the book to the shelf, I purchased it. That evening, as I read the history of Croatian pioneers, a story emerged which captivated me. And I discovered that my great, great uncles were patriarchs of the colony. My personal connection moved me to tell the story of a Croatian immigrant who helped turn Watsonville into the Apple Capital of the World. But after more research, I realized that was only part of a much larger story—one of global significance.

After finishing *Blossoms into Gold*, I contacted co-author, Donna Mekis, to discuss her book. Donna referred me to *The Slav Community of Watsonville, California,* which is a collection of newspaper clippings about local Croatians during the turn of the Twentieth Century. I found the pdf online and culled through over eight hundred pages of entries, offering a glimpse of life in those bygone days. Near the midway point, I learned the Austrian Counsel, a Slav from Slovenia, had come to town to discuss the situation in the Balkans. On his heels, several prominent speakers followed, urging local support for a Jugo-Slav state. The Croatian colony in Watsonville played a significant role in its creation. But who knew? This seemed to be a piece of lost history. And it changed the theme of my story from an immigrant who makes good to one who uses his wealth and influence to win freedom for his fatherland.

This is my second historical fiction novel about events in my hometown. I stand in awe of all that occurred there during the first half of the twentieth century. It is my hope *The Apple King* will give Croatians new pride in our compatriots' accomplishments. And that readers everywhere will find inspiration in this amazing story.

PROLOGUE

Freedom is not sold for all the gold in the world. Those are the words
inscribed on the entrance to Fort Lovrijenac (St. Lawrence
Fortress), which protects the city of Dubrovnik, formerly known
as Ragusa. Dubrovnik is at the southern tip of Croatia, sitting
high above the Adriatic Sea, surrounded by oaks from which it
derives its name. It was one of the most prosperous cities in
Europe, a cosmopolitan mercantile republic that had a self-
government and social system so enlightened it abolished slavery
in 1416. Lord Byron dubbed Dubrovnik the Pearl of the Adriatic.
When the Mediterranean sun shines, setting its limestone walls
aglow, Dubrovnik reigns as the jewel of the Dalmatian coast.

During the Middle Ages, Dubrovnik was a trading power-
house that practiced clever statecraft, allying with various
nations to preserve its freedom. Both Europe and the Ottoman
Empire had seen the advantages of an independent Dubrovnik
to balance the ambitions of the Venetians—earning it the name
City of Seven Flags. But its ships flew only one flag—Libertad.

Ragusa sent its favored sons abroad to be educated in the
best schools and when they returned, they added their knowledge of the world to Dubrovnik's form of government which was
already ahead of its time with a free public health system, public

pharmacy, one of the first orphanages, and a quarantine system to prevent the spread of the plague and other diseases. After freeing itself from one hundred fifty years of Venetian control, Dubrovnik prospered in freedom until 1808, when Napoleon conquered it by trickery and annexed Dubrovnik to the Kingdom of Illyria. With the help of Britain and Austria, Dubrovnik regained its freedom, only to lose it in 1815 to the Austrian Regime.

For generations, Nikola Markovich's family had lived in the village of Cilipi in the municipality of Konavle in the county of Dubrovnik, less than fifteen miles from the city of Dubrovnik. Nikola had been raised on the lore of Ragusa's fabled past which developed in him a patriotic pride rooted in his soul. However, the situation in Dubrovnik and all Croatia had deteriorated under the Austrian Regime. The people had become poor, uneducated, and desperate for a better life. First sons, the inheritors of the land, stayed, while second sons sought their future elsewhere, most commonly America, the land of the free, a country that shared Croatians' most cherished value—liberty, a value they would fight for, even to the death.

In 1881, this is the situation when Nikola Markovich contemplates his future.

CHAPTER ONE

Nikola struggled to catch his breath. The hot, stuffy hall of the Church of St. Nikola, filled with sweaty bodies and smells from roasted meats and seafood, was threatening to suffocate him. He had just danced three kolos at his sister's wedding reception and needed a breath of fresh air. Outside on the porch, he found his older brother, Ivan, in the midst of a smoke.

Ivan looked up when he heard the door open. "Nikola, sit down and share a cigarette with me."

"In a moment. I need some air first." A lock of Nikola's sandy hair fell across his sweaty brow, highlighting his green eyes, the color of jade. He brushed the hair back as he opened his jacket to cool off. His damp shirt clung to the muscles of his broad chest as it expanded with each intake of air.

"All right, have it your way." Ivan paused, lighting a cigarette, as he waited for Nikola to recover.

Ivan and Nikola bore a strong resemblance to each other, except for one thing—Ivan got the bulbous nose. He also sported a walrus mustache, which Nikola had not yet been able to grow. Otherwise, their similar familial traits left no doubt they were brothers.

"I've been wanting to ask you about your plans."

Nikola took a couple of breaths before answering. "Go to California, like a lot of other Croatians before me." He paused for a couple of inhales. "The Gold Rush is over but I've heard there are other ways gold can be found."

"I think you'd be smart to get out of the country. War is brewing. You're almost seventeen—you might be conscripted. That Timok Rebellion was just the spark of it."

"How they ever got the Serbian army to fire on their own brethren is beyond me."

"Money. Isn't it the root of all evil? People sell their souls for money, and certainly those soldiers did. You know the world has gone to the devil when a Slav turns on a Slav."

The church bells rang out. "Midnight," Nikola said. "Time to cut the cake."

Ivan stood and crushed his cigarette butt under his heel. "Let's go grab a piece before it's gone."

When they returned to the hall, Ana and Dmitry stood behind the three-tiered wedding cake, a silver knife clasped in their hands. Ana's long golden hair highlighted her pretty face, glowing in happiness. Nikola thought his sister had never looked lovelier in the lace gown their mother had fashioned for her. Nor did Dmitry ever appear more handsome in a dark suit that blended with his dark, striking features. Together, the bridal couple made the first slice through the white frosting, cutting a marzipan rose in half. Nikola winced. One less rose. Then they made a second slice, slid out a piece and each took a bite. That symbolic gesture was an important tradition. No Croatian wedding would be complete without a cake meant to bring good luck to the couple and the guests. Nikola always looked forward to his piece with great anticipation. The trick was to make sure he got a marzipan rose on it—the almond paste confection he could die for.

His mother had taken over the cake cutting and when it was Nikola's turn, she presented him with an extra-large piece with not one but two roses. She knew how to please him, and Nikola understood that this was to be one of her last gestures of love before he left—possibly forever.

Nikola took the plate and returned to his seat to savor every last morsel. After he finished, he surveyed the room filled with family and friends. He would miss his family, especially his favorite brother, Francis. But also, Ivan, who was destined to remain, because he was the family heir. The law of primogeniture tied him to the land and its hardscrabble life. In these times, the blessing had turned out to be a curse. The lucky ones could leave to seek their fortunes elsewhere. And that was what Nikola intended to do. He hoped Francis would follow him out to California and later Luka and Gabe, too. But his sisters, Marija and Dora, would have little choice but to stay and, if lucky, marry a first son.

The wedding lasted until the wee hours of the morning when the couple left for the groom's home for their wedding night. Nikola stood near the door until every guest departed as he said his last goodbyes. These neighbors had populated his entire life. But in a few days, they would be only memories, never to be seen again unless a turn of fate brought him home. But he'd never forget them.

The musicians picked up the rear, carrying their folk instruments with them—an accordion, a bagpipe, and the tamburica, a long-neck lute. Nikola caught wind of the tamburica whispering as she passed, "Always carry our music with you, and always remember the melody of Croatia, your Slavic homeland."

A week later, Nikola kissed his mother and sisters farewell and shook hands with his brothers, especially Ivan, who he left with his parting words, "You're the heir of the family, the keeper of our legacy. May you prosper as much as I hope to."

Ivan gave Nikola a big bear hug. "Godspeed."

Then Nikola climbed into the carriage with his father and brother, Francis. He glanced at the horses, noting they seemed in good spirits, a sign the ride would not take too long. If they were lucky, they would make the port of Gruz in less than four hours. Then it would be a short sail across the Adriatic to Venice, followed by trains to Le Havre. Nikola had a few hours to spare in Venice where he would explore the kingdom of his enemies. For centuries, Venetians had tried to conquer Croatia to take control of its coastline and did so one time. Venetians were superb sailors, like the Croats, and Nikola wanted to judge them himself.

They passed Dubrovnik on the way. Nikola gave the city he loved one last salute and kept watch as it receded into the distance. When they arrived at the port of Gruz, it was teeming with passengers lined up for the ships. Nikola reached back to grab his suitcase and bounded out of the carriage. His father handed Francis the reins as he held onto his straw hat and dismounted, reclaiming them while Francis jumped out.

Nikola knew he might never return to Croatia, depending on his new course of life in America. He took in a deep breath to bolster himself as he hugged his father, perhaps for the last time. He gave Francis a hug, and he whispered in his ear, "Remember, you promised to join me in California in a couple of years. I'm going to hold you to it. Together we will accomplish great things." Then Nikola shook Francis' hand as he nodded in agreement.

His father clasped Nikola's hand before he left. "Find your countrymen first thing. They will help you. And you can always trust them, besides."

Nikola locked eyes with his father, imprinting his image onto his memory. His father's face bore the ravages of a life lived without luxury. Yet, his limpid green eyes and wide smile brightened his appearance. As Nikola squeezed his father's hand in agreement, he felt the measure of the good man he was, the good father he had been. Then he turned away, moving toward the end of the line.

As Nikola took up his place, his gaze surveyed the other

passengers. Not all appeared to be headed for America. From the conversations he overheard, some were traveling to Venice on business or family visits. He also spotted young men, like himself, who he assumed were making the Atlantic crossing. No doubt there would be competition among his fellow Croats for jobs once he got to California. But Nikola had confidence in himself. In addition, he was blessed with a big, strong body that had known hard work. Besides helping his father tend the grapevines, he earned a few kuna at the port unloading cargo. With several ports on the Adriatic, Croatians had an active trade with neighboring countries. That was the only way they could survive since they could not make or grow everything they needed for themselves. Ports always needed extra men who could handle the heavy lifting. The port of San Francisco would need some, too. Besides a job, scuttlebutt around the port might prove useful.

At last it was time to board the sailboat for Venice. Nikola had never been far from home, so passing through Croatia's island chain, at last count over a thousand, was a real adventure. Nearby Korcula was one of the most beautiful and famous—it was the first place in the world to abolish slavery in 1214 and was believed to be the birthplace of Marco Polo. Although Venetians and Croatians disputed his birthplace, Venice's claims to his resting place were unchallenged. Nikola was a great admirer of Marco Polo who had a wanderlust that appealed to young men like himself. *I will try to find the Venice church to pay my respects to Marco Polo and ask that he watch over my travels.*

As Nikola's imagination soared with the new sights and sounds he was about to experience, he spotted an island that fit the description of Korcula, a stone wall protecting the Old Town. Then strong wind filled the sails, moving the ship at top speed, Korcula left in its wake. The ship made its way toward Split and the island of Brac, the largest Dalmatian island a short distance from the mainland. Nikola knew nothing about Brac, but he'd heard that Split had once been the site of Diocletian's palace and the modern city was built within the ruins. Perhaps they were not just preserving history but also trying to preserve themselves with walls that had been an age-old source of security.

Nikola sat back to enjoy the view and the beautiful spring day, sunny with a scant cloud in the sky. While his eyes were busy, he tried to keep his ears tuned to conversations around him, an attempt to pick up helpful information for his travels. The crew prepared for arrival as it slowed the boat's speed, reefing the sail. Nikola's first sight of the lagoon was astonishing, filled with boats following a traffic pattern that made no sense, unless you were Venetian. It appeared the crew knew its job as they called to each other in the Italian tongue. Choppy waves filled the lagoon, tossing boats to and fro, the sailboat among them. Without warning, a gondolier lost control, heading on a direct course for them, but the crew made a quick tact, averting disaster.

Despite the obstacles and rough water, the sailboat made it safely to the dock for passengers to disembark. Nikola hurried off the ship to explore Venice, not wanting to waste even a minute of his extra time. As he walked down the plank, he asked a crew member the way to the Church of San Lorenzo in his best Italian dialect. Although he had been understood, the words that shot out of the sailor's mouth were almost unintelligible. He shrugged, and the man pointed in the direction. Nikola would have to ask someone else for better guidance. Nevertheless, he put one foot in front of the other until he reached San Marco Square and the Basilica di San Marco, striking him with awe as a clock chimed out the hours. He would have to hurry if he wanted to find Marco Polo's tomb and arrive at the railroad station on time.

Racing over bridges and through alleyways, Nikola came upon the Church of San Lorenzo in record time. It was a simple, humble church—not at all where he expected the great Marco Polo to rest. He climbed the steps to the door and turned the handle—it was locked. As he turned around to leave, three ruffians appeared out of nowhere, menacing looks on their faces. Nikola felt adrenaline surge. He stood tall and pulled back his shoulders in a show of strength which he hoped would deter any mischief they might be up to. They taunted him as he tried to pass, grabbing for his suitcase. Nikola realized he had to do something before the situation went from bad to worse and the thieves made off with his belongings.

At the crucial moment, a priest appeared who yelled at the scoundrels while he raised his cane, prepared to strike. The trio did not stick around for a thrashing. Nikola bowed his head before the priest to thank him while he made the sign of the cross. "You may need my blessing to protect you in your travels. Good luck."

Nikola nodded, grateful for both the blessing and the narrow escape.

He arrived at the Santa Lucia railway station with only a few minutes to spare. After checking the board for the platform number, he ran until he reached the train. There were still seats available, and Nikola took the first one in his line of vision. He stowed his luggage on the rack above and settled into his seat. The engines revved up and, with a jerk, the train moved down the track. It was still daylight, the sun highlighting the country-side for Nikola to take in the show. He was moving farther and farther away from Croatia, the land of his birth, the land that he loved. He would miss it and his family, although they would abide in his heart forever. But the one thing he would not miss was the heavy hand of the Austro-Hungarian Regime that oppressed the people. He had a chance to change his family's future. With that thought in mind, he took a vow...a vow he would honor with his life.

The conductor appeared, asking for his ticket. "Change in Milan."

When the train pulled into the station, Nikola got out of his seat and reached for his suitcase. Passengers brushed by him, pushing and shoving toward the door. Nikola hurried into the main station to check the departure board. Platform 24. He checked the platform number closest to him. Eight. It was a long walk, so he had to make haste. He arrived out of breath and entered the first open door.

The train was crowded on the Milan to Paris route. Nikola walked through several cars before he found an empty seat next to a middle-aged man with his nose in an Italian newspaper. Nikola greeted him as he stowed his suitcase. The man did not look Italian nor French. *God help me if I've sat next to an Austrian.* Nikola tried not to disturb him.

When the man finished reading, he offered the newspaper to Nikola.

"No, thank you," he said in Italian. Nikola could scarcely read, even in Croatian, because there had been few schools available.

"You speak Italian, but you're not Italian."

"That's right. I'm Croatian. From Cilipi, near Dubrovnik."

"Where are you headed?"

"To America. I plan to make my fortune there."

"Well, I wish you luck."

"Thank you. I plan to work hard, but luck will certainly help."

The man turned away and pulled out a book.

Nikola looked around at the other passengers on the train. Many appeared to be businessmen from Milan. They were all reading, and if not reading, writing. *These people are a cut above most Croatians. If I'm to make it, I need to go to school. It's a pity there wasn't an opportunity to get an education in Croatia. But that was just one of the many ways the Austrians kept us down.*

When the train arrived at the Paris station, passengers rushed to get off, heading for connections or transport into the city. Nikola wished he had time to explore the City of Lights,

where the French Revolution occurred. Instead, he reviewed the
Le Havre train schedule and made his way to the platform. This
time, the train was less crowded, and he found a seat next to a
gentleman who was sound asleep. Nikola closed his eyes, hoping
that sleep would overtake him, too. If so, he would arrive
refreshed, ready for the next leg of his long journey.

Nikola didn't stir until the train wrenched to a stop. He
looked over at his seatmate, who was still sleeping but not snoring. *That's odd.* He leaned in for a closer inspection. The man was
not breathing either. He touched his hand—an icy chill shot
through him. Nikola pulled himself back. *What should I do? If I
report the dead man, they might think I killed him. Or at the very least
detain me for questioning.* Then something caught Nikola's eye. It
was the man's wallet, poking out of his pants pocket. A thought
crossed his mind. He dismissed it, and then it crossed his mind
again. *If I don't take it, someone else will.* Nikola blessed himself and
said a quick prayer for the man's soul as he reached for the
leather wallet and scrambled out of his seat to merge with the
crowd. He picked up his step until he reached the terminal
where he broke into a run for the exit.

As soon as he could, Nikola stopped to catch his breath out
of the public eye. He examined the wallet, recognizing genuine
leather from its touch and smell. Nikola opened it and thumbed
through the contents. *Sweet Jesus. There's a small fortune in krone
notes. And an Austrian passport.* Hearing footsteps, he stuffed the
wallet into his jacket pocket, but not before glancing at the
man's name. Izidor. A name not easily forgotten.

Nikola checked his ticket to verify the ship's name and
departure time. He walked along the port in search of SS *Le
Bretagne*, a behemoth of a ship, looming in wait of its cargo and
crew. A line had already formed. In a few minutes, it moved and
a short time later, Nikola had worked his way to the front.

A crew member took his ticket and welcomed him aboard.
Another crew member directed him to the steerage section in
the bowels of the boat. Nikola claimed a lower bunk, throwing

his suitcase on top. Then he headed back up to the deck to await departure. Once he heard the engines revving, he knew there would be no looking back. It was full steam ahead across the Atlantic to New York City, his first stop in the land of the free. Nikola was both excited and anxious about the unknown world ahead. But others had gone there and come out on top, so why not he? All it would take was patience and a lot of hard work.

CHAPTER TWO

Two and a half weeks later, *Le Bretagne* reached New York Harbor. The ship first pulled up to the dock and let all the Americans off. Then it traveled to the tip of Manhattan to Castle Garden, the immigrant processing center, and released the remaining passengers. Nikola took his place in the long, slow-moving line until it was his turn.

The agent scrutinized his Austrian passport and scanned his body from head to toe before passing him on to the medical examiner. Nikola had no worries—he was healthy and fit. He realized he had overcome every obstacle when the last agent said, "Welcome to America."

"Which way to the ferry?" Nikola asked.

The agent shrugged.

He repeated the question in Italian.

"Now, I understand." He explained the directions in rapid Italian with enough gestures that ensured Nikola would not get lost.

He arrived in time to catch the last ferry bound for Jersey City, and his muscles relaxed. As the ferry neared the shore, his anxiety rose again. The transcontinental railroad, connecting the eastern and western United States, would be the last leg of his journey. *Once I'm on the train, I'll be home free. California, here I come.*

Passengers pushed and shoved in their rush to get off the ferry. Nikola pulled his shoulders back and chicken wings up to hold his own in the crowd. Once on solid ground, he turned his eyes left, then right. *Which way to the train?* He asked a ferryman who was tying the boat to the dock. The man grunted while holding a cigarette between his teeth and pointed the way.

That's all the information Nikola needed to find the train station, running at top speed to get there. He could only afford a third-class ticket, which meant traveling time would be almost three times the four days it took for first-class passengers since third-class coaches had to stand aside for freight trains to pass.

Nikola had to wait several hours for the next train. In the meantime, he paraded around the waiting area in search of an empty seat.

A man reading a newspaper looked up as he passed and called out to him in Italian. "Aren't you the young man I met on the train to Paris?"

Nikola stopped and turned toward the voice, noticing the navy pinstripe suit before he glimpsed the face. He appeared to be his seat companion on the train from Milan to Paris. "I believe I am, sir."

"Then it looks like we will be traveling together again."

"Perhaps, but the one thing I know for sure is we won't be sitting next to each other. Unless, of course, you want to risk soiling your suit in a third-class boxcar."

The man gave Nikola the once-over, taking in his shabby jacket, baggy trousers, and scuffed-up shoes. "How far are you going?"

"All the way across the continent to San Francisco. That's my goal—where I'll make my fortune."

"Fortune, eh? Haven't you heard the Gold Rush is over?"

"There's still gold to be found from what I've been told, if only you work hard and, of course, luck is on your side."

"You should make a success of yourself if you're not afraid of hard work. San Francisco is full of immigrants—you'll not be alone. As I recall, you're Croatian."

"Officially, I'm Austrian. At least, that's what my passport says. But I'm Croatian by blood."

"Then you'll find a lot of compatriots in the city. In fact, the waterfront is lined with coffeehouses, restaurants, and greengrocers all owned and operated by Croatians. They'll be able to help you."

"Thanks for the tip."

"Do you have work lined up already?"

"No, not yet. But I will try to find a job right away to make some money for my bread."

The man took out a pen and scrap of paper from his satchel and began writing. When he finished, he handed the paper to Nikola. "Here. This is my name and business address. If you need work, I may be able to help."

Nikola looked at the paper. He couldn't read a word, but he knew this piece of paper might be a key to his survival. "Thank you, sir."

The man held out his hand. "Pero Loreto. I know my handwriting is hard to read. The nuns were always after me to do better. The address is 273 Mission Street. It's a main street—not hard to find. Ask anyone for directions."

Nikola smiled. Mr. Loreto appeared to be a successful businessman. He wore a classic navy pinstripe suit and shoes handcrafted of fine Italian leather. His black hair, cut in the fashion of the day, completed the look of a gentleman. Somehow, having this piece of paper from such a man comforted him. "My name is Nikola Markovich. I'm from Cilipi, Konavle near Dubrovnik."

"Dubrovnik...I know it well. My people and yours have been fighting to control it for centuries. But no matter. We're in a new country and we can be friends."

"I'd like that." Nikola continued walking through the station until he found the third-class waiting area. No one was attired like Mr. Loreto, although a few wore threadbare suits, most likely their Sunday best. Nikola had on traveling clothes. His one and only suit was packed away, awaiting church next Sunday and, hopefully, a social hour. Someone had mentioned the Slavonic Mutual and Benevolent Society sponsored get-togethers after Mass, where he could meet other countrymen...and also women. *I'm not ready for a wife yet, but there's no reason not to look.*

Nikola passed the time people watching. The third-class passengers appeared to be a mix of nationalities from Europe, several Croatians among them. He considered approaching a few, but decided against it because he didn't want to get tangled up with the wrong sort. He'd be better off alone until he took the measure of a man and his motives. Although he had heard many tales about the riches in California, he had heard just as many about misfortunes. One man from Konavle had been swindled out of two weeks' wages. Another had his wallet stolen in broad daylight on a busy street. Yet another had been cheated at cards, but he had no way to prove it. Nikola's father cautioned him to stay alert and avoid games of chance. He told him the only way luck can happen was by hard work. The more you work, the more you earn, and the richer you become. That's a fact of life, one that Nikola was banking on.

A line began to form, which Nikola joined. Pushing and shoving ruled the day as desperate immigrants fought their way to seats on hard wooden benches. They squeezed shoulder to shoulder until everyone had a place. Even before the train lurched forward, the car filled with a putrid smell from the passengers' body odor. Nikola suspected most of the men aboard had not bathed since they left home. He hadn't had a proper washing either—only a quick sponge bath in a public toilet. The way they smelled wouldn't bode well for a good job. But employers who hired immigrants fresh off the boat were probably used to it and wouldn't hold it against them.

The train started to move and Nikola felt every inch as the train rocked back and forth on the tracks, more a jarring motion than a lullaby. He wouldn't get a wink of sleep if this kept up. But then he found his eyelids closing as the sandman worked his spell. The tight packing would keep him in place while he snoozed. Even the loud snoring around him couldn't prevent him from sleep.

With a sudden jolt, the train came to a stop, brakes letting out a high-pitched scream. *Where are we? What's happening?* He glanced at the other passengers for a clue. Then the conductor walked through, announcing a wait for a freight train to pass. Nikola only understood the message when the conductor switched to Italian.

The train trudged its way across the plains in the heat of summer. Nikola had grabbed a window seat when a passenger departed, which offered him a view of endless wheat fields that would soon put bread on the tables of those who could afford a loaf. The heat in the car was stifling. Not even a breeze from an open window helped cool the car— the breeze brought with it more heat.

When the train stopped, Indians were waiting to sell their wares. Nikola took a moment to peruse their goods—turquoise jewelry, colorful handmade rugs, and baskets woven out of straw.

Next he sought shade under a nearby oak tree. Nikola had stripped down to his undershirt days ago, which didn't do much to hold down his internal temperature. How he wished for a swim in the Adriatic Sea—something he had always taken for granted. As soon as he reached the Pacific Ocean, he planned to take a running leap into it to cool off and cleanse himself.

Mountains appeared as if out of nowhere—the Sierra Nevada, high and majestic, yet an obstacle to their destination. Nikola had never seen any that compared. Even his train rides across Italy and France did not reveal mountains like these. The engine would have its work cut out for it.

It was slow going, but the train made it through the moun-

tains. Nikola learned Croatians helped build the tracks, along
with other nationalities—especially Chinese who did the most
difficult and dangerous work, tunneling and detonating explo-
sives. Mostly what Nikola knew of Chinese were from the tales
of Marco Polo, who spent seventeen years in Cathay, as China
was called back then. The Chinese must be good builders,
Nikola mused. They built the Great Wall of China and the
Grand Canal. And they were responsible for building much of
the track for the transcontinental railroad. Before the railroad,
California could be reached quicker from China than the East
Coast. Once the Chinese learned of work, they arrived in droves
and built a Chinatown in the city by the bay.

After nearly two weeks, the train pulled into the station—its
last stop San Francisco. As Nikola departed, he swore he would
never ride with peasants again. *I have to make money, there's no
doubt about it. Even in America, it's money that makes a good life.
Freedom can only do so much. It offers opportunity, but unless I seize it,
I'll not be much better off than in Croatia. At least in Croatia, I have
family and friends. But here? Nothing—unless I create it myself.*

Nikola headed straight for the waterfront to find Croatian-run
businesses, and hopefully, a warm welcome. He passed a green-
grocer and Dalmatian restaurant. A Croatian coffeehouse
appeared a few steps ahead. He reached into his pocket to feel
for the change he had been given at the immigration center in
New York and pulled out the coins. *I should be able to buy a cup of
coffee, at least.* Nikola opened the door and proceeded to an empty
table near the window to watch the activity on the waterfront
and take in the view of the bay.

San Francisco Bay was impressive, but on this foggy morning,
the water was gray, reflecting the cloudy skies, a complete
contrast to the brilliant blue of the Adriatic. As foghorns echoed
in the distance, a young waitress appeared with a menu and said
something in English that Nikola did not understand.

"Do you speak Croatian?"

Her face lit up with a smile. "Of course. Let me bring you the other menu."

Embarrassed he could not read other than a few words, Nikola ordered a coffee.

When she returned with the coffee, she also set a plate of fritule on the table. Nikola's mouth watered at the sight of the Croatian pastry, popular at holidays but also at breakfast time. *I could devour this whole plateful in less than a minute.* But he knew he had not ordered them and had not the means to pay for them either.

The girl recognized Nikola's hesitation. She had seen it before on new immigrants' faces, too numerous to count. "They're on the house."

Nikola returned her smile before biting into one. The girl waited at the table for his response. "Delicious. Just what I needed after my long trip. It hits the spot and reminds me of home." Nikola took another bite while the girl continued to watch. "I almost forgot my manners. My name is Nikola Markovich. I come from Cilipi, Konavle near Dubrovnik."

"I'm Lana Babich. My father owns this coffeehouse and I work here to help him."

"The last words my father said to me before I left was to find my people and, here I am, in a Croatian coffeehouse, talking to a daughter of Dalmatia."

Lana laughed, flashing a full set of straight, white teeth. She was a pretty, young woman with long golden hair and bright-blue eyes that sparkled whenever she smiled. "You're in a good place, I mean San Francisco, because there are many Croatians living here. You won't have any trouble finding a community that will help you get settled." Lana turned and headed toward the kitchen. She returned with a middle-aged man with thick gray hair, clear blue eyes, and a bulbous nose who Nikola assumed was her father. "This is my papa, Mateo Babich."

Mateo extended his arm and when Nikola extended his, he

grasped his hand in a tight, bone crunching, squeeze. "Welcome to America, where you can make a success of yourself if you only try."

"That's what I intend to do. My family is counting on me to help them."

"Yes, our poor relatives back in the old country have a hard time of it. I send money when I can, but it's not always easy to do. I have a wife and six children. Lana is the eldest, a true godsend. She works all day without complaint and then goes home to help her mother. We don't know what we'd do without her."

Nikola glanced at Lana and caught her blushing. *She must be shy and finds her father's flattery embarrassing.*

"Enough of my family burdens. You need some friendly advice. The best thing I can do is to point you in the direction of the Slavonic Illyric Mutual and Benevolent Society. There you'll get all the help you need."

"Thank you. How can I get there from here?"

"I will draw you a map. Lana, please fetch me a pencil and paper." Now, with pencil in hand, Mr. Babich went to work. "You are here. You need to go right and walk to the second intersection. Turn right again and you will find the building a few paces up on your right. If you make a left turn, you'll end up in the bay —a sure sign you're headed in the wrong direction."

Nikola looked at the map. "Thank you. This map will be the North Star guiding my way."

"You must come to the Slavonic Society this Sunday to meet everyone and have a good time. There'll be lots of food and music and, of course, dancing. Lana will be there with the family. She's a wonderful dancer. Isn't that right, Lana?"

"If you say so, Papa."

"In case you haven't noticed, Lana is a shy one, humble as a saint. I don't know what we did to deserve such a blessing."

Nikola pulled out the coins to pay the bill, but Mr. Babich waved him off. "Today, it's on the house. Next time, you pay."

CHAPTER THREE

After Nikola departed the coffeehouse, he stopped a minute to gaze out at the bay. The fog had turned to mist, allowing the sun to break through. Then, right before his eyes, a rainbow appeared. *Is it just a coincidence or am I being blessed?* He blinked twice to make sure he wasn't just imagining it, but the rainbow remained whenever he refocused his eyes. *There's supposed to be a pot of gold at the end of the rainbow. I'm about to find out if that's true.* Nikola turned right as he looked at the map again—Mr. Babich had drawn a good one that took him to his destination with no wrong turns or detours.

Nikola took out a handkerchief and wiped the grime off his face. Then he brushed the dust off his clothes and ran his fingers through his hair. He tried to make himself as presentable as possible, but knew he fell short. *I'm probably not the only immigrant they've seen looking like a bum.* He pulled back his shoulders before opening the door and stood as straight as he could. Now, confidence radiated from him. A smile would be the last touch, signaling friendship and good cheer.

As soon as he stepped inside, a young man dressed in a shirt and tie greeted him in Croatian. "Welcome, brother. I'm at your service."

Nikola knew all about Croatian hospitality but did not expect to receive it before he announced himself. "Hello. I'm Nikola Markovich, fresh off the boat from Croatia and the transcontinental train from New York."

"You have come to the right place. We can help get you settled. I'm Leo Horvat. Follow me."

"Horvat? I know some Horvats in Cilipi."

"It's a very common name. There are many of us all over Croatia and here, too."

Leo led Nikola to an office with the name Viktor Horvat on the door. *Must be Leo's father or uncle.*

Leo gave a quick knuckle knock on the door and opened it. A big man with bushy black eyebrows and grizzled beard sat at an oak desk, facing them. "I've got another one for you."

"Another Croat seeking his fortune in California. Please have a seat," Mr. Horvat said.

"His name is Nikola."

"Nikola Markovich."

"Leo, bring this man some coffee and kolache if there's any left, please."

Leo returned in no time and after the coffee had been poured and kolache passed, Mr. Horvat began in Croatian. "You should consider the Slavonic Society your home here in San Francisco. We can help you get set up with housing and a job. On Sundays, you will have a chance to meet other Croats in the area and have a little fun besides. Now, first things first. Work. What can you do?"

"I have some experience at a port. Perhaps I can start by loading and unloading cargo."

Mr. Horvat shook his head. "It's mostly Italians down on the waterfront—fishermen, primarily. You'd have to unload the catch of the day." He took a sip of coffee and paused. "Do you speak Italian, by chance?"

"Enough to get by."

Mr. Horvat wrote a name on a piece of paper. "Here, take

this down to the waterfront and keep your eyes peeled for the felucca *Santa Lucia*. Once you find it, ask for a man by the name of Tony Martino. He'll give you a job, no question about it."

Nikola took the piece of paper and read the name out loud. "Tony Martino."

"He pays by the day which will give you enough wages to get by. There's a boardinghouse down by the port where a lot of Croat men live. I suggest you try there for bed and board. If not, ask Tony for help." Mr. Horvat wrote the name of the boarding-house on another paper. "The Croatian checkerboard flag is posted out front. You can't miss it."

Nikola headed toward the port but stopped by the boarding-house before seeking a job. He knew he would be too tired to find a bed later, and he needed a good night's sleep. He hadn't walked long before he spotted the flag, fluttering in the wind. Nikola entered the boardinghouse where he found a matron in a black work dress standing watch. "Good morning. I need a room."

The woman eyeballed him before answering. "How many nights?"

"A week's worth at least."

"I have a bunk room, ten beds, bathroom down the hall. Will that suit you?"

"Yes, that will be fine."

"Pay now for the first night."

Nikola pulled the coins out of his pocket and set them on the counter.

The woman counted out the amount she needed and left the rest. "You also get breakfast and dinner. Breakfast starts at five in the morning, dinner at six in the evening. Be on time if you're hungry. You missed breakfast today, but if you go around to the kitchen, the cook might have some scraps saved. You can store your suitcase in your room, number thirty-four—up two flights on the left."

Nikola took the stairs two at a time to make it back to the

kitchen before the cook disposed of the leftovers. Hunger ravaged his stomach, and the few pastries did little to fill it. He was in luck. Platters with leftover eggs and burnt bacon sat on the counter while the cook busied himself with the dishes. "I just arrived and was told I could get a few morsels to hold me over until dinnertime."

The cook scowled at him and grunted. He handed Nikola a wet plate and pulled a fork out of the dishpan. "Here, help yourself."

Nikola didn't bother wiping off the plate. He scraped whatever he could find onto it. Then he looked around for a place to sit. Finding none, he stood to eat.

The cook shot him a frown. "Take a seat at the dining table and eat properly."

"Thank you for the food. I appreciate your kindness." Nikola left the kitchen in search of the dining room. Once he was finished, he carried his empty plate and fork back to the kitchen. The cook smiled for once. *I guess he's happy I bussed my own table.*

Nikola felt strong and confident after filling his stomach, and took long strides toward the port. *Mr. Horvat told me to look for a felucca. The port is filled with feluccas. Finding the* Santa Lucia *won't be easy. Maybe I should ask someone to direct me.*

The first few men only gave a shrug while they waved him off. They couldn't be bothered with the new immigrant who was not an Italian. Nikola asked a dozen people before one took pity on him and gave him the information.

He found the *Santa Lucia* tied up at the dock where men were busy offloading the catch of the day. He made a beeline for the boss who he assumed to be Tony Martino.

"So, Mr. Horvat sent you. You appear big and strong. Have you ever unloaded crates before?"

"Yes, back in Dubrovnik, I worked at the port, loading and unloading merchant ships. I know the hard work involved and I am up to it."

"Well, you seem to be able to speak up for yourself. I could use a young buck like you—always can. I pay by the day. But today you're starting late, so you'll only get half wages. In the morning, we start at six. Be here on time and you'll get paid for the entire day."

"You'll not be sorry you hired me." Nikola looked around for a place to lay his jacket. Somewhere it would be safe.

"You can toss your jacket in this bin for now. But I suggest you leave it behind next time because you don't want it stolen. Most of these guys can't be trusted."

Nikola was taken aback. In Croatia, men could be trusted. That was a virtue they practiced faithfully. No wonder his father cautioned him to stick to his own kind.

Nikola got in the mix, and even though the work was hard, it was made easier in the mild weather. He stood on the dock while men handed him one crate after another, which he stacked according to the type of fish it contained. The men became a machine as they did the same task over and over again until it was finally finished. Nikola took one look around at all the crates and wondered whether a wagon was coming for them. And sure enough, one appeared, and the loading continued. Afterward, both the boat and the dock needed to be swabbed. Someone tossed him a mop, and he went to it. Fish always left a stinking mess behind.

At the end of the day, he stood in line with everyone else to receive his wages. He looked at the coins but didn't know if he had received the correct amount. He vowed to learn about the money before someone cheated him. Tonight, at the boarding-house he would search out a Croatian who could teach him. *But at least for now I have a few coins to spend.*

Nikola had some time to spare before dinner. When he got into his bunkroom, he asked if anyone could explain the money.

"Come over here," a man resting in a lower bunk called out. "I'll school you."

Nikola hustled over.

"You see this coin here?" He held up a small brownish-colored coin. "It's made of copper and it's a penny—worth one cent. It's got the head of an Indian on it. There are one hundred of them to a dollar. This is a dollar bill. There are silver dollars, too." He next taught the value of nickels, dimes, and quarters. "Does it make sense yet?"

"Seems to."

"If you ever can't remember, just look at the coin. It has the value on it. The key point is that a dollar is made up of one hundred pennies or cents."

Nikola took his place at the dining table and waited while the benches filled up with men, hungry and tired after a long day of back-breaking work. As soon as everyone was seated, the cook and his assistant brought out the food. First, large caldrons of soup were placed at both ends of the table. The man nearest a caldron did the honors. Soup bowls were passed down the line until each man had one. Tonight's soup was cabbage and potatoes—hearty, nutritious, and satisfying. That was followed by a platter of fried cod, rice, and peas, then chocolate pudding for dessert. There had been plenty of food to go around, and now each man let out a series of loud belches. What better way to show appreciation for a good meal.

The next day was much the same as the last, except for the additional hours. Fewer clouds filled the sky, allowing the sun to heat up the day as men sweated and tempers flared. The least mishap set them off as they cursed and often came to fists. Nikola was glad when the workday ended and he could collect his full day's wages. After the man disbursed his earnings, Nikola moved aside to count the coins.

He was supposed to be paid two dollars. When he counted the money the first time, it appeared to be ten cents short. He counted again. Then, to be absolutely certain, he counted it a third time. Still ten cents short. "Excuse me," he said to the payer, "you still owe me ten cents."

"Don't bother me. Can't you see I'm busy? Next."

"Sir, there's been a mistake. I counted the coins you gave me three times and came up ten—"

"Leave me alone, if you know what's good for you. Next."

"All I need is ten cents and I'll be on my way."

A supervisor stepped up. "Kid, he told you to get out of here. Now, scram."

"I can't leave until I receive my full pay."

"Let's step over here and talk." He grabbed Nikola by the collar. "Get out of here, you dirty Croat, and don't ever come back."

"But he cheated me. Aren't you going to do anything about it?"

"Yeah, I'm about to." He whistled and three goons appeared. "Make sure this guy understands to not make trouble."

Now Nikola got the picture. Not only had he been cheated, but he was about to be taught a lesson. He turned to make a run for it, but the wind caught his jacket and a punk grabbed onto it, pulling him back. The next one kicked him in the groin as he called him a stinkin' Slav. The other kicked his backside until he fell down. "Take that, you barbarian."

Nikola caught a flash of silver. *A knife.* He rolled away and jumped to his feet and ran as fast as he could, leaving the others in his wake. He didn't dare go directly to the boardinghouse for fear they would follow him or stake him out. Instead, he hid until dusk fell, returning too late for dinner. Twice he'd been cheated today—once out of money and once out of food. *No one will ever swindle me again.*

The matron did a double take when he came through the door. "What in the world happened to you?"

"Thugs."

CHAPTER FOUR

Even though he had been hungry, Nikola slept in and missed breakfast. His stomach rumbled as he pulled on his pants and shirt. *Now I have two missions—get breakfast and find a job.* He hobbled down the stairs on the ankle he had twisted the day before.

Mrs. Popovich stopped him. "You owe me some money."

Nikola turned toward her. "I'll pay you tonight." Mrs. Popovich was no fool. She knew Nikola did not have the money, but he hoped she would take pity on him.

"All right then, pay tonight. But your fee includes two meals a day. You missed dinner last night and breakfast this morning. Go ask cook for some leftovers to tide you over."

Nikola saw a kind smile cross Mrs. Popovich's face. She wasn't as much of a hardened matron as he imagined. "Thank you. I'll do that."

With his stomach full, Nikola had accomplished his first goal of the day. *Now to find a job.* He considered returning to the Slavonic Society, but his pride kept him from it. Then he remembered the slip of paper the man on the train had given him, with his name and address. He rummaged around in his pockets until he found it. He pulled out the crumpled piece of paper that still bore Mr. Loreto's name and address. But because he couldn't read and didn't know his way around the city yet, he hadn't a clue how to get there. *I'll ask for help.*

Nikola entered the coffeehouse which was almost empty at this hour, and Lana came up to greet him. "I didn't think we'd see you again so soon."

"Me neither, but I need some help. Can you read?"

"Of course, I can read. Do you need me to read something for you?"

It embarrassed Nikola that he had to ask her for help. But the writing was in English, which Lana knew he didn't yet speak. She might not realize he couldn't read much at all. He handed her the piece of paper.

She looked at it a moment. "Where did you get this?"

"From a man I met on the train."

"Pero Loreto is a very important man in this town. The address on the paper is 273 Mission Street. That must be his business address. His home is on Nob Hill, near the railroad barons."

"I don't know beans about Nob Hill, but I have heard of the railroad barons. What would Loreto have to do with them?"

"He's an attorney for the Southern Pacific Railroad."

Lana's font of knowledge impressed Nikola. "Where do you get your information?"

"I read and keep my ear to the ground. It's amazing what you can pick up that way."

"I need to find Mr. Loreto. Can you point me in the right direction?"

"Let me get my father. He's better at directions than I am, and he can draw you another map."

The route took Nikola right to Mission Street. He walked a block until he came to 273, an impressive office building with an oak door and a brass knocker. Nikola ran his fingers through his hair before knocking, but knew it was a futile attempt to look respectful.

A woman opened the door and asked his business.

"I'm here to see Mr. Loreto."

"What is your name so I can announce you?"

"Nikola Markovich. Please tell him we met on the train to Paris. I'm sure he'll remember me."

"Wait here." She shut the door in his face. He knew she'd be able to get rid of him easier by keeping him on the stoop outside.

The woman returned with a smile on her face. "Sorry to keep you waiting, Mr. Markovich. Please come this way."

Mr. Loreto stood and reached out his hand to shake when Nikola entered his personal office. "It's a pleasure to see you again. What can I do for you?"

Nikola didn't mince words. "I need a job. Can you tell me where I can get one?"

Mr. Loreto studied Nikola before answering. "You look like a strong, young man. The railroad could use you building tracks. Does that interest you?"

"What does that involve? I've never built a railroad."

"First, it would mean moving up north. But I could get you a train ticket."

Nikola recalled what his father said about staying close to Croatians. San Francisco had a large colony and a Slavonic Society besides. He better heed his father's advice. "Many of my countrymen are here. If I leave, I would be on my own in a strange country, not speaking the language."

"Of course. I understand. Did I mention my sister-in-law's Croatian? Her parents had many of the same problems. All immigrants do, including my Italian forbearers."

Nikola relaxed. A broad smile filled his face. "Then we are compatriots of sorts. Where did your sister-in-law's family live in Croatia?"

"Split. The old town inside Diocletian's palace."

"I've heard of it but have never been there."

"Dubrovnik has its wall, and Split has the one left by Diocletian. A city built within a palace is quite something to see. Now, back to your problem. What about the fruit commission house? A lot of Croatians work there, sorting and packing fruit."

"Then I'll give it a try. Thank you."

Mr. Loreto scribbled a name and address on a piece of paper and handed it to Nikola. "Make sure you ask for Milan Vukovich. He's a good friend. My secretary will give you directions."

It was almost noon when Nikola arrived. He entered the building and spotted what appeared to be an office. Once inside, he asked for Mr. Vukovich. He was told to wait for him to come out from the back office. Nikola noticed a large man with a walrus mustache lumbering toward him, holding a cigar in one hand, a drink in the other.

When he reached Nikola, he took a puff and blew smoke rings into the air. "You asked for me? Make it quick. I'm busy."

Nikola swallowed hard. He was not easily intimidated, but his intuition told him to tread lightly around Mr. Vukovich. "I'll not waste your time. Mr. Pero Loreto sent me. I need a job."

"Well, that sheds a whole different light on things. Pero only sends me men who will work hard for their pay. And I noticed you're a Croat, like most of us here. You'll fit in."

Nikola nodded in agreement while he listened.

"I tell you what. Today is almost gone. Why don't you watch so you can become familiar with what we do here. Then show up tomorrow at six sharp."

"Thank you. I'll do that."

"Follow me. I'll introduce you to the foreman who'll assign you to someone who can explain everything."

The rest of the week flew by as Nikola filled his days with fruit packing at the commission house. And he kept Mrs. Popovich happy by paying her on time. By the end of the week, Nikola had a sense of accomplishment and was ready for a day of rest. Opening his suitcase, he pulled out his only suit, made of brown worsted wool, and laid it on the bed to smooth the wrinkles. He took his white shirt out and hung it on a hanger, along with his cravat. Cravats were a Croatian invention, and no self-respecting Croatian ever wore a suit without one. This cravat had the red and white checkerboard on it, patterned after the Croatian coat of arms.

Now for a bath. He hoped there wasn't a line because he wanted to be first in a fresh tub of water.

Nikola wasn't able to smooth all the wrinkles out of his clothes, but they would just have to do. He headed for the Church of St. Francis of Assisi, which he heard was even older than both the city and the state. Croatians held a deep devotion for St. Francis who walked humbly with the Lord, because that was their path as well.

Although they were humble, they were still proud. Before Nikola stepped into the nave, he pulled himself up and threw his shoulders back to display the pride he had in himself as an immigrant to this great country. He marched up the aisle and took his place in a pew near the front of the altar that would enable him to be fully engaged in the Mass. But first he knelt on the riser, made the sign of the cross, and prayed the Hail Mary and Our Father in gratefulness for his safe arrival and good start on his goal. When the Mass began, he stood with the congregation and in Latin sang the entrance hymn, "Be Not Afraid," in his best tenor voice as he internalized the hymn's message. *Be not afraid—* that would be his mantra, a few words to give him courage to face the unknown.

After Mass, Nikola headed for the Slavonic Society, where he had been told he could expect a good social time in the afternoon. When he arrived, he looked around the room and realized he didn't know a soul. He didn't even recognize anyone from the ship or his boardinghouse. But at least the room was filled with music, dancing, food, and, most importantly, his compatriots.

Hunger called, so he headed to the buffet table, laden with an abundance of Croatian specialties. Nikola filled his plate with savory pies and meats, along with a pork rind and egg spread seasoned with paprika, a spice inherited from the Hungarian Regime.

All he needed now was something to drink. He found the punch bowl at the end of the table, filled a glass, and brought it up to his lips for a taste. It was only fruit punch—he had hoped it would be spiked with rakija, Croatia's national drink, which was made from a variety of fruits and herbs.

Nikola took a seat at one of the round tables in the room. He nodded to everyone seated and dug in, making quick work of the tasty morsels that left him wanting more. *No reason to stand on ceremony. Besides, no one knows me, so I won't embarrass them or myself.* He returned to the table with a second helping and smiles from his table mates, who recognized a young man struggling to survive in the new country.

He was about to head back for a third round when someone tapped him on the shoulder. *Don't tell me I'm about to receive a warning from the buffet police.* He turned around to find Lana standing there. Nikola rose to greet her. "You are the first face I've recognized. I'm happy to see you."

"And I as well. Papa wanted me to invite you to join our family."

"I accept your invitation. Lead the way. But first let me clear these plates so the next occupant has a clean space."

Once Nikola arrived at the family table, Mr. Babich stood to welcome him and introduced him to the entire family. Mrs. Babich, a plump woman with hazel eyes and faded blonde hair, was surrounded by her brood. Lana was the eldest of six—she had three brothers and two sisters. Nikola felt at home with the Babiches. They were fun-loving people, and they seemed to have a lot of friends in the room.

He became nostalgic for the family and friends he had left behind only a few weeks ago, yet in some ways it seemed like an eternity. Until now, he had not realized how much he missed them, homesick for the way of life he'd forsaken. He wondered whether he had made the right decision by leaving. Everyone had told him that the streets in America were paved with gold. But, so far, he hadn't seen even a glimmer. Yet the Babiches and their friends were thriving here, which gave him hope that he would, too, one day—one day soon.

The band struck up music for a kolo, the Croatian circle dance. Men grabbed partners, leading them to the dance floor. Lana asked Nikola to dance with her. He took her by the hand and they found a place in the circle. From that point on, Nikola could have danced the rest of the afternoon, as if he hadn't a care in the world.

Lana beckoned Nikola back to the table. "I need a drink of water," she said, trying to catch her breath. "You are quite the dancer. Has anyone ever told you that before?"

"In my village, we are all dancers. You have to be to survive."

When the afternoon ended, Nikola was sorry to have to return to the boardinghouse. But at least dinner would be waiting. After all the dancing, he had built up quite an appetite.

Mrs. Popovich was at her station when he walked in. Eyes fixed on him, she said, "It looks like you've enjoyed your day."

"First church, then dancing at the Slavonic Society. Nothing could be better."

"Hurry and grab a seat. The cook already has the soup on the table."

CHAPTER FIVE

Nikola gazed around the commission house and spotted a man who he had seen there a few times before, wondering who he was. One thing was certain—he did not come to pack fruit. Judging by his attire, he was a businessman. He wore a suit, tie, well-polished shoes, and a pocket watch. To Nikola, a pocket watch separated a workman from a businessman. It was a sign that you had made it and were someone to be respected.

Nikola realized the man had made his rounds of the packing-house and had settled in to observe him. Whoever this man was, he knew he had to impress him if he wanted to move up the next step of the ladder. Nikola examined each piece of fruit before placing it into the packing box, rotating it to expose its best side. Both brokers and customers cared more about looks than taste, so he met their expectations.

A voice broke through the silence. "I'm impressed by your work. In addition, the manager sings your praises. What's your name?"

"Nikola Markovich."

"Karlo Rajkovich. Glad to make your acquaintance. When you're done with work, I'd like to talk. I have a business proposition for you."

"When I'm finished, I'll be at your service."

"Service. I like that. In fact, that's what good business is all about."

A tingle went up Nikola's spine as he awaited his meeting with Mr. Rajkovich. The rest of the day, he could think of nothing else, even though he forced himself to focus on the job at hand. He didn't want to ruin any future opportunities by making a mistake now. The hours dragged by until quitting time. He let out a breath of relief as he was about to learn what Mr. Rajkovich had in mind for him.

He found Mr. Rajkovich waiting out front, just as he had promised. "Let's go up the street to a coffeehouse where we can sit down and talk. It's owned by some friends of mine—they're Croats like us." He smiled at Nikola.

Nikola smiled back and tension seemed to melt between them. A smile always had that effect on him. He had to remember to do it more often.

The coffeehouse was small and cozy—just the spot for a friendly chat over a steaming cup of coffee. "Would you like something to go along with coffee to take the edge off? My eye is on a piece of apple strudel in the glass case."

"Strudel? It's been a long time since I've had any."

Mr. Rajkovich placed the orders with the waiter and made small talk until the coffee arrived. He was a gregarious man, with a head full of wavy, black hair, piercing brown eyes, and a bulbous nose that twitched as he talked. After a bite of strudel, he let out a happy sigh. He was a man who enjoyed food, his girth a testament to it. "So, Nikola—may I call you Nick? It's more American."

"Go right ahead."

"So, Nick, I understand you've only been in San Francisco a short time. How do you like it?"

"Reminds me of Dubrovnik—the sea, the hills, the harbor full of boats."

"Would you be up for making a change?"

"If it's the right opportunity."

"Then I have one for you. I need a foreman at one of my packinghouses down in Watsonville, not far from here. A little Croatian colony has taken hold there, which is continuing to grow. You'd be a real asset to them."

"Watsonville? I think I've heard of it. Some men from Cilipi used to go there to pack apples during the season. They returned with pockets full of money."

"The apple business is just starting to take off there. You could be part of it. Not only do you know the best way to pack, but I've noticed the men look up to you. The sky's the limit."

"I would need some time to decide."

"You have two weeks—that's when I'll be back and expect your answer. Now, I've got to run." He threw some bills on the table. "Dinner's on me."

Nick rose to shake Mr. Rajkovich's hand who clasped it in a tight grip. Then he slapped Nick on the back. "We're Croats. We stick together."

Nick picked up the change as he checked the time on the wall clock. He had missed dinner at the boardinghouse again. Rather than eat alone, he walked over to the waterfront to catch a bite at the Babiches' coffeehouse. After receiving Mr. Rajkovich's offer, Nick wanted some advice, and he felt Mr. Babich would be a superb source, not to mention a person he could trust.

Lana was busy serving other customers when he arrived, but she motioned toward a vacant table in the far corner. Nick glanced over at the next table crammed full of children and recognized Mrs. Babich's face. He stood to greet her and nodded to the children. He caught the middle daughter staring at him as if she had never seen a young man before. When he fixed his eyes on her, she looked away. Lana arrived after this little scene and gave Nick a kiss on each cheek.

It wasn't long until Mr. Babich came out of the kitchen to

wander the floor and check that his customers were satisfied.
"Nikola, what brings you here after a long workday?"
"Dinner, of course. I missed the one at the boardinghouse."
"Then you have to pay twice—not the way to get ahead.
Lana, please take this hungry man's order. After you've eaten, I'll
be back to talk."
Nick scanned the menu, wiener schnitzel catching his eye. It
was one of his favorite meals, even though it was an Austrian
national dish. He ordered it, hoping it wouldn't fall too short of
the wiener schnitzel he remembered back home. The schnitzel
arrived, covering the entire dinner plate it was pounded so thin.
Another plate of side-dishes accompanied it—parsleyed potatoes, cucumber salad, and butter lettuce with vinaigrette. Nikola
blessed himself, thanking God for the food set before him. Then
he took his knife and fork in hand and cut the veal into pieces.
The first mouthful was always the best, and he had only praise
for Mr. Babich's rendition of the dish.
When he came over at the end of the meal, Nick said, "I've
never had a better schnitzel."
Mr. Babich smiled, enjoying the praise. He looked over and
gave Lana a nod. In less than a minute, she was table side with a
large piece of apple strudel. "This is the perfect finish to a veal
dinner."
Two pieces of apple strudel in one day. Apples must be in my future.
"Mr. Babich, I wanted your advice on a business opportunity I
just received."
Mr. Babich pulled out a chair and sat down. "Tell me
about it."
"Do you know a man named Karlo Rajkovich?"
"The name is familiar, but I don't think I've had the pleasure
of his acquaintance."
"He's a fruit broker who visits the commission house. Today
after work, he took me out for coffee and offered me a foreman
position at one of his packinghouses."
"That sounds like it would be a winner. Why ask me?"

"Because I'd need to move a couple of hours south of here."

"If you're talking about Watsonville, I've heard of it, too. A thriving Croatian colony is developing there around the apple industry. Since the thirties, Croatians have come over to pick and pack fruit, but now my sources tell me there are more ways to make money. You should check it out. What have you got to lose? You can always come back."

"You're right. I have nothing to lose and much to gain. Thank you for helping me sort this out."

"As you will learn in life, most decisions are not set in stone. There are always ways to change course if you possess both desire and imagination."

Nick was anxious to give Mr. Rajkovich his answer, but he did not show his face. Day after day, Nick waited until the man finally returned. *Now, should he wait for Mr. Rajkovich to come to him or should he approach Mr. Rajkovich?* He couldn't very well leave his work station until the end of the day, which meant he would just have to bide his time. Nick was concentrating on the apples when he sensed somebody behind him. He turned to find Mr. Rajkovich there.

"I know you can't talk now. Meet me outside when you get finished for the day."

Nick was a bundle of nerves until quitting time. He hoped Mr. Rajkovich's offer was still open, considering much time had passed. *Sometimes you just have to seize the moment—carpe diem—otherwise, you've lost it forever.*

Nick found Mr. Rajkovich pacing while he smoked a cigar. "I've given you enough time. Do you have an answer for me?"

"I accept your offer. When do I start?"

"Let's go grab a coffee and talk over the details."

Mr. Rajkovich snuffed his cigar after blowing out a few rings to impress those within view. Then he ordered coffee and krafnes, a jelly-filled donut without a hole. When they arrived,

Karlo grabbed one and took a big bite. Red jelly oozed out, dripping onto his tie. "That's what cravats are for. Babies have bibs. Men have cravats. The pattern hides stains."

After observing Mr. Rajkovich attack the donuts, Nick took a more subtle approach, even though he was in work clothes, and avoided even one drop on his shirt.

"I see you have a better technique than mine."

"Not really. I just learned what not to do from watching you."

Karlo let out a deep belly laugh. "Yes, a man can be a role model of what not to do as much as the reverse. Glad you already recognize that wisdom. Now, let's get down to it. I recommend you give notice at your job and finish the work week. On Saturday or Sunday, you can catch a train down to Watsonville Depot. Right now, picking is still going on, so that's what you'll be doing until the fruit is ready for packing."

Mr. Rajkovich pulled a sheet of paper out of his suit pocket. "Here. This is the address of the Cullen Ranch. Ask for John Dudich. He'll set you up with a bed in the bunkroom and let you know when and where to get your meals. Gosh, I almost forgot. I took the liberty of buying you a train ticket." Rajkovich handed the ticket to Nick, knowing that he'd have no excuse not to fulfill his promise.

"Thank you for giving me this opportunity. You won't regret it."

"I should think not. I pride myself on being an excellent judge of character."

Nick checked the wall clock and realized if he hurried, he could make it back to the boardinghouse in time for dinner. Mrs. Popovich stood at her station as he whizzed into the dining room, almost bumping into the cook with a cauldron full of soup. "Pardon," Nick said, as he wiped a splash of soup off his shirt.

"Watch where you're going next time. Were you brought up in a barn?"

Nick ignored the cook's remark and took a seat in the middle of the table to avoid him. When Nick received his bowl, he inspected it with a smile—Dalmatian vegetable soup, hearty and tasty. He finished before anyone and looked for seconds, but the cook had removed all the cauldrons. Even so, the cook kept the platters coming—roast chicken, mashed potatoes, green beans, and rice pudding for dessert. All the burping in the room revealed the men were as satisfied as he was.

Now, he wanted to share his good news with someone, and the only person he had any connection with was Mrs. Popovich. But she wasn't at her station when he left the dining room. He'd get up early so he could catch her and give notice on his room at the same time.

The rest of the week seemed to drag as Nick anticipated his move. He wished he wasn't leaving on Sunday because he would have liked one last chance to attend the gathering at the Slavonic Society. He wanted to dance and sing and make merry with his compatriots one last time before setting off. But instead, he would take a lonely train ride to an unknown place, a small town somewhere on the coast. He was thankful it was near the sea and not inland, because the sea provided a sense of comfort, reminiscent of home. But what else would he find there? Mr. Rajkovich had mentioned a Croatian colony. Did they have a Slavonic Society? He doubted the colony would be large and thriving like the one in San Francisco. And what about the other people living there? He had not forgotten the Italians who had called him a dirty Slav and barbarian. He never wanted to hear those names again.

Nick found it difficult to pay attention to work while his mind raced with thoughts of the future. But when he spotted the foreman eyeing him, he knuckled down to his work. He still needed to make money, so he couldn't risk losing his job now. Some apples he picked up were bruised. Setting those aside, he culled through the lot and placed the good ones in the box with their best side up. Not all workers took the time to do that, but Nick already understood how fruit brokers judged a box. Just one bad apple could mean the difference between profit and loss. He took pride in packing a box for profit, even though no one would ever know who had taken the time to do it right.

The foreman came up behind him, grabbing his shoulder. "Keep up the excellent work."

Those few words motivated Nick to do an even better job and brought satisfaction to the workday.

When Nick returned to the boardinghouse, Mrs. Popovich was in the front hall. "I only need a bed for two more nights."

"Two more nights, you say? Are you not happy here? Where will you sleep after that? Can we not entice you to stay?"

Her barrage of questions took Nick aback. He paused a moment to gather his thoughts. "You've been very kind to me, but it is time to move on. I have a new opportunity away from this city."

"Is that so? Tell me about it."

"It's a job as a foreman in the apple business in a small town on the Monterey Bay. I need to find accommodations there."

"Good luck to you then."

CHAPTER SIX

After breakfast on Sunday morning, Nick packed his suitcase and headed down the stairs. He looked around for Mrs. Popovich to say goodbye, but she was missing. He ducked into the kitchen and waved to the cook, who only grunted as he scrubbed the stove. Then he stepped out onto the sidewalk, the warmth of the sun caressing his face.

It was gearing up to be a beautiful day in San Francisco, a rare occurrence—no wind, no fog, no chill in the air. Of course, he'd be on a train where he couldn't enjoy it. But he'd enjoy it while he could. He took a deep breath of the warm air and began his walk to the train station. Every once in a while, he glimpsed the bay filled with sailboats at a standstill, waiting for the wind to kick up.

Nick arrived at the train station with only a few minutes to spare. He felt for the ticket in his pocket and pulled it out. Then he checked the departure board for the track number. Three. He looked around for a nearby track. Twelve. He had a distance to cover to reach his track. Nick put himself in high gear, stretching his long legs into a fast walk, nearly a run. When he arrived at track three, he was the last passenger to board before the attendant closed the door. But the train was not crowded and Nick found an unoccupied seat next to the window. He wanted to take in the countryside to pass the time.

As the train bobbed and weaved, Nick kept his eyes fixed on scenery— stands of redwoods, oaks, and evergreens, giving way to glimpses of lush green fields and the royal-blue Pacific, presiding over California with its majestic presence. The coast-line alternated between white sand and rocky shore that waves crashed upon, sending up a plume of white froth before retreating for another attack. Nick had never seen waves so high and powerful, a mesmerizing force that transfixed him.

Compared to a train trek across the country, this ride was a short one. Nick was only one of two passengers to disembark at Watsonville Depot. A horse-drawn wagon picked up the other man, but Nick was on his own and no one was around to ask directions. However, there appeared only one way to go to reach civilization. He headed away from the ocean toward the Santa Cruz Mountains, bookends to the Pajaro Valley. The scent of apples in the air guided his way.

He came upon a few packinghouses and walked toward one that seemed occupied. It was a large wooden building with a double gabled roof and picket fence out front. Nick popped his head inside the wide, open door. "Which way to the Cullen Ranch?" A couple men turned toward him and shrugged.

Then another man walked up to him. "Cullen Ranch? I'm headed there and can take you. My wagon's in back."

Nick followed the man out and climbed aboard. "Thank you for this kindness."

"It's nothing. I'm going there, anyway. My name's Filip. Filip Tomasich. But people call me Phil." He was a lanky, rangy-looking man with straight brown hair topped with a cowboy hat to hide his bald spot. A cigarette dangled from his lips as he spoke.

"I'm Nick Markovich."

"Well, Nick, did you just arrive from Croatia?"

"Been living in San Francisco awhile."

"What did you do there?"

"Packed fruit at the commission house."

"Then you've come to the right place. We always need packers, and experienced ones get the jobs first."

"I have a job coming from Mr. Rajkovich. Do you know him?"

"Karlo Rajkovich? Everyone knows him. He's big in the apple business. What job did he offer you?"

"Foreman of a packinghouse."

Phil looked at Nick, confused. "So, what's your business at the Cullen Ranch?"

"Mr. Rajkovich is meeting me there in a few days. Meantime, I'll do whatever work I can get."

"Let me give you a warning. Cullen is an Irishman, and he's got a big, mean Irishman named Gallagher as a foreman. So, watch your step."

"What do you mean by that?"

"I guess you don't know, so I'll have to school you. The Irish run this town and don't look kindly on us Eastern European types moving in. They don't think we're good enough to shine their boots."

"I'm used to keeping my nose to the grindstone, so I don't anticipate any problems."

"No one ever expects problems, but they come, anyway. Just a warning—these Celtic types are tough and have fiery tempers. Anything can set off one of these red-haired devils. The only positive quality they possess is that they're Roman Catholic like us."

"At least we have religion in common. I'll invoke Our Lady if they give me trouble and keep on the lookout for red hair."

"Except they don't all have red hair. Some have black. They're known as the black Irish and can be even more menacing because they've got Spanish blood in them, too."

When they arrived at the ranch, Phil dropped Nick off near

the office. "You should be able to find Gallagher hanging around here."

Nick reached back for his suitcase and jumped down from the wagon. "Thanks again." He headed toward the office, mindful of the warnings. He rapped lightly on the door, but there was no answer. Then he called out. Still no reply. He took a chance and opened the door.

A fat, red-headed man with freckles sat in a chair. "What do you want? Don't you know it's Sunday—a day of rest?"

"I'm sorry, but Mr. Rajkovich sent me here. He told me to ask for John Dudich."

"Rajkovich, eh? Go to the bunkhouse around the corner and stake out a bed. Then report back to me first thing in the morning. The name's Gallagher."

Gallagher. That's the name of the man Phil warned me about.
"Thank you. But where can I find Mr. Dudich?"

"He's gone. Now I'm the man in charge."

Nick did as he was told. When he opened the bunkroom door, a room full of sleeping men was revealed. He tiptoed until he found an empty bunk—an upper one with a bunk filled with a body below. He carefully lifted his suitcase up onto the bunk, but as he let it down, the suitcase hit the bedframe which let out a groan.

Men jumped out of bed, ready for a fight. "What the hell?"

Nick went numb. He didn't know what to do. "I'm sorry," he said, with such a heavy accent that no one seemed to understand him.

Someone yelled, "Not another one of those heathens." Then men began to surround him, looking him over with menacing sneers.

A loud ringing broke the tension. It was the triangle bell signaling a meal was ready to be served.

"Let's forget about this vermin and go get lunch," a voice in the group said. "We can deal with him later."

Nick was saved by the bell, but not before the mean-spirited words worked their way into his psyche, wounding his pride. He was hungry, too, but he passed up this meal. He needed to get the lay of the land before he made another move—his life might depend on it.

Nick wandered around the apple farm somewhat aimlessly until dusk set in. As he approached the bunkhouse, he could hear voices but couldn't make out what they were saying. Nick waited until the lights went out to enter, hoping the men would be too sleepy from a big hearty meal to bother with him. Fortunately, a sliver of moonlight pierced the window, illuminating the room. He waited a minute for his eyes to adjust, removed his shoes, and padded quietly to his bunk. But when he got there, another body was lying on it and his suitcase was missing. He continued to walk up the row, searching for his suitcase and a bed, but he came up empty-handed.

Now he didn't know what to do or where to go. There was no space for him to sleep in the bunkroom, and all the belongings he had in the world had disappeared. He had a lump in his throat while he vacillated between tears and anger. Then he heard the snickering. *So, they're testing my mettle. Well, they'll find out what I'm made of and they won't ever test me again.*

Nick put on his shoes and stomped out of the bunkhouse, making as much noise as possible. He heard the yells among guffaws but chose not to react. He wouldn't give them the satisfaction. He headed for a barn that he had observed on his walk. A horse let out a neigh when he opened the door, but the other three stood silent. A couple of horse stalls were vacant and appeared to have fresh hay on the floor, which would make a decent bed for the night. He stepped into the stall and made himself comfortable. The body heat from the horses would provide enough warmth to hold off the night's chill.

Thoughts raced through Nick's mind, but he couldn't stop them. He wondered whether he had made a mistake coming to this town and, for that matter, to America. He came for a better life, but so far all he'd gotten was trouble. He couldn't help being Croatian, but apparently a Croatian was persona non grata.

The stirring of the horses woke up Nick early. The hay provided little cushion, leaving him with a backache. He left the barn before someone came to feed the horses. And now that the sun was out, he had enough light to search for his things. He moved toward the bunkhouse and walked its perimeter, but the suitcase was not nearby. As he retraced his steps, he noticed something in the trough. He hoped it wasn't his suitcase. But once he got close enough to touch it, there was no doubt it was a suitcase. Using both hands, he grabbed the slippery bundle and pulled it out of the trough's dirty water. The condition of the suitcase didn't bode well for its contents—they had to be a total loss. Now he wanted to cry.

Only one hinge held the suitcase lid to its bottom, so Nick opened it carefully. The entire contents were a wet mess. He pulled out socks and sweaters and shirts—all made of wool, which would be warm despite the dampness. He pulled out his cravat—no longer a tie but a long, wet worm. He dug underneath to locate his suit and pulled it out—a sorry sight to behold, all limp and stretched out of shape. He needed a rail to hang the suit out to dry. Then he remembered the horse barn. He could hang his clothes in a stall. They wouldn't have access to fresh air, but it would be better than nothing. He headed toward the barn and once he opened the door, the odor hit him. *They called me a heathen. What will they call me if I smell of horse manure?*

Nick walked around for a few minutes until he spotted some hedges bordering an outbuilding. He laid his clothes on the bushes where they would be in the sun. He'd come back after work to reclaim them. In the meantime, he needed some twine to hold his suitcase together. He shook his head in disgust. The new opportunity had only resulted in problems. He wished Mr. Rajkovich would show up soon so he could move on to the packinghouse to determine whether he would be any better off. If not, he would take the fastest rail back to San Francisco.

The triangle bell rang. Nick watched the men pour out of the bunkhouse and he followed, taking a place at the end of the row.

A man said, "We got the Croat at our table. Does that bother anyone else?"

Nick kept his eyes down to keep the taunting under control.

The man next to him leaned into him and made a loud sniffing sound. "It bothers me to have to eat next to a man who smells like horse shit. I guess he was raised in a barn, poor dirty Slav."

Nick had all he could do to restrain his fists. He wanted to punch that guy in the kisser to shut him up and teach them all a lesson. But he didn't want to bring more trouble on himself and end up in jail. They outnumbered him, and he knew no one would take his side.

Finally, platters of food arrived at the table. Nick smelled the bacon, which made his mouth water. But when the platter reached his end of the table, he watched the other men load their plates, leaving only scraps for him. After skipping dinner, he required more to sustain him, but he doubted he would find it at the table. As he got up to leave, two men nearby threw leftovers in his direction to antagonize him further. He wanted to pick them up and stuff them in his mouth, he was so hungry.

Once outside, he wondered where he could find some food. *The chicken coop.* He entered the coop and searched under the chickens for eggs. He remembered tales of his ancestors' wartime survival in the countryside, living on eggs. And he found a couple of warm ones under a hen who pecked his hand in objection. He cracked the first one, tilted his head back, and popped it into his mouth. The yolk had a creamy rich taste, which he savored for a few seconds before swallowing. He did the same with the next egg. Now he felt much better. He found a couple more eggs under another hen and made quick work of them.

He headed back to the horse barn, which had a trough filled with oats. He dug under the first layer to get a handful of clean oats while the horses watched, wondering why he was stealing their food. Between the eggs and the oats, Nick had energy for work. He followed the line of men to the orchard where he picked an apple to eat on the sly. The first bite sent out an amazing burst of flavor that left his taste buds wanting more. Nick had never tasted a better apple, and he didn't know whether it was because he was so hungry or because the apple was outstanding.

Nick lined up with the other men. The foreman, Mr. Gallagher, moved down the row, taking the measure of everyone. When he reached Nick, he said, "Coloreds in the other line over there."

Coloreds, Nick thought. *No one has ever call me colored. My skin's as light as most Irish. Maybe it's my green eyes they don't like.*

The man behind Nick nudged him. "Didn't you hear what he said? Get in the colored line over there." And he pointed in the direction.

The men in the colored line were a mix of nationalities— Chinese, Italian, Mexican, as well as Croatian. Mr. Tomasich had warned him about the Irish running the town and, Nick realized, this was how they kept the pecking order straight. Nick couldn't do anything now, but one day he would get his revenge. That was a promise he'd keep.

Nick was assigned to apple picking. He climbed a ladder and filled a basket with apples. Then he descended the ladder and gave the full basket to a man waiting to place the apples in a crate. A wagon carried the crates to the packinghouse.

Nick grabbed an empty basket and climbed the ladder again to fill it. He went up and down the ladder for hours without a break until lunchtime. To save time, lunch was served in the field which suited Nick just fine. He might have a better chance to get some food.

The men lined up with plates and waited their turn. The cooks ladled a portion of beef stew onto the plates, along with a piece of bread. Nick sat down on the ground and looked at his meal—it appeared hearty, but it wasn't anything he had ever eaten before. He didn't care. He just scooped up spoonful after spoonful as quickly as he could before someone took it away or knocked it out of his hands. He kept watch while he ate to make sure no one blindsided him. When the cooks called for seconds, he waited until the line was gone, but he was too late—nothing was left.

Nick hustled over to the bushes where he had left his laundry. It was still there, and the sunshine had done its work. He pulled out his suitcase from its hiding place and repacked the clothes. Then he took the piece of twine he had found in a shed and used it to bind his suitcase top and bottom together. He replaced the suitcase in its hiding place—he didn't want to risk losing it again. Next, he would have to do something about the clothes he was wearing. He took a whiff of his shirt sleeve. *That man was right—I smell like horse shit. I better put on a clean shirt.*

Day after day, Nick picked apples while trying to remain clear of the Irish bullies. He wondered whether Mr. Rajkovich had pulled a fast one on him and was never coming through with the job. One afternoon, he finally caught sight of him at the edge of the orchard, talking to Mr. Gallagher. Nick hoped he had not forgotten about him.

Mr. Rajkovich stood outside the bunkhouse. "I've been waiting for you, Nick. How's it been going?"

Nick's eyes darted from left to right before he spoke. "To tell you the truth, these guys have been pretty rough on me. I almost went back to San Francisco."

Rajkovich took an inhale of his cigar and let out the smoke. "The Irish don't like us Croatians coming here in so many numbers. They feel threatened."

"Well, they've been threatening me and calling me names like barbarian, as if we're descendants of Genghis Khan."

"Let me tell you something. Several years back, a newspaper printed an unflattering article about Croatians, calling us barbarians and clannish. That was ignorance talking. They have no knowledge of Croatia nor anywhere else in Eastern Europe. Ever since then, we've had an upward battle to prove ourselves."

CHAPTER SEVEN

The packinghouse was in full gear by the time they arrived. Men were unpacking the crates of apples from the horse cart, men were building boxes from redwood planks, men were culling apples, and men were packing apples in the fresh boxes made for shipping.

"Let me show you around, although from your work at the fruit commission, you should recognize what is taking place here," Mr. Rajkovich said.

Nick felt overwhelmed by the level of activity. The fruit commission in San Francisco also had a lot of activity, but it was in a much bigger building. Everything felt so intense here.

Mr. Rajkovich walked Nick by the men building boxes and those carrying out the filled crates to the wagons. "All these men know their jobs and they're good at them. So, you need not worry about them. However, keep a close eye on the ones sorting and packing. If just one rotten apple goes into a crate, it will spoil the others. Not only that, commission agents will reject the whole batch or downgrade them so much there'll be no profit. You especially have to watch out for the codling moth. It is the worst pest known to apples."

"How will I recognize the moth?"

"Check for larvae boring into an apple. The larvae make an apple wormy. Fortunately, in Watsonville, there's not much of a problem with the pest because the fog that the ocean brings in offers protection. But don't count on it too much. The best protection is good practices. Foremost, new boxes. Some packers reused boxes that had come over from Santa Clara where the moth persists, and the boxes brought it to this valley. Let that be a lesson to never let up your scrutiny."

"You can count on me to do a good job."

"I don't doubt that. Come over here and let's watch what these packers do." At a whisper, he added, "These guys will be on their toes now, so I don't expect to catch them making errors." Nick and Mr. Rajkovich stood watch for a few minutes, noting every step that went into a good pack.

Karlo reached over and took hold of one of the full crates. "Let's inspect this one. These apples are all Bellefleurs—one of the town's two favorite varieties. The other is Newtown Pippin. You'll notice the Bellefleur has a slight pinkish blush on its otherwise yellow skin. The packer did a good job displaying the blush which makes this apple more marketable. But some packers get lazy and don't do it. That's when you need to step in and make the correction. And if the packer continues to do it, you must send him packing." Karlo couldn't resist a chuckle at his own joke. "Please follow me to the office."

A man behind the desk stood as soon as Mr. Rajkovich and Nick entered. "Phil, this is Nick Markovich. He's the new foreman."

Phil held out his hand. "I think we've already had the pleasure." They shook hands while Karlo did a double take.

"That's right. You gave me a ride to the Cullen Ranch a couple of weeks ago, along with some friendly advice," Nick said.

"I hope it helped, because those Irish guys often give us Croatians a hard time."

"Unfortunately, I learned my lesson the hard way, but I will never forget it."

"Oh, yeah? Did they call you names and rough you up a bit?"

"Worse than that. They hid my suitcase in a trough filled with water. My only suit may be too far gone to wear again."

"Then the first order of business will be to get you some new clothes," Karlo said. "We can go downtown and purchase what you need before I show you to your accommodations."

They got into the carriage and Karlo drove the team toward downtown, a short distance away. "I know it doesn't look like much compared to the cities you've seen, but the town is growing and will have every amenity soon enough. But this is the real Wild West. At one time, elk and grizzly bears roamed all over this valley. In fact, every so often, they'd stage bull and grizzly fights right here on the lower end of Main Street."

"Grizzlies?"

"Believe it or not, some of these cowboys had the courage of a lion. They'd rope a grizzly, bring him to town, tie him to a bull, and let them go at it. Any guess on the winner?"

"If the bull was a longhorn, he probably won the match."

"You're right. The bear would strike down at the bull, but he couldn't get at any vital organ to take him out. The bull would lower his head and then, with a powerful thrust upward, aim for the heart. And more often than not, he hit his target."

"I'm amazed they held a spectacle like that right here on Main Street."

"It didn't happen often. Usually, they were staged in a corral in Corralitos, not far from here. It was a lot safer that way— protected the spectators who had come to watch."

"You won't catch me buying a ticket to one of those grue-some matches that harken back to Coliseum times. How did they separate the animals after the fun was over? The winner must have been too worked up to approach."

"The bear bled out from his wounds, which were too numerous to count since the bull repeatedly gored him. But once the bull tasted blood, his got spilled too because he would have gone after anyone who came near him."

Nick remained silent while he thought about the scene Mr. Rajkovich had described. He had heard nothing like it. *Of course, the Spanish have their bullfights, which they consider an art form. They have their cockfights as well. Then there are even dog fights. But none of those animals are restrained or tied together like a bull and bear. Only an evil mind could have conceived of such a match.* Nick felt the need to touch the crucifix that hung around his neck as he asked the Lord to bless him in this new, strange land.

"You've been rather quiet, Nick. A penny for your thoughts."

"Oh, I was just thinking about the poor bull and bear. I'm surprised they allowed it since the grizzly is a symbol of strength to Californians."

"Believe me, they didn't allow—they just did it. Out West, some people take action into their own hands. Many people are barbarians, just like us." Karlo glanced at Nick and winked.

Karlo halted the horses in front of a Western-style building, tied the reins to a post with a water trough nearby, and hopped down first. "Let's go inside." Nick followed him onto the plank board sidewalk and through the slatted swinging doors into a bar.

"First things first." Rajkovich sidled up to the bar. "Two slivovitzes." The bartender complied and Karlo handed a glass to Nick. "To your future. May it be as successful as mine has been." They clinked glasses and Nick took a whiff of his drink, remembering his homeland.

Karlo moved toward a table in the corner and took a seat. Nick followed. "This is it. Your new home." Nick shot him a perplexed look. "Not the bar, of course. You'll have a room upstairs. But the next room is where you'll take your meals—breakfast and dinner. Lunch is served at the packinghouse."

A barmaid stopped by and asked whether they wanted more drinks. "This will be it for now." Karlo waited for her to leave before he said, "Let's register for the room, and then I'll take you shopping for new clothes."

Karlo took Nick to Ford's department store down the street.

"This is where you can buy most items you'll need." A clerk greeted them and led them to the clothing section. "Look through here and find what you need. I'll be out on the porch, smoking a cigar."

Nick's eyes roved the entire store before he chose the items he needed. It was well stocked and even carried men's suits. He hesitated to purchase a suit until he was certain the one he brought with him could not be salvaged. When he had made his selections, he brought the goods up to the counter for purchase.

The clerk added up the cost, packaged the goods, and thanked Nick for the purchase. "But I need to pay."

"Mr. Rajkovich has taken care of it."

"One more thing. Where can I get a wool suit washed and pressed?"

"Right here. If you bring it in, I will send it off to one of our ladies who do that sort of work."

Nick left the store with his arms full of packages. Karlo relieved him of one and led the way back to the boardinghouse. They got the room key from the manager and climbed the stairs to the third floor. Nick's room was down the hall, on the side overlooking the street. Karlo inserted the key in the lock and held the door for Nick, who stumbled in, unloading the packages onto the bed.

"As you can see, this is a double room, so you might get a roommate. But you have everything you need—a closet, a sink with running water and a mirror, and a full bathroom down the hall. You should be comfortable enough until you make enough money to move into a house."

"This is more than I could have hoped for. Since coming to this country, I've been living in bunkrooms."

"I've told the manager who's a Croat that he should only put another Croat in this room. Now, let's get back to the packing-house. There's still work to be done."

On the way back, Karlo said, "You seem to have a basic under-standing of English. But you need to speak and write English as well as the Americans. I know a woman who gives lessons. She doesn't speak Croatian, but you might learn faster that way. You'll not get anywhere in this country without the language."

"I know the importance of language. Italian has already helped me out."

"Since you speak two languages, it shouldn't be difficult to add a third. You must have a talent for them." They arrived at the packinghouse in time for lunch. "Go get yourself some grub, then we'll talk."

Nick approached the cook, who stirred a big metal pot hung over a fire. *If the food is as good as it smells, I will be one happy guy.* The cook ladled a big helping of stew onto the plate and placed a biscuit alongside it. After grabbing a fork, Nick found a place to sit on a hay bale set out for that purpose. Most of the other men were on seconds or finished eating. He had to eat quickly to be back to work in time.

Karlo was waiting for him when he entered the building. "Let's go over here where we can talk privately. I want to school you about apples. The reason this valley can grow such good apples is because it's blessed. Like I told you before, it has fog that protects the fruit from the moths and it also has soil that doesn't need irrigation, which is helped by lack of a dry season. The trees grow rapidly here and produce good-size fruit. You may remember that the two apples grown here are the Newtown Pippin and Bellefleur. The Newtown is light green with a yellow cast to it. But it's the taste that the customers love—slightly tart, but hard to define because of other flavor notes. And it's crisp, besides. The Bellefleur is primarily yellow and may even have some tiny brown freckles. However, it's the pinkish blush that makes it so attractive to buyers. They are good eating apples, with a fruity flavor somewhere between sweet and sour. You gotta keep an eye on the men because they'll eat so many Bellefleurs that we won't have enough for market. Any questions so far?"

"Not yet."

"Then I'll go on. The packinghouses in this town are run by Croatians. Of course, they need to hire other workers to get the job done, but the foremen make sure the quality of the pack is maintained. As I said before, the apple crates are loaded onto carts and brought to the shed for packing. Workers have to cull out the inferior fruit and pack only the ones that meet our standards. This is where you must watch closely. Some workers don't pay attention, and that's when an apple ends up in a box which will do more harm than good.

"Once the boxes are packed, they're loaded onto a cart again and taken outside town to the stands of redwood trees where we store them in the shade so they won't rot. Apples can keep for a month of Sundays if they are stored in a cool temperature. Watsonville has a lot of advantages over towns on the other side of the hill that have pretty hot temperatures. If we store our apples properly under the trees, we can wait for the right market to sell them and, hopefully, make a killing. Do you follow me so far?"

"I think so."

"You'll pick it up fast. Just try your best and excellent results will follow. Now, let's look at what's happening in here. Tell me if you spot any problems."

"I've noticed a lot of apples set to the side. Why is that?"

"They have bruises or some other imperfection. In fact, about a third of the apples get dumped into the river unless a hog farmer wants them."

"That seems like a waste. Isn't there a way to prevent the bruising or find another use for the bruised apples?"

"At the moment, no. In time, maybe."

"So many people suffer hunger in the old country that it breaks my heart when I see food wasted. A poor person would be happy with a bruised apple."

"I'm sure there are hobos down by the river who scoop out a few. And then there's the fish. They don't all go to waste."

"I'd like to think some poor souls are benefiting."

"Consider it another way—the fewer the apples, the higher the prices. That's how the market works. Supply and demand."

"Golly, if we had too many apples, we'd be working more hours for less pay."

"Now you're getting it. Anyway, you've seen the operation. Questions?"

"What happens if I need more men? Where do I find them?"

"More than likely, they will find you. We have migrants coming through here all the time. They'll work for a few days and then move on. There's also an endless supply of Celestials."

CHAPTER 8

Nick left the packinghouse with his head spinning. There was so much to learn about the apple business. Growing up in Croatia —poor, oppressed, and uneducated—had not prepared him for this new life. Now he was expected to become fluent in English, a language totally unfamiliar to him. But he had no choice. He would have to learn it, or he would fail to reach the prosperity he yearned for.

When Nick reached the boardinghouse, he smelled dinner simmering on the stove and knew it would be some sort of stew again. He entered the side room, grabbed a plate and silverware, and got in line. The cook ladled a generous portion of stew on his plate filled with beef chunks, carrots, and potatoes in a rich brown sauce. Nick found a seat and dug into the medley, making quick work of it. When he finished, he looked for seconds, but the cook had already put the food away. However, he noticed some bread on the table and took the remaining piece. He broke off a chunk and dipped it into the sauce—now his stomach was full.

On his way back through the bar, a maid grabbed his arm. "Come sit down with me, honey." Using the element of surprise, she pulled Nick into a chair and plopped herself on his lap, her skirt completely covering his pants. She ran her fingers through his thick, straight hair and then kissed his cheeks.

Before she could get to his lips, Nick lifted her off his lap and set her on her feet. "No, thank you." He made a beeline up the stairs to his room, locking the door behind him.

And now he was in for another surprise—a roommate, fast asleep, sounding off the loudest z's he'd ever heard. Nick stepped closer to get a better look at the guy who appeared to be passed out. He hadn't seen him around before, but he caught the scent of whiskey on his breath. *He won't be worth a lick for work tomorrow. I hope he's not part of my crew.*

In the morning, Nick's roommate was still asleep. He was no longer snoring, so he feared the worst. But as he watched, his chest rose up and down—he was breathing. Nick moved to the sink and splashed some cold water on his face. He dressed and ran a comb through his hair before setting off for breakfast. Upon descending the stairs, he searched the room to make sure the coast was clear—not a barmaid in sight.

He took fast strides to the dining room, where he found no line and no diners. He assumed he was early, but the cook was ready to serve, so he stepped right up with his plate. This morning, the meal was the all-American breakfast—scrambled eggs, bacon, hash brown potatoes, and pancakes topped with sauteed apples, a cup of coffee the finishing touch. When he was almost halfway through his meal, an army descended on the dining hall. The peace of the morning gave way to loud chatter and rude grunts as the men chewed and belched their way through breakfast.

Nick took his chance on seconds. The cook looked up, gave him a wink, and loaded up his plate again. With a full stomach, he would be ready to take on the day no matter what trouble turned up.

On the way out of the dining room, a big, clumsy oaf bumped into Nick and said, "Watch where you're going, buster."

"You stumbled into me but no harm done."

The man stared at Nick with glassy eyes, weaving from side to side.

"Let me help you into a chair."

"I don't need no help. Just something to eat. Then I'll be fine."

"Coffee is what you require. Here's some to reboot your brain."

The man grabbed the mug out of Nick's hands, spilling half of it onto his lap. But he didn't seem to notice. He took a big gulp and spit it out. "That coffee is so goddamn hot it burned my mouth. I won't be able to taste my food now."

Nick set a plate of food in front of the man, and he began to eat. With each mouthful, he seemed to get better, more sober, until he came to his senses. "I guess I owe you for helping me out."

"You don't owe me anything. I'm sure you'd do the same for me if you have the opportunity."

"Don't count on it, kid."

"I'll leave you now. Best take it easy today."

"Easy. I have a job to do, too. You wouldn't be headed toward the packinghouses, would you?"

"Yeah. Why?"

"Do you have a buggy or are you hoofing it?"

"I'll be getting there under my own power."

"Then forget it. I need to find me a ride. I don't think I can walk today."

Nick arrived at the packinghouse early, but Phil was already there, banging boxes together. "I'm surprised to see you here already."

"It's my packinghouse. I'm almost always here."

"I didn't realize you were the owner. Mr. Rajkovich introduced you as the manager."

"Jack-of-all-trades—that's me. When you're in business, you do it all if you want to survive. See here, I'm building boxes so there's no reason we can't get to packing first thing. I was here all night working."

Nick hadn't realized everything that went into the packing business. When he first met Phil, he was driving the horse cart to the Cullen Ranch. When he saw him again in the office, he was doing paperwork. And now, he was sawing and nailing redwood boards together to create boxes for the fruit.

"Why don't you sit down and help me? You might as well learn all you can about the business. One day you might even own one of these packinghouses yourself."

Nick watched Phil for a couple of minutes. Then he imitated him until he had made a box. "How's this?" He held up his creation for Phil to inspect.

"Not bad for the first one. But make sure your corners are at right angles so they conform to the others." He held up two boards to demonstrate. "Try it again until you have the technique down."

Nick continued building boxes until the packing crew arrived. Apples fresh from the farm were already waiting as the men took up their places and began their tasks. First, they sorted the apples. Next, they brushed off excess dirt from the prime apples. Finally, they wrapped them in tissue paper and placed them into one of the new boxes. Nick noticed that half the men sorted and cleaned while the other half wrapped and placed the apples in boxes. The Newtown Pippin was a hard apple which didn't bruise easily. But the Bellefleur was more delicate, requiring extra care. A day in a packinghouse was long and got hotter as the afternoon progressed. Not much fresh air circulated in the cavernous building, but the high ceilings trapped the worst of the heat.

When the cook clanged the triangular lunch bell, the men tried to outpace one another to the line. Today, the cook ladled out a bean dish with some ground meat in it. Nick heard someone call it chili. He had never tasted it before, but it contained flavorful spices and was filling. A piece of cornbread accompanied it. He had never had cornbread either, but one bite turned him into a fan. The cook brought out a tray of dessert as Nick finished his meal. Chocolate pudding.

As he helped himself to a bowl, the cook said, "Chocolate tames the spices. Besides, it's good for you."

Nick dipped into the pudding, not even bothering to sit. He rolled it around his mouth before he allowed it to slip down his throat. The cook was right about the chocolate.

When Nick got back to his room at the boardinghouse, he found the man from downstairs sitting on the other bed, staring down at the floor.

The man looked up once he realized he was no longer alone. "I guess we're roommates."

"Appears so. Have you been sleeping all day?"

"Yeah, but I feel better now. Just need to get some food into me."

"Dinner's only an hour away. You don't have long to wait."

"It will be long to me."

Nick paused a moment before he spoke again. "Have you been around town for a while?"

"Just arrived. I was working the mines but gave it up. Spending the day in a dark cave was not for me. Not only that, there was not much air to breathe, which left me wheezing most of the time."

"Mining? I thought the Gold Rush was long past."

"It's silver now. Out by Nevada."

"What brings you here?"

"I heard there's work in the packinghouses, which might be more suitable to me."

"It's still hard work. And in the condition you were in this morning, you wouldn't get hired. The managers are strict and want a full day's work for the pay."

"Don't worry about me. I know the drill. Tomorrow I'll be up to the task—you'll see. Just need a good meal, a night's sleep, and a bath."

When the man returned from his bath, Nick barely recognized him. "You were right about the bath. You look like a new man. What's your name?"

"Jakov Kurtovich." He was a bear of a man, with an enormous belly and lumbering gait. His dark, moody eyes and coarse black hair and beard gave him a menacing appearance.

"Nick Markovich. I assume you're a Croat like me."

"From the Konavle region, near Dubrovnik."

"Me, too. Cilipi is the town I'm from. I've been told there are a lot of us here from Konavle."

Nick brought Jakov to work and introduced him to Phil. After they talked briefly, Phil told Nick to find a place for Jakov on a crew. There were always migrants on a crew who came and went at will, so there was always a place for a new hire. Nick put Jakov on sorting and cleaning. "This is the best place to learn about the fruit. Once you've mastered this job, I'll move you on to packing."

Nick kept an eye on Jakov because he had recommended him. So far, he was pleased with his ability to stay on task and the speed with which he could do it. When the workday was over, they walked back to the boardinghouse together. "You held your own today," Nick said.

"You can always count on me to do my part. I'm no Ivan Ivanovich. I'll not cheat anyone by slacking off."

"I can already smell dinner," Nick said. "Some kind of fish."

"Probably rock cod. They fish a lot of it from the bay. And it's cheap."

Men were in line when they reached the dining room.

"I must eat quickly because I have an English lesson." The cook had made a thick, creamy cod and potato chowder. One mouthful and Nick was in heaven. He lapped it up and went back for more.

Nick headed for Mrs. Bertucci's house, which was only a couple of blocks away. When he neared her place, the odor of fried fish filled the air. *No doubt she's a mackerel snapper.*

A matronly woman wearing an apron answered the door. "You must be here for English class, but you're a bit early."

"I apologize, but I didn't want to be late," Nick responded in Italian.

"It is not a problem. I am Mrs. Bertucci. And you are?"

"Nick Markovich."

"Pleased to meet you. You can wait in the parlor until I'm ready and the others arrive."

Two other men about Nick's age arrived soon after him. Now, Mrs. Bertucci was ready, her apron removed. She was a friendly matron whose brown eyes sparkled when she smiled.

She began, "I am Mrs. Bertucci. Since you are here to learn English, we will speak it during class." She set her gaze on Nick. "My name is Mrs. Bertucci. What is your name?"

He knew the answer, but wasn't sure how to put it in a full sentence.

Mrs. Bertucci gave a prompt. "My name is..."

Now that he was listening carefully, Nick had no trouble repeating the phrase. "My name is Nick Markovich."

"Very good. Now ask the man next to you his name." She paused, then gave the prompt, "What is your name?"

Nick repeated the prompt, and Mrs. Bertucci smiled in approval. After the three men had gone through that exercise, she began holding up objects and naming them. First, she held up an apple. "Repeat after me—apple." Mrs. Bertucci knew the men were in the apple business, so this vocabulary would be relevant. "This is a Newtown Pippin apple." Again, repeat. And thus, the lesson continued until its conclusion. "Gentlemen, we will meet three times a week after dinner at seven thirty. The next session will be Monday evening, followed by Wednesday and Friday. Have a pleasant weekend, and I will see you on Monday."

CHAPTER 9

On the walk back to the boardinghouse, Nick thought about his free day on Sunday. Of course, he could go to Mass. However, there would be no social life afterward since no eligible Croatian women lived in town. Although there were other women—Irish, for instance. But they looked down their noses at Croatian men, even if they shared Mass with them. If he wanted to dance and mingle with women, he'd have to go up to San Francisco. He'd take an early train that would get him to the Slavonic Society right after Mass let out. That would give him a full day before catching the train back. Nick smiled to himself as he moved along with a new bounce in his step.

Nick arrived at the Slavonic Society as it opened its door for the afternoon's festivities. A couple of tables were already laden with food that Croatian ladies had brought the day before and stored in the icebox. Nick perused the offerings, which featured many Croatian specialties. An empty place on the end of the buffet table with a big ladle resting nearby signaled soup would be on the menu. Nick moved to the drink table, pouring fruit punch into a glass, and gravitated to a corner to watch the people arrive.

Most came as part of a family group, although there were a few single men like himself. When the Babiches walked in, his heart skipped a beat. They were a sight to behold, with their many children—not as many as in his own family, but still a significant number. Nick finished his drink, placed it on a tray, and headed in their direction.

Mr. Babich held his hand out in welcome, and the entire family extended warm greetings. They were all glad to see him, especially Lana and her younger sister, Jelena.

"So, how is the apple business?" Mr. Babich asked.

"It's busy. The fall is the prime season. Our biggest challenge is keeping a good supply of labor. Each time a new man comes onto a crew, I have to keep an eye on him to make sure he does the job right. The packinghouse is quite large, so there's a lot of activity."

"And how do you like the town? What's life like there?"

"As you can see, I'm here today. That's because there's not much social life for Croatians since we're a colony of men. It appears I'll have to find a wife in San Francisco."

"A wife? Are you looking already?"

"No...I just mean when the time comes. Right now, I have to make money and make my way in business. When I'm stable, that's when I'll think about a wife."

The band had just struck up the music for a kolo. Lana looked in Nick's direction. He took her by the hand and led her to the dance floor. A group of young people formed a circle, so they had to break in. But there was always room for more.

Nick and Lana stayed on the dance floor for several dances after the kolo. By the time they called time out, they were exhausted and lunch was being served. The Babiches had staked out a table, which included an extra seat for Nick. Lana and Nick sat down to catch their breath before making their way to the buffet.

The rest of the family was in line, so Nick had Lana to himself. "How is the coffeehouse business? Any new immigrants come by?"

Lana laughed, which brought a sparkle to her eyes. "None since you. But I keep a watch out."

"Oh, you do, do you? Why is that?"

"You never know who you might meet that way. Some of these immigrants become rich in a few years. It's always good to know people who can lend you some money."

"That's true. Life always depends on money. Especially a good life." He paused for a moment while he considered the next topic. "Did I mention I'm taking English lessons?"

"No, you didn't. We should practice. That's how you get better."

"Today's my day off, so let's save it for another time." Nick looked up and noticed the family approaching, plates piled high. "We better get in line before there's nothing left."

Nick spied a pot of chicken noodle soup on the buffet. "Let's come back for the soup after we've filled our plates. I don't think we can balance both."

Lana chose her selections carefully and took only small portions, while Nick didn't hesitate to help himself to as much as he wanted. When they returned to the table, everyone was so involved in their meal that conversation had come to a standstill.

Mrs. Babich glanced at Nick's plate. "It appears they're not feeding you in Watsonville."

Nick finished swallowing before he responded. "I get a good amount of food. But I work hard, so I'm always hungry. Besides, we rarely get Croatian food. One day for lunch, the cook served a stew called chili. Have you heard of it?"

"Yes, it's a popular dish out West."

"It had so many hot spices, my mouth felt on fire. Chili is no substitute for a good Croatian stew."

"Well, you're in America now. You've got to adapt."

"What we need in Watsonville is a good Croatian restaurant.

If you run into someone who wants to open a restaurant, I would consider it a favor to send them my way."

"I'll keep that in mind. Now, Nick, the holidays will be here before you know it. You don't have family here, so we'd like to invite you to spend Christmas with us."

The kind offer took Nick aback. The holidays had not crossed his mind because he was so busy at work. But this would be the first holiday he would not be with his family. It would be sad, spending the day alone. He knew his heart would ache if he didn't spend the day surrounded by friends and good cheer. "I'd like that very much. Thank you for your kind offer."

"Christmas is all about kindness and brotherhood. That's why I keep the coffeehouse open as long as possible on Christmas Eve. Some poor souls have nowhere else to go or they have to work to provide the services we may need. But I close early so we can have a nice fish dinner before Mass. Then, on Christmas Day, we celebrate all day long. We have a good time, especially with all the younger children who anxiously await Santa Claus. It's best to celebrate Christmas with a family if you can," Mr. Babich said.

Nick left for the train ride back with a feeling of anticipation for the holidays. It would be good to be a guest of a family—one that wasn't too different from his, one that would bring back fond memories of Christmases past. With eight children in his family, Christmas was always a chaotic affair. And even though each child only received one gift, there were enough packages under the tree to create excitement at the abundance. Somehow his parents managed to give each child the perfect gift. He didn't know how they did it. Of course, the gifts didn't cost a lot of money and were often handmade, but they were just the gift the child hoped for.

One year, he received a wool sweater his mother had knit. Not only did it fit him perfectly, but it was just what he needed to get through the winter. He had outgrown his other sweater and had already passed it down to Francis. In fact, it was rare to receive a new piece of clothing in a family that made a practice of hand-me-downs.

As the train rolled along, its movement lulled Nick into a dreamlike state. He recalled more and more memories of his life back home. Living with family and friends he had known all his life had been comforting. He always knew he had people around him he could trust. But here in America, that was not the case. He had to keep his guard up with non-Croatians. Sometimes even his countrymen couldn't be trusted. Yet he sensed he had a great opportunity in America, and he would just have to put up with his petty grievances.

CHAPTER 10

An unfamiliar man in coat and tie wandered into the packing-house, looking for Phil.

"He's out at the Cullen Ranch, picking up a load of apples," Nick said. "Can I help you? I'm a foreman."

The man held out his hand. "Howard Dawson, editor of the *Pajaronian*. I'd like to talk with you about this year's apple harvest. We're doing a story on it for next week's paper."

Nick hesitated a moment while he assessed the man. He was of slight build, almost wiry, with short, dark hair, and a brush above his upper lip. "What do you want to know?"

"I'm after some facts and figures that can give the article credibility. For instance, how many crates of apples will this valley produce this year? How did the Bellefleur and Newtown Pippin fare? What do you expect the apples to bring at market?"

The English had gotten too complicated for Nick. He held up a finger for Dawson to hold up and left in search of a transla-tor. Once Nick understood the newspaper man's questions, he said, "Honestly, Mr. Dawson, I can't answer your questions. But I can tell you what is happening in this packinghouse."

"That'll get me started." He pulled out a pad and pencil. "Now shoot."

When Nick received the translation, he panicked. That's when he heard the wagon pull up and saw Phil heading through the door. He came right up to Mr. Dawson and shook his hand. "What can I do for you, Howard?"

Relief washed over Nick.

"I was just telling your foreman I'm doing a final story in our installment about this year's apple harvest and need some facts and figures, which I hope you can provide."

Phil's eyes darted back and forth between Nick and the translator, and he understood the situation. "Guys, thanks for your help, but I'll take it from here."

Nick nodded and walked away with the translator at his side. "I'm sorry, I didn't get your name."

"Paul Lovasich."

"Paul, where did you learn to speak English like that?"

"I just picked it up."

"Is that all?"

"Actually, I lived in the city for several years and took classes at the Slavonic Society. But I got a lot of practice when I worked in a restaurant."

"I'm taking lessons, but I doubt I'll ever be able to speak like you."

"It will take time. Take advantage of every opportunity to listen to English and speak it. Soon, you'll be speaking like a native."

That night as he walked home, Nick considered the experience with the newspaper man. It reinforced his effort to learn English and as quickly as possible. The next time he met with Mrs. Bertucci, he would ask her how he could learn faster.

Jakov sat on his bed with his head in his hands. When Nick walked into the room, he said, "How did you beat me back?"

Jakov straightened up. "Don't know. Just did."

"How's the job treating you?"

"It's been fine. But I want something more, you know?"

"Like what?"

"Something that's mine. Maybe my own packinghouse. A lot of guys are starting them up."

"That'll take some money."

"I've been saving. With a partner, I might be able to swing it."

Nick had misjudged Jakov. He had ambition and planned ahead. "When do you want to begin the business?"

"The season after next. That's when I should have my stake."

"If you need a partner, I might have a stake by then, too. Let's go to dinner and talk about it."

Jakov stood and followed Nick out the door. The line snaked around the dining room, men hungry from the day's work. The cook had made a chicken stew that tasted good and smelled even better, with a bold flavor note of sage. Before he dug in, Nick examined the stew for any surprises but only found the usual—potatoes, carrots, mushrooms, and green beans. Once he tasted it for himself, his tongue recognized the flavors of onions and garlic, too. The stew had a thick sauce that coated the stomach and satisfied every hunger pang. Tonight, apple pie fresh from the oven was dessert. Nick thought he had never had a better meal, even one his mother had made.

As he savored his food, Nick picked up some talk of a feast called Thanksgiving. From what he could gather, it would take place in a couple of weeks. He knew nothing about it, so he threw out a question.

A guy across the table took up the answer. "It's a holiday they celebrate in America near the end of November. They eat turkey that's stuffed with flavorful bread or rice and serve it with every imaginable vegetable from the fall harvest—corn, green beans, carrots, Brussel sprouts—along with cranberry sauce."

"Cranberry sauce?"

"That's right—they grow cranberries on the East Coast. The first Thanksgiving was held there. It had something to do with the immigrants from England being so thankful they made it to the new land."

"I'm glad I asked. Thanks for explaining it to me." Now Nick wondered how he would get a taste of turkey. Perhaps the cook would get his hands on a bird from the annual Turkey Shoot.

The apple harvest continued well into November. By the time it finished, it was nearly time for Thanksgiving. When Nick went to his English class the Friday before, he asked Mrs. Bertucci about the holiday.

"Some people consider Thanksgiving the best meal of the year. In my family, we switch off hosts and this year the feast will be at my house, which means I have the honor of cooking the turkey. But everyone helps out by bringing a side dish or dessert."

"I don't remember my mother cooking turkey. But around Zagreb, I've heard that people eat them."

"You can thank us Italians for that. An Italian bishop who introduced them, back in the sixteenth century I think it was."

"Our boardinghouse cook is serving a turkey dinner for Thanksgiving, which will give me a chance to taste the bird for myself."

"It won't be the same as with family. Would you like to join us?"

"I wouldn't want to intrude on your family celebration. Being a Croatian, I might not fit in."

"Thanksgiving is about sharing. Didn't you hear that the first feast involved the pilgrims from England and American Indians? So, a Croatian at an Italian table would be in keeping with the holiday spirit."

"As you know, I speak Italian, so maybe no one would guess I'm really a Croat."

"I hate to break this to you, Nick, but your heavy Eastern European accent is a complete giveaway."

"You're breaking my heart."

"I'm sorry, but it's true."

"Then tell me how I can get rid of my accent."

"Listen to native speakers and practice imitating them. It's the only way."

The doorbell rang. "Ah, the other students must be here. Let me go welcome them in."

CHAPTER 11

Nick took the train to the city to spend Christmas with the Babiches. He went a couple of days early to have time to shop for some gifts and also for a new suit. Washing and pressing had revived his brown suit, but it was still so ill-fitting he couldn't shake the fresh-off-the-boat image. Nick noticed that most men wore dark suits. He wanted a navy one which would make him look like a real American decked out in red, white, and blue. That would also require a red tie and new white shirt, with sleeves made for cuff links. Karlo Rajkovich wore cuff links, and so did Pero Loreto. The two men were his role models for success, and he wanted to imitate them.

When Nick arrived, he headed for the boardinghouse to arrange a bunk for two nights. Mrs. Popovich was at her station, surprised to see him again. "What are you doing here? Didn't things work out for you in the new town?"

"Everything's swell but I need a bed for a couple of nights. I'm here to visit friends and do a little shopping. It's still a wilderness outpost in Watsonville, with few shops other than the general store."

"Just two nights then?"

"That's right."

"Are you leaving here before Christmas?"

"Actually, I'll be the guest of some friends on Christmas Eve."

"Lucky you. I'll be stuck here making sure the guys get a wonderful celebration. The fresh Christmas tree is already set up in the parlor awaiting ornaments, which the boarders will put on. It gets them in the spirit, decorating the tree."

The more Mrs. Popovich talked of Christmas, the more nostalgic Nick became. The unveiling of the Christmas tree before dinner on Christmas Eve was always a highlight. In the early years, his parents had decorated the tree. But as time moved on, the older kids had taken on the task. Once he had his height, Nick placed the star. He was a good two inches taller than Ivan which had made it his honor. "Yes," Nick agreed, "it would get the guys into the spirit."

"Now about your room and board. A space freed up in your old room. Will that do?"

"It will be fine. But before I go up to my room to drop off my luggage, I'd like a recommendation of a men's store. I need a new suit."

"I'll say you do. That old brown thing has seen better days. Just turn right and right again away from the bay, and follow California Street until you get to Kearney. Make a right, then look for The White House on the corner of Kearney and Post. You should find an excellent selection of shops all around."

When Nick arrived at the correct intersection, he stopped in his tracks in awe of what stood before him. The White House was a behemoth of a building, wrapping itself around a corner of one of the busiest shopping districts in the city. Its awnings overhung the sidewalk which allowed sales assistants to protect merchandise they brought out for customers in carriages to consider. As Nick walked up to the store, he glimpsed the ladies waiting at curbside. They were as elegant as any he had ever seen, wrapped in furs on a chilly December day.

He hesitated, wondering whether he should enter a store that was so highfalutin'. But he was here—why not? Once he stepped inside, Nick's mouth gaped open as he perused a world meant only for the rich. The displays of everything from handbags to shoes to scarves and shawls were a feast for the eyes. He could only imagine their price tags.

He must have looked dumbstruck, causing a sales assistant in a three-piece suit to approach him mid-aisle. "May I be of service?"

"Oh...yes, thank you."

"Did you have something special in mind for the lady in your life?"

Nick smiled. "I only need something special for me—a new suit."

"Alas, I am sorry to say that we only carry women's clothing. But if I may suggest a fine men's store, Braun Brothers is on the next block after you exit left."

Nick allowed himself one last look before he turned to leave, impressing upon his memory every image he could. One day he would come back with the lady in his life and buy whatever was her heart's desire. And, if he was lucky enough to have a daughter, nothing but The White House would be good enough for her. Nick had never considered himself materialistic. But seeing these fine goods from Paris, which were out of his reach, created a desire in him that only money would fulfill. He had to not only work harder but smarter. To make the big money he had in mind, he would have to be in business for himself. He had to bide his time, but one day he would make it happen.

Nick came upon the men's store, recognizing it by the display of suits in the window. He spent some time studying the models, noting every detail, from choice of tie to cuff links. Then he walked in.

A clerk approached him. "May I help you, sir?"

Sir? Nick almost looked around for someone behind him. But the clerk had called him sir, the first to do so, and he liked it. "You certainly can. I need a suit, dark blue, made of wool." He had not forgotten his experience with his brown suit—wool had kept him warm.

"Please step right this way and watch your step."

Nick followed the clerk to an elevated platform at the rear of the store.

He quickly pulled out a tape measure and took Nick's measurements. "I'll select a couple of suits for you to look at and then we can go from there." He threw three suits onto the table and began explaining their selling points. "These suits are made of lightweight wool, which will serve you well throughout the four seasons we have in San Francisco. This first one has a Glen plaid pattern, a sporty look suitable for less formal occasions. If you are looking for a suit that can take you anywhere, the pinstripe and solid navy are the way to go."

Nick examined two suits because he had already eliminated the Glen plaid.

The clerk brushed his hand over the fabric. "Take a feel of it. Soft and yet warm, but not so warm you can't wear it in the summer."

Nick reached out and ran his hand up and down the cloth. It felt nothing like his old brown suit made of a coarse wool that was heavy, and so scratchy he was uncomfortable whenever he wore it. "I'd like to try these two."

The clerk showed Nick to the dressing room. "Let me bring you a shirt and tie to go with them."

Nick tried the pinstripe suit on first. He came out of the dressing room to observe himself in the three-way mirror. The clerk grabbed the jacket shoulders while noting the pant length. "It fits pretty well, only minor adjustments needed."

In a few moments, Nick came back out in the solid navy suit. "Again, only minor alterations. What do you think?"

Nick looked at himself again in the mirror. "I like this one. And it's more practical."

"You can't go wrong with a solid blue suit. It will take you everywhere in style. All you have to do is change the tie to give it a different look." The clerk scurried to the tie rack and returned with several selections. Holding each one up to the suit, he demonstrated how the ties changed the suit from casual to formal. "A plaid makes for a sporty look while a stripe is more elegant."

Now Nick talked price. The clerk showed him the tag, which he had not noticed before. It was too much. "I'm sorry for your trouble, but I cannot afford this suit."

The clerk turned to face Nick square on. "Tell me what you can afford, and I'll see what I can do."

Nick waited, not expecting to hear good news. But the clerk returned with a blue suit. "This suit seems to be about your size. It was returned for reasons I shall not disclose, but I think I can give you a deal on it."

Nick looked the suit over and felt the fabric.

"This is what we call a self-stripe fabric. If you look closely, you will notice a slight stripe in the same color as the fabric, but it's the different weave that makes the stripe. Try it on. I think you'll like it."

Nick came out of the dressing room with a smile on his face. The fit was nearly perfect.

"You can either take the suit as is or wait for alterations."

"Can you have it ready by tomorrow—Christmas Eve?"

"I can't promise, but we'll try."

Nick took another look in the mirror. "I'll take it as is."

Nick left with a package under his arm. The clerk had even thrown in a pair of silver cuff links that had been engraved improperly, advising him to tell anyone who noticed that they had belonged to his grandfather. Nick liked the wily clerk, who seemed to be able to cover any contingency. But he had forgotten to ask his name. He doubted the man would be at Braun Brothers the next time he was in the market for a suit. He really knew his business, marking him a man on the rise.

The streets were crowded with shoppers, all carrying bundles under their arms. At every street corner, a Salvation Army officer rang a bell to collect money for orphans and other unfortunate souls. Nick dropped a coin in the first basket but tried to avoid the bell ringers after that.

He hustled back to the boardinghouse as darkness descended. When Nick drew near, he encountered carolers making stops at every corner to spread some cheer. *A city really comes to life during the holidays. Dubrovnik, too. The Christmas market, the Stradun strung with garlands ablaze in lights, and merrymakers wandering through the Old Town, a sausage in one hand and a glass of rakija in the other. Christmas is made of memories and none are better than spending time with family.* Nick was glad he would be with a family during the holiday—although not his own, still a Croatian family who would celebrate all the traditions.

The carolers stopped in front of the boardinghouse to sing. When Nick walked through the door, they followed him in. Mrs. Popovich pointed the way, and they entered the dining room, where the men were assembling. One man with a tenor voice sang along, and the others joined him. Soon, everyone was singing.

The cook came out to take stock of the scene, creeping up to the doorway. No one noticed him at first, but when a bass voice resounded, heads turned, surprised to learn the voice belonged to the cook. Mrs. Popovich patted him on his back and joined in, her soprano voice cracking whenever a high note was called for. But she was like an old pro, not missing a beat.

Nick stole up the stairs while everyone was singing to place the package under his bed. After dinner, Nick climbed the stairs to his bunkroom, eager to take another look at his new suit and pack it away. He knelt beside his bed and reached under it—the package had moved. He bent over to inspect the space under the bed—the package was gone. In a panic, Nick jumped up to his feet, remembering what the Irish guys did to him at the ranch. He tried to calm himself while he considered how to recover his missing suit—his only suit for the holidays. At that moment, another man walked into the room. Nick turned, shooting daggers from his eyes.

"What's got you all bent out of shape?"

Nick took a deep breath before answering. "A large box with my new suit is missing from under my bed."

"Oh, is that all?"

"Is that all? It's my only suit, and it cost me a sizeable fortune."

"Go look under the tree. Some guy was gathering up the presents."

Nick let out a breath, but he would not be reassured until he had the suit box in his hands. He took a flying leap out the door, running down the stairs two at a time until he reached the living room, out of breath but relieved. The box sat under the tree, surrounded by several smaller packages. Once he removed it, the other packages looked rather trifling. A thought struck him. He headed back to his room, unpacked the suit, then repacked it in his luggage. He took an apple he had brought for the children's stockings and placed it in the box, setting it among the smaller packages under the tree. *Now the others don't look so sparse.*

Despite finding his new suit, Nick did not sleep a wink that night as he kept a watchful eye on it—he couldn't risk losing his new suit again.

CHAPTER 12

In the morning, Nick wore the suit to breakfast amid stares. He could hear the whispers as the men pondered why he was all dressed up. But wearing the suit was the only way to protect it from theft.

On the way to the Babiches', Nick realized he had some extra time and headed for Mr. Loreto's office to wish him a Merry Christmas. This time when the doorman answered, he let Nick in while he announced him.

Mr. Loreto stood at the office door. "I can hardly believe my eyes. You look nothing like the young man I met on the train." He shook Nick's hand vigorously and didn't let go until he finished talking. "That suit gives you the air of success." Finally, he released Nick's hand and offered him a seat. Instead of taking his place behind his desk, Loreto sat in the other club chair.

"I came to wish you a Merry Christmas and Happy New Year."

"Well, you just made my holidays. I have to assume the fruit commission house worked out well for you."

"It certainly did. And I apologize for not coming to thank you sooner. Mr. Rajkovich recruited me for a job as a packing-house foreman down in Watsonville."

"Mr. Rajkovich, eh? He's a real mover and shaker. If you've caught his eye, he'll raise you up. So, has the apple business been good there?"

"We're always busy and guys are building their own packinghouses."

"You should do the same one day. That'll put you onto the road to success faster than anything else."

Nick still had some time to kill. After wandering around and people watching, he ducked into St. Francis of Assisi Church, where choir practice was underway for midnight Mass. He slid into a pew at the rear of the nave, closed his eyes, and let the music wash over him. Anywhere in the world, the sounds of Christmas were familiar. Though they may be sung in different languages, the music was universal. He realized his family was attending Mass at that very moment, singing some of the same hymns. He felt so close to them, the miles between them dissolved.

Startled by an altar server, Nick checked his watch. *Almost time.* He picked up his luggage and headed for the Babiches' townhouse. Before climbing the steps, he stood back to take in the sight. An evergreen wreath with a big red bow was mounted on the front door and candlelight flickered in the windows.

A feeling of nostalgia overcame him. He took a deep breath of the chilly air and dashed up the steps. One knock was all it took for the door to open in welcome.

Jelena, the middle daughter, stood before him. "Papa and Lana aren't home yet. But please come in and make yourself comfortable."

Nick followed Jelena to the living room. "Don't you look festive in a red velvet frock."

Jelena gave Nick a subtle smile. "I inherited this dress from Lana. She got to wear it first."

"It looks very pretty on you, as I'm sure it did on Lana, too."

Mrs. Babich walked into the room just as the pair ran out of conversation. She approached Nick, giving him a kiss on each cheek. "I'm so happy you can join us for Christmas. Come with me, and I'll show you to your room."

Nick grabbed his suitcase and followed Mrs. Babich upstairs.

"This will be your room for the holidays. The boys are bunking with their brother."

"Thank you. I'm sure I'll be very comfortable here."

"Why don't you freshen up while I get back to the dinner downstairs. My husband and Lana should be home soon. The coffeehouse closes early on Christmas Eve, although not before we have satisfied the last customer. Mateo would never feel right shooing them out on Christmas Eve of all nights."

While preparing for the night's festivities, Nick heard a knock on the door. Opening it, he found Teo standing there.

"I need to get my socks out of the drawer."

"By all means, come in."

Teo went straight for the bureau, pulled out the second drawer, rummaged around for a minute, then pulled out one sock, and after much more rummaging, found its match. Teo held the pair up for Nick to inspect. "These are my Christmas socks. They have Santa embroidered at the top."

Nick stepped closer to examine them. "Did your mother do the needlework?"

Teo shook his head. "Santa gave them to me last year. They came all the way from the North Pole."

"Maybe he'll bring me a pair this year if I'm lucky."

After Teo left, Nick finished freshening up. He had bought himself a men's eau de cologne and splashed some on his face, rubbing it onto his neck. *This will give me the air of a proper gentleman.*

When Nick descended the stairs, he followed his nose into the kitchen where Mrs. Babich was stirring a pot on the stove.

She looked up, surprised. "We follow the tradition of the fish feast on Christmas Eve. I assume you like fish."

"What self-respecting Croatian doesn't?"

"Of course. It's soul food for us. What I'm making here is bakala en brodo." She dipped a ladle into the broth and held it up. "Try a little and tell me how you like it."

"Mm. It's very good. Just like my mother's."

"We probably use the same recipe, even though I'm from Split."

The door opened and in came Mr. Babich and Lana. Nick followed Mrs. Babich into the entrance hall to greet them. Mrs. Babich first gave her husband a kiss on the cheek and then Lana.

Nick held out his hand, which Mr. Babich grabbed, giving it a forceful shake. "Merry Christmas and welcome to my home."

"It's my pleasure to share the holidays with you and your family."

"When you show hospitality to a stranger, you could be entertaining an angel, or so the saying goes."

"I hate to spoil your fantasy, but I'm no angel."

Mateo laughed, full and hearty. "I should know. I've got three boys and none is an angel, at least not in our presence."

Vera interrupted the lively exchange. "The food is almost ready. Hurry and get changed so you can help me with dinner. And Lana, the same."

Once Lana and Mr. Babich were out of sight, Vera said, "I need your help until Lana comes to my rescue."

"I'm at your service."

Vera gestured "follow me" with a crooked index finger. "You're quite tall. Please hand me the soup tureen in the upper cupboard."

Nick pulled out a large, heavy, white porcelain tureen. "Where should I set this?"

"Right here on the counter next to the stove. I'll ladle the soup into it and then, please carry it into the dining room and set it on the table next to my chair, which, of course, is the one nearest the kitchen. Not until dessert and coffee are served, can

I rest even one beat. Mateo is very particular, so I have to be on my toes at all times."

Nick nodded. "It was the same for my mother."

"They say women's work is never done, and that's only the half of it. Ah, you see, I've gotten the tureen all filled up while we talked. It's good to have company in the kitchen. You can take it now, but be sure to use the pot holders over on the counter. The soup is quite hot."

Nick carried the tureen to the dining room and set it in its proper place, noting how lovely the table had been laid, with sterling silverware and crystal goblets sparkling in the light. White china dishes were set out on the buffet in order of battle, the soup bowls first in line. From all the dishes, it appeared to Nick that several courses would follow, a full-blown feast of the fishes. Italians started the tradition and introduced it in America. But Croatians, being fishermen like the Italians, had a similar feast on Christmas Eve.

Lana was in the kitchen by the time Nick returned.

"You have done your duty and can relax for a few minutes," Vera said.

Nick headed into the living room, where he found Mr. Babich lounging in an easy chair surrounded by his brood. "Ah, Nick, I'm just taking a little break. It was a long day at the coffeehouse. First, shoppers at the break of dawn. Then lonely souls who wanted some comfort and company before holding vigil alone. I didn't have one moment to rest. You can ask Lana if you don't believe me. But that girl never complains, just works and never stops. She'll make some man a good wife." Mr. Babich gave Nick a subtle grin.

Nick turned away and did not respond as Lana peered into the living room and announced, "Dinner is ready."

The boys elbowed one another to be first to choose a place. When Nick arrived at the table, Mr. Babich motioned to him. "Please take the seat on my right, Nick."

When Nick was seated, he found Jelena on his other side,

having just made a switch with her brother. Nick let his gaze travel around the table. Six children. Lana, the eldest, named after her paternal grandmother, as was the custom. Followed by Peter, named after his paternal grandfather. Jelena, named after her maternal grandmother. Pauli, named after his maternal grandfather. Then Teo and Marta, most likely named after a favorite relative or a saint on whose day they were born. The naming tradition ensured that the family name continued throughout the generations. Nick only knew his maternal grandfather through pictures, but his memory lived on through him, his namesake. *I've always felt a responsibility to live up to my grandfather's name.*

"Now, let us bow our heads in prayer," Mr. Babich said. Then he led the family in Our Father and Hail Mary prayers, followed by his own spontaneous words. "Let us give thanks for the food we eat tonight and remember the humble cod that has given its life to stave off our hunger and give life. Amen."

Lana jumped out of her chair to hand her mother the bowls on the buffet. Rather than passing filled bowls around the table, as it was done in the boardinghouse, Lana set one at each place, beginning with her father. Once everyone had their soup, they dipped their spoons and brought them to their lips.

"Vera, you have done it again. A toast to the cook." Mr. Babich raised his glass. "We are blessed to have such a wonderful cook before us. Thank you for this delicious meal." Glasses clinked around the table, while Mrs. Babich allowed herself a moment of pride before she blushed.

Several more courses followed the bakala en brodo. Next came the shellfish dishes—shrimp scampi, mussels Croatian-style, and crab cakes, made of Dungeness crab caught in the bay. Pasta was next—linguine with clams. And finally, the big fish—a salmon, stuffed with Dungeness crab, roasted, and topped with a lemon beurre blanc. Dessert was a simple apple strudel. For a fasting meal, it was decadent.

"If you don't mind me asking, what type of apples do you use for the strudel?"

"I make it a point to use Newtown Pippins because they have a citrus flavor with just the right amount of sweetness."

"They are very popular, and the best thing about them is that they keep for a long time."

"Now that Lana has brought out the coffee, she'll serve you and we can enjoy our dessert."

Nick couldn't wait to take a bite. "This is even more delicious than the strudel at your coffeehouse."

"That's because it's homemade, and I added more filling than would have been profitable at the restaurant."

"Mama always says that homemade is best. Now we know why," said Lana.

"No holiday meal is complete without a shot of slivovitz. Peter, would you do me a favor and bring out the bottle in the cabinet, along with a few glasses. Three, to be exact. Your reward for retrieving the bottle will be a little sip."

Peter smiled, bringing the bottle back to his father in record time.

Mr. Babich poured two full shots and a tiny quarter shot. He handed one glass to Nick, took one for himself, and motioned for Peter to take the other glass. Then he raised his glass. "To success in the New World." And they all tossed their portion back, gulping it down.

Lana helped her mother clear the table while Nick and the rest of the family gathered in the living room around the tree. They made quick work of the dishes and rejoined the group.

"Lana," Vera said, "please play us a few carols so we can sing."

Lana complied, seating herself on the bench while she thumbed through music on the stand. "Is everyone ready?" She began her medley with "Jingle Bells" and ended on "Silent Night," reminding everyone of the purpose for which they had gathered.

The mantel clock struck the half hour, cuing Mr. Babich to

ready everyone for church. "Wear your coats and mittens—it's chilly outside. And the church is notorious for being frigid for midnight Mass." In only a few minutes, everyone assembled in the entrance hall. "The church is not far. We can walk."

The church was farther away than Mr. Babich had calculated. The foggy air had caused the younger children to cough and wheeze. But once inside the nave, they recovered.

"Mateo, I'm worried that the walk home will not be good for any of us."

"Have faith, woman. God will protect us."

Mrs. Babich shook her head and said to Lana, "God expects us to use our good sense. That's why he gave us a brain."

Lana patted her hand, signaling her not to worry.

Once the organist started playing the prelude, the choir broke out in song and worries were forgotten. The church was packed as it always was for this special celebration, made even more mystical by the candles twinkling throughout the dark nave.

After Holy Communion, the soloist sang "Ave Maria," a musical version of the Hail Mary prayer. With so many Austrian Croatians at the Mass, the final hymn was "Silent Night," an all-time favorite first performed near Salzburg, Austria on Christmas Eve, 1818.

Nick again reflected not only the Mass, but the music connected Catholics no matter where they be. He had never felt so sentimental as tonight. Everything was about tradition, and tradition made life sweet.

Nick arose early on Christmas Day to add his gifts to the children's stockings. First, he selected an apple, polished it, opened the stocking, then slid it in. He repeated this for all six. Next he dropped a piece of Ghirardelli chocolate in each one, a reminder that life is sweet. The parents didn't have a stocking, so Nick left an apple and piece of chocolate on either side of the mantel clock. He still had one piece of chocolate left for himself, and he couldn't resist the temptation. He unwrapped the gold foil carefully, taking a bite and letting it melt on his tongue. The store clerk had told him that Ghirardelli chose only the best cocoa beans for his confections. Nick didn't know much about chocolate, but the taste was heavenly.

Nick heard footsteps creeping down the stairs, soft and stealthy. He turned toward the doorway and spied Mr. and Mrs. Babich with packages in their arms. Mateo held his forefinger up to his mouth, indicating for Nick to remain quiet. They placed six packages, all wrapped in brown paper and string, around the tree. One for each child. Then they turned toward the mantel.

"Ah, Santa has already been here," Vera said. Then she slipped a couple of surprises into each stocking and hooked a candy cane to the opening at the top. "There. Now, while we wait for the children, I'll prepare the hot cocoa."

Mateo signaled for Nick to sit down. He whispered, "Once Vera has everything ready, we can make noise. But until then we have to remain silent."

Lana was the next one to wander into the living room, wearing a pink terrycloth bathrobe and matching slippers. She gave her father a kiss on the cheek and waved to Nick. "I'll check if Mama needs help." She returned with four cups of hot cocoa and kolaches filled with apricot jam. She handed one cup to her father and another to Nick. Then she took one for herself, drawing it to her mouth for a sip. "It's still hot. Be careful."

Vera soon joined the others. "We need to make a little noise so we can get the children up. I can't spend all day waiting with cooking to be done."

"Oh, Mama. Just enjoy the peace and quiet for once. You know I'll help you and with two, the work will go quickly."

"The children were exhausted after midnight Mass. It's the same every year. I only hope no one got sick being out on a cold, foggy night."

They had just finished the hot cocoa when they heard the

children scrambling out of their beds and bounding down the stairs. The boys stopped at the doorway, stunned by the presents under the tree, which looked plentiful even though each child would only receive one. Jelena was the last to arrive, with Marta in tow.

Vera and Mateo hurried to the children and kissed each one. "Happy Christmas morning." The children knew they had to wait for their gifts until their parents finished the ritual.

"Now, sit down and we will pass you your present," Vera said.

Nick watched this happy scene that brought back memories of home. Even though the presents had been few, they reveled in one another, singing Christmas carols and sharing stories. Their stockings were nothing fancy like the ones the Babich children had. Instead, they were an old sock, similar to the ones St. Nicholas tossed through the poor girls' windows that first Christmas. But rather than gold coins, the Markovich kids received a piece of candied orange peel that their mother had made months before. Christmas morning was just one highlight of the day. The afternoon meal featuring a tender pork roast surrounded by potatoes and vegetables was another highlight. Nick recalled everyone had dressed in their Sunday best to show their appreciation for the meal and holiday.

While Nick had been caught up in fond memories, the children had unwrapped their presents—some toys, others clothing. He noticed the young ones received a toy—a doll, a truck, building blocks—while the older ones received a sweater or even pants or a pretty frock. Nick assumed the younger ones received hand-me-downs, so they did not much need clothes. But a special toy they had asked Santa for would thrill them.

Later that afternoon, when they sat down for dinner, Nick smelled familiar aromas coming from the kitchen. When Mrs. Babich brought out the suckling pig, he felt transported back home again, embraced by family—connected by food and through tradition.

After dinner, Mr. Babich said, "Nick, I've been wanting to

bring up the subject of citizenship with you. Have you thought anything about it? If you plan to remain in the United States, it would be important to have."

"Gee, to tell you the truth, I haven't looked into the requirements yet. But I guess I should make it a priority."

"Right now, it's pretty easy to get. In your case, you'd go to the Santa Cruz Courthouse and a judge would hear your case. You need to pledge allegiance to America and be able to speak English."

"My English is still not that good. Maybe I should wait."

"You speak as well as most immigrants. I wouldn't wait. You never know what might happen that will change things. Ask around. There's bound to be someone at the packinghouse who knows what's involved. You'd need a couple of witnesses, too, which I imagine wouldn't be an issue."

After dinner was over, Nick headed for the train station because he had work the next day. Being with the Babiches brought back so many memories of home that he wondered whether he wanted to stay in America forever. But if he did, it would make sense to become a citizen. He'd have to send another letter to Francis to encourage him to come out. *If I had my brother here, I wouldn't be so alone.*

CHAPTER 13

One spring day in 1886, a stranger showed up at the boarding-house, looking for Nick.

"I'm headed up that way," a man told the stranger, "and will let him know you're here."

All the man told Nick was that someone was waiting to see him. He had no idea who it could be. But dinner was about to be served, so a trip downstairs would serve two purposes. When Nick saw Francis in the lobby, he did a double take. The last time he had seen him, he was still a boy and now he was nearly a man—tall and broad-shouldered with dark, wavy hair, and eyes the color of the Adriatic Sea.

"Francis, aren't you a sight for sore eyes!" Nick wrapped his arms around him in a big bear hug. "It's so good to see you here. Come, let's sit down in the dining room, and you can tell me about the family. It's difficult to get any news, and I don't send letters often since I need help with writing."

The boardinghouse clerk followed them into the dining room, a frown on his face. "This is not a soup kitchen and no guests are allowed. Take your friend down the street to the diner if he wants something to eat."

"I apologize, but this is my brother, Francis. He just arrived from Croatia."

"I don't care if he's the king of England. He still can't eat here unless he's a boarder."

"Of course. He will need a room."

"That's more like it. I will try to find him a bed."

"We'd like to room together."

"That's out of the question. I have only one bed available and the other bed in the room is taken. If you convince the boarder to make a switch, all the more power to you."

Nick took the key and guided Francis to his room. "Leave your suitcase in the room and let's go down to eat. Maybe we'll run into your roommate or mine, and we can ask them to switch."

"I'm fine as it is, so don't knock yourself out."

"It's as much for me as for you. I want to have someone I can really talk to and who better than my favorite brother? It's been a long time since I've had family around."

Once Nick and Francis had eaten their fill of dinner, Nick said, "Let's go into the bar so we can talk. I want you to tell me all the news about the family." As they sat down, Nick signaled the waitress to bring two glasses of slivovitz. He held out his glass to Francis. "May God bless both you and me." They clinked glasses, slugging down the liquor in one gulp.

Francis filled the glasses again. "So, what do you want to know?"

"First off, how are Ma and Pa?"

"They're about the same and even though there are fewer children around, the grandchildren are filling the gap."

"Grandchildren? How many are they up to? Ivan had two when I left. Has Ana had one already?"

"Two. And Ivan's up to three. It doesn't take long for us to multiply. Ma and Pa's record confirm it."

"What about the others? Are Luka and Gabriel planning to come out here next?"

"Everyone is well and growing up. But as far as Luka and Gabriel, I believe they're too young to have a plan."

"That's true. I still haven't made my stake, although I have a little put away to start my own packinghouse."

"Your own business?"

"That's right. It's my dream and you'll be my partner. I can't go it alone, at least not at first."

"You'd be taking a big risk with me. I know nothing about the apple game yet."

"You will soon enough. Mr. Rajkovich is encouraging me to do it, and with him on my side, how can I lose?"

"If the man understands the business, then he would be a suitable partner."

"That's not his interest. He's an important man who can't spend too much time in one packinghouse. He is a mover and shaker of the entire apple industry. Some call him Mr. Apple, but not to his face."

The next day, Nick took Francis to the packinghouse and introduced him to Phil. "So, you want to become an apple packer, too, huh, Francis? Mind if I call you Frank? It's more friendly."

Frank gave a smile in agreement.

"Well, Frank, you've come to the right place. And, if you're half as good a packer as your brother Nick, you'll do very well here. Make a lot of money. Maybe one day you and Nick will have your own packinghouse and go into competition with me."

Frank nodded.

Nick glared at him. "Phil, pay no attention to him. He's scared and only trying to be agreeable."

"What's he scared of?"

"You know...all the new things he has to learn. He doesn't have his confidence up yet."

"Well, he better crank it up if he wants to succeed. No one achieved anything without believing in himself first."

"He will soon enough. He just got here, so he needs some time to adjust."

"Fair enough. Go take him around and show him the ropes. Once he starts performing, that'll build confidence. Just look what it did for you."

Nick took the morning to give Frank a tour of the packinghouse and explain all the various tasks the workers were doing. He noticed Frank was overloaded by the time the lunch bell rang. "Let's go get some grub. Then we can talk, and I'll answer all your questions."

Lunch was chili and cornbread. Nick watched as Frank inspected his food suspiciously. "This is really good, Frank. Try it. You're gonna like it. Ma made nothing resembling it, but it's hardy and spicy, tasting of hot peppers."

Frank dipped his spoon in and scooped a little on it. Then he brought it to his mouth for a taste. "It's different. I'll grant you that." But he was so hungry he cleaned his plate and went back for seconds.

Nick always got a chuckle out of the new immigrants, remembering he acted the same way when he first arrived. Of course, that was a few years ago and now he was practically an American. That reminded him he had an appointment with the judge at the Santa Cruz Courthouse later in the week. He'd better tell Phil that he wouldn't be at work on Friday.

When Nick appeared at the packinghouse wearing his blue suit, he set off wolf whistles which could be heard for miles. Everyone realized something was happening, but it was a mystery. Some assumed Nick was a pallbearer at a funeral, while others suspected he had to make a court appearance for some offense. But no one guessed the correct reason.

Phil had offered to take him to the train station, and he already had the team hitched to the wagon. When he gave the signal, Nick followed him to the awaiting wagon. Phil climbed aboard first, taking the reins in hand. Then Nick bounded into his seat. Once they were underway, Phil said, "Are you ready for any question the judge might ask?"

"Mrs. Bertucci prepared me. My only concern is English. I don't speak it that well yet."

"You're better than most, so you have no worry there. You should do just fine and the next time I see you, you'll be singing 'Yankee Doodle.'"

Nick had only a brief wait for the train, which carried few passengers this early in the day. While he rode, he went over the answers to the questions his attorney had told him to expect. His memory was almost photographic. After one time through, he had the answers impressed upon his brain.

The Santa Cruz Courthouse was only a short walk from the train station. Nick's attorney instructed him to wait outside courtroom number three, where he would meet him and his two witnesses. Finding a pair of witnesses who could travel to Santa Cruz during the work week proved equivalent to finding a needle in a haystack. But when Mrs. Bertucci learned of Nick's desperation, she volunteered herself and her husband.

Nick didn't have to wait long for them to appear. The Bertuccis were all dressed up for the occasion. Mrs. Bertucci wore a crimson suit with a matching hat and white gloves. She had the air of a businesswoman, she was so properly attired. Her husband wore a classic dark-blue suit, white shirt, and red tie. Together, they looked like the Star-Spangled Banner.

"Thanks for coming." Nick shook both their hands. "I didn't see you on the train."

"We came up yesterday to make the most of our trip. We have fond memories of summers spent on the beach in Santa Cruz with our children and wanted to pay our respects to relatives we hadn't seen in a while."

Nick's attorney appeared. "I'd like to introduce you to my witnesses, Mr. Bertucci and Mrs. Bertucci, my English teacher."

Mr. Costa extended his arm to shake hands. "Haven't we met somewhere before?"

"Perhaps," Mr. Bertucci said.

Mrs. Bertucci chimed in. "It was years ago, at my uncle's wake. You were quite young then."

"Now I remember. I think we're related somehow."

"That's right," Mr. Bertucci said. "We Italians have a long line of relatives. I believe my wife's uncle was a fisherman operating out of the port here."

"That explains our connection even better. My father, too, was a fisherman, like so many Italians on the coast.

"Now that introductions are out of the way, let's go over what to expect in court." Then he clued them in. "We have to wait for our case to be called. In the interim, I'll excuse myself because I'm due in court on another case. Don't worry. I'll be back in time."

To Nick, it appeared he had to wait an eternity until he and the Bertuccis made their way to the courtroom where Mr. Costa was standing by. "Nick, remember to let me do the talking until the judge questions you."

"All rise," the bailiff said as the judge entered the courtroom, taking his place on the bench. He was an elderly man who peered over his spectacles at the courtroom, settling his gaze on Nick, who met the judge's eyes with a self-assured stare. Once they unlocked eyes, the judge began the citizenship procedure. "Remain standing and pledge allegiance to our flag."

Mrs. Bertucci had drilled the pledge into him, instructing him to practice it every day until it became second nature. Now, he had his chance to show that he had learned it well. "I pledge allegiance to the flag of the United States of America..."

The judge smiled, pleased by what he heard. After questioning Nick for a few minutes, he called him and the Bertuccis forward. "Mr. Markovich, please place your hand on the Bible and repeat the Pledge of Allegiance once again in the presence of your two witnesses." Then the judge proclaimed Nick a naturalized citizen of the United States of America. Afterward, there were handshakes and kisses, as well as applause from the gallery of spectators.

"I need you all to follow me," Mr. Costa said, "to make it official by signing paperwork necessary for your certificate."

After they finished the legal requirements, Mrs. Bertucci said, "We'd like to treat you to a fish lunch at a relative's restaurant near the pier. Please say you'll join us."

"Of course, I will. Thanks for your kind offer."

When Nick arrived at the boardinghouse, the commotion in the dining hall signaled dinner was underway. Forgetting he still wore his new suit, Nick walked into the room, causing heads to turn while applause rose up, along with shouts and whistles. He caught Frank waving him over to a seat he had saved. When he reached Frank, they embraced in an outward sign of brotherhood.

"I am so proud of you. My brother, the American. How does it feel to no longer be a citizen of that nasty Austro-Hungarian Regime?"

"I feel free. For the first time in my life, I can be my own man."

CHAPTER 14

The next day, Nick and Frank got back to the job. The packing-house was handling plums until the end of July, when the apple harvest would begin. But packing plums was not much different from apples. In fact, it was a little easier because the skin did not show as many bruises and blemishes, making for quick work.

Near the end of July, the apple harvest began, heralded by the arrival of an international array of fruit tramps, as they called themselves. Single men from near and far made the journey, which often involved a sail around the treacherous Cape Horn with huge winds, high waves, and hazardous currents—along with the occasional iceberg. Those with less fire in their belly chose the overland route, crossing the Isthmus of Panama while bushwhacking through the jungle. Poor men, desperate for wages to survive, took the risks to get here.

When Nick saw the men showing up for work, he didn't know what to make of them or whether they could even do the job. But he needed laborers, so he took a chance and hired them. Phil told him they'd depended on fruit tramps for years, and that was the only way they could handle the harvest.

Most of the men spoke little English, which made managing them a challenge. However, the vast majority had worked the harvest before, so they knew what to do. And, if one compatriot was a novice, the expert clued him in.

Nick could communicate with the men from Croatia, who came over in high numbers. At lunchtime, he would sit among them, listening to them reminisce about home or tell tales of their voyages on sea and overland. Because the sea had baptized most Croatians, they opted for the route around the horn. Nick loved hearing about their adventures and how they cheated death over and over again. Some Croatians would jump off the boat in Chile, settling there instead because the coast reminded them of Dalmatia.

The apple harvest was an intense time between the work that must be done and the fruit tramps who needed to be taken care of while they were here. Bunkhouses were available on the farms, but the fruit tramps required an entire system of support, from cooks to transportation and, of course, entertainment. More often than not, the fruit tramps would walk to work. Those at more of a distance got a lift in one of the empty apple wagons. The townspeople looked forward to the fruit tramps' arrival, lending what they considered to be a cosmopolitan air to the town. They enjoyed hearing the wide variety of tongues spoken on Main Street when the fruit tramps were out and about on a Sunday after church, even if the men were shabby dressers and had boorish manners.

Nick made sure the tramps who worked for him obeyed the rules set out, such as no fraternizing with the womenfolk. They had whorehouses set up for their pleasure. But money was the factor that kept them in line. These men understood they had a brief window to earn their stake before they headed back home. Most of their families barely scraped by. Their only hope was the return of a husband, brother, or son with his pockets full of dollars.

Sometimes fruit tramps would move on before the harvest was finished, but Nick learned there were always others to take their place. However, training never stopped and he never let up his supervision. Mostly, the men who came to town valued work, and they gave it all they had.

The harvest was about halfway through the night it happened. Nick remembered cleaning up after the crews left for the day and heading back to the boardinghouse with Frank for dinner. Nick had arranged for his roommate, Jakov, to make a swap to allow him to share with Frank. Once they got up to their room, they were too exhausted to talk. Their heads hit the pillows, and they fell fast asleep. Not long afterward, bells rang out and voices shouted, "packinghouse fire."

Nick and Frank leaped out of bed, threw on their clothes, and ran down the stairs. They found men milling around in confusion. "Follow me. The firemen can use all the help they can get," Nick said.

Then it was a stampede out the door. When they reached the row, several packinghouses were aflame, including Phil's, which seemed to be completely engulfed. Nick found Phil in front of his packinghouse, looking helpless and beat.

"This is the end."

"It's not the end. You can rebuild."

Phil shook his head. "This is not the first time. I've been through this before, but never in the middle of the harvest. We've probably lost everything."

Nick patted Phil on the back. "It will be all right. You'll see." He grabbed a bucket, handing another to Frank, and they took up places in the water brigade. As they passed buckets of water along the line, Nick kept his eye on Phil's packinghouse. He feared it would be a total disaster, and he was right.

Nick stood vigil with Phil throughout the night until only a few embers were left smoking. "How much did you lose?" Nick asked.

"It's a total loss. Must have been nearly seven thousand boxes of apples, besides several thousand empty boxes, four horses, a harness, two large fruit wagons, and the winter's hay. Not to mention, all the paperwork in the office, which included cash to pay the workers."

"You kept most of the paperwork and cash in the safe. Surely, that survived."

Phil was so dispirited he could not reply, but instead blessed himself and clasped his hands in prayer, casting his eyes toward heaven.

Nick noticed someone listening to their conversation and when he shifted his full gaze to him, the man reached out to shake hands. "Howard Dawson from the *Pajaronian*. I think we've met before."

Now Nick remembered. *The newspaper editor. Of course, he would be after a story.* After Mr. Dawson shook Phil's hand, he said, "What do you need from us?"

"A list of the loss. A couple of quotes. And speculation on what started the fire."

Phil was so beat he nodded to Nick to take over. "You probably overheard us discussing the items we lost."

"I wasn't eavesdropping, if that's what you mean. But I picked up a couple of words. Why don't you go over them again?"

Nick repeated the list Phil had come up with.

"What does the loss mean for this year's harvest?" Dawson asked.

Nick waited for Phil to respond. "Mean? Isn't it obvious? We're out of business."

"For how long? A month? The season? Forever?"

"I don't know. I can't think too far in advance right now. First thing I have to do is file an insurance claim. I won't have the money to rebuild until they give me a settlement."

"You had insurance?"

"It's a good policy through the Croatian Fraternal Union. Without them, I would have been out of business years ago."

"Can you explain? I'm not following."

"This is not my first rodeo. I lost a packinghouse a few years back. You may not remember, since packinghouse fires seem to be a regular occurrence around here. But when it happens to you, there's no forgetting."

"I'm sorry. I didn't realize you had been hit before. There's speculation that this was the work of a firebug. What do you think?"

"Could be. Someone's carelessness started the last fire. It's hard to control. Sometimes these tramps just arriving or passing through seek shelter in a packinghouse. Maybe I should post guards during the season."

"That's not a bad idea. Why take a chance on being hit a third time?"

"Maybe I won't rebuild. Then I won't get hit again."

"You'd have to be crazy not to rebuild with the gold mine you're sitting on."

"Perhaps it's only fools' gold."

Nick did not return to the boardinghouse that night, preferring to stand watch until daybreak. He knew that when the sun shined its light, problems grew smaller. Although, in this case, that didn't prove to be true. What hadn't been visible in darkness was now in full view, not leaving one thing to the imagination. Reality smacked him in the face, right between the eyes—the packinghouse was a total loss, as Phil said it would be.

Nick grabbed the fire marshal as he walked by. "When can we check for salvageable items?"

"The embers are still hot. We'll let you know. But prepare yourself for the worst. I've seen packinghouse fires before, and there usually isn't anything left. You're down to scratch."

"There was a safe in the office that contained important business papers. Do you think it survived the fire?"

"That is the only thing that would. I'll tell the fire chief to be on the lookout for it."

Nick walked around the back of the building, hoping to find Phil keeping a watch there. But he was nowhere to be found. A terrible thought crossed Nick's mind. He had to search him out before something worse happened. He found Phil at the little house he rented, still awake, smelling of slivovitz and slurring his words. *Drunk. No doubt about it.*

Nick made a pot of strong coffee and got Phil to take the medicine. He also checked the refrigerator for beer and offered the brew to Phil, who guzzled it down in record time. The hops in beer could lessen the effects of a katzenjammer. And once Phil had finished, he had recovered enough to talk.

"The fire marshal said that the safe likely survived the fire."

"That would be one answer to my prayers. I can't rebuild without money."

"Couldn't you get a loan?"

"That takes time. And the bankers also consider if you're a good risk."

"Why wouldn't you be?"

"Because I've had more than one packinghouse fire. Makes people suspicious."

Nick reflected a minute. He couldn't imagine anyone believing Phil would set a fire in the middle of the apple harvest that was almost certain to make him a small fortune. "What's your next step?"

"I'll rebuild. What choice do I have? But if I wait for the insurance check, I'll lose out on this season."

"Maybe a loan is the answer."

"No. A partner is. What about it, Nick? Do you want to cast your lot in with mine?"

"Me, a partner? I don't know. I might not have enough of a stake yet." The wallet he snatched suddenly came to mind. *And do I want to join my fate to Phil's. It might be better to wait and pick a partner, or even go it alone until Frank is ready.* There were a million things to consider before making this commitment. But then again, there was power in seizing the moment. "I'll have an answer for you tomorrow." *By then, the safe may have been recovered and that'll put a whole new slant on the situation.*

Nick left once he was satisfied that Phil could take care of himself. When he opened the door to his room at the boarding-house, Frank was waiting for him. "Where have you been? It doesn't look like your bed has even been slept in."

"I waited until the sun came up so I could get a clear view of the fire damage. Then I went in search of Phil, and he was nowhere to be found. That sent me into a panic. Guys have been known to do away with themselves over misfortune. I went out to his house, where I found him in a drunken stupor. There's no way I could leave him like that, so I got him sobered up."

"Will he be okay?"

"He's certainly not up to dick. I don't know if he was talking crazy or not, but he asked me to be his partner."

"Do you have enough of a stake?"

"I might. The bigger question is, do I want to go into busi-ness with Phil?"

"Only you can answer that."

"This could be my big break. Kind of like finding that first gold nugget that leads to a vein of rich golden ore."

"If you want my two cents, the apple business seems to be a sure thing here. If you bet on it, you can't lose."

"My thinking as well. If I take the plunge, I can make big money. Then, in a few years when you're ready, we'll start the Markovich Brothers Packinghouse."

"I like the sound of that."

"Me, too. We've missed breakfast. So, let's grab some grub at the bar and then find us some jobs. We've got to make money to survive."

As they ate lunch, they planned out their job search. "We need to be strategic about it since this is not just about the job, but our future business. We should work for the best so we can learn from them. I've made a mental list of the best packers in town. You take three, and I'll take the other three, and hopefully, we'll get hired by two of them. What do you say to that idea?"

"I like it."

"This fire disaster is taking on a whole new patina. It may be a blessing in disguise. Let's go up and change. It helps to look your best, even when applying for a job packing apples." Nick took a whiff of himself. "Ugh. I smell like smoke. A bath would go a long way too, but there's no time for it. Maybe the smoke will garner me some sympathy."

Nick and Frank changed their shirts, and Nick doused himself with cologne. He took another whiff of himself. *Double ugh. I smell worse. Fresh air should take the edge off the stench.*

"Okay. Ready. Let's go."

It didn't take long for Nick to return to the boardinghouse, but Frank had beaten him back. He sat at a table, a smug smile on his face.

"How did you get back so fast?"

"The first one on the list hired me. I start tomorrow."

"That's great. The foreman hired me on my first try, too, but pulled me into speculation about the fire. There's a rumor that it was arson."

The next morning, Nick and Frank walked to packinghouse row together until they had to part for their workplaces.

"I may miss dinner tonight. I need to track down Phil and give him my answer."

"You've decided to take his offer?"

"That's if he agrees to a couple of my...I won't call them demands...more like requirements."

"Like what?"

"I'll tell you tonight when I come back."

Nick found Phil at home in a state of depression—a bottle in one hand, a cigarette butt in the other. "Welcome to my lair," he said.

They headed toward the living room, a scene of utter squalor. Nick cleared a chair of old newspapers and sat down. When he had Phil's attention, he began. "Yesterday, you asked me to be your partner. Did you mean it?"

"Sure, I meant it. I don't ask everyone to come into business with me?"

"You weren't in the best condition, so I wanted to confirm it was a genuine offer."

"Do you have an answer for me? You promised you would today."

"First, I need to discuss a couple of matters. If I'm to put my hard-earned stake at risk, I want an assurance from you we will rebuild the packinghouse this season."

"That may be too soon. It takes money."

"We'll get the money. I just need your commitment."

"If you can get the money, I'm in. What else?"

"That if you want to sell your share of the partnership, you'll only do so with my blessing. And I'll do the same."

"Of course, I would. You didn't even have to ask."

"You've got a deal. Let's shake on it." Nick reached out and grabbed Phil's hand in a firm grip. "Partners. Now, about the money. What will it cost to rebuild? If they recover the safe, will you have enough to share the expense?"

"I still owe wages to the men. After that, there may be little left."

"What is the number we need to get started?"

"Five hundred at least."

Nick hoped the safe contained the bulk of it because he didn't have even half the amount in savings. But he would not let Phil know that. "That's a start."

"Do you think you'll be able to match my share?"

"Let me worry about that. If I can't, I'll raise the money." *Or use the windfall in the wallet.*

Phil stared at him, as if he hadn't a clue what Nick was thinking.

Nick spotted Mr. Rajkovich at his workplace the next morning. Before he could even wave hello, Karlo had made his way to him. "Glad to see you've got a new job. But I wanted to find out what you know about the fire. Let's meet when you have your lunch break."

As he sorted apples, Nick wondered why Mr. Rajkovich was so interested in the fire. While he awaited their meeting, he let his mind ponder the question.

The triangle bell sounded for lunch, and Nick's meeting with Mr. Rajkovich, who he found out back waiting for him. "Tell me what you found out about the fire."

"I can't add anything to what you read in the *Pajaronian*."

"Do you think anyone had a beef with Phil?"

"Not that I know of."

"Everything points to arson. It could be personal or it could be business."

"Business?"

"It's the height of the apple season. The fewer packing-houses, the more profits for those still standing."

"I can't believe anyone would be that greedy."

"Believe it, because it's true. When it comes to money, men can lose their moral compass."

Karlo's words brought the Timok Rebellion to Nick's mind, and he nodded sadly as he thought of his brother Slavs and their betrayal.

They rebuilt the packinghouse in record time, enabling the part-ners to make the most of the latter part of the season. Because apple

crops were purchased from farmers in the spring, Phil owned the
apples regardless of their use. But not having money to pay pickers
and packers meant ripe apples fell to the ground, where they rotted.

Nick said, "A lot of fruit has gone to waste over the fire. First,
the seven thousand crates of fruit that were awaiting storage.
And then the mature fruit that couldn't be picked and packed
properly."

"I try not to think about it. Just makes me more depressed,"
Phil said.

"You're in the money now. And any day, you should receive
the insurance payment."

"Last I heard from the insurance company, they're awaiting a
decision on the cause. Since arson is now a possibility, they're
holding off for the culprit to be caught and made to pay so they
don't have to."

"Do the police have any good leads?"

"Not a thing."

"Then the insurance should pay out."

"We'll see."

Nick was pleased with how well the end of the season turned
out and even more pleased with Frank. He was one of his best
workers, perhaps because he was working for a family business
that he might have a share in one day, and Nick made him a
foreman in short order.

The next two seasons, Nick saw his income rise. He realized
by taking a chance, luck had followed.

One November day, Phil called Nick to the office. "I have
received bad news from home. My mother is on her deathbed,
and I must return to Croatia immediately. She wants to spend
one last Christmas surrounded by her entire family, and I cannot
deny her that."

The news blindsided Nick. He had not foreseen this possibility. "What about the business?"

"I've sold my share to Jakov Kurtovich."

"Jakov? Our deal was that I had final approval of a partner."

"I had to act quickly. Couldn't wait for you to post a help wanted ad and then start interviewing. I knew Jakov had a stake from his work in the silver mines, so I made him an offer he couldn't refuse. Besides, I thought he was a friend. You brought him here for his first job."

Nick's anger rose, and he waited to respond as he tried to calm himself with a few deep breaths. "The issue isn't Jakov. The issue is that you didn't honor our bargain."

"Under the circumstances, it wasn't practical. I have to leave right away. You know how long the journey is. My mother may not even be alive when I return. But I still have to try to get there in time."

"My brother, Frank, might have been a better choice. He's building up a stake, and I'm sure we could have figured out a way to get what you needed."

"It didn't even cross my mind to consider Frank. But it's all water under the bridge now. You'll not see me again for a long time."

Nick realized there was no sense in beating a dead horse. And it would be far better to part company on good terms. "I wish you Godspeed." But he felt Phil owed him one. And if Phil returned, he would collect on it at an opportune moment.

Nick waited until he and Frank were alone in their room to reveal what happened with the business.

"He betrayed you."

"I prefer to think of it as he didn't live up to our bargain. Regardless, holding a grudge doesn't do anyone any good. I have to move on and make the most of it."

"You're a better man than I'll ever be."

"Not true. I've learned to move forward in life. No one became a success by looking back. And doesn't the Bible caution about that?"

"That's right. Lot's wife did, and she turned into a pillar of salt, remaining forever at a standstill."

"My first step forward will be to meet with Jakov. I plan to ask him to come to our room after dinner. It would be best if it's just the two of us. I don't want to put him on the defensive with you there."

"Say no more. I'll find a drinking buddy at the bar."

"Did anyone ever tell you you're the best kid brother?" Nick reached out and ruffled Frank's hair.

CHAPTER 15

The boardinghouse clerk handed Nick a large, white envelope. He took it up to his room, wondering what it contained inside. The handwriting on the envelope was done in a type of calligraphy, indicating an important message. While he was studying the envelope, Frank came through the door.

"What's that you've got in your hand?"

"I've been asking myself the same question."

"Open it and find out."

Nick pulled out his pocketknife and ran the blade under the flap. He carefully pulled out the card inside and when he saw what it was, his heart skipped a beat.

"What is it? Are you okay?"

"It's a wedding invitation. Lana Babich is getting married."

"The one you've been sweet on up in San Francisco?"

"The same. But it was all one-sided, because I never made a move. The timing wasn't right."

"Will you go to the wedding?"

"I think I have to, but it will be a bittersweet affair for me."

"You can't blame Lana for moving ahead in her life since you didn't offer her any reason to wait."

"I know that. It's just that whenever I saw her and the family, I felt so good."

"Perhaps it's the family you're afraid you'll lose. But since you and Lana can still be friends as you've always been, it seems you can stay close to her family, too."

"I wonder who she's marrying."

"Doesn't it have his name on the invitation?"

"It does, but I don't recognize it."

"When is the wedding?"

"Next month—February. Do you want to come? It says I can bring a guest."

Nick and Frank arrived at the Church of St. Francis well ahead of the family and sat in a pew behind the one reserved for them. When Mrs. Babich was escorted down the aisle with her brood, Nick and Frank stood to greet her. Nick thought she put on a good show in a rose-colored gown with a matching hat and shoes. She wore a corsage of pink and white roses over her heart. Nick bent forward to kiss her cheeks before she took her seat and noticed she already had tears in her eyes.

"Thank you for coming to share this special day with us." Nick nodded as Mrs. Babich set her gaze on Frank. "This must be your younger brother I have heard so much about." She extended a gloved hand in greetings and then turned to face the altar.

The church was almost full when the organist struck up "Here Comes the Bride." Everyone stood and turned to watch the bride walk down the aisle on the arm of her father. Lana wore a classic Victorian wedding gown made of lace, with a high collar and long sleeves. Her face was covered in a short tulle veil, a longer one trailing behind.

Nick wished he could have seen her expression at that moment, but it was obscured. However, he caught a tear rolling down Mr. Babich's face after he took his place in the pew, having just kissed his daughter and presented her to the groom.

The congregation bowed their heads as the priest initiated the Mass. When it was time for the vows, a hush fell over those assembled, allowing the voices of the couple to be heard. After they exchanged rings, the priest said the familiar words—"I now pronounce you man and wife. You may kiss the bride." Nick watched as the groom tossed back Lana's veil and kissed her.

Lana was beaming as she processed back down the aisle on the arm of her groom to the tune of Mendelssohn's "Wedding March." The Babiches and the groom's family followed the pair as guests exited the pews behind them. Once everyone assembled on the steps of the church, the bride and groom appeared as they hurried, amid showers of rice, to a waiting carriage decorated with flowers and streamers.

Nick and Frank walked the distance to the Slavonic Society, where the reception was being held. By the time they arrived, the bride and groom, and their wedding party and families, were assembled in a line to receive their guests. When Nick reached Lana, he thought he had never seen a bride look so lovely and told her so. As she blushed, he kissed her on each cheek and then proceeded down the line to her groom—a tall, good-looking man with thick, dark hair and brown eyes. "I'm Nick Markovich, a friend of the family."

"Steven Pekich. Pleased to meet you."

Nick introduced Frank to Lana and then to Steven and the entire Babich clan. Then they moved into the hall to take their place at the long table that had been set up for the wedding party. No sooner did he pull up a chair, then he found Jelena moving into one next to him. Nick had recognized her fondness for him a few years ago, but he expected her to be over it. "Are you my dining partner today?"

"Mama said I should make you and your brother feel welcome. So here I am. Frank can take the chair on my other side."

Nick cast his eyes over Jelena. "You have grown up since I last saw you and have become a real beauty."

Jelena blushed as she offered Nick a smile. "Did you expect me to stay a kid forever?"

"Of course not. But since I don't see you often, you caught me by surprise."

As soon as everyone was seated, waiters brought out the soup. Tadich's Restaurant, the oldest restaurant in the state, catered the event. The Babiches had become good friends with John Tadich over the years they had dined in his restaurant. And they knew Tadich's would rise to the occasion for their daughter's wedding. They were experts at cooking fish as well as grilling meats. And both would be on the menu today.

When the meal was over, the band started up. Nick loved to dance and asked Jelena to join him on the dance floor. When Nick took her into his arms for the waltz, his heartbeat quickened, but he tried to ignore it. Jelena was still a young girl, and he was an older man of twenty-six.

Lana and Steven had moved to the dance floor to do their traditional first dance. As Nick watched, he could see how much in love they were and he felt happy for the couple to be so blessed. A kolo dance was next, as guests surrounded the couple in the center and danced the circle dance. Nick and Jelena found each other together again. And, finally, the dance Nick had looked forward to all day—the dance with the bride herself. Jelena held a pot to deposit money in, and Nick waited in line until it was his turn. He put in as much as he could afford to buy him time for a long dance with Lana in his arms.

When he finished, he returned to the sidelines, and Frank patted him on the back. "You made a good show, brother."

Another man approached, also patting him on the back. "Remember me?"

"Mr. Loreto. Of course, how could I forget? You got me started in the apple packing business and now, believe it or not, I own my own packinghouse."

"I realized from the moment we met, you were a young man on the rise. I'm glad to know that you've already made a success of yourself."

"I'm on my way. That's for sure. But I have more plans still. How are you acquainted with the bride and groom?"

"You may recall that my brother is married to a Croatian woman. Steven is her nephew. And you? Are you a Babich cousin?"

"No. Just a friend. I met Lana and her father right after I arrived in San Francisco at their coffeehouse, and we became friends."

"We should see more of each other at these family gatherings."

"I hope so. Mr. Loreto, you are an attorney for the railroads, if I'm not mistaken."

"That's correct. Why do you ask?"

"At some point, I may need your help with a transportation matter."

"Please come by any time. But check with my secretary first to make sure I'll be in the office."

The wedding party ended late—too late to catch a train back to Watsonville. Nick found a hotel nearby where he and Frank could spend the night. When they got to their room, the brothers were too wound up to sleep.

"So, how did you like the Babiches?"

"They're nice. Just like people from home. But you better watch out for Jelena—she's set her mark on you."

"It's just a schoolgirl crush. She'll get over it when she meets a nice boy her own age."

"I don't know about that. Just keep your guard up—unless, of course, you'd rather let her get around your defenses."

CHAPTER 16

When Nick and Frank arrived at the packinghouse the next morning, Jakov intercepted them. "Someone's waiting in the office to speak with you. I think it's that newspaper editor, Mr. uh..."

"Dawson?"

"That's it. I don't like him snooping around here."

"Don't worry. I'll take care of it." Nick took long strides toward the office and caught Mr. Dawson scribbling in his notepad. "Howard. What can I do for you today?"

"I need some information for an article I'm doing for the *Pajaronian* on the codling moth."

"The codling moth—he's a fiendish critter. What do you want to know about him?"

"Word is that he's a growing problem. He destroyed an orchard in Santa Cruz."

"If we get a good fog, that'll kill him off."

"But if you don't..."

"Then he's just one of many problems to contend with."

"Could you elaborate?"

"I could give you a long list, but I'll keep it short. Indirect railroad schedules that result in spoiled fruit from the long ride.

Supply and demand that is ever changing. Labor shortages. Commission men who try to bamboozle us. And then, of course, the codling moth. Ever since someone brought it into the valley in used packing boxes, we've been fighting the pest and there isn't a pesticide available that can kill it without harming the trees, too."

"I assume you're staying on top of it the best you can because that red scale disease back in the 1870s wiped out the entire apple crop in Santa Clara."

"And their loss was our gain. If that hadn't happened, Mr. Rajkovich wouldn't have come over the hill looking for a new source of apples. Now, if that's all you need from me, I have to get back to work. Even in the winter months, there're tasks to do."

"One more thing. I'd like to invite you to take part in a regular roundtable to discuss the apple industry. It would be good for you to meet some leaders in town."

Nick knew that the town fathers considered the Croatians a clannish bunch. But they couldn't fault their success. *It's our reliance on one another that has made us a force to contend with, not only in this town but in the state.* "Give me the date and time of the next roundtable and I'll try to be there."

Another fancy envelope was waiting for Nick when he returned to the boardinghouse.

Frank took a glance at it and said, "You might be off the hook, and Jelena is getting married."

"We'll find out soon enough." He tore into the envelope, not even bothering to cut it open with his pocketknife, and found a picture of a baby staring back at him.

Frank saw the stunned look on Nick's face and took a peek over his shoulder. "Someone must have had a baby."

"It appears that way." Nick opened the envelope and read, "Mr. and Mrs. Steven Pekich invite you to the christening of their son—Lana had a baby boy."

"What did they name him?"

"Tomas. After the paternal grandfather, of course."

"So, the naming pattern has survived in the New World."

"Traditions die hard."

"Will you attend the christening?"

"I wouldn't miss it. It will give me a chance to take another look at Jelena and see how she compares to the single Croatian women who are finally joining the colony."

"I might ride up with you and take a tour of San Francisco since I haven't had much of a chance to experience it yet."

"In the evening, we'll paint the town red."

After the christening, Nick made regular trips up to San Francisco on Sundays to court Jelena. It had dawned on him she was a woman now—one who was ready for matrimony. But he planned to take his time while he built another stake. He wanted to make sure he had something good to offer her besides his ambitions, especially a house of her own she could make into a gracious family home.

CHAPTER 17

The recent problem facing apple packers was supply and demand. They had established the habit of buying the crops in early spring from the orchardists, even before it was known if the crop would be a good one or not. But this year, the packers had decided as a group to not buy all the orchards available so they could control demand. The orchardists called a mass meeting to determine their response to the packers' action.

"Those Croatians are a greedy bunch," said one farmer. "They've been making money, hands over fists, with the apples we grow. And now they're hanging us out to dry. I, for one, may not be able to weather the storm they've created." Cheers went up among the orchardists gathered.

Then one put forth a proposal. "Let's pick and pack our own. We'll show them they aren't that smart."

Nick walked into the office where Frank was waiting to question him. "Did you hear about the farmers' meeting last night?"

"Yeah. I knew they were all worked up about us not buying some of their crops outright."

"And do you know what they're doing about it?"

"I heard the complainers are planning to pick, pack, and

distribute their own. Good luck to them. Once they do it, they'll realize how hard it is to make a buck that way. And if you don't have a knack for it...forget about it."

"Do you think they have any chance to compete with us and destroy what we've built here?"

"Not a chance. We're too far ahead. They've been angry for a month of Sundays that we Croatians have a monopoly on the packing business. It's not like the orchardists are very diverse themselves."

That night, sirens could be heard throughout the town, heading for packinghouse row. Frank woke up first and poked Nick. "Fire! Let's get going. I'll grab Jakov and meet you downstairs."

When the trio reached the row, they found several packing-houses on fire. Nick pulled the fire chief aside. "What do you make of this?"

"Someone called the fire in and when we got here, it had just begun. My take is it was arson. Anybody have something out for you guys?"

"Let me think about it." Then he went over to where Frank and Jakov stood to relay his conversation with the fire chief. "My take is that this was a warning. Those Irish farmers mean to play hardball with us."

"I wonder why they didn't set our packinghouse on fire?" Frank said.

"Because they want to leave me in suspense. They know I'm one of the leaders, so they want me to be on edge until they strike again."

"Do you think they'll do it again soon?" Jakov asked.

"My guess is if we don't yield and buy their crops, they'll strike during the height of the season. They know we haven't forgotten the damage done to Phil's packinghouse, and the losses incurred when he was put out of business."

"What do we do about it?" Frank said.

"Post guards...starting now. I'll take the first shift tonight while you both get some sleep. Daytime shouldn't be a problem. We can hire a couple of guys to guard the place. Policemen like to earn extra bucks working security. I'll talk to the chief about it."

"But aren't most of the policemen Irish? Which would mean they'd side with their own kind," Frank said.

"You're right. We'll have to find security patrols among our own."

"Sticking together—that's the way we've prospered so far," said Jakov.

Just as Nick predicted, another packinghouse fire broke out in the fall when apple production was at its peak. By the time Nick, Frank, and Jakov arrived, three packinghouses were engulfed in flames—among them one of the most prosperous.

"Our security guard saved us," Nick said. "But where in Sam Hill is he?"

"I'll check around for him," Frank said. He came running back, out of breath. "Our guard has been beaten up. He's barely conscious and hurting bad."

"Let's go," Nick said. Frank and Jakov followed. At the sight of the guard, he said, "We've got to get him to the hospital, fast."

"Help me carry him out front where we can signal for transportation," said Jakov.

"I don't think we should move him," Nick said. "A medic should make that call. Frank, find one fast."

Frank brought back a medic with a stretcher they loaded the watchman on to move him. They carried him out front and put him in a wagon for transport to the hospital.

"He's lost a lot of blood," said the medic. "I hope we can get him to the hospital in time."

Nick, Frank, and Jakov gave one another a foreboding look, fearful of what his death would mean in a small town caught up in petty grievances and prejudices.

When Nick turned around, he came face to face with Howard Dawson. "I'm not surprised to see you tonight."

"A newspaper man goes where the stories are. And tonight, this is a big one, especially with an assault adding to the drama."

"Tonight, it's an assault. Tomorrow, it may be murder."

"From what you just said, I assume the guard is in critical condition."

"We all better pray that he makes it. Because if he doesn't, this town will explode."

"You never accepted the invitation to meet with town officials. Perhaps, the time is now."

"It's the height of the season. Besides, Roger Bennett, the president of the Board of Trade, is one of the businessmen who's planning to go in with the dissatisfied orchardists to form a cooperative. I couldn't stomach the sight of him right now."

CHAPTER 18

The season had been a profitable one for Nick and Jakov. And the watchman survived, although he was still on the mend. Now Nick turned his thoughts to his future family and felt ready to make a commitment to Jelena. He planned to ask her to marry him at Thanksgiving.

Nick arrived in the city a few days ahead of the holiday and used the time to shop for an engagement ring Jelena would treasure—one that would always hold loving thoughts of him. He found the precise ring he had in mind at a small jewelry store down the street from The White House. Mr. Zeller had been very helpful. He showed him the latest art nouveau designs as well as recent Victorian ones. Both focused more on the setting than the gemstone, with designs inspired by nature. But Nick was old-fashioned and had always felt the stone should be the most important element of any engagement ring. When Mr. Zeller showed him a diamond in a Tiffany setting, Nick's quest ended.

"Notice how the stone sparkles," Mr. Zeller said. "That's because Mr. Tiffany, in his cleverness, set the diamond above the band. Since introducing his design a few years ago, it has become all the rage and certain to become a classic. How can you go wrong?"

Nick still had to decide on the size of the stone. Not too small. Yet not too big. He didn't want the townsfolk to accuse them of putting on airs. A one-carat diamond of good cut, clarity, and color would be perfect. He chose yellow gold for the band, a reminder of the Gold Rush that had inspired him to come to California. And he had struck gold in a land so rich that it yielded up its treasure faithfully year after year.

"I'll make the prongs on the band platinum to not distract from the diamond," Zeller said.

Nick walked out of Zeller Jewelers anticipating the evening ahead. He had dinner reservations at the Palm Court in the Palace Hotel, one of the finest hotels in the city. Jelena was not easily impressed, but he knew tonight she would be.

Nick set out for a visit to Pero Loreto about the problems the packers were having with the railroads. *If there's anyone who can help, he can.* Before he knew it, Nick had arrived at 273 Mission Street. He climbed the steps and knocked on the door, announcing himself to the doorman. Unlike years ago, when he was a recent immigrant, he was granted access immediately.

"I will tell Mr. Loreto you are here to see him."

Pero came out of his office to the reception area to greet him and lead him to his office, where they sat down in club chairs angled toward each other. "To what do I owe the pleasure of your visit?"

"To be quite frank, I need your help with the railroads."

Mr. Loreto uncrossed his leg and sat erect. "Exactly what kind of help are you looking for?"

"As you probably know, we ship apples to Chicago and New York, but that can take over two weeks and the fruit could spoil. At least that's what some commission men make us think so they can swindle us. We need to get the Southern Pacific to take our fruit out East on a direct route. At the rate we're going, the apple business won't ever be able to reach its potential."

"I thought the beauty of apples is that they can hold up for a long time."

"That's only true if they are stored under the right conditions. We also need refrigerator cars."

"You've thrown out a number of issues. Let me reiterate them. Rail routes. Refrigerator cars. Dishonest commission men."

"That about sums it up."

"The Big Four live here in San Francisco. I'll be attending a cocktail party tonight at Leland Stanford's home, where they should all be gathered. It might give me a chance to casually broach the subjects of rail routes and refrigerated cars. But, as for dishonest commission men, you'll have to find someone else to help you there. That's way out of my wheelhouse."

"All of us packers would be grateful if you can help us with our railroad problems."

"I'll give it the good old college try, but I can't promise any results. Now what's this I've been hearing about you and Jelena Babich being an item?"

"It's true. I'm here to spend Thanksgiving with her family, and tonight I'm taking her out for a special dinner."

Pero lit up. "Special, huh?"

"I can't say more than that right now."

"I'm an attorney who you've just asked to represent you with the railroads. Our attorney-client relationship is one of confidentiality, meaning I can keep secrets."

"Gee. In that case, I plan to ask Jelena to marry me tonight during dinner at the Palace Hotel."

"The Palace...that should impress her."

"I also have a diamond ring to clinch the deal."

"No woman can say no to a diamond. And you can break down any barriers first with flowers and chocolate, two things women love most. That is, after diamonds."

Nick had a couple of more stops to make before returning to his
hotel to shower and change for dinner. First, he stopped by
Ghirardelli's shop and picked up a box of chocolate. Next, he
found a flower shop and purchased a dozen long-stemmed red
roses. When the clerk asked if he would like them sent, he said,
"Yes, of course." But he wouldn't have thought about it on his
own. The roses were scheduled to arrive about two hours before
he did, so they would create anticipation—never a bad thing
when you were dealing with affairs of the heart.

By the time Nick had run all his errands, he had just enough
time left to shower, shave, and dress. He pulled his blue suit out
of the suitcase and hung it up to allow some wrinkles to fall out.
After he had taken care to groom himself properly, including
pomading his hair, combing his walrus mustache, and applying a
liberal dash of cologne, he was ready to dress in his one formal
suit—a suit Jelena had seen too often. Tomorrow, he'd make it a
point to go back to Braun Brothers and buy another one. He had
earned the right to be a two-suit man.

Nick was feeling so good he hustled down the stairs two at a
time until he reached the lobby. He gave the doorman the ticket
for the carriage he had rented, even though he would have to be
the driver.

Nick allowed the horse to nuzzle him, then he hopped up
into the seat and grabbed the reins. He gave the horse a pat on
the neck before heading off. He had learned that horses respond
better if they were treated right. A pat, a nuzzle, a carrot was all
it took to keep them happy. When Nick arrived at the Babiches'
townhouse, he parked the buggy right in front.

Mrs. Babich answered the door, giving him the usual
welcome. Then she called upstairs to Jelena, who only kept him
waiting a minute before she made her appearance. She wore a
green jewel-tone gown that complimented her chestnut hair and
blue eyes. It was a Victorian style, with a high neck and long

sleeves that nipped at the waist. Nick had never seen her look so alluring.

When she descended the stairs, Jelena greeted Nick with kisses on both cheeks before setting her eyes on his. "I have looked so forward to this evening and at last it's here."

Nick had not told her where they were headed because he wanted it to be a surprise. So, when he pulled under the Palace Hotel's porte cochère, she let out a gleeful cry. "I always imagined what this hotel is like inside and here I am, about to see it for myself."

Nick continued to drive the horses forward through the doors and into the Grand Court. "What are you doing?" Jelena exclaimed.

"Just wait and see."

A doorman greeted them. "Welcome to the Palace Hotel." He helped Jelena down as Nick handed the reins to the other attendant and jumped out of the carriage.

As soon as he got around to the other side, he offered Jelena his arm. "I'm relieved they didn't arrest you."

"That's how it's done here." Nick escorted Jelena into the hotel.

Her eyes swept over the Grand Court. "It's even more spectacular than I imagined."

Nick led her through the lobby to the restaurant where the maitre'd seated them at a banquette table, side by side. While the waiter stood with their menus, Nick leaned over to whisper in Jelena's ear. "You are the most beautiful woman I have ever seen."

Jelena kissed him on the cheek as a sign of her appreciation and love.

The waiter said, "We have some specials tonight, fresh from the sea. Sanddabs pan fried or stuffed with crab and abalone."

Upon hearing abalone, Jelena turned toward Nick. "I've never had abalone."

"Then that's what you shall have."

Both Nick and Jelena were fish lovers, so they ordered a crab Louie starter, a San Francisco tradition. "And since we're having fish, let's go with a bottle of champagne."

"We have Mumm's, will that do?" Nick approved, and the waiter left, returning with a wine bucket filled with ice. In an instant, he was back twisting the cork and filling two flutes with chilled champagne.

"To our future," Nick said as he looked into Jelena's eyes. But he refrained from pouring his whole heart out, saving it for tonight's climax.

Once the Grand Marnier souffles arrived, Nick knew it was time. He touched the box in his pocket for courage and took Jelena's hand in his, stroking it for a few moments. "Jelena, we've been courting for some time, and at last I'm ready to ask you to be my wife. Your father has already given me permission for your hand. I truly love you, and pledge to give you the best life possible. Now that my packing business is doing well, I have something substantial to offer you. Will you marry me, my love?"

"Oh, Nick. You know I've always wanted to marry you from the first time I saw you as a young girl."

"I thought that was just a silly schoolgirl crush that girls get for older men."

"It was no schoolgirl crush, I can vouch for that. I've been waiting so long, I thought you'd never ask. But once Lana was out of the way, I finally had a chance."

"Lana...I've always liked Lana. But it's you I love. Never think you were second best. But you had to grow up first, so that took time."

"And now that I have, I don't want to waste any more time. Yes, Nick, I will marry you. And I want to do it soon."

Nick bent in for a kiss on the lips. Then he reached into his pocket and pulled out the box. When he opened it, Jelena let out a little squeal of delight. "Oh, Nick, it's a beautiful engagement ring."

"Now give me your left hand so I can put this ring on your finger as a promise of our love."

Once the ring was on her finger, Jelena held out her hand out for both she and Nick to admire. The facets caught the candles' glow, sending light dancing all around them in an eye-popping show. Jelena responded by giving Nick the most passionate kiss of his life. When she let him up for air, he said, "Sweet Jesus. After that kiss, I need another drink before I take you home. Besides, I want to talk with you about the wedding plans before anyone else puts in their two cents."

After Nick paid the bill, he led Jelena into the hotel's stylish lounge where they ordered a couple of nightcaps. When the hot toddies arrived, Nick took a long sip and let out a satisfying sigh. Jelena followed his lead, but not being used to whiskey, grimaced at the first taste. "It's all right if you don't like it. I'll finish it and you can order something else."

"Just tea. The champagne made me light-headed."

After the tea arrived, Nick began, "Darling, you mentioned you want to get married soon. It would work well for me, and the plans I've made, to get married right after Christmas."

"That will give us enough time to plan a wedding Mother approves of. And I can use a red and white theme, the colors of Croatia."

"I'm glad you mentioned Croatia. I would like to take you there for our honeymoon. We'd spend our honeymoon night in San Francisco, then catch the transcontinental the next day for New York before we take a ship to Le Havre, France. And from there, trains and another boat. I want to introduce you to my family. I haven't been back since I left home almost ten years ago, so it would be like a big reunion."

"It all sounds too wonderful. Listening to you, my head is spinning."

"It's settled then. A wedding after Christmas. And a honeymoon in Croatia."

By the time Nick returned Jelena to her doorstep, they were

both floating on air. He did not want the night to end. But a chill was in the air as fog had crept in, covering the city. He drew Jelena close and gave her one last kiss to sleep on. "I love you so much and can hardly wait to make you my wife."

When Nick arrived for Thanksgiving, Mr. and Mrs. Babich exchanged stealthy smiles, and Matteo pulled Nick aside. "I hope she said yes."

"Of course. Why would you ever doubt it?"

"Good. I'll announce your engagement when we sit down at the table after we say grace."

Lana, her husband Steven, and their son Tomas, made their appearance next. Nick kissed Lana on her cheeks and held out his hand to shake Steven's. "How's the grocery business?"

"We're doing very well. It helps to be along the wharf with other Croatian establishments, since so many Croatians frequent the area. They prefer to buy from their own countrymen, and we make it easy for them to do that. Besides, we carry specialty items that they can't find easily elsewhere."

"I hope you're selling a lot of Watsonville apples."

"That we are. And all the housewives have been buying them up for Thanksgiving. They prefer apple pies to pumpkin, which they consider an acquired taste."

Mr. Babich said, "Go sit down in the living room and make yourselves comfortable. I'll bring out the drinks. And Lana, can you help Mother with the appetizers? I'll watch little Tomas for you."

As usual, the family enjoyed lots of conversation, and laughter as they awaited dinnertime. Once they were all seated around the table, Mr. Babich led them in grace. Then he nodded to his son, Peter, who opened the champagne and began filling the flutes set on the table.

Once everyone had some bubbly, Mr. Babich raised his glass. "It is my honor to announce the engagement of my daughter,

Jelena, to Nick Markovich. Vera and I couldn't be more pleased with Jelena's choice of a husband, and we wish you all the blessings a happy marriage can bring." Then he clinked glasses with his wife and went around the table to clink the others. When he had finished, he said, "Now, let our Thanksgiving meal begin with even more gratefulness for the new member we are about to have join our family."

Nick had been holding Jelena's hand under the table. He released it and stood to respond to all the kind words Mr. Babich had expressed. "I want you all to know that I love Jelena very much. She is my heart. And I will always do my best to be a family member you can trust and depend on, no matter what comes. With Jelena at my side, I look forward to only happiness." When Nick took his seat, he was almost at tears.

CHAPTER 19

On the train ride home, Nick's mind was spinning. There was still much work to do, even though apples were over for the season. He had to find a cottage that Jelena would find acceptable and purchase basic furnishings, leaving the finishing touches to her. He knew the basic furniture he would need to buy, but he had no idea about the items for cooking and dining. He remembered girls back home, like his sister Ana, always kept a hope chest that they would fill with tablecloths and linens and other necessities for the time they would have their own household to assemble. Added to that, wedding gifts of china, silverware, and crystal would cover the rest. He felt relieved knowing that everything would not be up to him—just the essentials, which most men could handle.

When the train pulled into the station, Nick was the first one off. He walked as fast as he could toward packinghouse row, hoping to find someone who could give him a ride. He was in luck and a short time later, he arrived at the boardinghouse. He bounded up the stairs to his room and threw the door open. "I want you to be my best man."

Frank rubbed his eyes, trying to wake up from his nap and refocus. "I take it Jelena accepted your proposal of marriage."

"That she did."

"When's the wedding to be?"

"Right after Christmas."

"So soon?"

"Yes, it won't interfere with business and give us time for the honeymoon I've got planned."

"Oh, yeah?"

"I guess I didn't tell you. I plan to take her to Croatia to meet the family."

"I hope you're back in time for apple season. Jakov and I can't manage without you."

"Don't worry. I'll be back. But I'll also do a little business on the way."

"What kind of business?"

"I'll meet with some fruit commissioners in New York, and on the way back, we'll stop in Chicago to do the same. I want those boys to have a face to put with our name and understand I'm no fool. It's time we put a stop to their cheating ways. And when I meet them, I'll be able to size each one up. Anyone who fails the test will not get our business. I can assure you of that."

"I hope Jakov will back you up."

"If he doesn't, we'll have to part company. I won't continue working my tail off while some scoundrels make off with more than their fair share."

At the sound of the bell, Nick and Frank headed for the dining room. The cook had made a turkey stew from the leftovers. Frank took one look and turned to Nick. "Third day. First excellent. Second good. Third—who knows?" But when they dipped in for their first taste, both Nick and Frank approved.

"The cook knows how to transform leftovers into its own dish. That's not just a skill but a talent," said Nick. And then he wondered whether Jelena knew how to cook. He'd seen Lana helping her mother, but rarely Jelena. He'd have to speak to Mrs. Babich about it and make sure Jelena was prepared to feed her husband right from the start.

After dinner, they joined Jakov in the bar. "Just want to let you know I'm back, and I'll be at the packinghouse tomorrow. If you'll be there, we should go over the finances together."

"I think the finances can wait. We've got more pressing issues."

"Do you know what Jakov meant by more pressing issues?" Nick asked Frank. "I don't want to be blindsided tomorrow."

"I think it's about the firebug. The police have a suspect."

"Who is it?"

"Ask Jakov, because they didn't confide in me."

Nick and Frank arrived at the packinghouse before Jakov. As soon as he came in, Nick cornered him. "Frank tells me they caught the firebugs."

"That's right."

"Tell me who they are?"

"A couple of fellas from the Cullen Ranch."

"Why in the world would they want to set packinghouses on fire? We buy their orchards every year without fail."

"But we don't buy some of their countrymen's, and that appears to be the motive. Besides, they were a pair of Irish hotheads who had too much to drink and came our way to let off some steam."

"It was more than steam—arson, assault, attempted murder. Are they being held at the town jail?"

"Somehow made bail. And word on the street is they grabbed a boat in Oakland, headed for the Emerald Isle."

"Then good riddance to them. We don't need their kind around here."

"I feel the same. So, how were things in San Francisco?"

"Wonderful. I asked Jelena to marry me, and she accepted. That's what I wanted to talk with you about."

"I'm listening."

"First, of course, I want you to be one of my groomsmen. But

I'll be taking Jelena to Croatia for our honeymoon, so I'll be away for a couple months."

"When is all this happening?"

"The wedding will be soon after Christmas, and then we'll leave for the East. I also plan to make some visits to fruit commissioners in New York City and Chicago. In addition, I'll be talking up the opportunity to come to California with young men in my village. We need to get some young, strong workers who can put in long hours to keep the orchardists from cutting into our business. As you know, the Chinese we depend on are getting old and slow and they're not being replaced by younger ones because of the exclusion laws."

"It sounds like you plan to accomplish a lot. I hope your bride doesn't get in the way and spoil things." Jakov let out a big belly laugh.

"If anything, she'll resupply my energy."

"I can't wait to meet the lucky lady. Do you have a date for the wedding?"

"We're working on that, but you'll be among the first to know."

"Count me in as a groomsman. And make sure you have plenty of young ladies available. I haven't danced in a long time, and I want to make the most of it."

CHAPTER 20

The wedding was set for January second at the Church of St. Francis, with a reception following at the Slavonic Society. Jelena chose a red and white color scheme, patterned after the Croatian coat of arms. To carry off the checkerboard effect, the groomsmen would wear white jackets and the bridesmaids, red dresses. Jelena planned to carry a bouquet of red roses while the bridesmaids would hold white ones.

Nick and Frank went up to the city the day before Christmas Eve to spend the holidays with the Babich family and attend to last-minute errands for the wedding. They spent the week between Christmas and New Year's getting measured for their tuxes, reserving a room at the Palace Hotel for the wedding night, arranging passage on the transcontinental railroad, and a host of other items that Jelena and her mother assigned them.

On the wedding day, the bridal party arrived before eleven o'clock. In keeping with tradition, they sequestered Jelena in a room off the vestibule of the church. Nick accepted a red rose boutonniere from Lana and took his place at the front of the church as guests arrived. Jelena's family took the first two pews on the left side of the church. Nick felt a pang in his heart when he looked at the empty pews on the right. He wished his parents could be here to share his joy. But he consoled himself with the thought they would see them soon.

The organist struck up Wagner's "Wedding March" and Nick got the first glimpse of his bride, wearing a Victorian lace gown with a pearl tiara and full-length tulle veil. Nick had never seen Mateo look prouder than with Jelena on his arm. It seemed the walk down the aisle took forever as Nick awaited Jelena's presence. Mr. Babich handed her off to him with a kiss. The bridal pair climbed the steps to the altar and knelt before the priest to exchange vows. After the priest pronounced them man and wife, Nick lifted Jelena's veil and kissed her amidst her tears. *There'll be enough time for passionate kissing tonight.*

Nick and Jelena processed down the aisle to Mendelssohn's "Bridal March" and made their way to the steps of the church under a shower of rice—a symbol of prosperity, fertility, and good fortune. Frank had the carriage ready out front, decorated with flowers and streamers and a big sign in back that announced "Just Married." Nick helped Jelena into the back seat and went around to the other side to join her.

Then Frank tapped the horses with his whip and took off for the Slavonic Society. They were the first to arrive and assembled themselves into a receiving line. Once the last guest had made their way through, the bridal party took their places at the head table and the meal began. Nick reflected on Lana's wedding reception and then to his sister's, and the many others he had attended in Croatia. Tradition connected them all. And now he and Jelena were part of that same tradition.

Near the end of the reception, Jelena and Lana slipped into a dressing room so Jelena could change. Jelena reappeared in the red jewel-tone frock Nick had purchased for her at The White House.

"I've never been able to resist a lady in red," Nick said.

Jelena shot him a coy smile. "I plan to wear this dress to meet your family, too."

The carriage and driver were waiting when Nick and Jelena

left the reception. Even with a rabbit stole, Jelena shivered in the chilly night air. Nick held her close as they rode to the Palace Hotel, giving her soft kisses to keep her warm.

When they got to their room, Nick popped the champagne while Jelena changed into her wedding night attire. As soon as she emerged, Nick put his arms around her and kissed her so passionately she almost swooned.

"Is it time?" she asked.

"Not yet. Let's have some champagne and relax. We had a big day." The champagne did the trick, putting Jelena in a giddy mood. He scooped her up in his arms and set her on the bed.

"Oh, Nick, I so love you," she said.

"And I love you." He began caressing her to make her feel cherished. When she was distracted, he slid out of his pants. Then he remembered his shirt would not be so easy with those blasted cuff links. But he was certain they would not interfere with the main event.

"Be gentle with me, Nick."

He covered her mouth with his and made slow, sweet love to her. After it was over, she melted in his arms. The two had become one.

When they awoke the next morning, they were still wrapped in each other's arms. Nick realized he should have booked the room for two nights—a honeymoon in a sleeper car might take the romance right out of it. He got up while Jelena lingered in the afterglow and called room service. The breakfast cart, laden with muffins, fruit, and coffee, appeared less than an hour later.

"Time to sit up and greet the day." Nick handed Jelena a cup of coffee with cream and sugar—just the way she liked it.

"Oh, Nick, you're spoiling me already."

He leaned into her for a kiss. "I think it's mutual."

After the leisurely breakfast, they hurried to make the transcontinental. When they arrived at the station, Nick paid the carriage driver and hailed a porter to tote the luggage to the train. Nick took Jelena's arm to lead her safely through the crowds. He helped her up after the porter had put their luggage on board. A train conductor wasted no time asking for their tickets, and Nick pulled them out of his pocket to display them.

"You have a sleeper car. Very nice accommodations. Follow me."

Nick looked at Jelena and smiled.

When they got to their assigned compartment, the train conductor handed Nick the key. "I think you'll find everything you need. The dining car is two cars back. Dinner is served at six o'clock."

Nick turned toward the door, slid in the key, and unlocked it. "Ladies first." Nick stepped in next, bumping his head on the doorway. "Ouch." With two of them inside, there was no room to maneuver. Nick looked around and saw nothing resembling a bed. But there was a handle right in front of him, so he pulled it and down popped a bed...of sorts.

"Remember, Nick, these are very nice accommodations."

"I'd like to see the ones that aren't so nice."

"I think you already have...on the way over here."

"That's right—the boxcar. By comparison, this is a major step up."

"How many nights are we spending on the train?" Jelena asked.

"I think it's three nights and four days. Do you think you can manage?"

"Do I have a choice?"

As soon as the train pulled into Jersey City station, Nick hustled Jelena and the luggage off the train. He hailed a carriage to take them to the ferry and from there, another carriage to take them to the new Holland House hotel at Fifth and Thirtieth Streets. The Italian Renaissance hotel featured an enormous staircase fashioned out of Siena marble with a bronze railing. Chippendale furniture upholstered in satin damask dyed to match the marble decorated the lobby.

After the bellman left, Nick and Jelena took a nap—they were completely exhausted after the long train ride. When they heard catering carts rolling down the hallway, they woke up with a start.

"What time is it?" Nick jumped out of bed and threw back the lace curtains. "It's already dark." Then he checked his watch. Four o'clock. He remembered he had not advanced it three hours. "Let's get ready for dinner. It's seven o'clock already." He scooped Jelena out of bed and set her on the floor, wrapping his arms around her for a kiss. "Let's make the most of our time here. You take a shower first."

After they had both gotten dressed, they headed for the elegant dining room. "I don't care what they have on the menu as long as this room doesn't rock," Jelena said.

Nick laughed. "I don't think we'll have to hold on to our plates and brace ourselves here."

Dinner over, they made haste for their room. "After that miserable bunk, I want to make good use of this comfortable bed tonight." Nick pulled Jelena toward him. As he kissed her lips, her face, her neck, he unbuttoned her dress and slipped it off her shoulders. "This will be a night you won't forget...even better than our wedding night."

"You're grinning like a Cheshire cat. How was your meeting?"

"It worked out pretty well. They understand our concern and will work on the problem, which may result in a fruit commissioner taking up residence in town."

"That's wonderful."

"And London wants our Newtown Pippins. We've going big time. I can't wait to share the news with the folks."

"They'll be so proud of you, just as I am."

"Let's go downstairs and have dinner, and I'll tell you everything."

"We're on the *La Gascogne*," Nick said to the carriage driver as they approached the pier, lined with a variety of ships from tugboats to seafaring steamers.

"I know the *La Gascogne*. It's tied up at the south end."

When they arrived at the ship's bow, Jelena said, "I feel dwarfed by this magnificent ship."

"I grant you, it is a monster in size but that is what will make it seaworthy when we get large swells or, heaven forbid, encounter a storm at sea."

"Storm at sea—"

"It could happen this time of year. When I made my first crossing, it was the spring, and *Le Bretagne* had a calm time of it."

"How long will we be on the ship again?"

"About two weeks. But don't worry about a storm. The worst potential disaster will be sea sickness. You haven't yet proved you're seaworthy."

"I've never been at sea, so how would I know?"

"You wouldn't but you'll find out soon enough."

Once Jelena developed her sea legs, it was smooth sailing the rest of the way. When they pulled into the port of Le Havre, she let out a sigh. "I look forward to setting my feet on terra firma. You might have guessed I'm a landlubber, and I don't think there's any hope I'll ever change."

"Maybe the return trip will make a sailor out of you."

"Return trip...do I have to?"

"Sorry, darlin', but there's no other way to get back."

After less than a three-hour train ride, Nick and Jelena were in Paris by the afternoon. Nick hailed a carriage outside the train station and directed the driver to take them to the Hotel

Dupuis, a small French hotel on the Left Bank within walking distance of Notre Dame Cathedral. The doorman carried their luggage to the third floor. Jelena let out a joyful shriek when she stepped into the room filled with a canopy bed.

After a nap, Nick and Jelena prepared for dinner at a restaurant recommended to them on the Champs-Élysées. The carriage took them near the Arc de Triomphe, which Nick wanted them both to see because it was connected to the history of Dubrovnik. "Napoleon had this monument constructed after his greatest victory against the Russian and Austrian armies—the Battle of Austerlitz. That was the beginning of the end for Ragusa, the Kingdom of Dubrovnik, because Napoleon's army marched into the Old Town after tricking our officials into letting them through the gates and took over."

"That's terrible."

"It was one domino falling after the other. After several years, the Croatian people rose up, and the French were defeated with the help of the British and Austrian armies. But instead of honoring our treaty of independence, those powers put us under the thumb of the Austrian Regime in 1815, where we remain to this day."

"You sure know a lot about history for a fella who had little schooling."

"It's not history. It's family lore. Both my grandfathers and too many uncles to count fought with rebels for the Republic of Ragusa."

"Do you think Dubrovnik will ever regain its independence?"

"We pray for it all the time, and we scheme. One day...one day soon, I hope...we will be free again. The flag we'd flown on our ships was Libertad—freedom. That's what we all want and why many of us have left and moved to places where we can have freedom—especially America."

"Croissants and coffee come with our room. Let's go downstairs for a real French breakfast, and then we can go to Mass at Notre Dame Cathedral, followed by some sightseeing."

Nick and Jelena walked the mile and a half to the Eiffel Tower, taking the route along the Seine River. For a January day, the weather was mild, which invigorated them. Once they spotted the tower in the distance, they increased their pace. This structure was not like anything they had seen before, and they felt insignificant before it.

"It was built for the last World's Fair, held in 1889. Hey, here are some stairs leading to the first platform." Nick stood aside while Jelena took the first step, remembering that a lady goes up first and down last to allow the man to break her fall. Once they reached the platform, they got a bird's-eye view of Paris.

Jelena put her arms around Nick's neck and pulled his head down to give him a kiss. "Thank you for bringing me to this romantic city on our honeymoon. I'll never forget it."

Nick responded with a passionate kiss of his own. "It's time we get back to the hotel for a nap," he said with a sly smile. "We missed it yesterday."

On the way back in the carriage, Nick told Jelena that the upcoming World's Fair would be next year in Chicago. "They're calling it the Columbian Exposition in honor of Christopher Columbus' 400th anniversary of the discovery of America. That's one reason I've arranged for us to stop in Chicago on the way back. Watsonville plans to present its apples to the world, and I want the complete lowdown to make it a success."

CHAPTER 21

"Hurry. We don't want to miss our train." Nick led Jelena to the departure board to check the track for their train to Milan. "This way," he said as he gave her a tug. When they reached their seats and stowed their luggage, they both breathed a sigh of relief. "Well, you just ran through the Gare de l'Est, one of the oldest rail stations in the world. Congratulations."

"You seem to know how to do it, so I could easily follow."

"We're retracing my steps from my trip out." Then he remembered the last time he ran through a train station. It was after he discovered the man next to him was dead. He had tried to push that shameful memory away. Not that he had anything to do with the man's death, but that he had benefited from it. *Without that ill-gotten gain, I wouldn't have my packinghouse. I should have gone to confession at Notre Dame. Those priests might have the special grace to forgive my sin.*

"One more train to Venice, then the boat to Croatia."

"When it's time to return home, I may stay behind. I don't think I can handle another trip like this so soon."

"Believe me, you'll be begging me to take you back to your world of creature comforts and, most of all, freedom. Besides,

Croatia is not nearly as lovely in winter. Now, if it were summer, I don't think I'd stand a chance of uprooting you."

"Next time, we must come in the summer."

"No chance of that as long as I'm in the apple business."

When the train arrived in Venice, Nick gave Jelena a brief tour. "I wish we could spend some time here. It's so charming... maybe even more so than Paris."

"If you're a good girl, I'll try to make it happen." He gave her a smile.

"And just what qualifies as a good girl in your book?"

"If you think about it, the answer will come to you."

They walked past the lagoon on the way to the harbor where their ship was waiting. "Let's stand here a minute and watch the boat traffic. It's a wonder they don't crash into each other the way they're maneuvering around."

"I know nothing about sailing, but it makes no sense."

"And if you learn nothing else, you'll learn that a lot of things Venetians do don't make sense. They've been one big pain in our patoots for centuries."

"That settles it. I have to spend some time here to judge for myself."

Once the sailboat was underway, Nick and Jelena nestled together to stay warm. The side benefit was they could steal kisses when the other passengers weren't looking. Nick tried to point out sites along the way, especially Split, where Jelena's parents were from.

"We'll visit Split, won't we? My parents will be so disappointed if we don't."

"That's the plan." Jelena gave Nick a kiss on his cheek, her way of thanking him.

Once they disembarked at the port of Gruz and had gathered up their luggage, Nick arranged for a carriage to Cilipi. "We're less than four hours away from my home now."

When they got to Dubrovnik, Nick gave Jelena a history lesson as they passed. "See those thick, high walls? Only the

French got in, and trickery did it, not force. Those Venetians tried repeatedly to defeat us but for the most part, those walls kept them out. Let that lagoon be proof they have no organization."

Jelena laughed in agreement.

"Ah, welcome to Cilipi. If you look to your right, you will see The Church of St. Nikola and the town square. Every Sunday, when the weather permits, we go there and dance. Of course, we bring food and drink and make a party out of it."

Jelena's eyes grew wide as she surveyed the town. There was no doubt in her mind that the people were poor. But everything looked neat and clean and buildings were in good repair, unlike some areas of San Francisco where people dwelled like the wretched.

Finally, Nick told the driver to halt. "This is it. Home sweet home."

Jelena stared at the small, stone house with a red tile roof and white shutters. She knew the garden must be filled with flowers in the summer, but now it was in repose. She spotted an arbor over the doorway with grapevines growing on it. A stand of Italian cypress trees stood on the right side of the house. She knew to expect a humble home, but she hadn't realized it would be this humble. She could only wonder what it looked like inside.

Nick helped Jelena out of the carriage and grabbed the suitcases as they walked up the dirt path. He didn't need to knock, as his family had been watching for their arrival.

His mother, wearing an apron and babushka, swung the door open and wrapped her arms around Nick so she could kiss and hug him after missing him for so long. Then she released him and greeted Jelena with kisses on both cheeks. "Welcome to our family." She didn't speak a word of English and Jelena didn't speak a word of Croatian, so Nick translated.

Jelena realized it would be a long few weeks with no other way to communicate between them. *What kind of honeymoon has this turned out to be?*

Mr. Markovich had been waiting behind his wife to welcome the newlyweds. He gave Nick a bear hug and handshake, and kissed Jelena softly on her cheeks. The rest of Nick's siblings were waiting inside.

Mrs. Markovich said, "Come in. Come in. It's cold outside."

When they stepped into the living room, a fire was roaring in the hearth as if it had been set just for them. It was a cozy room with a beamed ceiling and walls of stone.

Once they had met everyone, Nick said, "Let's go get settled." And he led Jelena to the rear of the house to a small bedroom with a hall bathroom nearby. "This used to be my bedroom. First, I shared with Ivan and then with Frank. I sent my mother some money to fix it up for us."

The room had the same cozy feel of the living room. A full-size bed was the major piece of furniture, along with an armoire and a small table with a lamp. Lace curtains hung from the two windows that were shuttered against the winter cold.

"Let's unpack later so we can visit with the family. I know my mother has a meal of some sort planned. She's been preparing all week for our arrival."

When they entered the living room, the family was assembled around the hearth. "We have so many questions to ask you about your new life in America," Nick's father said in Croatian.

Nick took a moment to assess his father. His hair had grown whiter since he had last seen him, but his eyes were still a somber shade of green, and he had not forsaken his walrus mustache, which still had some streaks of brown. "What would you like to know?"

"First, how is Francis doing? We don't hear from him often."

Before answering, Nick translated the question for Jelena, which he would do throughout the conversation, along with his answers. "Francis is fine. He's working with me at the apple packinghouse and doing quite well. One day we plan to have our own packinghouse. Perhaps we'll buy out my partner Jakov."

"Do you have your home ready for your return?" asked his mother. She had removed her babushka to reveal gray hair arranged in a bun.

"Actually, Francis is handling that for me. I had so many other details to attend to between the wedding and the business, that I lost track of time to look for a house to purchase."

His mother frowned, and her blue eyes sharpened their gaze. "What about the furnishings? Did you leave them up to Francis, too?"

"Just a few of the basics. Jelena's mother and sisters are coming down to get everything set up for us."

Nick's sister, Marija, a dark-haired beauty with a cheerful demeanor, had been waiting to ask a question, so he called on her next. "Tell us about the wedding since we missed it and have never been to one in America."

"We got married at the oldest Catholic church in San Francisco, St. Francis of Assisi. It was founded before the city and even the state. Jelena looked beautiful in her white lace dress and floor-length veil. All the bridesmaids wore red, and the groomsmen wore white jackets. It was Jelena's idea to look like the Croatian checkerboard coat of arms."

"Chessboard," corrected his father. "That's the name our countrymen prefer because we play chess, not checkers. In fact, legend has it that King Stephen played a chess match against the Venetian Doge and won his freedom after defeating him. From that time on, the red and white chessboard was part of our coat of arms."

"I apologize. Of course, we're a nation of chess players. It's taught us to be watchful of our enemies in all directions."

"Please finish telling us about the wedding," Marija said.

"All right. The wedding ceremony was very similar to what I remember of Ana's—even the music. We had the reception at the Slavonic Society and again, everything was familiar. We're still steeped in Croatian traditions."

"Where did you spend your honeymoon?" another sister, Dora, asked. She was a replica of Ana—blonde, blue-eyed, and almost as serious.

"So far, we've spent our honeymoon getting here. But we did enjoy one night in San Francisco and a couple in Paris."

"Paris! Was it as beautiful as—"

"I think that's enough talk for now. We will be having a big dinner, which your mother has underway, and we can talk until the cock crows. But let's give Nick and his bride a chance to relax and freshen up before then," Mr. Markovich said.

Once they got back to the privacy of their room, Nick said, "Well, what do you think of the family?"

"They all seem very nice, and I can tell how much love they have for you."

"And for you, too."

"I hope so. My only regret is I don't speak Croatian. I'll miss out on so much without the language."

"As long as I'm nearby, you can rely on me to translate. Suddenly, I feel tired. I'd like to take a nap before dinner."

Jelena responded with an understanding smile.

Nick pulled Jelena to his chest and gave her a deep, passionate kiss. "I love you for coming here with me for our honeymoon. You have made my family very happy and what makes them happy makes me happy. Did I ever tell you you're a good girl?"

"Good enough for an overnight or two in Venice?"

"I'll work it into our schedule, as long as you continue to behave. Now, about that nap."

Jelena dressed in the red frock Nick had purchased at The
White House. When she and Nick walked into the living area,
they noticed the kitchen and dining room tables had been
pushed together to accommodate everyone. "Ask your mother if
there is anything I can do to help," Jelena said to Nick.

"No, please make yourselves comfortable in the living room."

Nick took Jelena's hand and led her to the sofa in front of the
hearth. Soon, other family members joined them. "Will Ivan and
Ana and their families be dining with us tonight?" Nick asked
Marija.

"I'm sorry, but they cannot be here tonight. However, they
will come to dinner at the restaurant tomorrow."

"That's good. But I am disappointed they won't be here
tonight."

Mr. Markovich came into the room and announced, "Dinner
is ready. Please take your places."

The tables were set with matching plaid tablecloths in a red
and white check. Small bouquets of holly with red berries added
a seasonal touch. Nothing was fancy. No crystal. No sterling. But
the overall effect was pleasing as candles spread their soft light
over the family table. Mrs. Markovich brought out the soup first,
made of a rich chicken stock and filled with seasonal vegetables.
Roast pork was the main course, accompanied by roast potatoes
and carrots. A mincemeat pie finished the meal, an attempt to
add apples to the menu.

"Please, tell your mother everything was delicious," Jelena
said to Nick.

Paulina beamed as she nodded, accepting the compliment.

"Now, for the slivovitz," Mr. Markovich said. "Luka and
Gabe, please do the honors."

Luka and Gabe looked as different as day and night. Luka
was light, with straight blond hair and piercing blue eyes. Gabe
had dark curly hair and green eyes like his father. But both were
kind-hearted and had fun-loving spirits. Nick planned to do his

best sales job to convince them to join him and Frank in California.

When Luka returned with the bottle, Gabe had the glasses ready to fill. All he needed to do was pour. When everyone had one, Anton raised his glass. "To Jelena and Nick. May you have all the blessings of a marriage made in heaven."

Nick clinked Jelena's glass first, then did the same with everyone around the table before slugging the liquor down in one gulp.

Then Nick got up, grabbed the bottle of slivovitz, and began filling the glasses a second time. "Now, it's my turn to offer a toast. To my bride, Jelena, who I am pleased to have join our family. You have given her a warm welcome and for that I am grateful."

When Nick and Jelena returned to their room, it was past midnight. After they changed into their nightclothes, they fell into bed, where they snuggled until morning, wrapped in each other's arms.

CHAPTER 22

Nick hitched up the buggy to take Jelena to Old Town Dubrovnik. It was a blustery day when they arrived at the Pile Gate as the wind whipped off the water, although the walls would protect them from the worst of it. Nick tied the reins to a hitching post and helped Jelena to her feet. Then he led her over the bridge and through the gate. "That's our patron saint, St. Blaise, in the niche up there, watching over the town."

Jelena cast her eyes upward. She had heard of St. Blaise but didn't know much about him. They continued walking down the stone path until they reached the Stradun, the main road through the Old Town. "I've never been to a city like this before."

"That's because it's medieval. The walls were built in the thirteenth century as a defensive measure. Remember, I told you no one ever got through them until the French tricked one of our officials into letting them in? Because of the wall, Dubrovnik is known as the Pearl of the Adriatic."

"I've never seen walls like these before. They're so thick and high."

"That they are—limestone over eighty feet high. Later, if the wind settles down, we can take the stairs and walk around on the ramparts. You'll get a splendid view from there."

Nick led Jelena to the end of the Stradun, then ducked through a covered alleyway that opened onto a port, and searched for a restaurant with a view. "Let's try this one," Nick said.

The waiter seated Nick and Jelena at the window, with a view of the harbor encircled by the wall. "In summer, this place is teeming with visitors. And restaurants set out tables on the sidewalk to handle the demand."

"Even on a day like this, it's beautiful. There is a lot about Croatia that reminds me of California—the hills, the sea, the rockiness near the shore. I finally understand why so many Croatians felt comfortable settling in San Francisco and other towns along the coast."

"After this trip, I think you'll understand your heritage better, as well as your husband. This is the place that formed me and it still continues to shape me, sometimes in ways I don't even understand."

Nick picked up his menu and scanned it. "Whenever I'm near the sea, I always crave fish. Ah, they have mussels on the menu. Of course, they'll be cooked Croatian-style—just the way I like them."

"How is that different from the way they are usually prepared at home?"

"Croatians start by sauteing the mussels in lots of garlic, parsley, and olive oil. Once they open up, they add wine. They finish the dish off by adding some bread crumbs to the sauce, which thickens it. I haven't had mussels done this way since I left home."

When the waiter returned, Nick ordered mussels for the two, along with a bottle of white wine. Even before the mussels arrived at their table, Nick could smell the familiar aroma of garlic mixed with the rich mussel flavor. When the waiter set the bowl in front of him, Nick leaned in to take a deep inhale. "Smells always stay with you wherever you go."

Jelena pulled a mussel out of its shell and dipped it into the sauce. "I don't think I'll ever eat mussels any other way. This dish has spoiled me."

"Before we leave, I'll ask my mother to teach you how to make it, along with my other favorites."

"Oh, I finally understand...you had a sneaky motive for bringing me here." Jelena gave Nick a playful smile.

"That certainly was one. But the other was to educate you about my native country. While Croatia is now under the Austrian Regime known as the Kingdom of Croatia, Slavonia, and Dalmatia and the Triune Kingdom—it was the Ragusa Republic that governed itself. Dubrovnik had a reputation for wealth, which it built through its maritime trade. Trade seems to be in our blood. That's what's building the apple business back home—not farming. Of course, the product is important, but without Croatian trading know-how, the farmers would not have found so many markets for their fruit."

"This is all news to me. It seems I've only learned the social aspects of my heritage but not much of the history."

"Maybe immigrants don't talk about the history often because it's so confusing. I don't pretend to know it well either. And, besides trade, Dubrovnik was good at diplomacy. Too good, perhaps. With the French, playing nice backfired big-time." At that, Nick sat silently, and stared into Jelena's eyes. He could tell his words had made an impact.

After exiting the Old Town, Nick said, "While there is still light, I want you to see the Fortress of St. Lovrijenac."

"What?"

"I'm sorry. The Fort of St. Lawrence."

Nick led Jelena to the western side of the city. Rising one hundred twenty-one feet above the sea, the triangular stone fortress stood on a rock promontory, protecting both the oldest harbor and western entrance of Dubrovnik.

"I have to tell you the story of how this fortress came about. Word got back that the Venetians planned to build a fortress on this very spot where they could not only control shipping in and out of the Adriatic, but also us. But we beat them to it. In only three months' time, Croatians had constructed the Fort of St. Lawrence and when the Venetians arrived, they had no choice but to turn around, having been outsmarted."

"What a tale."

"Let's climb the stairs and I'll share more of the lore." After crossing the drawbridge, Nick pointed to an inscription above the gate. "That translates 'Freedom is not sold for all the gold in the world.' It sums up our greatest value."

They stood silent, meditating on the words Croatians have lived by for centuries. When Nick moved Jelena inside, he put a fist to a wall and pounded it. "These are thirty-nine feet thick except on the side facing town, which are only twenty-four feet. The Croatians wanted to be able to destroy the fort with cannon balls if their enemies ever occupied it. Another clever thing they did was to put rails on the stairs leading down while leaving the upward side free of them. This would enable the city's defenders to draw their swords while the enemy heading downward would be prevented."

"Ragusans were shrewd people."

"We had to be to survive."

On the way back, Nick stopped at the Konavle Kafe. "I'll just be a minute. I want to check on dinner for tonight since I'm hosting it for the family. Hold on to the reins."

When he returned, he hopped into the seat and took the reins from Jelena. She sighed with relief.

"I apologize. I didn't realize you'd never held the reins before."

"There's always a first time. But if the horses had taken off, I would have been at their mercy. Anyway, is the restaurant all set for tonight?"

"It seems to be. I want everything to go well so my parents and siblings can relax and enjoy themselves for a change."

That evening, the family gathered at the Konavle Kafe. Ana and Ivan and their families joined them. Nick introduced Jelena, but other than kisses and smiles, they could not speak to each other. Later, Nick whispered to Jelena, "They think you're beautiful. And congratulated me on choosing well."

"You better set them straight. I was the one who put the target on your back."

"True. One day we'll tell them the story."

Nick had ordered a full-course meal, beginning with mushroom soup, followed by seafood risotto and the main course, roast lamb with a medley of root vegetables. Dessert featured a choice of Sachertorte or linzertorte, both made without fresh fruit—not easily available in winter. Nick only wished he'd been able to ship a crate of apples over because apple strudel was the crowd favorite. One day...one day soon he would manage that.

Nick invited his brothers to join him for a drink. But Ivan begged off because he had to get his wife and children home. His father stepped up to the task to allow his sons some time to themselves.

After saying their goodbyes, Nick led his brothers to a tavern down the road, across from the town square. Once they had a bottle of slivovitz on the table and their glasses were filled, Nick began. "We have a lot to talk about. First, I'd like to know what the situation is like in Croatia these days. How are the Austrians treating you?"

Ivan answered first. "There are always tensions. The Serbs and Turks seem to have settled down. But the Austrians always make life difficult. We won't rest until we have our freedom back."

"You know, Napoleon built a monument in celebration of his

success in the Battle of Austerlitz. It's right on the big boulevard in Paris. The Arc de Triomphe is what it's called."

"It could also be a monument marking when the Austrians double-crossed us and we lost our republic—and our freedom, to boot."

"That's the difference between Croatia and America. We have freedom and opportunity. I'll be rich one of these days. But if I stayed here, I would just be another poor peasant."

"Like me, you mean," Ivan said.

"You inherited the land. That's worth something."

"Not much. I can barely scratch out a living and the young 'uns keep coming."

"I thought Petra appeared to be with child."

"It'll be here before the summer."

"What about you, Luka and Gabe? Any plans yet for your future?"

"I thought I might marry a first daughter with no brothers. Then we'd inherit the land," Luka said.

"You'd be required to change your last name to hers. Do you want to give up your birthright?" Nick asked.

"I forgot about that slight complication. No matter. I haven't met a first daughter yet with no brothers."

"And what about you, Gabe?"

"I might go out to Canada to homestead. It would be one way to get my own land."

"We've thought about taking the plunge together," said Luka. "The Canadian government has sent agents here to promote their program."

"Frank and I were hoping you'd join us in the apple packing business. Since we've already paved the way, you'd have nothing to lose and everything to gain."

"We're more interested in farming than packing fruit. Besides, we'd get land out of it."

"Just remember, the offer is always open. The four of us

would be a real powerhouse. In fact, other Konavle brothers are making good in the apple business. You'd fit right in."

"Sorry to disappoint you," Luka said. "But your dream is not our dream."

"And I have no dream. Just need to make the best of it," said Ivan. "No matter. It suits me, living here where I grew up. Someone needs to help Ma and Pa in their dotage, and then there're the sisters to still marry off."

The brothers joined in a hearty laugh. Nick knew being the first-born son was not all it was cracked up to be. He'd take his freedom any day.

CHAPTER 23

Nick took Jelena around to visit with other relatives and friends as much as their time would allow. Whenever he could, Nick joined his father in the vineyard, leaving Jelena to his mother's care. Even though Jelena could not converse with her, she could watch and learn how to make Nick's favorite foods.

After spending three weeks visiting family in the Dubrovnik area, Nick and Jelena said their goodbyes, with a promise to visit again in a few years. Nick knew it would be a promise unlikely to be kept—too many of life's events would intervene.

Luka and Gabe drove the pair to the port of Gruz, where they would take a ship to Split to spend a few more days visiting Jelena's relatives, none of whom she had ever met.

As he was about to depart, Nick said, "Remember, my offer to come to California and be a part of our family business still stands. Don't jump too quickly at a chance for land. Nothing is ever free in this life. You pay one way or the other." Luka and Gabe nodded, but Nick knew their minds were already made up. Homesteading in Canada seemed more of a sure thing. But he had said his piece, and maybe his words would come back to them at some point to reverse their decision.

Nick and Jelena boarded the sailboat just before the crew

untied the lines for departure. A couple of mates hoisted the mainsail, and the winds filled it, sending the ship on its way. Jelena leaned into Nick to snuggle as the sailboat tacked its way up the coast. "I believe the island coming up on our left is Brac. Many Croatians in town are from there."

Once they passed Brac, Split was in sight. They pulled into the harbor and a couple of mates tied the ship to the dock before putting out the gangway. Nick gathered up the suitcases and grabbed Jelena's hand to lead her off the ship. They walked around the perimeter of the harbor until they found the entrance to the Old Town. After passing through an open space with columns all around, they ducked under an arch that led to a narrow passage filled with twists and turns.

"We'll get lost in this maze," Nick said. "Let's stop and ask someone for directions." Up ahead, Nick spotted a cafe. "Maybe someone can help us there. I could use a snack as well. How about you?"

"A coffee would be nice."

When the waitress appeared, Nick ordered two coffees and walnut rolls to go along with them. Nick cut off a piece of the walnut roll with his fork and put it in his mouth. "Yum. This is almost as good as my mother's."

When Nick paid the bill, he asked the cashier for directions to the aunt's house. Although he understood what she was saying, he knew he wouldn't remember the turns to take on the complicated route and asked for her to draw him a map.

Nick inspected the map and led Jelena through the maze of alleys. He stopped twice to double-check his directions, but they found the address was at the top of a long set of stairs. "Perhaps I should climb up to make sure we're in the right place and someone is home. No use dragging these suitcases all the way up there if this is the wrong address."

As they were discussing what to do, an older woman, carrying a bag of groceries on one arm and a loaf of bread under the other, stopped at the stairs. She turned and asked whether they were the Markoviches she was expecting. Beaming, she set down her groceries. Then it was hugs and kisses as she welcomed them. Finally, she said, "Please follow me."

Aunt Rosa gave a knock at the top of the stairs, and a young woman about Jelena's age opened the door. "Sofija, these are our guests from America. Your cousin, Jelena, and her husband, Nick Markovich."

She leaned in to give each kisses on their cheeks, then held the door open wide for them to enter.

"Just set your bags there by the door and come in and make yourselves comfortable. I'll join you in a minute after I dispatch the groceries and put on a kettle for tea. Sofija, entertain our guests in the meantime."

Nicked looked from Jelena to Sofija, trying to note the family resemblance. They were first cousins, so they should have some resemblance. But Jelena was light while Sofija was dark, which made any resemblance difficult to detect. While they waited, a bedroom door opened and an older man stepped out.

"Papa," Sofija said. "Our guests have arrived."

Andro Novak was wearing an undershirt and pajama pants. He padded barefoot to the living room and shook hands with Nick. Then he bent over Jelena to give her a kiss.

"Papa, you need to dress properly for our guests."

Andro cast his eyes downward. "My apologies." He shuffled back to his bedroom to make himself presentable.

Rosa appeared with a tray full of goodies and set them down on the coffee table. "Please, help yourselves. I'll be right back." She returned with cups full of tea, setting cream and sugar on the table, along with a pot for refills. "Now then. How has your visit to Croatia been so far?"

Before Nick answered, he said, "Jelena does not speak Croatian, so I will translate for us. To answer your question, we had a wonderful visit with my family in Cilipi, and we spent time in the Old Town of Dubrovnik as well. My family fell in love with Jelena, as I knew they would."

Andro entered the room, wearing a proper shirt, pants, and shoes. "Again, please excuse me for my appearance earlier. I did not realize company had arrived."

Rosa handed Andro a cup of tea. "Baked goods are on the table but restrain yourself. You overdid it during the holidays."

Andro shot Rosa a frown, taking several pieces of kolache, anyway.

"So, tonight, I'll fix dinner for us here. And tomorrow night, we'll meet the others at a restaurant. The family has grown so large that it's difficult to accommodate everyone at home."

Jelena smiled while Nick replied, "Thank you. I hope it's not too much trouble."

"Trouble? You're my dear brother's children, who I have never once laid eyes upon. We have to celebrate. Everyone is looking forward to meeting you."

After tea, Rosa said, "Now, you must spend some time touring Split. Sofija has agreed to be your guide. But first, I'll show you to your room so you can get organized."

Rosa opened the door to the guest room. "My boys used to share this room. As you can see, there's not the least thing feminine about it."

Nick looked at Jelena and smiled. The room had bunk beds. He leaned over and whispered, "I'll flip you for the top."

Sofija waited for them by the door. After they walked down the stairs, she turned to the couple and said, "I'll just have time to show you the highlights. Follow me."

Sofija led them through a labyrinth that opened onto a public square. "We call this Fruit Square because this is where women used to sell their fruit. The statue in the center is of the father of Croatian literature, Marko Marulic. Have you heard of him?"

"Can't say that I have," Nick said. *I'm not about to admit I can barely read Croatian.*

"As we walk around, you'll notice the city built inside Diocletian's palace. It is a wonder to architects, who often come here to study."

"What prompted people to build a city within a palace?"

"All I know is the palace was badly damaged in a war. However, the people living nearby took refuge in what was left of the fortress and just continued to build their town within until we have what you see today."

"That's incredible."

"We're coming upon St. Dominus Cathedral, the oldest Catholic cathedral in the world. But before it was a cathedral, it served as Diocletian's mausoleum. The bell tower is a symbol of the city. Every May seventh, we celebrate the feast of St. Dominus, who is our patron saint."

Sofija kept up a fast pace as she moved Nick and Jelena around the city. "Now we are coming upon Diocletian's cellars, which he used for storage, but as you can see, it's now a gallery of shops. If you'd like to buy a souvenir, this is a good place. We still have some time before we're due back, so you can browse if you like."

After Jelena received Nick's translation, her face brightened as she turned toward a jewelry shop to explore. She settled on a medal of St. Dominus that she could wear on a charm bracelet.

By the time they headed back, darkness had fallen and the torch lights were lit, marking their way. Sofija had gotten them back just as Rosa was pulling a roast from the oven. One whiff of the aroma told them chicken would be on the menu.

"Hurry and get freshened up," Rosa said. "We'll be eating soon."

Andro was waiting for them at the head of the table when they returned, and Rosa was ladling soup into bowls, which she set at each place. Andro motioned for them to sit down, and then both Rosa and Sofija joined them. "Let us say grace," Andro said. And he bowed his head.

Andro took a spoonful of vegetable soup and proclaimed it delicious. "So, how was your tour with Sofija?"

Jelena turned to Nick to answer. "You live in a very interesting city. I don't think I've ever heard of one built inside the ruins of a palace before."

"Nor have I, but that means nothing. It was the people of Salona, Diocletian's hometown, who sought safety here from invasions by the Avars and Slavs. Even their city walls with towers where guards were posted didn't protect them."

"They should have hired Dubrovnik's architects. Those walls have survived many invasion attempts."

"Yes, but they were built much later—thirteenth century, I think. Salona was an ancient Roman city—the capital of Dalmatia. Its walls were built around the second century BC. Your people had about fifteen hundred years to learn how to do it right."

"Thanks for setting me straight."

Rosa changed the subject to family. "How is my younger brother, Mateo, doing? He doesn't write often."

"He has a coffeehouse on the San Francisco waterfront, which does well enough to support his family. He has a grandson already."

"Yes, we're aware of the grandson, Tomas, I believe his name is. He's Lana's son, correct?"

"That's right. By this time next year, Jelena and I may have added another grandson to his line." He glanced at Jelena, who had not understood by her placid smile, and he did not bother to translate.

"Tomorrow night, you will meet the rest of our family at dinner. I have two sons and two other daughters who are all married with children. But you must also visit the aunts and uncles before you leave. They are looking forward to meeting you."

Nick and Jelena were exhausted from all the visiting by the time they took the boat across the sea to Venice. "I'm glad we have a few days to ourselves," Jelena said.

"I agree. It will give us a chance to rest up before the return voyage. Let's hope it's smoother sailing."

After they arrived at the dock, Nick hired a gondola to take them to their hotel. "Baglioni Hotel Luna, per favore." The gondolier paddled through a series of canals until he arrived at the dock entrance to the hotel, only steps away from San Marco Square. A doorman stepped up to help Jelena and Nick disembark and handle their luggage. He guided them to the reservations desk where a clerk was awaiting them with a smile. "Buongiorno."

The clerk did the required paperwork and checked their passports. Then he handed a large bronze key, attached to a disk bearing the number 314, to the bellman who already had the suitcases on a cart, ready to go.

"Follow me, per favore."

Their room had a canal view. It was small but elegantly decorated with damask wallpaper in gold tones. The full-size bed had a provincial headboard and duvet that matched the wallpaper. A beautiful Aubusson rug covered most of the hardwood floor. Nick was quick to tip the doorman, who knew to take his leave. Then he wrapped Jelena in his arms. "Our honeymoon is about to take on a new dimension."

"I think it's time to see the sights," Nick said. "You take a shower first."

"Oh, do I have to? I just want to linger awhile longer."

"When we get back to the room, I promise you, we will linger the night away."

On their way out of the lobby, they passed the Marco Polo ballroom. "Look, the door is open. Let's take a peek."

A peek was not enough for Jelena. She had to step into the room. "Oh, my God." The walls were covered with frescos by students of Tiepolo and ornately framed mirrors. As their eyes moved upward, the massive fresco that covered the entire ceiling captivated them.

"I picked this hotel because of its history, back to the twelfth century. But I had no idea it contained such beautiful art."

"Everywhere else I've been pales in comparison."

"True. I wonder if they entertained the Knights Templar in here? I heard they stayed at the hotel during the Crusades." Nick saw Jelena's face go blank.

"The Knights Templar consider themselves soldiers for Christ. They protected Christians who were making a pilgrimage to the Holy Land from Muslim attacks."

"Oh. There is so much I don't know."

"Nor I. But we'll learn together."

In only a couple of minutes, they were in San Marco Square after walking over a series of canal bridges. Even on a winter evening, the square was full of people. They headed toward San Marco Basilica, entering the cavernous, decadent space.

"They call the basilica the church of gold. Venetians built this to show off their wealth and power, even as they were sacking cities around them. Look at those mosaics and you'll see what I mean."

Jelena gazed up at the dome, which was like a golden sun shining its blessings down on those gathered below. "Venetians must have been very rich at one time."

"They got rich from trade and wars. But eventually God got even with them. He sent the Black Plague, which wiped out nearly everyone in the city."

Nick took Jelena's hand when they reentered San Marco Square. "Come on, there's something else I want to see. I missed it the last time." They walked through alleyways and over canals until they came to the Church of San Lorenzo. Nick tried the door. "Locked again."

When they got back to the hotel, Nick asked the clerk, "Why is the Church of San Lorenzo always locked when visitors come to pay their respects to Marco Polo?"

"I regret to reform you. If Marco Polo's tomb ever rested there, it was lost when the church was rebuilt over three centuries ago."

"Lost?"

The clerk shrugged. "It happens."

Nick shook his head and turned to Jelena. "That's Italians for you. They may make great art but they lack organization."

"I would not say it's lost but missing. I suspect it was stolen."

"No doubt. Venice has long had a shady side—namely, gambling and prostitution. Croatians learned the hard way not to trust them."

The sun peeked through their window the next morning, shooting a beam into Nick's face. He rubbed his eyes and shook Jelena. "It's our last day in Venice. Rise and shine so we can make the most of it."

Jelena got out of bed and went to the window to take a glimpse of Venice at daybreak. "I can see the dome of St. Mark's Basilica from here. Come, take a look."

Nick moved in beside her. "You may remember from catechism classes that churches contain relics of the saints they're named after. Of course, this one contains St. Mark's."

"Did he die near Venice?"

"Actually, he was buried in Alexandria, Egypt. Venetian merchants stole some of his bones and brought them here."

"I guess it's good they did or they wouldn't have built St. Mark's Basilica."

"An example of God making good out of bad—the history of the world."

CHAPTER 24

The following morning, Nick and Jelena caught a train to Milan, then another to Paris and yet another to Le Havre, where their ship was waiting while officers checked passengers aboard. They were taking *La Gascogne* again for the return to New York and from there, the train to Chicago.

Nick and Jelena rode a carriage to the Palmer House hotel in downtown Chicago. Upon arrival, a bellman set their luggage on a cart, leading them to the reservations desk in the opulent French-inspired lobby, a grand staircase the centerpiece.

After checking in, the bellhop guided them to the elevators. "These were the first of their kind in Chicago. Of course, New York had them much earlier."

Once the bellhop left their room, Jelena collapsed on the bed. "After two-and-a-half weeks at sea in that little cabin, this feels like a palace."

Nick pulled out his pocket watch. "You relax in luxury while I go off to my meeting. When I return, we'll take a stroll before supper."

Nick hailed a carriage outside the hotel and gave the driver the address of his destination. It took him less than half an hour to get there. When he reached the building, he noted the office was on the fifth floor—not an elevator in sight. The stairs proved to be a steep climb, but he had been up to it, not even breaking a sweat. Nick entered the office and announced himself to the secretary.

"I'll let Mr. Caputi know you're here."

Nick made himself comfortable while he waited and leafed through the newspaper.

When the secretary returned, she said, "Follow me, please, Mr. Markovich."

Mr. Caputi welcomed Nick into his office. He had a swarthy complexion and a handlebar mustache. With a wide, toothy smile, he said, "I hope you're enjoying our city."

"Actually, we only just arrived. But my bride is very pleased with our accommodations at the Palmer House after a train berth and ship's cabin."

Mr. Caputi let out a laugh. Then he reached for a humidor, opened it, and offered Nick a cigar. He took one for himself, cut off the ends, struck a match and lit them.

Nick took an inhale. Mr. Caputi did the same but let out three smoke rings while Nick watched, remembering Karlo's trick. *I have to learn how to blow those.*

"Now, I know you're here to talk about the World's Fair. By the way, Bertha Palmer is in charge of the Women's Building. She's the owner of the Palmer Hotel, where you're staying."

"A Women's Building? That's a new one on me."

"Yes, Bertha's quite a feminist and has big plans for it."

"I also have big plans, but for apples instead."

"California's products will be showcased in their own build-ing. They're in charge of all the displays—it's out of my hands. Contact someone in the state. I recommend either your state senator or an official at the agriculture department. And if you run into a problem, get back to me and I'll make sure your apples are displayed."

"They'll be the best in the world soon. Your visitors will be the first to know."

"We always like to be ahead of the curve. Now, what else can I do for you?" While he waited for Nick to respond, Caputi sat back and blew some more smoke rings into the air.

"We've had some problems with fruit commissioners in this town. They don't give us a fair shake."

Caputi bolted upright, his bronze eyes blazing. "What do you mean, they don't give you a fair shake?"

"Since they don't take ownership of our apples, they let them sit and rot. Then they say they aren't worth much."

"I see—"

"If we can't trust your commissioners, we'll find—"

"Not so fast. Let me check into this and see what I can do to right it. I doubt you will have any more problems. I give you my word on that."

When Nick entered the hotel room, Jelena seemed in much better spirits. She sat in a club chair with her feet propped up on an ottoman. "I've been reading a brochure about the hotel. Did you know this is the second Palmer House Hotel?"

"What happened to the first?"

"It burned down in the Great Chicago Fire of '71, only a few days after it opened. Can you believe that?"

Nick shook his head. "How did it start?"

"They're not sure, but it spread like wildfire because most of the buildings were made of wood."

"Croatians are lucky a ready supply of stone is available to build with. But now that you mention it, I think San Francisco also has a lot of wood buildings." He banished the thought that crossed his mind.

CHAPTER 25

Frank had a buggy waiting for them when they arrived at Watsonville Depot. He helped Jelena into the back seat, then loaded the luggage in the rear compartment while Nick jumped up front. "Next stop, home sweet home." Frank clicked his tongue and shook the reins. "Giddyap, you two."

Nick had given Frank instructions to purchase a house for him and Jelena. Mrs. Babich and Lana volunteered to furnish it with the basics, permitting Jelena to do the rest to her taste. The California Craftsman-style bungalow was within walking distance of the packinghouse. Jelena hesitated a few moments before disembarking as she took in the full view of the house. It was one story with stairs leading to a wide front porch and another small porch on the side. *So different from the townhouse I grew up in.* She noticed a chimney, pleased there would be a hearth in the parlor.

After she alighted, Nick led her up the path while she took in the front and side yards that separated neighbors. After climbing the stairs, he slid the key into the lock and opened the door but hesitated. She didn't understand why. Then, in a swift motion, he scooped her up into his arms to carry her over the threshold.

"For good luck," he said. Before he set her down, he gave her a sweet kiss.

Jelena's eyes roved around the room. It felt spacious, with the freshly painted white walls and simple furnishings—a sofa, two chairs, and a coffee table. Enough to get started. As she moved through the room, she ran her hand across the back of the blue velvet sofa, sensing its softness while admiring its tufted style. She stopped at the coffee table and took a deep inhale. Someone had set a vase of red and white roses on the table. "Are you responsible?" Jelena asked as she fixed her eyes on Frank.

"Guilty as charged."

Jelena gave him a kiss on the cheek. "Thank you. It means a lot to me."

Jelena walked through the parlor which led to the dining room and then into the kitchen. "This is a very modern kitchen. My mother must be envious." A small oak table covered with a floral oilcloth sat in one corner, with four chairs surrounding it. She inspected everything — opening cupboards and drawers and assessing the size of the ice chest. "This is more than I will ever need."

"Don't be too sure." Nick took her in his arms and kissed her again. "I couldn't resist this opportunity while Frank stepped out." He leaned in for another kiss, but when he heard boots on the porch, he let up. "Give me a rain check. I'll make it up to you tonight."

"And I'm holding you to it."

Frank came in with the luggage. "Should I put these in the master bedroom?"

Nick motioned yes and guided Jelena into their bedroom.

Her eyes opened wide when she saw what her mother and sisters had done in there—a wrought-iron bed with a floral duvet, lace curtains, and an armoire painted a soft white with gold trim. And something no Catholic couple would do without —a crucifix over the bed.

Frank gave Nick a quick glance and shot him a smug smile.

Jelena caught him. "I know what you're thinking—it's too feminine for Nick. But he'll get used to it."

Nick and Frank stole another look, which Jelena missed.

"So, what's new around town?" Nick asked.

"Well, for one thing, I have a girlfriend."

"Don't stop there—tell us more," Jelena said.

"She's a sister of a couple packers from Cilipi. Her name is Helen Kordich. Her brothers are Victor and Vlad."

"Victor's in business with some cousins."

"That's right. I don't know the others."

"How did you meet her?"

"At church. Her brother introduced me."

"I'm glad to learn there's another young Croatian woman in town," Jelena said.

"She's not the only one. Several have arrived and more are coming."

"If I'd known that, I would have waited rather than trekked all the way up to the city."

Jelena gave Nick a poke in the ribs.

"Ouch. That hurt."

"There's more where that came from, if you don't watch yourself," she said with a wink.

"How was the trip to Europe and the visit with the folks?"

"I'll tell you all about it later. Now, what about the second thing you mentioned?"

"Let's save that for later, too. I don't want to spoil your homecoming."

Nick walked into the packinghouse and gave it a quick once over. Frank was already there, knee-deep in boxes. "I see you got a lot of boxes made up while I was away."

"We tried to get ahead of the harvest. Besides, there's a lot of pressure to use new, clean boxes."

"A rumor I picked up in New York is they want cedar boxes, not redwood. Be prepared for that change."

"When it happens, we'll deal with it."

Nick looked around the packinghouse again. "Where's Jakov?"

Frank put down his hammer and approached Nick. "Jail. It's the second thing I wanted to mention."

"What's the charge?"

"Murder—he killed a man."

"Who, for God's sakes?"

"An Irishman named Doyle. They were arguing about apple packing and before you knew it, Doyle pulled out a blade and lunged at Jakov. He dodged the knife but grabbed a bottle of slivovitz off the table and cracked Doyle on the head with it, making him see stars. He fell to the floor with the biggest clunk you ever heard, ending up dead as a doornail."

"That sounds like self-defense to me. So, why are they holding him?"

"For the arraignment date."

"Has he retained a lawyer?"

"Not yet. But he wants you to get him one."

"I'll see to it after I talk with him."

"It better be a good one. The odds are stacked against a Croatian in this town. Especially one who killed an Irishman."

Nick headed for the office and Frank followed. "I was hoping to talk about the family with you this morning. But instead, I have to deal with Jakov's problem."

"Why don't you go see him now and when you get back, we can eat lunch and talk."

Nick walked the two miles to the jailhouse so he could clear his mind and think. *Where can I find a lawyer? The ones in this town are loyal to the Irish establishment. None will take Jakov's case, but if they do, they'll make sure to lose it. I have to get an out-of-towner. Pero*

Loreto. He doesn't do criminal law, but he probably knows a lawyer who does.

By the time he figured it out, he had arrived at the jailhouse. Nick announced himself, and the jailer took him to Jakov's cell. "Do you want to tell me about it?"

"Not much to tell. Got in an argument. The guy pulled a knife, and I bopped him on the head with a bottle. I think he bought the farm when he hit the floor."

"You can beat the rap with a good lawyer."

"Good luck finding one in this town."

"Not here. San Francisco. I have a good contact who I'll cable today."

After he left the jail, Nick sent a telegram to Pero and walked back to the packinghouse. Frank was waiting for him. "How did it go?"

"As expected. I sent a telegram to Pero Loreto for names of defense lawyers."

"Smart thinking. Now, tell me about the family. How are Ma and Pa?"

"They're quite robust for their ages, but get plenty of help from Marija and Dora, who are still at home."

"What about Ivan?"

"He knows his responsibility and lives up to it. Believe me, he does."

"And Ana?"

"She's busy being a mother and housewife, which seem to suit her. She takes more after Ma than I ever thought possible."

"What about Luka and Gabe? Did you convince them to change their minds?"

"I did my best sales job, but they have their hearts set on homesteading in Canada. Apparently, agents are scouring the country and making offers young men can't refuse. They told me they'd rather farm than pack apples any day."

"It's settled then. It's just the two of us."

The courtroom was filled on Jakov's arraignment day with one side Irish, the other Croatian. The lawyer Nick had secured from San Francisco was slick—too slick for the town's country lawyers, and he convinced the judge to reduce the charge to manslaughter and give Jakov bail.

My only choice is to spring him, Nick thought. And he put up the bail money.

Nick and Jakov took the carriage back to the packinghouse where Frank was waiting. "We need to double security," Nick said. "I smell a packinghouse fire in the making."

"The crowd was angry."

"You can say that again." He turned to Jakov. "You better take every precaution from now on. They'll be gunning for you. It's what they call out West frontier justice—taking the law into their own hands."

"Believe me, I'll watch my back."

"Move out of the rooming house," said Frank. "Find some place where they won't be able to find you."

"Excellent advice. If you don't mind, I'll gather up my belongings and lie low for a while."

Nick and Frank watched Jakov leave, already looking beaten.

"You need to step up now. We can't count on Jakov to pull his load."

Nick and Frank did a double take when they stepped into the office for their morning coffee—the safe was standing open. Nick squatted while he did a quick inventory. "All the important papers are here, but the cash is gone." He stood and faced Frank. "There's only one explanation."

A few days later, Nick received a telegram. "Gone back home. I owe you one." It was unsigned. And the telegraph office registered a name he'd never heard of. But he knew it was from Jakov. He showed Frank the message. "After he absconded with the money, he must have boarded a ship in Oakland. That's easy enough to do, especially if you're willing to spread some green-backs around."

"It's too bad. I liked Jakov, and he worked hard. Without his stake, we wouldn't be in business."

"I should have known a tiger wouldn't change its stripes."

"But he pulled himself together."

"Temporarily...I knew partnering with him might end up a bum deal, but yet it was an opportunity, so I had to take it and make the best of it."

"Which you have."

"First thing we do is change the sign to Markovich and Markovich Packers."

"I like the sound of that."

"It'll cost you."

In less than a week, the sign was up—Markovich Bros. Fruit Packers and Shippers.

"I see you changed the wording," Frank said.

"That way I don't have to redo the sign if Luka and Gabe join us."

CHAPTER 26

Jelena had not been feeling well. Nick set her up with a family practitioner he had used from time to time. She had talked her symptoms over with her mother and sister, so she was not completely surprised when Dr. Klein declared her pregnant. Jelena was thrilled and knew Nick would be, too. "When will the baby be born?"

"Let me do some calculations. Your last period was January nineteen, so forty weeks from that would be November first."

"All Saints' Day."

"Don't count too much on it. Babies come on their own time. Some are early. Some are late. Most aren't born on schedule."

When Nick arrived home that night, Jelena served him his favorite meal while candles flickered their light between them.

"To what do I owe the honor of this special dinner?"

"I have some good news to share."

Nick set down his fork and swallowed the seafood risotto to listen more closely.

"We're going to have a baby."

Nick let out a whoop, jumped out of his chair, pulled Jelena out of hers, and wrapped her in a bear hug before kissing her until she was almost faint. When he let go, he was full of ques-

tions. "How do you feel? When should we expect it? What
instructions did the doctor give to follow?"

"Slow down. My head is spinning. Let's sit and catch our
breath. Then I'll answer your questions one at a time. But this I
can tell you—the baby is due at the end of the apple harvest—
good timing, if I do say so myself." She couldn't resist a smug
smile.

Frank and his girlfriend, Helen Kordich, came for dinner on
Sunday. She was a classic Croatian beauty, with long blonde hair,
blue eyes, high cheekbones, and bow lips that always seemed to
smile.

Introductions over, Nick could contain himself no longer.
"We've got something to share. Jelena's in the family way."

Frank gave Nick a couple of slaps on the back. "I knew you
wouldn't be shooting blanks on your honeymoon." Nick beamed
a wide, proud smile. Not that he needed it, but his manhood had
been validated in every sense of the word.

"I have the table set and dinner will be out of the oven in just
a minute. Please take a seat in the dining room."

Jelena left for the kitchen where she filled a tureen to the
brim with mushroom soup, setting it on the end of the table. She
began ladling it into bowls, which she passed. Helen couldn't
resist leaning in for a whiff of the aroma. "It smells delicious."
Then she tasted it. "What's your secret?"

"A few porcini mushrooms add a woodsy flavor. I learned that
trick when we visited Venice, so I brought some back. I don't
know if you can get them here, but if anyone has them, it would
be the Italians."

"I must remember that."

Jelena returned to the kitchen to remove the chicken from
the oven. She had filled it with a sage stuffing, accompanied by
side dishes of carrots and peas. After making the gravy, Jelena
called Nick into the kitchen to carve the roast. The juicy slices

of chicken surrounded by the green and orange vegetables were a delight to the eye. Nick passed the platter, and Jelena set the dressing and gravy on the table for everyone to help themselves.

After they had their plates filled, Frank said, "Helen and I have some news ourselves."

Nick and Jelena gave him their full attention.

"We're engaged."

"That's wonderful news," Jelena said. "You'll be so happy. I can tell by looking at you."

"Helen, Frank told me your brother Victor is in the packing business."

"Yes, and I have another brother here named Vlad. I came over with him."

"Do you have a date for the wedding yet?" Jelena asked.

"We're thinking about doing it in December or January. The winter timing worked out well for you in more ways than one." Frank gave Nick a wink when the girls weren't watching.

"The end of the year will be busy, that's for sure. Did I mention I spoke with the fruit commissioner in Chicago about the World's Fair they'll host? We have a lot of work ahead to prepare for it."

"When does it open?"

"May first."

"That's bad timing for us."

"I haven't spoken to anybody else about this, but I assume we can send the apples out to be exhibited. There'll be a California building, after all."

"World's Fair. I'd like to see it," Jelena said.

"Maybe we both can go at the end of the harvest. Closing ceremonies will be on October thirtieth."

"What about the baby's first birthday?"

"Of course, we'll work around it."

"Or, better yet, bring him with us."

Nick rolled his eyes.

After Frank and Helen left, Jelena said, "I like her. I think we'll be good friends."

"I hope so. I don't want anything to spoil things with Frank."

"She doesn't seem like the type of girl who would. I think she'll be a true partner, like me."

"Leave the dishes until morning and let's partner up."

CHAPTER 27

1892 seemed to fly by with so many events competing for their attention. Jelena gave birth to a baby boy on November first, the forecast due date. Following the Croatian naming tradition, they christened him Anton, after Nick's father. They gave him the middle name Mateo after Jelena's father.

Nick was beside himself with joy. "With Anton, I have put down roots in America that will eventually run as deep as the Croatian ones."

After all the hoopla over Anton's birth, the holidays came and went in a flash. Then it was on to Frank and Helen's wedding, held at the Valley Catholic Church. Nick, of course, served as best man, and Helen asked Jelena to be her matron of honor. Frank didn't have the time or money for the type of honeymoon Nick had taken, so he opted to spend it in San Francisco—a city he and Helen had rarely visited. They painted the town red whenever they weren't holed up in the bridal suite of the Palace Hotel, which Nick had helped fund.

Upon their return, Frank got his bride settled in the cottage he had rented, then made tracks for the packinghouse. Nick was having a serious discussion with someone he didn't recognize. When Nick spotted Frank, he said, "Come over, I want to intro-

duce you to someone special. This is Mr. Keller. He's the representative the commissioner from Chicago sent to help ensure
our apple deliveries out East go well, especially the load
earmarked for the World's Fair."

Howard Dawson caught Nick on the way out of the packinghouse. "What's this I hear about your apples being displayed at
the World's Fair?"

"It's true. Markovich Brothers and other packers will be
sending apples to showcase in the California building. People
from all over the world will attend, which could mean more
international markets for us."

"I'd like to do a story on this for the *Pajaronian*. Let's meet so
we can talk properly."

"I'll try to clear some time for you."

By early April, packinghouse row was a hive of activity as all the
packers did their best to box displays of their fruit for the fair.
Mr. Keller made the rounds daily to ensure only the best packs
would be sent East. He made extra certain that the boxes bound
for the fair were top quality, knowing new markets could be
theirs for the taking if they were smart.

The cooperative packers were also busy, but it was widely
known they could not keep up with demand. And because of
that, their packs suffered. None of the Croatian packers wanted
the cooperative's fruit displayed with theirs—it would be a
disgrace to all they had worked for.

It didn't take Mr. Keller long to understand the apple politics
in town. He inspected the cooperative's apples frequently and
often rejected the pack—they had cut corners to make up for
lost time.

"I'd like to see the World's Fair," Jelena said one evening at
dinner. "Can I come along?"

"I'd love to have you with me. But the baby—"

"He wouldn't be any trouble."

"Maybe you could leave him with your parents, and we could make a second honeymoon of it."

"Honeymoon? Remember what happened last time."

Nick and Jelena took the train to San Francisco with baby Anton, where Mateo had the carriage waiting. He pulled aside a corner of the blanket that Anton was swaddled in to give him a kiss. "I just love babies. Vera and I are looking forward to having him to ourselves for a week."

Nick and Jelena boarded the transcontinental for Chicago—a three-day journey. When they arrived in their compartment, Jelena pulled down the bed. "Even worse than I remember."

"Once we partner up, you'll forget all about it."

The train pulled into Chicago's Union Station in the afternoon. By the time Nick and Jelena arrived at their room, they were weary. "Let's rest and get a fresh start on the fair tomorrow," said Nick. Of course, they did not rest, both eager to relive the highlight of their honeymoon, until they had totally exhausted themselves.

A bell ringing at a nearby church awoke Nick with a start. He grabbed his pocket watch, noting the time was already past seven. "Jelena, wake up. If we want dinner, we have to hurry."

When they returned to the room after dinner, both realized they were not tired after their long nap, so they made the most of what remained of the evening until they fell asleep, cuddled up close.

Nick and Jelena arrived at the fair as the crowd waited for the gates to open. Once inside, Nick led Jelena by the hand to the center where a large reflecting pool was situated, symbolizing Columbus's voyage to the New World. The pool was surrounded by neo-classic style buildings—all painted white, which earned the temporary town the name White City. At one end of the pool, the Republic Statue, Big Mary, stood watch. She held a globe with an eagle perched on it in one hand, a staff with the word *liberty* encircled by a laurel wreath in the other.

"I've been told that Frederick Law Olmsted was a designer of the exposition's layout. They call it City Beautiful and expect it to be a model for cities of the future."

"Wasn't Olmsted the architect of Central Park? He did a masterful job with this landscape," Jelena said. "It is just breathtaking."

"Let's not dawdle here too long. There's a lot to see. We have to be on the lookout for Columbus's three ships that were built in Spain and sailed here, just like Columbus did on his voyage."

"I noticed some state buildings ahead. California must be among them. Now I see it—up on the right." She pointed the way.

Upon entering the building, they were taken aback by a tower of oranges that served as a beacon. "Now why didn't we think of that?" Nick said. "Then again, oranges have the right skin for it—all shiny and bright."

They found the apple exhibit on the other side of the orange tower. Nick examined his display as well as those of the other packers, noting all the ribbons they'd won. "This show has put us on the map. Next, I'd like to view New York's apple exhibit. They're one of our chief competitors."

That evening, Mr. Keller had arranged a dinner with some key fruit commissioners in the city. Nick and Jelena rode the elevator to the hotel's top floor. "Keep your eyes peeled for a hospitality suite." When they entered the room, the cocktail party was already underway, guests smiling and chatting as they imbibed.

Mr. Keller spotted Nick and grabbed his hand in welcome. "Order whatever you like from the bar." When the dinner bell rang, Mr. Keller approached Nick again. "I'd like you and your beautiful wife to sit next to me for dinner. We can kill two birds with one stone that way."

As they were enjoying coffee after dinner, a hotel employee walked up to Mr. Keller and whispered something in his ear. Nick saw his face go white but hesitated to inquire about the message. Mr. Keller bowed his head, and when he raised it, he took his spoon and hit his glass to get everyone's attention. "I have some terrible news. The mayor of Chicago has died." He waited a moment for the news to sink in. "A lone gunman shot him dead." Upon hearing those words, the group gasped and speculated among themselves.

After a respectful pause, a guest asked, "What does this mean for the fair?"

"I don't know," Keller said. "But I'm sure we'll find out in the morning."

When they learned the closing ceremonies were cancelled, Nick changed their train reservations and arranged a sleeper car for the next morning.

They arrived in San Francisco before lunchtime and headed for the Babiches' townhouse, where Vera welcomed them with the baby on her hip.

"Anton, come to Mommy." Jelena took him from her mother and smothered him in kisses. "Look, Papa's here, too."

Nick patted him on the head and gave him a kiss on the cheek.

"You made it back for his birthday. We're celebrating tonight at the coffeehouse. I finished making the cake this morning. And it's about time for Anton's nap."

"I'll take him upstairs and put him down. He likes me to sing a lullaby which helps him go right to sleep."

When Jelena left, Nick said, "I hope Anton was good for you."

"He's a boy, so you know how that goes. Even though he's only crawling, he moves like a racehorse—it's hard to keep up with him. I don't know how I ever raised six when one seems to be too much now. Listen. Jelena's singing Brahms's 'Lullaby.' It's the one I used to sing to her."

Nick stood quietly and listened as he thought about life and how it repeats itself. *One day, Anton might sing this same lullaby to his child.*

After Anton awoke from his nap, it was time to get ready. "Everyone is meeting us at the coffeehouse. I just have to bring the cake and our presents," Vera said.

"Our present was too big, so we left it at home. We got him a rocking horse."

"He'll love it. Your brothers had one, and we thought they'd never outgrow it they rocked so much."

Mateo had pushed several tables together to create one big table, which was almost filled with guests by the time they walked into the coffeehouse.

"I'll hold the baby on my lap," Jelena said to Nick.

"We can take turns." They took seats next to each other.

Mateo stepped out of the kitchen to greet everyone. "No ordering off the menu tonight. I have prepared a special four-course dinner. We will begin with the appetizers which are almost ready. And then we'll finish with Vera's delicious Madjarica cake."

Everyone clapped to show their appreciation for the meal to come. Not to be left out, Anton banged a spoon on the table. That got everyone's attention and left Nick wondering what else they could expect from the birthday boy.

"Tell us about the fair," Lana said. "What was the most exciting thing you saw?"

"For me, it was an electric kitchen that even had a dishwasher," Jelena said.

"Doesn't that beat all," Vera said.

"What about you, Nick? What did you like best?"

"Of course, the Electricity Building was a glimpse into the future. I can't wait to have my own electric car. But then Buffalo Bill's Wild West Show was a fascinating glimpse into the past.

We had nothing like that back in Croatia. Now I believe what I've been told about bear and bull fights on our own Main Street. Oh, I almost forgot to mention the ride we took on a contraption called a Ferris Wheel that gave us a bird's-eye view of the fair when the wheel reached the top right before it tumbled down."

"It was quite a thrill, but I still don't know how you talked me into it," Jelena said.

"I'm sorry you had to miss the closing ceremonies," Vera said.

"They did not go on. But I can't imagine them greater than what we saw."

"It probably would have been a bunch of politicians congratulating themselves," said Mateo. "They would have come up with something big but would've steered clear of fireworks. Chicago had that big fire in '71 and during the fair, a fire broke out at the cold storage building that killed sixteen people. Chicago can rightly claim the title Fire Capital of the World."

Vera brought her Madjarica cake out from the kitchen with one candle blazing in the center. She set the cake in front of Anton, who sat on Jelena's lap. "Now, let's all sing happy birthday."

Jelena helped Anton blow out the candle, then Vera cut the layer cake filled with chocolate frosting, and began passing the pieces.

"Mama, what does Madjarica mean?"

"Hungarian girl. I never knew why they called the cake by that name because it is a traditional Croatian recipe."

"So, we have a mystery," said Jelena. "Perhaps the original recipe came from a Hungarian girl."

"Maybe. All I know is that whenever I serve it, people love it."

Jelena spooned some cake into Anton's mouth. He smiled and pointed for more. After another spoonful, he had eaten enough and squirmed.

"You can let him have his freedom. No customers are around to bother," Matteo said.

Jelena sat Anton on the floor. Once everyone had given him their attention, he stood up and took his first steps.

"Did you see that?" Nick said excitedly. "My son just walked for the first time, as if he planned his debut tonight for the crowd."

CHAPTER 28

Frank met Nick, Jelena, and Anton at the train depot. As soon as they were in the buggy, he announced, "Helen's in labor. I've got to get home."

"Go to the whip so we can get to the house quickly and get Jelena settled, and I'll come with you."

After dropping off Jelena and Anton, Frank gave both horses a crack on their rumps, forcing them into a fast gait which they kept up until Frank reined them in, panting and sweaty.

"You run in while I take care of the horses," Nick said. He led them to a trough and let them drink for a few minutes. Then he tied them up, checked his pocket watch, and planned to be back again soon to offer them more water. He didn't want to lose two good horses by neglect.

Frank was pacing in the living room but took a seat when Nick arrived. "How long has Helen been in labor?"

"About four hours, but the doctor told me she has a few more to go."

"How is she doing? Any problems?"

"The usual. It's shaping up to be a hard labor."

"Women's curse. But God knew what he was doing when he gave them the job instead of us men."

"Truthfully, I wish I could take her place."

Silence stood between them for a few moments before Nick said, "Did I miss anything while I was gone?"

"One big thing. The orchardists have given up the packing business."

"It's about time. One less thorn in our side."

"How was the World's Fair? Did our apples take any prizes?"

"Our town packers swept most of the categories. But the best we did was second."

"So, there's room for—"

The doctor appeared. "I'm happy to announce your wife delivered a healthy baby boy and is doing fine."

Nick jumped out of his seat and gave Frank a hug. "A boy! You have a son, too."

"When can I see them?"

"In an hour, give or take. The nurse is getting them ready now."

They christened the baby Anton Josip a month later, with Nick and Jelena serving as godparents. "Another Anton," Nick said.

"Followed the naming tradition."

"It'll get confusing real fast."

"We can always call him AJ." And it stuck.

On Christmas Day, Frank, Helen, AJ, and Helen's brothers, Victor and Vlad, joined Nick and Jelena for the holiday feast. Jelena found herself in the kitchen for the first time. "This is why I prefer to go to Mother's," she said to Nick.

"We'll see them for New Year's. But I think it's nice we're entertaining Frank's family. It's a chance for us to get to know Helen better, and Victor and Vlad, too."

Helen appeared in the kitchen. "Can I help?"

Jelena looked at Nick and then at Helen. "I can use all the help I can get."

After the dinner of suckling pig followed by coffee, dessert, and shots of slivovitz, Victor and Vlad took their leave. The rest of them settled in the living room, the women on one side with the babies, the men on the other, sitting within whispering distance of one another.

"I think the business is about to explode. We need to expand," Nick said.

"What do you have in mind?"

"I'd like to build a new packinghouse, and I want to move it to Alexander Street."

"Why Alexander?"

"Location, of course. I also plan to build Jelena a new home, but don't mention it to her. It's a surprise."

CHAPTER 29

That spring, the codling moth threatened again. The orchardists met, pointing fingers at the packers. "They want us to spray while they have poor practices that cause the apples to become infested," one of them said.

"What should we do about it?" a voice shouted from the crowd.

"Inspect." No sooner were the words spoken, then loud hurrahs and clapping hands filled the hall, demanding the appointment of an inspector charged with making his rounds at the beginning of the new season.

Chuck Cranford pulled up to the Markovich packinghouse, catching Nick by surprise. He was tall, blond, and tan, his body bulging with muscles developed from manual labor.

"What's your business?"

"You know what my business is."

"I'd like to hear you say it."

"Your packinghouse has an infestation of codling moths, according to—"

"That's where you're wrong. Now get off my property."

"The law says you must comply with my inspection."

"Over my dead body."

Cranford took up the challenge and continued toward the door. Nick ran ahead and blocked the entrance, spreading his arms wide across the opening. "I'm not letting you in."

"We'll see about that." Cranford attempted to force Nick aside, but Nick had more strength and weight on him.

"Try that again and I'll flatten you."

"All right. Have it your way. But this packinghouse will be inspected whether you like it or not."

Nick waited until Cranford's car was out of sight before he entered the building. He found Frank in the office. "Did you catch any of that?"

"What?"

"My head knocking with the new inspector?"

"No. What happened?"

Nick explained as he tried to contain his anger. "We need to build that new packinghouse sooner rather than later and put locks on that no one can pick."

That evening when Nick and Jelena were having dinner, someone pounded on their front door. Jelena put down her fork and fixed her frightened eyes on Nick.

"Stay here. I'll go see who it is."

When Nick opened the door, he came face-to-face with a cop. This could only be bad news. "What is it, Officer?"

"You're under arrest."

"What's the charge?"

"Refusing to allow access to a state horticulture inspection officer."

A pregnant Jelena appeared. "What's this all about?"

Nick took a deep breath. "There's been a misunderstanding. I'll go down to police headquarters to set them straight."

"Sorry to bother you, ma'am. Just doing my duty."

Nick gave Jelena a kiss and a pat on her tummy. "Don't worry. It'll be fine. But if Frank stops by, let him know where I am."

Jelena did not wait around for Frank. She checked on Anton, who was fast asleep in his crib, grabbed her shawl and headed out the door, holding the rail as she descended the porch stairs. Frank's house was only a couple of blocks away, which would not take long to walk. By the time she arrived, she was out of breath but gave Frank the message.

"I'll hitch up the buggy and take you home before I head to the police station."

Frank helped Jelena out of the buggy and up the stairs. As he climbed back into the buggy, he heard a scream and jumped back out. He found Jelena sprawled on the sidewalk, crying out in pain. Frank knelt beside Jelena and tried to soothe her. "Where does it hurt?"

"It's the baby."

"I'll carry you up the stairs and put you in bed. Tell me if I'm hurting you, okay?"

Frank slid his arm under Jelena, and that's when he felt it— the dampness, and knew her water had broken. He carried Jelena into the bedroom and laid her on the bed. "I'll bring Helen here and then go for the doctor."

"Don't leave me. I'm scared."

Frank didn't know what to do. He had to get a doctor, but he feared for Jelena. "I have to get help. I'll run to your neighbor next door." He bent over Jelena to feel her forehead. She was hot and sweaty. He had to hurry. In no time, he was back with Mrs. Savich, while Mr. Savich had gone for the doctor. "What can I do to help?"

"Boil some water and round up a bunch of rags."

Frank dashed out of the room to take care of the assignments. *Nick should be here. Somehow, I have to get Nick.* When the doctor arrived, Frank saw his moment of escape. Fortunately, the horses hadn't taken off with the buggy while it was left unhitched. He jumped in and whipped the horses into a gait faster than a trot. In the darkness, the quarter moon provided scant light, but Frank knew the route blindfolded and made it to the jailhouse in record time.

He burst into the station in a fit of anxiety. "Where's Nick Markovich? His wife had an accident."

"He's in the back and can't leave until someone posts bail."

"Take me to him right now."

"I'll get the keys."

Nick stood at the front of his cell, hands gripping the bars. He breathed a sigh of relief when he saw Frank. "Thank God you're here."

Frank turned to the jailer. "Give us a moment." When the officer left, Frank said, "I have bad news."

"What? I want you to get me out of here."

"I'm working on that. But Jelena's had an accident."

Nick's face went pale.

Frank paused a moment, then continued. "She took a fall, and the baby is coming."

"I need to go to her. Get that jailer to open this door now."

Frank left to reason with the jailer. "I'll sign an IOU and bring the money tomorrow. But Nick's wife and child need him now. If you are a man of God, you'll let him go."

The jailer stared at Frank for a long minute, then he blessed himself and threw Frank the keys.

Frank ran back to the cell and let Nick out. As they hustled out of the jailhouse, Frank tossed the keys to the officer. "Thank you and God bless."

Frank jumped into the carriage and took control of the reins, whipping the horses up to speed and driving them hell-for-leather back through town.

Even before he brought the buggy to a complete halt, Nick
bolted out and ran up the stairs into the house. He took a few
moments to collect himself before entering the room where
Jelena lay weeping. Nick pushed his way in to her bedside. "I'm
here, darling. Everything will be all right now."

"The baby. It's too soon."

Nick turned to the doctor, who remained silent. "Do everything possible to save the baby."

The tiny body was already entering the world. When it
emerged, the doctor cut the umbilical cord, turned it upside
down, and gave it a slap on its buttocks. The baby only
whimpered.

"Hand me one of those towels." Dr. Klein began rubbing the
baby boy all over to stimulate it. Then he turned it upside down
again and gave it another smack.

Nick looked on in despair. The baby was so tiny and its skin
so sheer that every vein, muscle, and bone was visible to the
naked eye. He wanted to hope, but knew only a miracle could
save his son.

The doctor handed the baby to the neighbor woman and
turned his attention to Jelena, who was bleeding profusely. He
worked until the bleeding stopped.

In a weak voice, Jelena said, "Give the baby to me. I want to
see him."

Mrs. Savich glanced at the doctor, who nodded, and she set
the baby in the crook of Jelena's arm. Nick moved in to comfort
them both. Jelena gazed at the baby's face and kissed it tenderly
on its forehead while the infant struggled for breath until its
little body trembled and all signs of life ceased.

"No..." Jelena clutched the baby to her breast, sobbing
uncontrollably.

Nick leaned in closer and stroked Jelena's head as he tried to
hold back his own tears.

The doctor gave them a couple of minutes, then moved in to

take possession of the baby's body. Jelena would not release him. "He's my baby. You can't have him."

Nick signaled the doctor to retreat and gently removed the baby from Jelena's grip. As Nick handed the little body to Dr. Klein, his eyes searched out Frank whose face reflected his pain. After the doctor sedated Jelena, Nick left the room, collapsing into Frank's arms.

"My son is dead. It's not right. And I'll not forget who brought this about." Later, he would blame himself for the anger that had sparked the events leading to his son's death and Jelena's depression. *If only I had remained calm and reasoned with the inspector, perhaps I could have held him off until we could get the packinghouse ready for inspection. But no, I let my anger get out of control. From now on, I have to let my head rule.*

Once Jelena's nurse arrived, Nick left to take care of a grim task. Later, he told Frank, "I arranged the funeral with the priest for two days from now. After lunch, I'll pick out a plot, a headstone, and an itty-bitty casket for my son to rest in until the end of time."

The funeral was held at the Valley Catholic Church. Because of the circumstances, the service was private, only family attending. Frank and Jelena's three brothers served as pallbearers. After the Mass, they carried the little casket to the plot on a rise overlooking the valley. Nick held Jelena close as they watched the coffin lowered into the grave and, together, they threw the first shovel of soil onto it. *Mother Earth gives life and cloaks death. She's the eternal embrace, lavishing us with her love.*

Afterward, everyone gathered at their home for lunch, which Mrs. Babich and Lana had prepared. It was a solemn affair, but shots of slivovitz lifted spirits. They all understood death as part of life, and once the deceased was mourned, it was time to live again.

CHAPTER 30

Nick pulled Frank aside. "As soon as Jelena is well enough to travel, I'm taking her to Tassajara Springs. Those hot springs in the beautiful Ventana Wilderness will restore not only her body but her soul."

"In the middle of the apple season? Can't your trip wait?"

"Remember what we were taught—family first. If Jelena doesn't get well, everything in our lives will suffer. Then, the business won't matter. Money can't buy every kind of happiness."

"Maybe you should take her parents along and come back for the harvest."

"This is something I have to do alone. Jelena would never forgive me for not being there—for shirking my responsibility."

Frank dropped Nick and Jelena off at the station. Anton was staying behind with Helen so they could truly relax. They took the train to Monterey and from there a stagecoach took them up a narrow road curving through the Los Padres National Forest, just southeast of Carmel Mission.

"If we have time on the way back, we'll visit Monterey.

Maybe even stay overnight in a hotel with a view of the bay. How would you like that?"

"Let's wait and see."

Wait and see. This is not the Jelena I married. She was always game, so full of life. I hope all she needs is time and tender loving care, which I will do my best to give her for the next couple of weeks. They say rest and relaxation work wonders—I'm pinning my hopes on that.

By the time they arrived at the resort, it was past Noon. After checking into their room, they headed for lunch. Three of the four dining room walls were plate-glass windows, offering views of the Ventana Wilderness. Nick noticed Jelena took in the scenery but did not comment on it. He would leave her alone with her thoughts for now.

The hostess seated them at a table alongside a window and handed them menus, which Nick scanned for fish. "They have abalone on the menu. So, I'm all set. What would you like?"

"That sounds fine." Jelena hadn't even opened her menu.

After placing their orders, Nick said, "Do you want to talk about it?"

Jelena gazed at her hands and twirled her wedding ring.

When the wine arrived, the waiter poured Nick's first for him to approve, and attempted to pour Jelena's, but she covered her glass with her hand and shook her head.

"I'm sorry. I thought you'd like a little wine to start our getaway."

"Not now."

After they finished their lunch and were relaxing over coffee, Nick asked again, "Would you like to talk about it?"

"Not really."

"I've been wondering how the accident happened."

"All right then." She hesitated. "There's not much to tell. I walked down to Frank's to tell him you'd been arrested. He brought me home and when I was about to go into the house, I remembered something I wanted to tell him. I turned around and caught my foot in the shawl, tumbling down the stairs. The rest you know."

"What was so important to tell Frank?"

"I don't even know. And to think…I lost my baby over something so unimportant."

"It was a freak accident. We just have to accept it was God's will."

"I don't believe God wanted our baby to die. I'm to blame for my carelessness."

And I'm to blame, too. Even more so. But I can't own up to it now. It's not that I'm a coward—it's that Jelena is too upset to hear my confession. I'll talk to a priest. If anyone needs forgiveness, it's me.

Jelena wanted to stay in the room after lunch to rest, but Nick coaxed her out to take a bath in the healing waters. By the time they were ready to leave, Nick knew the cure had worked because Jelena had received him lovingly the night before.

They were both eager to see little Anton and made haste for home. Their son was overjoyed to have them back, but once the effects of their getaway wore off, a spark still seemed to be missing from their family life. Later that week, Nick brought a surprise home for Anton, which he carried rolled up in his shirt. He called the boy to him and the bundle let out a yap. Nick unrolled his shirt to reveal a puppy with black and white spots— a Dalmatian, happy and loving and a little mischievous. They named him Split for his origin and two-tone color. In medieval Biblical art, dogs are depicted as healers, licking wounds to cure them after a sin is confessed. Nick was betting on that.

CHAPTER 31

Jelena loved her new house on Alexander Street with the large kitchen, gracious formal rooms, and plenty of bedrooms upstairs for guests or another child she so yearned for. Nick knew her heart ached for another baby. And every time Helen got pregnant, her pain seemed to intensify. Not that she was jealous, only that it was a reminder of her loss and barrenness. By the turn of the century, Frank and Helen had four children—one boy and three girls. But they had only one.

For the rest of his life, Nick would carry the guilt over the loss of their second son which may have caused Jelena's inability to conceive again. At least that was what the doctor assumed. But guilt can be a powerful motivator and it had helped propel him to success, not only in the apple business but in civic affairs. With only one child, he could devote time to multiple causes, especially political ones which were near and dear to his heart.

In 1901, WN White of London, representing fruit auctioneers, came to town for consignment on Newtown Pippin apples, and Markovich Bros. Fruit Packers was one of the first packing-houses he visited.

"Welcome, Mr. White," said Nick. "This is my brother and partner, Frank. We'd be pleased to show you around and answer any questions."

"It goes without saying, the firm I represent is impressed with the apples you produce in this valley."

"The orchardists do a fine job, but without the rich soil and favorable climate, they wouldn't have an apple worth talking about."

"This little Pajaro Valley is certainly blessed. They tell me farmers grow all different types of crops, from strawberries to beets to lettuce, and they all do well."

"And it's not just this valley," said Frank. "The entire state seems to produce a gold mine of agricultural products. Nowhere else in the world can even compete."

"I think you're right. But the primary reason I'm here is the Newtown Pippin. It's flavoring and coloring hold up even when shipped across the ocean. Besides, Londoners have taken a fancy to its crisp taste which gives them something to sink their teeth into. There's demand, I tell you. Mark my word. Watsonville is on its way to becoming the Apple Capital of the World."

"Cranford's at it again," Nick said.

Frank looked at him, perplexed. "What do you mean?"

"His attack on Slavonians at the World Fruit Conference. Can you believe he would have the nerve to say such things in San Francisco, of all places, where most of the fruit business is comprised of Slavonians?"

"I must have missed it. What on earth did he say that's got you so riled up?"

"He denounced us as a race. That *Pajaronian* article by the local orchardist whose name rhymes with mud must have emboldened him. That guy's a real mudslinger, all right. He called us anarchists and criminals and worse names I dare not repeat. I thought we had put all that discrimination behind when we got away from the Austrian Empire. But it followed us here.

"There was a newspaper article circulating when I first arrived calling us barbarians. And they accused us of clannishness because they noticed it helped us prosper. Those orchardists in town resent that Croatians control the packing business where the real money is made. That's why they tried to start their own packing business, but it failed because they lacked the talent."

"So, what are we going to do about it?"

"I think we should circulate a petition that refutes his remarks, stating our good character and honesty and work ethic. Our results speak for themselves."

"Who will your get to sign it?"

"To start, businessmen and orchardists."

"What about Cranford?"

"He claims he was misquoted. If he wants to prove it, he can be the first to sign. In big, bold letters."

Tensions subsided in town to work together for the sake of the harvest. But there was always some foe lurking about, and it often came in the form of a firebug. Although there had been many packinghouse fires over the years, some more destructive than others, the worst hit in the spring of 1903. It caused the destruction of the Earle Fruit Company's packinghouse and the Pajaro Valley Fruit Exchange. Other packinghouses were caught up in the pyre, including Nick and Frank's. By the time they got to the scene, only embers were left. Not only was the building lost but also tools, packing papers, and thousands of boxes that had been made ready for the harvest.

"We've been here before," Frank said.

"Yeah, but it's getting old."

"We have no choice but to rebuild. Our families are counting on us."

"Fortunately, I saved the plans to the packinghouse in the new safe. It's guaranteed to be fireproof."

As they were about to leave, Howard Dawson came up to them. "What do you make of it?"

"Why ask us when the fire marshal's here?"

"He thinks it's a firebug. Do you agree?"

"It appears so. How could a fire move this fast if someone hadn't set it?"

Despite the firebug, the apple business moved ahead after developing new markets around the world, dismissing dishonest commissioners, negotiating better train schedules and rates, developing a cold storage plant, and creating a label to distinguish Pajaro Valley apples from its competitors. And last but not least, outsmarting the codling moth with orchard spraying and good packing practices. Finally, all obstacles had been outmaneuvered, and the future seemed assured.

CHAPTER 32

In the wee hours of April 18, 1906, the world changed. The ground trembled and shook as the earth along the San Andreas Fault broke, sending out shock waves that would devastate the city of San Francisco and be long remembered as the greatest earthquake ever recorded on the Pacific Coast.

Nick and Jelena were jolted out of bed by the disturbance and ran to Anton's bedroom to protect him. They led him to the dining room where they all huddled under the table, awaiting aftershocks or even the main event that may not yet have occurred. Nick put one arm around Jelena and the other around Anton as he pulled them close. Anton cried uncontrollably at first. But as fear took hold, he grew silent. "Don't be afraid. Mama and Papa are here and we'll keep you safe."

Nick knew little about earthquakes except that they could be deadly, although he had never experienced one until now. Old-timers in Croatia often told stories about the 1667 quake that was so devastating it almost destroyed the city of Dubrovnik and killed five thousand people.

Once the shaking ceased, Nick said, "Stay here. I'll take a look around." The first thing he noticed was that the china cabinet was open and some of Jelena's prized teacups lay on the floor in pieces. He walked into the kitchen and turned on the water but didn't suspect any leaks. Next, he checked around outside and found that his chimney had fallen down, along with those of his neighbors. In the distance, he heard sirens and assumed fires were blazing around town. Or maybe they were ambulances, transporting the wounded to the hospital for treatment.

Nick reentered the house, where Jelena cowered with Anton. "I think the worst is over now." Then he relayed what he saw. "But I should go and offer my help."

"We need to find out about Ma and Pa and Lana and—"

"I'll stop by the *Pajaronian* to ask what they know."

"How long will you be gone? I don't want to be here alone in case—"

"Not long. But get back under the table at the first sign of more shaking." He fixed his eyes on Jelena—she was scared to death. He put his arms around her and held her tight. "Don't worry. I'm sure the worst is over." But he really wasn't so sure.

Nick was glad he had purchased a Ford Model B a couple of years ago. Now it would be worth its weight in gold, as it could out-clock a horse and buggy any day of the week. First, he went by Frank's house to check on them. Frank was in the yard, surveying his property.

"Jump in and let's go offer our help."

Frank motioned no. "Helen is all shook up."

"Are she or the kids hurt or anything?"

"No. Just afraid."

"Then our help may be needed elsewhere. Get in."

"I'll be back in a minute."

Nick drove to the packinghouse first. "You take the outside; I'll take the inside." In a few minutes, they were back in the car, satisfied that the packinghouse had held up to the strain.

"Now where?" Frank asked.

"Let's drive down Main Street and check it out on the way to the *Pajaronian*."

"Why go there?"

"Jelena is anxious about her family in San Francisco. If anyone has news...they should."

Once they drew near Main Street, the full force of the destruction revealed itself. Flooding covered the street and the Pajaro bridge had collapsed.

"I don't know if the car can handle all the water on the road."

"Try to stay on the ridge near the edge."

They crawled down Main Street, noting cracked windows, fallen facades, and various objects thrown about, including a storage shed behind Ford's department store. When they finally reached the end of the street, they stopped in their tracks, setting their gaze on St. Patrick's Church, dedicated only three years before. One of the gables had been damaged and the spire had been lifted off its base.

"I can only imagine the damage inside with so much stucco and ornate decorations."

"Repairs will be costly."

"Nothing another fundraising drive won't fix."

Nick made a couple of turns and pulled into the parking lot in front of the *Pajaronian* offices. When they stepped inside, the place was abuzz with activity as people rushed to and fro, almost in a panic. Howard Dawson emerged from his office to join the burst of activity, and Nick grabbed him by the elbow. "Howard, I realize you're busy, but I need to find out about San Francisco. My wife's family lives up there."

Howard came to an abrupt halt and homed in on Nick. "Give me a minute."

Nick looked at Frank, who wore the expression he was feeling—fear. They walked to Howard's office and waited in silence.

"San Francisco got it bad." He paused as he let those words settle on the pair. "I'll give it to you straight, if that's what you want."

"I need to know."

"You asked for it. As we speak, the city is on fire. Hundreds of buildings have collapsed. Thousands of people have been killed. San Francisco has gone to wrack and ruin." He threw a copy of a San Francisco newspaper at him to read for himself.

"*Not in history has a modern imperial city been so completely destroyed,*" author Jack London wrote in the catastrophe's aftermath. "*San Francisco is gone. Nothing remains of it but memories and a fringe of dwelling-houses on its outskirts. Its industrial section is wiped out. Its business section is wiped out. Its social and residential section is wiped out.*"

Frank put his hand on Nick's shoulder to steady him.

"What about survivors?"

"Everyone's leaving the city. No one can live there right now."

"Where to?"

"They're taking boats across the bay to Oakland, which fared better."

"How can we find out what happened to our relatives?"

"Your guess is as good as mine."

"Are the roads passable to Oakland?"

"I haven't heard otherwise."

When Nick left the office, he was trembling inside, but even Frank didn't realize it since he had it well camouflaged. *I can't tell Jelena the truth, but I have to find out about her family. I guess I'll drive up to Oakland and try to locate them.*

"Where to now?" Frank asked.

"Oakland."

"Do you think this little car will make it up there?"

"No. We need the wagon. Let's go back to the packinghouse and hitch it up."

Before leaving, Nick had no choice but to tell Jelena the news. He left out the part about thousands dying and even all the buildings collapsing. All she really needed to know was that residents were clearing out of the city and crossing the bay. "I'll search for your family and bring them back here."

"Oh, Nick." Jelena sobbed. "Be careful. I don't know what I'd do if something happened to you."

"Don't worry about me but say a prayer that I'll find your family, especially your parents. At their age, they won't deal well with hardships."

As Nick was about to leave to pick up Frank, he spotted him hustling up the block with Helen and their four children in tow. It was a relief to know that the women and children would be together while they were away on their mission.

"It's certainly slow going," said Frank.

"We didn't have a choice. This wagon is big enough to carry Jelena's entire family."

"Do you think the horses will make it there and back?"

"If we give them enough rest and water."

They headed over Mount Madonna and linked up with the Camino Real, which was the old trail built to connect the missions during the Spanish period. "I don't know how those old priests did it."

"Those Spaniards were made of hearty stuff. And to think—most of the time, they hoofed it."

As they drew closer to Oakland, they saw more and more evidence of the earthquake's wrath. "I hope Oakland was spared," Nick said.

The sun began to set, which meant they would have to wait for sunrise to continue their journey.

"I'll keep my eyes peeled for a place to spend the night," Frank said.

They pulled off the side of the road into a grassy patch where the horses could graze after being watered. Once the horses had been taken care of, they rummaged through the provisions to find something for dinner. Beef Jerky. Apples. Bread. Enough to satisfy their hunger. And wine for thirst and comfort.

"We need to leave at sunrise, so let's hit the hay now."

They spread out the blankets in the wagon and climbed in.

"Not bad. Certainly, I've had it worse. And you, too. Remember the ship?"

"How could I ever forget?" said Frank. "At least in the wagon, we won't get seasick."

At dawn, Nick and Frank hitched up the horses and got back on the road. They still had a long stretch before they'd reach Oakland. By the time they did, only a few hours of daylight were left. They parked the wagon as close to the bay as possible while Nick went down toward the dock to scan the arriving passengers. Frank stood guard over the wagon but kept an eye out for the family as well. At dusk, the last passenger boat of the day made shore, releasing its weary load.

Nick edged his way through the waiting crowd until he could identify each face enough to know whether it was the one he was looking for. He heard people emerging from the crowd saying, "Come with me. I'll take you to a place where you can stay and eat." Nick felt overwhelmed by the kindness he witnessed. Finally, out of the masses, the face of Lana emerged on the other side from where he stood.

Nick pushed people out of the way and when he was within earshot, he yelled her name, "Lana! Lana!"

She turned at the sound, but the face was not the one he remembered. This face was stricken with shock, as if she had escaped the depths of hell. Nick grabbed her by the hand and pulled her into his arms as the terror she experienced swept through him, assaulting all his senses. Her four children were trailing behind. And then he saw her parents—bent over, bereft, and beaten. They were the image of refugees who had just fled an unspeakable horror.

Once they reached the wagon, Nick breathed a sigh of relief. Frank helped him load their belongings into the wagon. "I've been told there's a meal to be had in the hall over there."

Nick looked at the group. They needed warmth and sustenance, and so did he and Frank. Besides, it was dark now and they couldn't start back until morning.

As soon as they got some hot food and drink and sat down, Nick asked, "Where is the rest of your family?" He was wondering about Lana's husband, Steven.

Mateo spoke up first. "We hope they survived and got out. All we know is Steven perished as he was trying to help firefighters rescue people from the blaze."

Nick looked at Lana, her head hanging down in defeat. He understood she couldn't let her eyes meet his. Words seemed so useless, but he had to say something. "I'm sorry, Lana. Your husband was an excellent man."

She kept her head down and nodded to acknowledge Nick's expression of sympathy.

"When we're done here, we'll spend the night in the wagon and leave at dawn. It will be a full day's ride, but barring any mishaps, we should be home by nightfall."

In the morning, as they prepared to leave, refugees were again arriving and townspeople were lined up to receive them. Nearly three hundred thousand people poured into Oakland, a city a third the size of the refugee numbers, but the residents managed to care for all the poor souls.

Nick watched and marveled over the pure goodness he witnessed firsthand. "Are you sure the rest of the family will be okay?"

"I think so," Vera said. "They have other relatives in Oakland."

Frank hitched up the horses while Nick got the family settled in the wagon. Then he took the reins and turned the horses back to the road out of town. Soon, they were on the El Camino Real, but all anyone had to do was turn in the direction of San Francisco and they could see smoke rising from what was once the great city on the bay. As he glanced back into the wagon, Nick's heart warmed at the sight of the Babiches surrounding Lana and her children with their arms—arms that not only embraced but provided security in these uncertain times.

Nick made a couple of stops to feed and water the horses and to let the Babiches stretch their legs as well as have a bite to eat. When the group finally reached the top of Mount Madonna where they could gaze over the valley all the way to the sea, they all breathed a sigh of relief and said a prayer to Our Lady in thanksgiving. Although they had experienced terrible losses, they knew they were lucky to be alive.

As soon as Jelena and Helen heard the wagon pull up, they ran outside to greet it. Tears ran down Jelena's cheeks as she hugged her parents, Lana, and her nieces and nephews. Without thinking, she let the words, "Where's Steven?" slip from her lips. In the moment of silence that followed, she covered her mouth to hold back a scream.

Nick rescued the situation. "Let's go into the house where you can get comfortable."

"Yes, I have food prepared and rooms ready," Jelena said. "And the tub is full of warm water for baths." Jelena put her arm around Lana and led her up the stairs.

Helen and Frank followed, a child on each arm. Nick and Mateo helped Vera up the stairs, knowing she needed their support to prevent her collapse. They set her down on the sofa where her body dissolved into the overstuffed cushions. Mr. Babich sat down beside her so she could lean on him and gain some strength.

The next task was to find out what happened to the rest of the family. Nick made a daily trek to the *Pajaronian* to get an update from Howard.

"It'll be a mess up there for a month of Sundays. Eighty percent of the city has been wiped out. Even in my wildest nightmares, I never could have imagined such a wholesale calamity."

"We're still trying to locate family members. Do you have any suggestions?"

"Wait until they contact you. There's no way to track them down without knocking on doors. Besides, your help is needed here."

The town had not waited to begin relief efforts. Frank took a position on the committee because he could focus all his efforts on the town, not having immediate relatives in San Francisco. There was so much to be done, but not one person expressed disillusionment. On the contrary, everyone took on their tasks with renewed hope for the future.

A few days later, Jelena received a telegram. It was from her sister Marta, informing her she was safe and staying with her husband's relatives in Oakland. Over the course of the next few weeks, more telegrams arrived from Jelena's brothers—they all had survived the earthquake.

CHAPTER 33

Just when they thought they had received word from everyone, a cable arrived from Ivan.

We have been afraid for you after hearing the terrible reports that San Francisco and surrounding towns have been submerged and fissures are swallowing up cars and trains loaded with passengers. We've seen pictures of San Francisco that bring to mind the apocalypse. In fact, Mount Vesuvius erupted two weeks before, spreading ash all over the Dalmatian coast which gave rise to Biblical prophesies.

All of us have been praying for you, especially the ladies at St. Nicola's, who are doing novenas nonstop. May God be with you at this time of great challenge.

Yours in brotherly love,

Ivan and family

"I'm off to the cable office to send a message back to Ivan that we are better off than the reports he's received." Upon his return, Nick said, "I've got more news."

Jelena sat at the table, enjoying coffee with her parents. "Tell us."

"Those Irishman didn't wait long. A fundraising campaign is already underway to repair St. Patrick's Church."

"I hope you made a donation."

"Gave enough for our name to be on a plaque right below a stained-glass window. Although, they would have preferred that I gave a little less, so they didn't have to see our name every time they attend Mass."

"Speaking of churches," Vera said, "did you learn anything about Nativity of Our Lord?"

Nick looked at Jelena to determine whether he should answer the question truthfully.

She grimaced. "It's time."

Nick sat on a chair and stared into his mother-in-law's eyes. "It burned down the day of the quake."

Vera burst out crying. "We just built our church. It took us years to save the money. And now, after only two years, you're telling me it's just a pile of ashes."

"I'm sorry. But they are planning to rebuild it, too."

"And how long will that take? And what important events will be missed—marriages, baptisms, First Communions, Confirmations, funerals. A church tells the stories of the families who worship there. Now our story has been ripped apart."

"They tell me the church will continue to meet somewhere. And they, too, have already begun a fundraising campaign. I will make a nice donation so you and Mateo can have a plaque."

"I don't want a plaque. I want my church back. I want my city back. I want my life back." Vera covered her face with her hands while Mateo tried to console her, rubbing her back and reassuring her with soothing words as she continued to weep.

After Vera calmed down, Mateo led her to the sofa in the living room. Once they were sitting side by side, Mateo enveloped Vera in his arms and held her tight.

"It pains me to see them like this," Jelena said. "I don't know if I can take it much longer."

Nick didn't know whether he could either. The house was not big enough to contain all the daily drama that unfolded. "I should make a trip up to the city to scope out the damage for myself. Some businesses are open again. Maybe your father can get back in business, too."

The earthquake had moved the railroad line about four feet, but it had been realigned and the train was operating. Nick and Mateo left together to survey the damage and determine whether there was any way they could move back to the city. They took the train as far as Oakland and then a ferry across the bay which deposited them on the San Francisco waterfront not far from the coffeehouse.

"Would you look at that? A lot of Croatians are back in business. Leave it to them to find a way," Mateo said.

When they arrived at the coffeehouse, Mr. Babich took out his key and opened the door. He let out a sigh. "It looks like the earthquake just happened."

Nick took a quick check of the restaurant. "I'll grant you it's a mess, but structurally it looks sound. After we get a cleaning crew in here, I'd be surprised if you couldn't go back into business."

They walked through the restaurant, dodging debris as they made their way to the kitchen. "All my equipment is still here. But all the pottery has been smashed to smithereens."

"That can easily be replaced." Nick inspected the kitchen, looking for any signs of broken pipes, and turned on a faucet to test the water line. Next, he turned on a stove burner, which lit immediately. "Most things appear to be working. But you'll need an inspection to be on the safe side."

"I'd like to walk up to the townhouse. It was made of stone, solid to the core, which is the reason we're still here. Those wood numbers collapsed and burned. Remember that lesson, Nick, and the next time you build a house, make it out of stone."

As they walked backed down the waterfront, Mr. Babich poked his head into store after store to offer his greetings. Every owner was glad to see him. "We've missed you. Come back and join us."

When they got to Lana's grocery store, they stopped abruptly. Even with the wall acting as a barrier, they could smell the decay. Fruits, vegetables, and meats were disintegrating, giving off a foul stench. As he glimpsed through the window, Mateo said, "I don't want Lana to see her store until we get it cleaned up. She can't take any more blows."

The army was present in every direction, keeping order and taking part in the cleanup. They passed a soup kitchen, with survivors standing outside in a line that stretched around the corner. "It breaks my heart to observe people in my city in such a state. Eastern Europe was notorious for breadlines. But America is supposed to be a land of riches where everyone can always fill their stomachs."

"Hard times are hard times. It doesn't matter where they occur. But in America, everyone will get a meal."

"Every day, I am so thankful that Jelena settled in Watsonville with you. In one of the psalms, there's a verse that states one survives by transplanting. You have helped us survive."

"I never thought about that before, but scattering helps families survive, especially during hard times—be they disaster or war."

They arrived at 635 Lyon Street before they knew it. "It's still standing, just as I expected it would. Let's go around back and peer inside." All they could glimpse was the kitchen, which was much as they left it. "We should be able to live here soon. Now, let's go check out Lana's house and keep our fingers crossed."

They walked around the corner and even after all the devastation they had seen, they were not prepared for this. "It's as I told you. Wood doesn't hold up—especially to fire. Lana will be so sad about her home when she learns what happened to it. She has no choice but to move in with us."

As Nick gazed at the pile of ashes, he recalled the good times he had spent there among Lana's family. An image emerged of

Steven standing at the doorway in welcome. Then, before his eyes, the image faded, and another flashed—it was Steven, a ghastly look of horror on his face. Nick couldn't wipe that image out of his mind, nor the agonizing sound emanating from it— Munch's *The Scream* had come to life, echoing across the eerie wasteland.

"Are you all right?" Mateo asked. "You act like you've seen a ghost."

Nick snapped back to reality. "Let's get out of here."

They took a different route back to the waterfront, which passed by the Church of St. Francis. "My God. It was spared," Mateo said. When they got closer, they realized that was not entirely the case—a fire had gutted its insides. "But the stone walls did not succumb. St. Francis protected his church."

On the train back to Watsonville, neither man spoke. Nick still had a picture in his mind of the San Francisco that greeted him when he arrived and his wedding night at the Palace Hotel. And now the hotel would have to be gutted and rebuilt. Opera star Enrico Caruso had spent the night there following his performance of *Carmen*. Upon exiting the city, he vowed never to return.

Fortunately, Nick thought, *San Franciscans are made of sturdier stuff*. Most of the immigrants had known hardship and had fought against fate itself to forge a life in the New World. The great earthquake was just one of many obstacles they faced on the way to their American Dream.

CHAPTER 34

Residents proved themselves up to rebuilding their city. Within three years, twenty thousand buildings had risen from the ashes. It called for a party, and San Francisco threw the grandest one the city would ever know. They called it the Portola Festival after the explorer Gaspar de Portola, who discovered San Francisco Bay one hundred forty years before and served as California's first governor. It was a five-day celebration, from October 19 to 23, 1909, designed to showcase the city, announcing it was back in business as it bid to host the 1915 Panama-Pacific International Exposition.

Nick, Frank, and their families took the train to San Francisco to join the festivities. They stayed at the Fairmont Hotel on Nob Hill which had opened in grand fashion exactly one year following the earthquake with its own lavish celebration, featuring rare wines and exotic hors d'oeuvres. The family headed first for the waterfront to view Portola entering the city by boat, surrounded by navy warships from around the world.

President Taft kicked off the celebration with a toast to the town. "Since Portola looked through the Golden Gate on the descending sun, San Francisco has twice become the Imperial City of the Pacific; first, by the energy of a pioneer race and steady growth into the Western metropolis; second, after complete destruction by the greedy flames and in the face of insurmountable obstacles by a regeneration so rapid and complete as to be the wonder of the world. May her future growth be as remarkable as her past, and may her civic righteousness and the individual happiness of her citizens keep pace with it."

Frank said, "Remember that letter Gabe and Luka sent after the earthquake? Well, if they could see San Francisco now, they'd regret not moving out here with us."

The various Babiches took turns playing host, leading them to one event after another—parades with floats and bands, concerts and carnivals, athletic competitions from wrestling tournaments to automobile races, and the biggest sporting event of them all—a bloodless bullfight between the Festival King and a snorting hoofed beast with deadly horns.

Nick said to Jelena, "Can you imagine if that designer Daniel Burnham had had his way? San Francisco would have looked like Paris, with wide boulevards and traffic circles—its character lost."

"I agree. But after what it's been through, it could use an Arc de Triomphe."

Then there were balls—one formal, the other masked—and couples danced into the night. The five-day party concluded with a parade up Market Street that featured electrified floats showcasing historic scenes while bands accompanied the parade and people danced in the streets, as a volcano-float spewed confetti over the onlookers and fireworks lit up the sky. San Francisco was back, and the Portola Festival did its best to spread the word around the world.

CHAPTER 35

With the earthquake behind them, town officials began looking to the future. Watsonville was now the biggest producer of apples in the world, and it was time to show off the valley where they came from. The president of the Board of Trade, Roger Bennett, proposed the town hold an apple show similar to the one Washington had every year. The proposal received the nod, and a committee was formed, with Nick as a member. No one wanted to recreate the wheel. Instead, they asked Spokane for their plan. Now they understood what was involved and, how much it would cost. The first order of business was to build a pavilion big enough to hold the exhibits. One member suggested a bond, and it passed at a special election in April, giving them funds but little time for all the preparations needed.

A site near Main Street was chosen for the pavilion. They soon realized the pavilion would not be big enough to contain all the exhibits. So, they purchased large circus-size tents to put up alongside it. They had to arrange to house and feed all the attendees and pressed residents into service. Many residents agreed to open their homes once local hotels were filled to capacity.

Marketing, which Croatians knew was the key to success in any business endeavor, was a big part of the plan. They enlisted an artist to create a poster to display in surrounding towns, featuring the slogan "An Apple Show Where Apples Grow." They had exhibits at the state fair and Ferry Building in San Francisco to spread the word far and wide. Button Day was another effort to raise awareness and additional funds. They drafted every teen in town to cover Main Street, asking shoppers to both purchase and wear a button. They also toured Santa Cruz County, promoting the buttons. A week beforehand, a whistle-stop campaign aboard a special Southern Pacific train was scheduled, making stops in Santa Cruz, Los Gatos, and San Francisco, where they stopped for lunch at the Palace Hotel and listened to pep talks. Afterward, they crossed the bay to Oakland, San Jose, and Gilroy, and all along the way, promoters marched to the tune of the town's band while they handed out leaflets and tossed apples to the crowds.

A few weeks before the apple show, twenty-seven carloads of apples were entered, and they knew the Apple Annual would surpass Spokane's national show.

"We should send an invitation to Gabe and Luka and their families to be our guests," Frank said. That night, he wrote a letter asking them to come.

The two brothers and their wives showed up on Thursday afternoon, the day after the whistle-stop campaign. Nick and Frank picked them up at the train station and divided the couples—one would stay with Nick, the other with Frank. But Jelena took charge of the dinner which would also include Marija and Dora and their husbands. And she put on a feast worthy of the crowd.

As Nick surveyed the faces that graced his table, a lump came into his throat. Most of his siblings were gathered together. Only Ivan and Ana were missing. It had been many years since he had laid eyes on Luka and Gabe. They had grown into real men, with brawny bodies and hefty hands, a result of physical work. Like Marija and Dora, they were opposites on the color wheel. Luka light. Gabe dark. One blue-eyed, the color of the Adriatic Sea. The other green-eyed, similar to his father. Both high spirited, kindhearted, and a joy to be around.

The next morning, Nick and Frank arranged a sightseeing tour of the town. They took Luka and Gabe down Main Street and talk turned to the earthquake. "We have all the repairs done. St. Patrick's is back holding court on the corner. And you should see what they've done in San Francisco. It's too bad we don't have time to take you up there. The city was wiped out and to see it now, you'd never guess what it had been through. Those engineers put up twenty thousand buildings in three years."

"Dubrovnik, too, had to be rebuilt after the earthquake in 1667. And they made it better than it was before," Luka said.

"In San Francisco, they used new earthquake-resistant methods," said Frank.

"But we won't be able to tell if they work until another one strikes," Nick said.

"Earthquakes—a natural disaster we have to contend with. But I'd take one over a war any time," Gabe said.

"Do you think there'll be another war soon?" Nick asked.

"Reading between the lines of Ivan's last letter, it seems rumors to that effect are spreading like wildfire."

They drove up to the packinghouse and parked in front. "I like your sign—Markovich Bros. Fruit Packers and Shippers. It has a nice ring to it," Gabe said.

"Maybe we should put out a sign—Markovich Bros. Farms," Luka said. "That also has a nice ring to it."

"No sense standing out here when we can go inside and show you our operation," Nick said as he led the way. The season wasn't over, so men were still busy packing apples. "Let's walk around and I'll explain what we do." After the tour, Nick said, "Well, what do you think?"

"I'd still take a nice piece of land over a packinghouse," Gabe said.

"Yeah," Luka said, "we're peasants. We like land. At first, we each got one hundred sixty acres for a small fee and then, after we met the requirements on that land, they gave us another one hundred sixty acres to homestead. Together, we own over six hundred acres."

"We own land, too," said Frank. "But the land doesn't own us. Instead, it works for us."

The brothers each shot a perplexed look their way.

"Let me explain," Nick said. "We invest some of our profits in land and make money from the sale. We have investments on Main Street as well as housing developments around town. The businesses on Main Street provide us rent, but eventually we'll make a good sum when we sell at the right time."

Saturday night, a gala dinner dance was held at Rappe Hall with a Croatian band from Oakland providing the music and thirty Eastern bankers in attendance. The women wore satin ball gowns in jewel tones, and the men rented tuxes for the occasion.

"I'm a fish out of water in this penguin suit," Gabe said.

"I understand what you mean," Luka said. "It just doesn't have the comfort of overalls."

Nick and Frank exchanged glances, as if to say *we've come a long way*.

The evening proved to be the event of the season. The band struck up one kolo after another, and all the Croatian couples joined in the familiar circle folk dances. When Nick and Frank spotted some non-Croatian men on the sidelines, they grabbed them and their wives and drew them in. Howard Dawson, Roger Bennett, and Chuck Cranford discovered dancing feet they never knew they had, and their wives were happy about it.

On Sunday, church bells rang out in every quarter of the town, announcing an outdoor religious service at the high school, with music provided by the orphanage band. Next, the grand parade marched down Main Street, featuring sixty horse-drawn apple wagons, bands and majorettes, and cars decorated with balloons and streamers carrying dignitaries, such as Hiram

Johnson who would be elected governor the next month, and the Austrian consul from San Francisco. The Native Daughters of the Golden West showed their support, assembled behind a hand-sewn banner appliqued with apple blossoms bearing the slogan "An Apple Show Where Apples Grow."

Apples filled the exhibition halls. A replica of the high school that teens had made out of the fruit caught Jelena's eye. "You should have made an apple tower, Nick," she said.

"Remind me next time."

Nonstop events filled the hours, from horse racing to football games to apple packing contests. When the day was over, they gathered in Nick's living room to take stock of it all.

"We still have four more days to go," Jelena said. "I'm not sure I'll be able to make it."

"Our train leaves for Canada Wednesday morning. So, we'll be cutting it short." Gabe said.

"You're here now. Let's not spoil it by talking about your departure."

"I want to mention a special event you're all invited to," Frank said. When everyone was listening, he continued, "I've arranged a dinner with Dr. Joseph Vidmar, the Austrian consul, and the leading Croats in the Austrian Benevolent Society for Monday night. Vidmar has had an interesting life serving as a diplomat for the Austrian Crown in Vienna, Berlin, Paris, Odessa, Bucharest, Condenza in Romania, Jassy in Moldavia, and Belgrade where he was posted to work on the new Russian and Balkan policies. The managing editor of the *Jadran*, the only Croatian newspaper on the Pacific Coast, will attend, too—a Mr. F.F. Akacich."

"Tell me," Nick said, "what purpose you have in mind for getting an Austrian diplomat together with a bunch of Croatians? Are you looking to start an international incident?"

Frank laughed. "Pardon me. I should have explained. Vidmar is a Slav—Slovenian, the only Slavs allowed to serve in the Austrian diplomatic corps."

"Now that I understand, I congratulate you on arranging what should prove to be a very informative evening. I look forward to learning about the Balkan policies for which he was tasked."

By the time Nick, Luka, Gabe, and their wives arrived at the Morning Star Restaurant, most seats were already filled. Nick did not know why Frank had picked this restaurant—there were better ones in town, but none had a proprietor who resembled Franz Joseph, sporting mutton chops to full effect.

Now he approached them, waving hello as he posted a sign *Closed for Private Party* on the door and locked it. Next, he walked over to the blinds and drew them shut. If this didn't signal a clandestine meeting, Nick didn't know what would. *For years, we've tried to live down the clannishness label and now we're gathered together to listen to a fellow Slav discuss politics in the Balkans. Once word gets out, and it will, we'll all be under suspicion again.*

Frank had saved Nick a seat at the head table next to the guest of honor, a middle-aged man with a walrus mustache, graying hair, and a paunch that no one in politics could avoid. They exchanged a few words before dinner was served, but did not engage in real conversation.

After slivovitz was placed on the table, Frank clanked his glass with a fork and moved to the lectern. "Welcome, everyone," he said in Croatian as cheers rose up from the crowd. Nick knew Frank had struck the right tone with this group of compatriots. "It is my honor to introduce you to Dr. Joseph Vidmar, Austrian consul in San Francisco. Dr. Vidmar has served in many Eastern European cities, most recently Belgrade, which qualifies him as an expert on the political intrigues in that part of the world. Tonight, Dr. Vidmar will discuss his work on the new Russian and Balkan policies our Austrian Crown, in its fiendish wisdom, is undertaking. I have one caution for Dr. Vidmar before he takes the podium—

watch out for Franz Joseph. He's lurking around here
somewhere."

That brought a laugh from the crowd and lots of clapping as
heads turned to pinpoint the proprietor. On cue, he emerged
from the kitchen, decked out from head to toe in a Hussar's
uniform—black military jacket and red breeches, both adorned
with gold brocade, shiny black boots, and a military hat with
plumage rising from the crown. A fur-trimmed pelisse, draped
over one shoulder, completed the costume. Franz Joseph paraded
around the room amid applause, then took his seat in the front
row, across from the podium where he could make faces at the
speaker.

Dr. Vidmar played along with the joke. "I must speak in code
so our esteemed emperor will have no clue what we're talking
about." That brought more applause, as everyone knew that was
the modus operandi in Croatia. "Tonight, as you heard, I am
here to speak about Austria's schemes as it applies to Balkan
policies. But first, a bit about myself. I'm sure you're wondering
why I was asked here tonight to speak to a group of Croatians.
Let me explain that my last name is somewhat of a subterfuge. I
am a Slav, like you, one from Slovenia. As you may be aware,
Slovenes are the only Slavs allowed to serve in Austria's diplomatic corps. My uncle was a member of parliament. After I
received my law degree and was at loose ends, his wife suggested
the foreign service. Thus, here I am. But in some ways, I think I
would have been better off if I had remained in my village in the
Austrian Alps. Ah, fate...it always intervenes and we must play
our part."

Dr. Vidmar reached for a glass of water and took several big
gulps before continuing. "I am here to tell you tonight to expect
war in the Balkans. As one of the most important Croatian
communities in the United States, as well as one of the wealth-
iest in California, you can influence its outcome. No doubt you
have concern for the family you left behind and fear for their
future. If we work together, we can positively impact that future.

"I spoke of Austrian intrigues before. Well, we need to have some intrigues of our own—it's the only way to combat them. While I serve the Crown, as a Slav, my heart is with our people. God has placed me in this position to do His will. And that is my only mission. The Crown moved me from Belgrade to San Francisco as punishment for my implacability. All Slavs are implacable, and that's what makes us strong.

"But it's here I can be the most helpful, by mobilizing good Croatians like yourselves to our cause. Not only do you have a passion for your fatherland, but you have wealth. Money is not the root of all evil if it is used justly and with compassion. Then it can be a force for good. My other uncle, the banker, taught me that."

When Dr. Vidmar sat down, Nick made small talk. "So, your uncle was a banker. I know a lot of bankers. Maybe I met him sometime."

"I doubt that. Uncle Izidor died twenty-seven years ago. They found his dead body on a train on his way from Paris to Le Havre. Can you believe that?"

A shiver went through Nick. "Wh...what happened?"

"They found him slumped over in his seat. But since he didn't have any identification on him, it took a while to get him home for burial."

How many people die on a train? Nick wondered. *And on that route, twenty-seven years ago?* He tried to recall the name on the passport but couldn't. One thing he knew for certain was the man had an unusual first name.

"How did you finally do it? Get him home, I mean?"

"My other uncle, who had served in the parliament, had connections. We knew Uncle Izidor's route and once we put out the word, we got a call from a morgue."

"I'm sorry." *More sorry than you'll ever know.*

"Of course, to lose a loved one in the prime of life is always devastating. But this was even more so."

"I don't understand."

"Without an ID, they treated him like a vagrant...nothing more than a common bum. He did not deserve that—he was such an elegant man in life."

"Did you catch his killer?"

"He died from a heart attack. I assume some opportunist noticed his wallet and had not the common decency to leave it alone."

Upon hearing those last words, Nick left for the bathroom to collect himself. He took some deep breaths and not until he had calmed down, did he return to his seat. Then he said to Jelena, "I think it's time we get home. Luka, Gabe, and their wives have to catch an early train."

Once everyone was sound asleep, Nick crept down to the basement where he kept a box of personal mementos. The wallet was stashed in the middle, out of sight. He felt around and retrieved it. Then he took the passport over to the light so he could make out the letters. Just as he feared—Izidor Joseph Vidmar. *Now what?* His mind raced as shame overwhelmed him. He stowed the wallet back in its hiding place and dragged himself to bed, tossing and turning until dawn.

CHAPTER 36

"Come up and visit us sometime," Luka said to Nick before he boarded the train for the trip home.

"Unfortunately, when I have the time, your land is covered in snow with temps below freezing."

Luka exchanged a glance with Gabe. "We'll find a way to get you up there."

Nick waited until the train was out of sight to head to the apple show. It was early Tuesday morning, a time he didn't expect a crowd. He made his way to the pavilion to get a better look at the exhibits because he had been preoccupied with so many other details until now. When Nick rounded a corner, he bumped into Karlo Rajkovich. "You came."

Nick reached out to shake hands, but Karlo wrapped him in a bear hug first. "Wouldn't miss it."

"I heard you'd been under the weather."

"The reports of my demise have been greatly exaggerated."

Nick laughed as he took in the robust figure before him. "Can I buy you a cup of coffee?"

"I can always use one."

Nick led Karlo to a coffeehouse, resembling ones in Croatia. There were plenty of empty tables. Nick chose one in a quiet corner. After the waitress brought the coffee and apple kolache, they settled in for a talk.

"When did you get here?"

"Last night. I'm staying at the Central Hotel."

"Excellent choice—Frank owns the building. But you'll be my house guest for the rest of the time you're here."

"I appreciate that. Say, there seemed to be some big doings in town last night. I tried to have dinner at the Morning Star Restaurant, but it was closed for a private function. I thought the apple banquet wasn't until later in the week."

"That's something I'd like to talk to you about. Do you know—"

"Karlo, where have you been keeping yourself?" an apple packer said as he approached the table.

"Mostly been on the other side of the hill. How's it been with you?"

"You must judge for yourself. Stop by my exhibit at the pavilion."

"I'll bring him by later." Nick gave him the bum's rush politely.

"Now, where were we?" Karlo said. "Ah, I remember. You were about to tell me about the event at the restaurant last night."

"Frank arranged it all. He wanted key Croatians in town to meet Dr. Joseph Vidmar, the Austrian consul up in San Francisco."

"Why was that? Is something brewing?"

"Could be. But I wanted to ask you about Dr. Vidmar. What do you know about him?"

Karlo leaned back in his chair as he put a forefinger to his temple. "Let me see. Oh, yeah, he has recently been assigned to the consul office—came over from Belgrade, I believe."

"That's right. Is he a good guy? You know...one you can trust with your life?"

Karlo bolted upright. "Underneath that last name beats the heart of a Slav—he's a brother."

"Now I feel even worse."

Karlo locked eyes with him. "Tell me what's wrong."

At that moment, Frank walked in the door and made a beeline for their table. "I've been looking all over for you." Then he noticed Karlo. "Well, I'll be. You've shown up at the right time. We need another apple judge to replace the one who called in sick after he tied one on last night."

"I'll be happy to oblige."

"Come with me."

Karlo turned to Nick for his consent.

"Go ahead. I'll catch up with you later and we can move you into my spare room."

Nick knew Jelena was not happy about having another house guest. But she put on a feast for Karlo, a lifelong bachelor who took most of his meals in restaurants. After the apple pie was finished, she herded Anton upstairs for a bath and bedtime.

Once they were out of sight, Nick pulled out the slivovitz and filled a couple of tumblers. He held up his glass. "Cheers." They clinked glasses.

Karlo raised his. "My belief in you has been brought to fruition. I think you've earned a new name—The Apple King."

Nick guffawed. "Thanks for the sentiment, but a lot of guys are just as deserving of the title."

"Maybe so, but you're one of the patriarchs. Don't ever forget it." They clinked glasses again and slugged the plum liquor down in one gulp.

Nick refilled the glasses. "Let's move to the living room where we can be more comfortable." He gestured for Karlo to take a club chair in the corner and he took the other, setting the slivovitz on the table between them.

"Your apple show is the best I've ever seen, and coming from me, that's quite a compliment. I've been to a whole slew of them but only the best."

"It was high time we had one now that we're the Apple Capital of the World. Did you hear Markovich Brothers took the sweepstakes prize for best one hundred box lot of Bellefleurs?"

"You've accomplished a lot during the time I've known you."

"If it hadn't been for your mentorship, though, I would not be where I am." *Nor would I be here without the money in that wallet.*

His face bore an expression that Karlo couldn't ignore. "Is something wrong? Something you want to talk about? It seemed this morning you had something on your mind."

"You have a gift for reading people. I don't know where to start."

"It helps to start at the beginning. Or even in the middle, if that's the heart of it."

Nick took a deep breath. "Okay. I've held this in for twenty-seven years, although I managed to squeeze it in with some other sins when I went to confession."

"Twenty-seven years ago? My advice is to let sleeping dogs lie. We all do things we regret later. But now my curiosity's up, so get it off your chest."

"Last night at the Morning Star Restaurant, I learned that Dr. Vidmar's uncle was a man named Izidor Vidmar."

"Why is that important?"

"Because I sat next to a man by that name on my way out here to immigrate."

"And..."

"As I got up to leave, I thought he was still asleep. But he was dead."

"I'm not following you."

"When I realized he was dead, I spotted his wallet halfway out of his pocket. I didn't want to do it...I thought twice about it...but a little voice told me to snatch it instead of leaving it for other sticky fingers. There was a lot of money in that wallet. It gave me a stake for my first packinghouse."

After that admission, there was only silence until Karlo spoke again. In a soft, low voice, his words reflected mercy, not condemnation. "I think God is using you as a tool. As we learn from life, his ways are often mysterious. You are in a position to be a force for good for our people because of your position as a patriarch in this town and your wealth. God will use your shame as motivation to achieve his goals. My advice is to pay attention. You and Dr. Vidmar have been joined together for a purpose—a purpose that is only in God's mind right now, since he is above time and knows the future."

"Are you saying what I did wasn't a sin?"

"Now we're getting into a gray area. An opportunity was placed before you, and you took it. Better you than some scoundrel. You've built a worthy business with that money. I'm reminded of Prometheus, who stole fire from the gods and gave it to humans. His act became a blessing to us."

"Do you think I should confess to Dr. Vidmar?"

"In a word, no. There's nothing to be gained by it and possibly much to lose. But I think you owe Dr. Vidmar your allegiance. The two of you are in positions to help our people by helping each other."

Nick did more than show his loyalty—he gathered as many Slavs together as he could to attend the reception at the St. Francis Hotel honoring Dr. Vidmar as the newly appointed consul of Austria-Hungary for the Pacific Coast. It was the first assembly of Slavs of every nationality in California. And to mark the occasion, they feasted on traditional Slavic fare, followed by rakija in a variety of fruit flavors, especially plum and grape.

Once waiters departed the banquet room, their job done, Dr. Vidmar took to the podium once again. Now he engaged the audience in the true purpose for their meeting. "Austria and its ally Germany want to crush pan-Slavism. In order to do that, they either need to expand control over the Balkans or engage in a war with Serbia, which will draw in Russia. They had plans to wage war against Russia after it was weakened by its defeat in the Japan-Russian war, but the right opportunity did not present itself. They still have designs on partitioning the great Slav state among themselves to further German control. Mark my words—war is coming. And if I learned anything while posted in Belgrade, it will start in the Balkans."

CHAPTER 37

"The situation over in Austria doesn't look good," Nick said.

"I can't believe the Crown suspended the Croatian constitution over a little complaint. And now it seems there will be war in the Balkans," Frank said.

"It's like Dr. Vidmar warned—the Austrians are looking for a way to start a war to put an end to pan-Slavism."

"Are you going to San Francisco on Tuesday to discuss fundraising for the Balkan War?"

"Wouldn't dare miss it. Besides, it will give me another chance to touch base with Dr. Vidmar. I want to offer my services."

The meeting on October fifteenth was about more than fundraising. Forty thousand Croatians in the state had organized themselves into the Croatian League with the goal of winning independence for Croatia. The plan was to send fighters to the country to join their brethren in the cause. Timing would depend on the Balkan War. Balkan League countries of Serbia, Montenegro, Bulgaria, and Greece had banded together to drive the Turks out of Europe. Croatians knew war would occupy Austria's attention, and they intended to take advantage of that opportunity. Bay area men from Balkan League countries readied themselves to depart in a few days. And as soon as war was declared, Croatian men would follow to their own battle.

Nick pulled Dr. Vidmar aside to have a word with him. "How can I help you in this effort?"

"First, I am sure you understand that the war of independence has to be kept quiet. And in my position, they could try me for treason."

"Of course."

"That being said, men and money will be required. Through our network, I will get you the specifics."

"You can count on me."

"But for now, we all need to appear to be focused on the Balkan War. And, it is important to us, too. Austria and Germany have a Mittel-Europa plan to squash the Slavs. They know Russia will not hesitate to step in to protect their Slav brothers, and once they do, that will open the door to all-out war. Ultimately, they plan to partition Russia among themselves."

"I don't understand."

"They've done it before. Remember Poland? They partitioned that Slav country right off the map."

Nick was speechless. All this was too much to process.

Vidmar caught his astonishment. "Now maybe you understand what we're up against. Our very identity is at stake."

On October twenty-one, a steamer loaded with Serbians and other Balkan League nationalities left San Francisco harbor for the war. The First Balkan War was short-lived, ending after only ten weeks on December third, with a victory by the Balkan League. This victory came as a surprise to Austria and Germany, which were hoping a defeat would crush Serbia and open the way for Mittel-Europa.

The war had been a bloody one, leaving thousands homeless and without basic necessities—especially women and children. The Slavonian colony in Watsonville planned a grand ball to raise funds. At a meeting of the Austrian Benevolent Society, Nick stood up and said, "Everyone should buy a ticket to help. They're only fifty cents, and women come for free."

Peace negotiations hit a snag, and the war resumed on February third, waging until the second armistice was reached on April fifteenth. Then, on June twenty-ninth, Bulgaria made a surprise attack on its former allies and the Second Balkan War broke out. This war was even shorter than the first one—a six-week struggle with more bloodshed.

"Those Balkan Wars were total lunacy," Frank said as he reviewed paperwork in the office.

"The worst of it was they didn't give us enough time to launch our bid for independence. We just couldn't get over there fast enough."

"It seems this won't be the last time there's an opportunity while Austria is distracted with war."

A few weeks later, Frank came into the office, waving a letter. "King Nicolas responded."

"You've lost me."

"Don't you remember? I sent him a telegram on his capture of Scutari from the Turks?"

"Now it's coming back to me. I thought you were off your nut for sending a telegram to the king of Montenegro."

"He expressed his thanks and reinforced the brotherhood of Croatians and Serbs."

"When we have a common enemy, we unite. Austria never fails to offer herself. Suspending our constitution created the first bond. Now, the Balkan Wars, which we all know Austria and Germany were behind, have created another."

"And if Dr. Vidmar's prediction is right, a big event will soon happen to bond us even more tightly."

CHAPTER 38

A Serbian man named Jack Stepanovich opened a cigar shop in town. Frank took Nick over to buy some smokes, even though he was reluctant. "I don't understand what is so special about this store. We've always had cigar stores in town."

"You'll see in a moment." The sign read *Jack's Cigar Store,* and Jack stood sentry at the counter. "This is my big brother Nick."

Jack's luminous, dark eyes with a big bulbous nose set between them stared at Nick, taking in every last inch. "Your reputation has proceeded you." He held out his arm and they clasped hands in brotherly friendship.

"I think you know why we're here," Frank said.

"Habanos. They're still expensive. High tariffs."

"Nothing's too rich for our blood."

Jack reached under the counter and pulled out a polished wooden box with a brass latch that was inscribed *Habanos. Hecho en Cuba. Totalmente a Mano.* He handled it like fine china, setting it softly on the counter. Then he unlocked the latch and lifted the lid as he bent down to take a deep inhale. "Ah...smells so sweet." He removed a cigar, sniffed it, and handed it to Nick for a whiff.

Nick jerked back. "It almost bowled me over. What's in this thing?"

"Cuban black tobacco. Made entirely by hand. Habanos are pure Cuban-made."

Jack took another cigar out and handed it to Frank to sample. "Now give them to me." Jack took out a knife, making a careful slit on the ends. Then he handed them back, struck a match and lit them. After Nick and Frank took a few puffs, assuring him that the cigars were well lit, he said, "The guys are in the back."

Nick glanced at Frank, who nodded at Jack. "Cigars are the first reason I brought you here. And now you are about to discover the second." Frank walked past the counter and pushed open the swinging doors as he stepped aside for Nick to enter.

Once his eyes adjusted to the dim light and smoke-filled room, Nick let out a holler. Most of his packer buddies were there playing poker and kibitzing about politics.

"Pull up a chair," one of them shouted. "We'd like your take on the situation in Serbia."

"You must mean the assassination of Archduke Franz Ferdinand."

"The one and only."

"No doubt the Austrians and Germans will use it to set off another war that will draw Russia into the web they've been weaving." Nick threw a few coins on the table. "Deal me in." After playing a few hands, he gathered up his winnings and stood. "Ready?" he said to Frank.

Frank swept his eyes around the table. "Yeah."

When they passed Jack again on their way out, Nick said, "What's your two cents about Serbia?"

"Austria will give them nothing but grief." He paused, and when there was no response, he said, "Next time, you can leave by the rear door so you don't run into any regular customers."

Once they were out of the store, Nick asked Frank, "Do you know what he meant by regular customers?"

"Non-Slavs. The back room is private."

Nick slapped Frank on the back. "Timing couldn't be better."

Jack's Cigar Store became a habit. The following week, Nick stopped at the counter. "Are you going to Rappe Hall tonight?"

"I wouldn't miss it. The Serbian consul in New York City and a Columbia University professor wouldn't be sending a Serb around the country to speak to the likes of us if it wasn't important."

"I'll be there, too, with a contingent of Croatians to get his take on the war." When Nick walked into the back room, the Slavs were talking about nothing else. He took an open seat and waited for his hand to be dealt while he kept his ears cocked. Not only were the guys discussing the war, but they were also discussing the problems they were having as immigrants from the Austrian Empire, especially those who had not yet become citizens. They were all under suspicion as to where their loyalties lay.

Nick let the talk get him all steamed up. Finally, he had to break his silence. "We need to educate our neighbors. They don't understand we're not ethnic Germans but Slavs, some of us Croatian, others Serbian, as well as other nationalities. They haven't a clue how oppressed we are under the Austrian Regime and only want our freedom."

Nick and Frank went to Rappe Hall together. Every Serbian in town was in attendance, even though their numbers were far less than Croatians'. Nick spotted Jack Stepanovich right up front. Tudor Demitrigevich began by discussing Austria's role as the bully of Europe and, in her thirst for power, had coerced Slav states into her realm. "But the Serbian victory in the Balkan Wars has put an end to her dreams of dominance with the port of Salonika awarded to the Greeks and the creation of Albania, which ends Austrian ambitions of access to the southern Adriatic."

Next, he turned to Serbia's dream of a Slav empire, which would bring the scattered Slavs, a diaspora almost as large as the Jews, together in one homeland. "To do this, they need to reclaim the Old Slav Empire lands taken by the Turks. In the Balkan Wars, Serbia doubled its territory, a good start but still short of the goal. Serbia also convinced Montenegro, a Slav nation, to share a parliament while retaining their kings. These are two steps toward Slav unification that have fueled a passion among the Serbs."

Finally, Demitrigevich got to his key point—fundraising. "I will not lie. We need money for the Red Cross efforts. And we need men to serve on committees that will further aid our fatherland." After he concluded his remarks, the hat was passed and volunteers lined up to help the cause.

CHAPTER 39

Jelena handed Nick a letter bearing a Cilipi return address as
soon as he walked in the door. Before he opened it, his eyes met
hers, worried and full of fear. He tore the envelope open, not
bothering to use a letter opener. "It's from Ivan." His eyes moved
rapidly down the page. "He's been conscripted."

"Conscripted? My God, he's nearly fifty years old. And he's
got five children and a wife, as well as elderly parents who
depend on him."

"Do you think the Austrian Empire cares? They just want
men to fill their rank and file. Ivan wrote they sent army officers
out to scour the country for men between the ages of eighteen
and fifty. He didn't know where he'd be stationed, but he left for
the war that morning."

"And when was that?"

Nick glanced at the top of the letter. "July twenty-seventh."

"He's been at war more than a month."

Nick didn't respond. He just stared off in space. "I have to
tell Frank right away. Don't bother holding dinner for me." He
kissed Jelena goodbye, flew out the door and jumped into his
automobile. He was at Frank's house in a matter of minutes.

Bounding up the steps, he didn't even bother to knock as he

threw open the door and caught Helen by such surprise she screamed. "What's wrong?"

"I need to talk with Frank. Where is he?"

"He's upstairs. I'll call him."

"Don't bother." Then he dashed up the stairs, two steps at a time, and caught Frank with his pants down.

"Give me a minute to do my business, brother. And calm down. It can't be as important as all that."

"I'll let you be the judge." Nick went back downstairs to cool his heels.

When Frank appeared on the landing, he was still buckling his belt as he descended the stairs. "Whatever it is, must be pretty important. Do you want a drink before or after?"

"After. This can't wait any longer." He handed the letter to Frank.

"What kind of heartless people would draft a fifty-year-old man with children?"

"Austrians—that's who. Ivan's been at the Eastern Front for over a month. And we have no idea where he's been deployed."

"Old Franz Joseph will discover he has soldiers with no heart for war. He'll be sending men into battle who won't fight against their brother Slavs. What a pea brain. He's never understood his southern empire full of Slavs, who represent a couple dozen different nationalities and speak a whole slew of different languages. This time, these downtrodden peasants will fight for their independence and their own Slav state."

"Frank, we have to do everything we can to support the cause for a Slav state. Our people have suffered enough since getting under the thumb of the Austro-Hungarian Regime nearly a century ago. There has to be a way…it can't continue much longer."

On the heels of Ivan's letter, they received another from their sister Ana announcing the death of their mother.

"We must do something to honor her life," Nick said.

"A gravestone and prayers would be appropriate."

"Better yet, a Mass at Nativity of Our Lord. We'll gather every Croatian on the coast to say prayers in her memory."

Paulina Markovich lived her life as a follower of Mary. And as a good Catholic woman, she gave birth to many children, eight who survived her, and a few who did not. Nativity of Our Lord, a Slavic church dedicated to the birth of Christ, was filled with images of Mother and Child—an appropriate venue for her memorial service.

The turnout filled the church to overflowing. Nick and Frank were gratified that a large contingent of Croatians from Watsonville came to pay their respects. They had placed a small photo of their mother wearing a babushka near the altar, but it was only visible as communicants approached. The entire Mass was celebrated in Croatian. Their mother spoke no other language and when she worshiped at the Church of St. Nikola, it was always Croatian prayers she offered up.

Nick and Frank each took a turn eulogizing their mother, who had created a family that was the bedrock of their lives. By her humble example, they had learned the most important values in life which had always served them well.

After the service, the group moved downstairs to the hall, which Dora and Marija had decorated with their few family mementos. Tadich's restaurant catered the funeral lunch. During the meal, conversation often involved the war and speculation about the outcome. Nick and Frank had agreed that they could not let the event end without speaking about events in Eastern Europe. Everyone gathered had a stake in it and they felt even their mother would have approved.

Nick stood and clanked his glass to get the group's attention. "My mother had known nothing except life under the Austro-Hungarian Regime, but had often heard her parents reminisce about Croatia when it was free. The country had a long history of accomplishment until Napoleon's troops pulled a fast one, allowing them access to the city of Dubrovnik, which they seized. Not long after, Austria gained domination which has continued to this day. Croatia had once been a maritime power-house known for its wealth and also diplomacy, which it used skillfully to balance its interests between Venice and the Ottoman Empire. This is not the time to sing all of Croatia's praises, but mark my word, the time is coming. Today, the best use of our time is to develop a plan that will once again secure Croatia's freedom."

When he sat down, Nick said to Frank, "It's too bad Dr. Vidmar is not the consul here anymore. He could have added a lot to this gathering."

"The Crown called him back in April. I heard he's been reassigned to the embassy in Berlin."

"Then he'll be in the thick of it." *I only hope they don't discover where his loyalties lie.*

CHAPTER 40

Both Anton and AJ were students at nearby Santa Clara College, and AJ's siblings were not far behind. The one worry both families had was the draft. Although America had not yet entered the war, their sons were of prime age to fight it. "I fret over what the future holds for our sons," Frank said.

"If called up, they must do their duty. They'll have no choice."

"With all the talk they've heard about freedom for Croatia, my guess is they'll volunteer."

Nick sat in silence, reflecting on Frank's words, and then nodded in agreement.

Not long after, Uncle Sam posters appeared—a white-haired goateed man dressed in red, white, and blue peering out from under his top hat's band of stars while pointing a forefinger outward, as if proclaiming the words printed below—*I Want You for the US Army.*

In the spring, Frank invited Nick over for cocktails. When he arrived, Dr. Vidmar was waiting in the living room. "I thought they stationed you in Berlin."

"I've been around long enough to realize that it would be my ruin. I'm in too deep to keep my activities secret from their spies. I resigned from the foreign service."

Frank joined them and put a tray holding slivovitz and tumblers on the table. He filled the glasses and handed one to each of the others.

"What's your next move?" Nick asked.

"Work for the Allies. We have spies all around this country, too, and I'll ferret them out."

Nick glanced at Frank and then looked back at Dr. Vidmar. "And just how do you propose to do that?"

"I have my sources. But I'll build a network all across the country, starting with California, where so many Austrian sympathizers live." Dr. Vidmar raised his glass to his lips and took a sip before finishing his answer. "We all understand that there are a few here."

Nick's mind raced as he feared the conversation's end point. *I hope he doesn't ask me to be a snitch.*

Dr. Vidmar did not wait for Nick's reply. "You once offered your services. Now I'm asking for your help."

This is my penance. He took a calming breath. "What do you want me to do?"

"I'll not only find spies but build an organization to support our freedom effort. Of course, you could be of great assistance in both areas. But discretion is most important."

The conversation turned to the *Lusitania* which had been en route to England from New York when it was torpedoed on May seventh by a German U-boat. The ship sank within minutes, killing nearly two thousand people. One hundred twenty-eight Americans had been aboard.

"Wilson will have to get into the war now," Frank said.

"Perhaps. But it will be on his timetable," Vidmar said.

"He won't stand for the killing of Americans when the ship was only carrying passengers," Nick said.

Vidmar gave a cunning smile. "Was it now?"

"Are you trying to tell us something?"

"Let's put it this way. There was more in the *Lusitania*'s hold than passenger trunks."

"If you know something, just spit it out." Nick reached for the bottle of slivovitz.

"You must realize I still have my sources. It was carrying four million rounds of small round ammunitions, among other materials for war."

"How can you be so certain? Did spies pass on the intelligence?"

"Since you brought up the subject of spies, they found three German-speaking stowaways after departure who they interviewed and put under house arrest. Later, they discovered an Englishman believed to be a turncoat who had been observed meeting with German agents before the ship got underway. No doubt they passed on information about the cargo."

"Are you saying the Germans were justified in sinking the ship since it was not neutral?"

"I'm not drawing any conclusions. I leave those to you. I am only laying out the facts as I know them. But, as always, I insist on your discretion."

At that moment, Helen walked in the door, loaded down with packages. Frank hurried to relieve her burden, setting the packages on the kitchen table. Then he ushered her into the living room. "Look who's here."

"Dr. Vidmar! I thought you left us for good."

He stood as he was taught to do whenever a lady entered a room. "Fate had a change of mind."

Helen gave him a kiss on each cheek. "Welcome back. If I didn't know better, I would think you timed your return to coincide with recent events."

"Alas, I am no longer in the foreign service. Berlin did not suit me."

"Prince Alexander, Regent of Serbia, told a newspaperman in London he hopes for a new Slav state when the war is over," Nick told the men at the Austrian Benevolent Society. "Besides Serbia, it will include Croatia, Dalmatia, Istria, Slovenia, Bosnia and Herzegovina, and the old Serb Empire south of the Danube. And he wants all the Balkan questions put to rest."

"Aye, aye," voices from the crowd responded, signaling their approval.

"As you probably heard, the Serbs routed the Austrian Army twice. According to the prince, it's the force of patriotism that's made his men successful. At first, they were fighting to maintain their independence. But now, they're fighting for the long-awaited dream of a Slav state and the liberation of Croats and Slovenes from Austrian oppression."

The men stomped their feet in agreement until the room was full of thunder and let out another, "Aye, aye."

"The prince said he wants intellectual, commercial, and industrial development to sustain our race. He expressed gratitude for the aid America has given his people. And he cited the Red Cross for their noble work in treating the wounded and protecting the rights of the Serbian people on the battlefield.

"Gentlemen, the words of the prince should give us the encouragement we need to continue our support for the great Slav cause. I'll pass the hat and ask that you be as generous as possible. Our brethren back home are counting on us in their hour of need."

Jack stood at his post when Nick and Frank entered the cigar store. "That prince of your homeland is inspiring. With his powers of persuasion, he should be able to bring about a Slav state."

Jack stared off in space, not responding.

"What's wrong?" Frank said. "Aren't you happy about it? And to think, the Serbian army routed the Austrians twice."

"But not a third." Jack's eyes drooped downward.

Nick and Frank stole a glance at each other. "What do you mean, not a third?"

"I assume you haven't yet heard. News of the war in Eastern Europe is often slow to reach our shores. The Austrians and Bulgarians orchestrated another attack, and the Allies could not reach the battlefield in time to support the Serb Army. So, they did the only sensible thing."

"Retreat?" Frank asked.

"That's right. They retreated, intending to hole up in Montenegro, but their foes had blocked the way."

"What did they do then?" Nick asked.

"The soldiers hiked over the mountains in the dead of winter, hauling civilians and Austrian prisoners with them."

"What could the commanders have been thinking? Those are some of the highest, most treacherous mountains in Europe. You'd have to be immortal to survive a trek like that."

"Prince Alexander did. But half of the group was lost. Imagine—two hundred thousand people died from starvation, disease, freezing conditions, and even attacks by Albanians who still held a grudge over the Balkan Wars."

"Where are they now?" Frank asked.

"Once they made it to the Adriatic, Allied ships picked up the ragtag group and ferried them to the island of Corfu. Prince Alexander has set up a Serbian government-in-exile there. Serbians are calling this horrific episode our Albanian Golgotha."

"Let's pray it leads to a resurrection," Nick said.

"We need more than prayers."

As they walked toward the back of the shop, Nick pointed to a poster on the wall.

COMING
SATURDAY NIGHT
I.O.O.F. HALL

7:30 P.M.
MILAN MARJANOVICH
SLAVONIAN SPEAKER on
'THE FORMATION OF A SOUTH SLAV STATE'
ADMISSION FREE
ALL SLAVONIANS WELCOME

"We can't miss that."

The Odd Fellows Hall was packed to listen to Mr. Marjanovich,
a long-time former editor of a Dubrovnik newspaper who they
knew and trusted. In his post as vice president of the Jugo-Slav
Committee in London, he traveled America to discuss the
formation of a Slav state encompassing more than fourteen
million people from Serbia, Montenegro, Bosnia, Herzegovina,
Istria, Carniola, Dalmatia, Syrmia, and Slavonia. He emphasized
nine million Slavs lived under oppression by the Austrian government, which pocketed fifty-six cents on every dollar paid in
revenue. And he set forth the dream of a Slav state that would be
one of the greatest in Europe, with its rich copper mines and
fertile lands for wheat and fruit.

"The state will control certain zones in the Adriatic through
its four hundred miles of coastline, ports in Rijeka and Split as
well as smaller ones."

The crowd listened spellbound as Mr. Marjanovich touched
on the long-held hopes for their fatherland. He said that both
the British prime minister and US secretary of state were
committed to the Slav state, which they considered an impera-
tive solution to the peace process.

Marjanovich left his primary purpose for last. He wanted to
gauge whether the Slavs favored a republican or monarchial form
of government.

Nick stood up. "The only two kings I know of from that

group of countries are King Nicholas of Montenegro and King Peter of Serbia, who is quite old. Croatia has not had a king for a long time, even though it has been under the Austrian monarchs, and does not wish to be under the thumb of another foreign monarch, even if the king ends up being Prince Alexander, who is greatly admired."

Jack stood up next. "As most of you know, I am of Serbian descent. My fear is that so many countries merging into one would cause chaos, since most did not have self-rule under the Austro-Hungarian Regime. We don't want to end up like Poland which left itself open to invasion and partition because of its weak government. I vote for a powerful leader like Prince Alexander. He also has a good relationship with the Russian monarchy, which would not hesitate to come to his aid if another power threatened. A monarchy would be the wisest course."

After Jack sat down, Nick gave Frank an elbow in the rib and shot him a frown. Jack had presented his case well, but most of those in the room wanted freedom for the people, even if it was messy.

By the end of the meeting, several people had spoken in favor of a republican government. Of course, most in the room were also of Croatian descent. Even under the Austrian Regime, Croatia had maintained a parliament and had an alliance with Serbia for mutual benefit. They understood the politics of the region well and knew that a Serbian king would not be good for Croatia.

As Nick and Frank left the meeting, Howard Dawson stepped out of the shadows. "Buy you a drink?" When he got no response, he clarified himself. "I'm doing a story for the *Pajaronian* on the meeting tonight and what's at stake. I need some background information on the history of Croatia."

Both Nick and Frank chuckled. "How long do you have?" Nick asked.

Now Howard didn't understand.

"It's a complicated history that even the best scholars don't understand, much less us peasants. But we can give you a bird's-eye view."

Once they were seated in the bar and a bottle of slivovitz was on the table, the talk resumed. "Let's start off with the meeting. What was the upshot?"

"Mr. Marjanovich wanted to know if we favored a republic or king for the new Slav state," Nick said.

"And what was the consensus?"

"Since most of us are Croats, with many from the Republic of Ragusa, we voted for a republic."

"How many were for a king?"

"Jack the Serb spoke on behalf of a monarchy. Of course, he wanted King Peter or his son Prince Alexander on the throne."

"Prince Alexander seems like he would be a good ruler."

"Perhaps, but you have to remember we Ragusans live by our motto—'Liberty is not sold for all the gold in the world.'"

Howard became silent as he reflected upon Nick's words. Frank broke the ice. "What do you want to know about Croatia's history?"

"I know it's been complicated, so let's start from the present and work our way back," Howard said.

"Complicated is an understatement. But first, your readers should understand some basics. Even though we immigrated with Austrian passports, we are Croats by ethnicity, a south Slav subgroup." Nick thought it important for their neighbors to know they were neither Austrians nor Germans. "Austro-Hungary is just one of the many empires that have dominated us over the centuries. Frank and I, along with many others, come from the Republic of Ragusa, the Dubrovnik area. Most of the rest are from Dalmatia, the historic region along the Adriatic Coast, spanning from the island of Rab all the way to the Bay of Kotor in Montenegro. Croatia is north of Dalmatia, and Slovenia lies to its east. People call all of us Slavonians, but those are only the people from Slovenia. However, Slav could refer to Slavic since we are all part of the south Slav race," Nick said.

"You remember Dr. Vidmar. He's a true Slavonian from Slovenia. In fact, Slovenes, yet another name, are the only Slavs allowed to serve in the Austrian diplomatic service," Frank said.

"And why is that?" Howard asked.

"Beats me. However, they have had a long history of diplomatic service in Europe," Frank said.

"Now, we're a bit off topic. Let's get back to the history of Croatia. Currently, we're ruled by the Austro-Hungarian Empire. Before that, Napoleon snuck up on us. The entire fifteenth century and for some years on either side, the Ottomans rode herd over us. But they let us be, as long as we paid our taxes. Venetians conquered us before that. And on and on it went throughout our history. But despite many masters, Ragusa kept much of its clout and even its parliament. It had become such a maritime powerhouse that its conquerors respected it. The Ottomans, for instance, engaged Ragusa to ferry goods between Constantinople and Italian ports. After America was discovered, the spice trade no longer used Mediterranean routes, and that was the beginning of the end for us and also the Venetians."

"What a history," Howard said. "I'm overwhelmed by it all. Most of us only know about Western European history. What's gone on in Eastern Europe is the stuff of action adventure stories."

"And spy novels. Let's not forget about all the spies."

"Do you think spies are at work here?"

"Spies are at work everywhere, although I don't have any firsthand knowledge of any."

"It's getting late, so I don't want to keep you much longer. Is there anything else?"

"The key thing is to get our ethnicities right. In this town, most of us are Croats with a few Serbs and Montenegrins thrown in. Most Croats come from the Konavle area of Dubrovnik, while others hail from Dalmatia, especially the island of Brac. You can call us Slavs as long as you're referring to our dominant race. But never call a Croat a Serb, or vice versa. That will bring the wrath of God down upon you."

"I thought you considered each other brothers."

"Brothers, yes, but just like Cain and Abel, we don't always see eye to eye."

CHAPTER 41

A few days after the Slav state meeting, Dr. Vidmar paid a visit to Nick.

"Did you come to rehash that San Francisco Preparedness Parade bombing? I hope you're hot on the trail of those radicals. Killing and wounding innocent people to make a point is the devil's work."

"I couldn't agree with you more. Thank goodness there wasn't more carnage. That was the biggest parade ever held in the city, with over fifty thousand marchers."

"My in-laws watched the parade. They said it was pure mayhem after the bombs went off and their nerves are still shaky."

Vidmar shook his head. "I read the piece in the *Pajaronian* about Croatian history and the desire for a Slav state. Well-spoken."

"Thank you. But did you see this?" He handed Vidmar a later edition of the *Pajaronian*. "One of our local packers has been circulating a letter he received from a brother in the war. And somehow, it ended up in print." Nick waited while Vidmar read.

"Interesting. He was met by cheering crowds in Ragusa when he returned from furlough. Must be a popular guy."

"The brother believes Austria is winning the war."

"He's a good soldier. He has to believe in the cause. But his packer brother doesn't. I should have a talk with him."

"Do you think he could—"

"I won't know until we have a tête-à-tête."

Nick hoped Vidmar's little talk would lead up a blind alley. Although, now that he reflected on it, Butkovich was not at the meeting. Every patriotic Slav in town had been there. *Why not Butkovich?*

"Tell me, where I can find this fellow?"

"He has a packinghouse on the row just a few down from ours."

"I wonder if he holds American citizenship."

Nick just stared back at him.

"Don't look at me like that. Spies are everywhere. Didn't you hear about the Black Tom explosion?"

"No, but I expect you'll fill me in."

"Black Tom is an island in New York Harbor. German agents blew up munitions intended for the Allies."

"I...I didn't know."

"Now you do. Maybe it will finally convince you that the enemy is on these shores, making mischief at every turn."

Signs that America was about to enter the war appeared. Watsonville's Company L, Second Infantry, mustered sixty-eight members to support the National Guard. The Citizens League formed to watch over family while their men were away. And then a telegram reported the Cunard liner *Alaunia* was sunk in the English Channel, along with a Pajaro Valley shipment of apples. This news shook up the apple packers, and they held a meeting.

"We must protect our overseas shipments," said Nick. "America hasn't yet entered the war and they're targeting us."

"That's because we're shipping to England, which is in the

war. They want to keep supplies from reaching them," a packer said.

"Well, I guess we're in the war, too, and if we want to win, we have to keep shipping apples. In fact, I got a telegram from a commission agent in New York and he wants to increase his order of Newtowns. The English only want Newtown Pippins—they like their apples crisp when they sink their teeth into them."

"Besides insurance, we should require more convoys to escort our apples," Frank said.

"Write your congressman," a voice in the crowd yelled out.

Despite the loss, the apple season had been good, even better than the previous year, as evidenced by packers building new packinghouses to accommodate the increasing crops. Nick bought himself a Studebaker Model 17-4 touring car. And not long after, other packers were tooling around town behind the wheel of a Studebaker, too.

CHAPTER 42

When Americans got wind of the Zimmerman Telegram, they were up in arms. Germany had sent a message to Mexico urging their alliance in return for the states of Texas, Arizona, and New Mexico. Germany hoped a pact with Mexico would incite a conflict between the two neighbors that would keep the United States out of a European war. But their hopes were dashed when Mexico remained neutral in the Great War.

In fact, the Zimmerman Telegram had the opposite effect—Wilson declared war on Germany on April 6, 1917, igniting war fever. Anti-German sentiment flared across the country. German schools were closed. German books were banned. Germany businesses were boycotted. And Germans were taunted with names like Hun.

The Enemy Alien Act went into effect, naming unnaturalized Germans enemy aliens. They could not own firearms, fly a plane, or operate a wireless radio. They were forbidden from traveling, taking part in beach activities, and moving homes. When America declared war on Austro-Hungary a few months later, Austrian-Hungarians were also named enemy aliens.

Nick estimated two thousand in Watsonville could be affected. He had noticed that in the lead up to the war, the *Paja-*

ronian listed men who had become naturalized citizens, many of
them Croatians who had been Austrian subjects. Every time he
saw a name he recognized, he breathed a sigh of relief and hoped
citizenship would be enough to protect them. But he wasn't so
sure. Dr. Vidmar had confided that the Austrian and German
governments had for years been setting up an American network
of sympathizers. This did not bode well for the rest of the
Germans and Austrians, even though they swore allegiance to
America.

And what about Luka and Gabe in Canada? Nick wondered.
They never discussed citizenship when they were here for the
Apple Show in 1910 because it didn't seem important at the
time. Canada, as part of the British Empire, entered the Great
War in 1914. He had heard nothing from them, so he had to
assume they were holding up. They were farmers, and the
country needed farmers to supply its war machine.

Anton came home for the weekend unexpectedly. Nick assumed
something was up, so he was not taken by surprise when Anton
cornered him in his office. "I want to talk to you about an important matter."

Nick turned and assessed his son, trying to discern what he
was about to say before he said it. A few things flashed through
his mind—one good, another bad. "Go ahead. I'm listening."

Instead of coming right to the point, Anton beat around the
bush. "I've been reading a lot about the war. It seems to be
pretty important to our people...the cause for a Slav state."

"It definitely is. Several prominent speakers have come to
town seeking our advice, and I'm giving them my wholehearted
support."

"But if the Allies lose the war, there won't be a Slav state."

"There won't be much of a world either."

"Pa, I can't stand by and let others carry the load. I want to
enlist."

"Enlist—"

"I've made up my mind."

"Can't it wait?"

"Troops are leaving any day. I want to be with them when they land."

"It's almost dinnertime. And I need to talk to your mother later."

"Fine. But I'm not changing my mind."

Bedtime was not the moment Nick wanted to approach Jelena with their son's desire to go to war. He knew after their talk she would be in no mood for romance, and romance was what he most desired right now. But fatherhood beckoned, and he had no choice but to answer. "Jelena, I had a talk with Anton this afternoon."

She turned to look at him. "Oh...is that why he came home?"

Jelena was only half dressed and Nick found it difficult not to focus on her body, which was still attractive to him after all these years. "As a matter of fact, yes."

Jelena slipped her cotton nightgown over her head and pulled it down. "So, tell me what he had on his mind."

"Come over here and sit next to me on the bed." Once she was in position, he took her hand in his. "There's no soft-pedaling it. He wants to enlist."

"Enlist? You mean, the army?"

"That's right. If not the army, then the navy."

"But why? Once he graduates, he can practice law."

"He feels it's his duty."

"It's not his—"

"He's a man now, Jelena, and men do their duty. It's just how we're made."

In May, General John "Black Jack" Pershing took command of the American Expeditionary Force. It had been less than two years since he lost his wife and three daughters in a fire at the

Presidio in San Francisco. Miraculously, his only son survived. Because of this personal tragedy, Pershing not only had the public's sympathy but admiration for his ability to rise like a phoenix. Pershing's forces landed in France in June, Anton not among them. His father had convinced him to wait to be conscripted.

On July twentieth, grim-faced officials gathered in Senate Office Building Room 226 to draw names of eligible men between the ages of twenty-one and thirty years for the draft. President Wilson had expected a million men to volunteer to serve in the Great War, but only seventy-three thousand enlisted. Falling far short of the number needed to wage war, he resorted to the draft.

Secretary of War Newton Baker, a pacifist, had the dubious honor of drawing the first number. He stood before a glass bowl, blindfolded, and pulled out a capsule containing a serial number. The drawing continued until the wee hours of the next day, not a single capsule remaining.

Newspapers throughout the country publicized the first round chosen. Before Nick read the morning paper, Jelena spread it out on the kitchen table, searching through the names. As he walked into the room, Jelena screamed, "AJ is on the list." She gazed into Nick's eyes and he recognized the fear, not only for their nephew but also for their only son. Nick embraced Jelena and tried to soothe her.

When Anton heard the news, he roared, "I can't let my cousin, who's like a brother to me, go it alone. I'm enlisting now and you can't stop me."

"I guess we're in it in a big way now," Nick said to Frank. "We need to push the Liberty bonds more than ever. It takes money to win a war, and I'm not sending our sons to the battlefront without every supply necessary to beat the enemy."

"We must shake down every Croat packer. They know this is not only a war to defeat the Germans, but also a war to win a state for the Slavs. Anyone who doesn't contribute is no longer a friend but a foe."

Nick let Frank's words percolate a few moments. *This could be one way to uncover German and Austrian sympathizers.* "I want you to keep a list of everyone who refuses to give. It may come in handy at some point."

"Vidmar," Frank said as the silence grew thick.

When the day arrived for the Pajaro Valley draftees to depart for American Lake training camp, a parade and ceremonies gave them a proper sendoff. Families, friends, and townsfolk gathered at the plaza where eleven soon-to-be soldiers sat on the bandstand as the chairman of the County Exemption Board called out their names. Amid cheers and tears, the young men marched off to catch the 4:19 p.m. train headed north while the St. Francis Orphanage Band played "God Bless America" in farewell.

"He's really off to war," Jelena said. "I was hoping it would end before he had to fight. I know you think of him as a man, but to me Anton will always be my baby. And now he's leaving for the unknown where even a mother can't protect him."

"We have to put our faith in God's plan."

"At times like this, I wonder if he even has a plan. It seems he just sits up there and watches us make a mess of things."

"Good always triumphs over evil, and it will again."

CHAPTER 43

"Can't you hear someone pounding on the front door?" Jelena trembled. Ever since her son had gone off to war, she worried that an army representative would show up to deliver bad news.

"Stay right where you are. I'll get it." Nick hustled toward the racket and cracked open the door. "State your business." He had not put on the light, so he could not make out the figure on his porch.

"It's me. Luka."

"Luka. For land sakes. What are you doing here? Come in, come in." Luka showing up out of the blue could only mean trouble. And if that wasn't enough, his appearance gave him away. He was smelly and dirty and skinny, clothes hanging loose on his body—a uniform of some sort.

Jelena ran into the entranceway. "What's the matter? Why are you here?"

"They interned Gabe and me. I escaped, but Gabe's still behind bars." Jelena let out a gasp and covered her mouth.

"Let's go into the kitchen and sit down. Jelena, can you make up a plate for Luka? Now, let's slow down and start from the beginning."

"Canada entered the war in 1914. After that, anti-German

sentiment began to build. The government encouraged neighbors to snitch on each other. That's when our trouble first started. Both Gabe and I got called in to determine our allegiance. They knew we had immigrated from Austria because of our passports. And even though we both became citizens, they viewed us with suspicion. One day, the authorities showed up and moved us to an internment camp."

"They imprisoned you?"

"That's right. They built several internment camps across Canada. They sent Gabe and me to Castle Mountain near Banff National Park. They treated us like slaves, forcing us to make park improvements."

Jelena set a plate of cold cuts and bread before Luka. "I'm sorry I don't have something better. Soup will be ready in a minute."

Nick watched as Luka gorged himself on the ham and cheese and Italian bread. When Jelena put a bowl of chicken noodle soup down, he lapped it up and burped out his satisfaction.

"Do you feel better?" Jelena asked.

"Much. But I could still use some rakija."

"You stay here with your brother. I'll get the bottle." When she returned, she set the tray of shot glasses and slivovitz on the table. Then she kissed Luka on the cheek. "I'll leave you now. If you need me, I'll be upstairs."

"Could you keep Luka company a minute? I want to pick up Frank and bring him here."

Frank wasted no time getting into the Studebaker. On the way, Nick filled him in on what he knew so far of Luka and Gabe's ordeal.

"This is incredible," Frank said.

When they walked into the kitchen, Jelena was patting Luka on the hand, trying to soothe him as he put away shot after shot.

"Thanks, Jelena. We'll be fine now."

She gave Luka a pat on the back and said good night. "I'll get a room ready for you."

"Did the slivovitz help?"

"Always does."

Nick grabbed a glass and handed one to Frank, which they both filled to the brim. "Now, where were we? Oh, yeah...something about the camp—"

"Castle Mountain. But it won't be a camp much longer. They're closing it down and moving the inmates somewhere. That's how I escaped."

"Is Gabe still there?"

"Unfortunately. I just seized my chance when it presented itself, slipping through a hole in the fence."

"What about your families?" Frank asked.

"They're still on the farm. Mostly, they interned men."

"When was the last time you saw them?"

"Back in 1915 when they took us away."

"You didn't attempt to see them after you escaped?"

"I didn't want to endanger them. Besides, Rita wouldn't have let me come down here if she had laid eyes on me after all this time."

Nick glanced at Frank to determine what he was thinking about this mess. "Okay. We can get more details in the morning. But I think we need a plan to get Gabe out."

"We could ask our congressman for help."

"Or Dr. Vidmar. He seems familiar with these things."

"Let's have another drink and sleep on it. In the morning, we'll view the problem from a fresh angle."

"I sent a telegram to the congressman, but I doubt this problem is in his wheelhouse," Frank said as he took a seat in Nick's kitchen. He eyed a fresh batch of kolache on the table and grabbed one, sinking his teeth into it.

Nick poured him a cup of coffee. "We should contact Vidmar," Nick said.

"I already did that."

As expected, the congressman could not help, but Dr. Vidmar headed down to Watsonville as soon as he received the telegram. They all gathered around the kitchen table again as he laid out a plan.

"I have an operative in Seattle who can do the job. I'll send him a telegram after our meeting. But plan to be on the next train north. I'll tell him to meet you at the train station and drive you to the outskirts of the camp. He will be in charge of the operation, but my guess is he'll need your support. He doesn't know your brother from Adam. Luka may have to reenter the camp to help find him. If the camp is being moved, there's got to be some confusion. As Sun Tzu said, 'In the midst of chaos, there's also opportunity.' Our agent will figure out how to take maximum advantage of that. I have no doubt."

"There's a train up north in a few hours. We'll be on it."

"I recommend that Luka arrive first and sit alone. Remember, there are spies among us."

The brothers shot each other glances across the table.

"Speaking of spies, how is your work on behalf of the Allies shaping up?" Nick said.

"It's progressing. The internment camps are filling up."

"Don't tell me America has an internment camp," Frank said.

"Four, to be exact. The one in Georgia has a contingent from the Boston Symphony. But they're making the most of it. They recently performed Beethoven's *Eroica* for the inmates and since most of them are German, they got a standing ovation. I hear the next concert should be a sellout."

Nick hid Luka in the back of his Studebaker, then transferred him to an apple wagon at the packinghouse. He dropped Luka off near the station, cautioning him to stay out of sight. Then he went back for Frank and got a helper to give them a lift to the station. The train was behind schedule, which provided some anxious moments until it arrived.

Once all three were on board, Nick breathed a sigh of relief. "It's going to be a long train ride. After we change in San Francisco, I suggest we get some shut-eye so we'll be fresh for what lies ahead."

When they arrived in Seattle, it was the wee hours of the morning of the following day, the sun still below the horizon. Nick and Frank waited for Luka to depart, then they left.

Luka stood to one side of the station house and Nick and Frank on the other. The night was so silent, not even a hoot of an owl dared disturb it. Then, out of the silence, they heard *psst* and turned toward the sound. A figure lingered in the shadows and they moved toward it.

Suddenly, a man stepped forward, his size and appearance threatening. "Vidmar sent me. I'm Alex."

"This is Frank and I'm Nick. Our brother Luka is standing in front of the station." No sooner had he uttered those words, than Luka appeared.

"It seems we are all here. My car's over there." It was an unassuming black Ford—perfect for the mission. "It'll take better than two hours to reach our destination." He tossed a couple of bags in the back to Frank and Luka, and the other to Nick in the seat next to him. "This should sustain you until we can get breakfast." Then he stepped on the accelerator and screamed out of the parking lot.

As they approached the border, Nick became apprehensive, not knowing how they would get across without proper identification. Alex pulled up to the window and handed the agent some paperwork. Within moments, they were ushered through. "Whew," Nick said. "That could have been a close one."

"Not so close. My friend is well paid."

They drove on in silence for what seemed like hours but was only about two. "We stop here and eat. Then we talk."

The diner was the Canadian version of a greasy spoon, but it served up hearty grub. Each man ate his fill of ham and eggs, along with hash browns and muffins lathered in butter and apricot jam. "They buy the jam fresh from farmers. There's nothing better," Alex said as he shoved a muffin into his mouth. After they all had a fresh cup of coffee in front of them, Alex pulled out a pack of cigarettes and shook it until cigarettes popped up. He gestured toward each of the men. "Join me in a smoke."

Nick was the first to accept the offer, and the others followed. He preferred cigars, as did Frank, but with the stress he was under any form of nicotine was a godsend. Alex pulled out a match and lit one, holding it out for the men to use before he set his own afire. He shook out the match and took a long inhale on the cigarette, blowing out rings to impress his company. "Now we talk."

It took almost an hour to reach their destination. Alex parked the car out of sight and exited. "Stay here." When he returned, he tossed a bag to each of them. "I want you to put these on. Luka, you need to wear double."

"What for?"

"Your brother will need one. You can't go carrying a suitcase into camp, now can you?"

Luka didn't answer, and his brothers kept mum as they did as they were told.

"Good. You proved you can follow orders. Understand—I am the only one who gives them. Let's go."

They walked toward the camp and once they were within spying distance, Alex halted. "We stay here and watch until sunset. Let me know if you spot your brother. Luka, tell me again where the hole was that you escaped through."

"It's near the southwest corner."

Alex pulled out binoculars and searched the perimeter of the camp. When he reached the southwest corner, he stopped. "Luck is with us. It's still there."

"What do we do now?" Nick asked.

"Wait. Sleep. But we take turns."

Nick and Frank laid back on the grass, hands cradling their

heads. They were exhausted from the long train journey, and the anxiety of not knowing what lie ahead drained whatever reserves they had left. Before long, they were cutting z's as sleep overtook them.

Alex handed the binoculars to Luka. "Let me know when you spot Gabe."

Luka was familiar with the camp routine. It was almost lunchtime and Gabe would have kitchen duty. He focused his view on the kitchen door until a group of men appeared. "I found him."

"Let me have a look."

Luka passed the binoculars to Alex. "He's the tall, thin one walking with a limp."

"Limp? No one said anything about a limp."

"He twisted his ankle. That's all."

"That's all we need for this mission to fail." A sober silence fell between them as Alex continued staring through the field glasses. "What else have you failed to tell me?"

"That's it."

"So, we have a problem. Now we need a solution."

Luka watched Alex as he contemplated the problem.

"Are you wearing an undershirt?"

Luka hesitated before answering yes.

"Good. Take it off."

Luka hesitated again.

"I don't want to repeat myself. Follow orders."

This time Luka made quick work of removing his two black shirts to get to his undershirt.

"Hand it over."

Luka watched as Alex pulled out a hunting knife and began shredding the shirt. Once he had several strips, he held them up for examination. "These will do."

"I'm not following you."

"Your brother has a weak ankle. It needs to be reinforced. Let me show you how. Take off a boot and extend your leg toward me." Luka complied. Then Alex wrapped his ankle, weaving the strips under the foot and around the ankle until they provided a strong reinforcement. "Now stand and tell me how it feels."

Luka stood. "My ankle won't give out with this wrap on."

"That's the idea. Now sit down and take it off." Alex removed his boot and extended his leg. "Now it's your turn. One of us will have to wrap Gabe's ankle, and it most likely will be you."

Luka began wrapping as Alex coached him. "Make sure you overlap the pieces and wrap them tight. We have one chance to get your brother out and we have to do it right. I don't want to end up tossing him over my shoulder and carrying him like a sack of potatoes." When Luka's wrap was finished, Alex tested it. "Not bad. Now you'll do it again and again and again until it's second nature." Alex unwrapped the strips and handed them to Luka. "Understand?"

Luka grimaced as he took up his task, this time wrapping faster.

"See that? Practice makes almost perfect. Try again."

The sun lowered toward the horizon, a bright orange glow in its wake. "It's almost time. Let's go over the plan once more. Luka and I will go in. You two will wait outside as backup. You may need to assist Gabe back to the car. Luka revealed to me he has a sprained ankle. He won't get far on it in this terrain, even with it wrapped. Now, follow me and stay low."

They inched their way toward the fence on all fours, taking one long, slow step after the other—rocks and divots obstacles they could not see to avoid. Finally, they reached the southwest corner.

"The men will be coming out of their tents soon for their evening constitutional," Luka said. "How are we supposed to get Gabe's attention?"

"We'll have to keep on our toes and improvise." Alex looked up at the armed guards stationed on the towers. "We have to avoid the searchlights to keep from getting shot. Now, let's move out." Alex forced his large, muscled body through the hole and Luka followed with a mere wiggle. They crawled along the perimeter while Nick and Frank watched, helpless.

"All we can do now is pray," said Frank.

"The time for prayer is over. Action is the priority. Keep your eyes peeled for anything that could interfere with the plan," Nick said. They stood watch as men lined up to use the outhouses, knowing that Luka and Alex had to be nearby, hidden from view.

"When you see Gabe, you need to signal him," Alex said.

"How am I supposed to do that without alerting the rest of the men or, heaven forbid, the guard?"

"Have you ever played baseball?"

"Yeah, why?"

"Then you must know how to throw. Try to hit Gabe with a rock to get his attention." Alex handed Luka a rock he had been carrying in his pocket. "Here. Try this on for size."

Luka rolled the rock between his palms. "This will do."

They continued to wait and watch. Suddenly, Luka elbowed Alex in his side. Alex surveyed the situation, then said, "Now."

Luka threw the rock, hitting Gabe on his bad ankle. They heard him let out a grunt and the man next to him said, "What's wrong?"

"I must have kicked up a stone, and it hit me in a sore spot." Gabe waited a moment and looked in the direction the rock had come from. He could make out a figure in the shadows but didn't know who it was. Luka had been missing from the camp for about a week. He wondered whether he had returned to rescue him. Gabe coughed. He stepped out of line and continued to make a gagging sound as he moved in the direction of the rock. Then a hand grabbed him and pulled him back.

"It's me, Luka, and this is Alex. Quick. Put these clothes on." Gabe wasted no time dressing in the black stealth clothing. Then Luka made him sit down while he wrapped his ankle. "How's that?"

Gabe stood and tested it. "Good. It will hold."

"Let's go. Follow me and stay low."

As they neared the hole in the fence, Frank spotted a guard surveying the camp with field glasses. Next a handheld searchlight shot a beam over the field in their direction. "We've got to draw attention away from them," Frank said.

"I'll move down the line and create a distraction," Nick said. He crawled along the fence until he got far enough away. *A distraction?* He knew wildlife lived in the area, including coyotes and wolves. *A wolf howl. That's what I'll do.* Nick put his hands around his mouth and let out his best imitation. The searchlight changed course in his direction. He had accomplished his aim. He drew back from the fence, moving like a wolf to avoid detection, and continued on toward Frank.

He spotted a guard heading toward the southwest corner. No doubt he was aware of the hole. He turned and saw Luka, Gabe, and Alex coming from the other direction. *They'll converge on the hole at the same time and there's nothing I can do about it but hope for the best.* Nick made his way back to Frank just in time to witness the scene.

The guard pointed his rifle and shouted, "Halt. Who goes there?"

Silence.

"I said, who—"

Alex sprang up and kicked the gun out of his hand, spun around, kicked the guard in the stomach and as he was clutching his belly, gave him a blow to his head that knocked him down and out.

"Come on. We have to get out of here fast." Luka and Gabe went through the hole first, followed by Alex. "You two," Alex pointed to Nick and Frank, "support your brother on either side and let's move." They each took a side, placing Gabe's arms around their necks, and took off toward the car. When the trio reached the vehicle, they collapsed beside it, panting for air.

"We're not yet home free. Get him in the car." When

everyone was settled, Alex shot the car forward, having backed it in for a quick getaway. Once he was on the road, Alex checked the rearview mirror to make sure he wasn't being followed. "We're not in the clear yet. We still have a couple hours until the crossing, and we won't be stopping for food in this direction."

Luka spoke up in alarm. "We can't go back before seeing our families."

"Families? This is the first I've heard of them. They're not part of the bargain."

Luka and Gabe looked at each other and then at Frank, who sat between them in the back seat.

"The homesteads aren't far from here. They can't leave without seeing their kin."

"They'll be in danger if they stay," said Gabe. "We have to bring them with us."

Under his breath, Alex mumbled, "When I see Vidmar, I'll give him what for."

"What did you say?" Nick asked.

"Nothing important."

"The turnoff for our farms is coming up," Luka said.

Alex didn't answer, but he made a hard right that threw the passengers off-balance. "I'll drop you off. But don't count on my return."

"You can't leave us stranded," Nick said.

"Want to bet?"

"How much?"

"Say it again?"

"How much do you want? Aren't bribes the way you do business?"

"Sometimes."

"Make it this time."

"Save your money for when it's needed. How many people will you be?"

"Two wives, nine children, plus the four of us."

"Total fifteen. Too many. No can do."

"Think again. You can and you will do what's required. There is no other option."

"Stop your squawking about options. I'm the master of them. I just need a moment to think."

The first house they came to was Gabe's. He threw the car door open and hobbled to the front door. Instead of knocking, he shouted to avoid frightening the family. "Lucy, it's me, Gabe. I'm out." The brothers gathered behind him as the door narrowly opened.

"Is it really you, Gabe?"

"Let me in and I'll prove it."

Lucy recognized his voice and swung the door open wide, falling into his arms as she smothered him with kisses. "Did they let you out?"

"My brothers rescued me. You and the children must get ready to leave. We're going to California with Nick and Frank until the war's over."

"And leave the farm?"

"We have no choice. It's a matter of survival."

Luka's house was just a few steps away. Rita, too, was over-joyed but reluctant to leave everything behind.

"I'll give you twenty-four hours to get ready. Only bring the bare necessities. If I'm not back on time, go it alone," Alex said.

"Do I need to remind you again that you have only one option?" Nick said.

"And do I have to remind you that families were not part of the bargain?" In a hushed voice he added, "Wait until I get my hands on Vidmar."

"We'll be ready and waiting for you tomorrow night."

Alex left the group in a haze of dust as he peeled out of the driveway.

The families worked all day, preparing to leave. They packed a few clothes and personal items, setting aside the most difficult task for last—the animals. They only had a few farm animals, but they also each had a dog who had been a loyal friend. Unfortunately, they did not have a choice. They all had to be left behind. They freed the chickens and cows and goats, providing enough water and feed to sustain them until they were claimed by neighbors. They brought the dogs together and set their bowls, side by side, on Gabe's porch.

"Do you think we should leave a note?" Gabe asked.

"Anyone who comes upon your farm will figure it out," Nick said.

"Farmhands will be back in a few days. They'll know what to do. And then there are neighbors not far down the road," Luka said.

Nick glanced at the two dogs sitting on the porch and went over to give them a pat. *Man's best friend. If that were true, they couldn't leave them behind.*

Everyone's ears perked up when they heard the racket made by a vehicle coming their way. It was a Packard jitney bus with Alex at the wheel.

"How did you come up with this thing?" Nick asked.

"I have my sources. Ready?"

"I think so."

"Then let's pack up and get moving." One by one, they climbed into the bus with their belongings. As they were about to pull out, Alex turned his head to the right, appearing to take one last look at the farmhouse. "What? Are you not taking the dogs?"

"How can we? We're riding a train," Luka said.

Alex turned off the engine, bolted out the door and whistled. The dogs came running. When they reached him, he held out his enormous arms, and they jumped up on him, licking his face. Then he mounted the steps and signaled for them to follow. The family members looked from one to the other, not knowing what to make of this scene.

"Don't you know dogs are special spirits? Some people

believe they are angels who have come to protect us. I will take them home." The dogs let out a bark as if voicing their approval.

Alex drove through the night until he reached the border. He handed the agent the paperwork and exchanged a few words before they were allowed to pass. He drove on to the Seattle train station where he deposited the group. "You're on your own from here."

"We can make it now," Nick said. "Thanks for getting us this far. We couldn't have done it without you." Luka, Frank, and Gabe all joined in expressing their gratitude.

"What can we do for you?" Frank pulled out his wallet.

"Put that away. I already have my reward." He patted both dogs on their heads. "Just one thing I need."

"What's that?"

"Dogs' names. We'll become friendly faster if I call them by the names they know."

"Hansel and Gretel."

"Huh? What kind of silly names are those for magnificent animals?" Both dogs were big, furry creatures, most likely a cross between a Newfoundland and retriever of some sort.

"The kids named them. They come from the fairytale. The dogs were lost when they found them, so they thought the names fit."

"I'll rethink names, in that case. A guy like me can't be calling dogs named after fairy-tale characters."

As they walked toward the train station, the brothers couldn't help guffawing whenever they thought about Alex calling his dogs. They looked back over their shoulders and had no doubt the dogs would be in good hands—Alex was sharing his beef jerky with them and they were gobbling it up.

CHAPTER 44

It was afternoon when the train pulled into Watsonville Depot. Nick and Frank walked back to the packinghouse to pick up a wagon. Once they had the horses hitched up, they returned for the group.

"I apologize for the transport, but it's the best we can do since you are so many," Nick said.

"We've had worse," Gabe said.

"Toss in your gear and hop aboard," Frank said.

Once everyone was in the wagon, Nick led the team to Frank's house. He turned back toward the group. "We'll split you up tonight. Tomorrow, we'll move you to the hotel."

Helen heard the commotion, opened the door and ran down the steps to greet them. She made the rounds of hugs and kisses before leading her unexpected house guests into her home. "Please set your bags here in the hallway and make yourselves comfortable in the living room. I'll put the coffee on and bring it right out."

"I'll take my leave, so I can get Luka's family settled for the night," said Nick.

Frank walked Nick out. "I'll go by the hotel later and reserve rooms."

The next morning, Nick returned with Luka's family in the back of the wagon. After Gabe and his family were aboard, he and Frank drove down Beach Street past the plaza and made a turn off Main Street to the Appleton Hotel which had been built a few years before for Apple Annual guests.

"What a lovely hotel," Rita and Lucy said in unison.

"It was designed by the excellent architect, William Weeks. He built many of the town's landmarks, including St. Patrick's Church where we worship," Frank said.

"The church is near the end of Main Street. Of course, Main Street USA is where most small towns site their most important services, whether they be shops, restaurants, or churches," Nick said.

"I've got an idea," Frank said. "Why don't we give you the town tour after we arrange for your rooms and drop off your bundles? Some things have changed since you were here last."

"That sounds great," Luka said. "I'm sure Rita and Lucy would like to get the lay of the land again. You know how women are—shopping is a top priority."

All the rooms were on the second floor overlooking the street, a rollaway in one for the fifth child in the family. "This is the best we can offer in our one-horse town."

"We'll be very comfortable, won't we?" Luka said. And everyone smiled their agreement.

"Okay. Downstairs and back into the wagon. Frank and I will give you the best darned town tour you'll ever have."

After the tour up and down Main Street, they ended at the packinghouse. "We want to show you the operation in full swing," Nick said. By the time they made it around to all the stations, it was time to eat. "Lunch is on the house," Nick said. They walked into the yard and got in line with the workers.

"Looks like the chef made his world-famous chili especially for you," Frank said.

"We can smell the spices," Luka said.

Once they had filled their plates, the families sat down and dug in. "It's a little too spicy for me," Gabe said. "We Canadians like our food on the mild side."

"You'll get used to it," Frank said.

"What is that supposed to mean?" Luka said.

"It means you may be here awhile. No one knows when the war will end."

Luka and Gabe went to work at the packinghouse, but their hearts weren't in it. Nick and Frank worried about them, but circumstances left little choice. A few weeks after they had been packing apples, Nick had a talk with his brothers.

"Sorry," Luka said. "It's not for us. We're farmers. We miss the land."

Nick relayed Luka's words to Frank. "Heck, they can farm here. In fact, better than almost anywhere else in the world and especially Canada, where the ground is frozen half the year."

An idea suddenly struck Nick. "We need to turn them into orchardists. Let's go scout the farms for sale."

"I know one that would be perfect—the Sullivan place. It's been for sale awhile but he's asking too much."

"Hop into the Studebaker and let's take a ride out there."

They caught old man Sullivan in his orchard, taking stock of the fruit as he leaned on a cane for support.

"Mr. Sullivan," Nick said, "we've come to make you an offer. Let's talk business."

Sullivan blinked a couple of times then mumbled, "Business?"

"Yeah, business," Frank said. "We might want to buy your farm." Nick and Frank already knew everything necessary to make the purchase. It was just a matter of agreeing on the price.

"I'm old and can't farm much longer. As you can see, even my overalls are in tatters after all the wear. Name your best price and we'll have a deal."

Nick and Frank did a quick consultation, then put forth their best offer, which they felt was a fair one. And Mr. Sullivan agreed to the terms. "We'll have our lawyer contact you to draw up the contract. How soon do you think you can vacate the premises?"

"I only need to get rid of all the old junk and sell off the rest. My daughter has been begging me to come live with her over the hill. Her husband grows grapes."

"Don't sell anything until we have a look. We may take all the furnishings with the house and most of the farm equipment, too."

The deal went through, and Luka and Gabe began their new careers as orchardists.

CHAPTER 45

"Don't forget about the meeting tonight at the Odd Fellows Hall," Nick said to Frank. "An important representative of the Southern Slavic National Council will be speaking."

"I wouldn't miss it for the world. How are Luka and Gabe getting there?"

"I'll pick them up."

"By the way, Dr. Vidmar will be there. Tomorrow night, I've planned a little dinner with him so we can rehash the meeting."

Mr. J.B. Mihaljevich told the group he was in town to organize a local branch of the Washington, DC-based Southern Slavic National Council which aimed to help Croatia attain independence with a republican form of government modeled after America. "Croatia would become part of a south Slav state to include Montenegro, Serbia, Bosnia and Herzegovina, Slovenia and Macedonia. We plan to organize all southern Slavs living in the United States for this purpose, and the additional aim of fostering a love for America and its way of life."

He went onto say that King Peter of Serbia, the most democratic monarch in Europe, was in favor of the movement and willing to abdicate in favor of a republican form of government. "As you may know, Prince Alexander and the Serb government are in exile in Corfu where they signed an agreement with the Jugoslav Committee to form a south Slav state with a constitutional monarchy led, most likely, by a Serbian king."

Mihaljevich reminded everyone of President Wilson's Fourteen Point speech in January, which gave support for self-determination for the people of the Austro-Hungarian Empire. He ended his talk with remarks about the persecution people living under the regime have endured since the war began with men away and women and children left to starve.

Dr. Vidmar rose from his seat. "If I may interject. Word has come to me that forty thousand Slav children are starving in the empire. Representatives of Slovenia and Croatia petitioned the Crown to feed them if they could be excused from providing food for the military. Of course, Austria refused the request. But our compatriots were not to be deterred. With the help of a Franciscan priest in Zagreb, Father Didak Buntic, they took the ragamuffins from Istria, Bosnia, and Herzegovina into their homes. It did not matter whether a child was Catholic, Muslim, or Orthodox. They only wanted to save as many children as possible for the Slav race."

When Dr. Vidmar sat down, applause rose up and continued for several minutes until Mr. Mihaljevich retook the podium. "After Dr. Vidmar's glaring remarks, there is not much left to say, but the time has come to break the Austrian yoke."

As the group departed, Nick said to Frank, "I guess this means we have to step up the sale of Liberty bonds."

"Right. Not only will it help the war effort but show Slav loyalty to the country. What are the latest results, anyway?"

"Oversubscribed. I heard it was a real shock to Germany and sent a message that America is in this war to the end."

"It should also send a message about our patriotism. I worry about some fellows in town."

After dinner with Dr. Vidmar, Nick and Frank sat around the dining room table with him, drinking rakija and discussing the war. "There's a serious problem with enemy aliens, some so close to us we call them friends, even relatives," Vidmar said. He let that comment marinate. Then he continued. "I have knowledge of an editorial that will see the light of day soon in the *Pajaronian*. The upshot is that America has been too lenient on those who are not its friends."

"What does the government propose to do about them?" Nick asked.

"Everyone not born here who has American citizenship will be given a hearing to determine his loyalty."

"And what happens if he proves disloyal?" Frank asked.

"He'll be interned, stripped of his citizenship, and sent back after the war."

Nick stood and paced. "What about those who are not American citizens?"

"They'll be locked up until armistice is declared. I hope your brothers have applied for asylum."

"An attorney is working on it."

"Good. Back to enemies. A prominent member of the Monterey County Council of Defense is promoting harsher measures."

"If they're deserved, that's one thing. But a witch hunt would catch about two thousand men here in the cross hairs."

"It's war. We have to be vigilant to keep enemies and spies from aiding the enemy. It not only will help those on the home front but protect our boys fighting overseas."

"We're on your side and are doing our part to ship apples across the Atlantic and sell Liberty bonds. Croatians here have been generous."

"I don't mean to cast a distrustful eye on those you consider friends, but the threat is real. Remember the refinery fire at the Spreckels sugar plant? Authorities received warnings, but their hands were tied. That factory contained half the state's sugar supply. And then there was the case of the Monterey man who threatened to blow up army officers and government officials. The case ended up being dismissed because the suspect was a naturalized citizen. People need to understand that citizen or not, there are people here who support the Kaiser and will even go to great lengths to undermine our noble cause."

"We need laws that allow us to deal with these foes," Nick said.

"Laws take time. The patriots among us must remain vigilant. This is where I can still use your help."

"Just name what you need and we'll supply it."

After Dr. Vidmar left, Frank said, "Why did you lie about the attorney for our brothers?"

"Because I had to."

Nick and Frank doubled their efforts to aid the war. They raised money for the Red Cross and shipped apples overseas. But they focused on the sale of Liberty bonds. Every week, names of purchasers were listed in the paper to recognize their generosity and encourage others to buy the bonds. They had heard that money to sustain the war was the critical element now that they had enough men to fight it.

They posted Liberty bond posters in visible spots around town. One featured the Statue of Liberty with the slogan, "You buy a Liberty Bond lest I perish!" Another with a picture of fighting men read, "Beat back the Hun with Liberty Bonds." And yet another designed to pull at the heartstrings depicted a lone soldier with the line, "Lend him a hand. Buy Liberty Bonds."

In April, Hollywood Stars Mary Pickford, Douglas Fairbanks, and Charlie Chaplin went on a country-wide tour in their Three-Star Special promoting Liberty bonds with stops in Chicago,

New York, and Washington, DC where they were special guests at a White House dinner. By the time Mary returned to Los Angeles, she had sold forty million dollars' worth of Liberty bonds and been named Uncle Sam's most successful saleswoman.

With this momentum behind them, the Liberty bond parade for the third loan was the greatest pageant ever seen in Pajaro Valley. The parade of patriotism spanned a mile and a half and included every organization in town as well as businesses and lone patriots led by a military band. The parade passed the bonfire just as the sun was setting and marched on down Second Street to the auditorium, which was already filling. The enthusiastic crowd was more than it could hold—so much so that not even standing room was available.

Nick sat among the men on the rostrum, which included the mayor and other members of the Liberty Loan Committee. After rousing speeches, the vice chairman of the Liberty Loan Committee stood. "I challenge you to raise two hundred fifty thousand dollars tonight for our patriotic cause, especially our young fighting men. Those of you who cannot enlist can do your part by purchasing a Liberty bond. America needs money now more than men. The men need the supplies your money will buy to continue the fight for freedom."

When the subscriptions were totaled, they had put the town over its quota—with pledges of $286,050. However, the hundreds of people who had been turned away would have made the evening an even bigger success. And later they did just that.

"Congratulations on the success last night," Frank said to Nick as they took a coffee break at the packinghouse.

"I was pleased with the results. The two banks each contributed twenty-five thousand dollars—much more than expected. And so far, the Austrian Benevolent Society is in for ten thousand dollars. That should put questions about our patriotism to rest."

"Maybe. Did you catch the tone in the *Pajaronian* article?"

"I must have missed it."

"They credited the Austrian element in our midst for making a good showing. They went on to say they were gratified to see the Jugo-Slavs show support for the country that had been so good to them."

Nick shot a frown at Frank. "Not only is that condescending, but it hints at disloyalty. No matter how hard we try, we can't live down the suspicion and—"

"I spoke to a lawyer—"

"About what?"

"Asylum."

"What did you do that for?"

"We could lose everything if we're caught aiding and abetting the enemy."

Nick shook his head in disgust at the word enemy. "Who's the lawyer?"

"Pero Loreto. He thinks he can work it out."

Nick let out his breath in an enormous sigh of relief. "If anyone can get asylum, he can. On another subject, next week we're holding a meeting of apple packers and growers to discuss the labor shortage. Not only did we lose men here to the war, but workers are not coming from overseas for the season."

"That is a big problem. Any suggestions floated yet?"

"The main one gaining legs is to raise the hourly wage."

"That'll cut into profits."

"We all know that, but we must get the harvest picked and packed. Otherwise we won't make any profits."

After the men finished lunch, Nick called them together. "I have some news for you. We're raising your hourly wage to thirty-three cents." The men let out a cheer.

Nick waited until they had settled down before continuing. "Packinghouses and orchards throughout the valley will do the same. But with the war on, we have a serious labor shortage. Every man here who can put in a ten- or eleven-hour day should do so to not only ensure the harvest but to help the war effort. Our apples are in demand in England and every time one of our shipments gets torpedoed, we end up working twice to replace it. Those of us on the home front can help win the war by doing our part. Now, the chef has prepared a special dessert and after you've partaken, let's get back to work."

CHAPTER 46

On a beautiful summer day in mid-July, Nick and Frank headed for Jack's Cigar Store, along with dozens of other Slavs in town. Jack looked at them with tears in his eyes. "The tsar was our protector...and his beautiful family, too."

The world had only just learned that Tsar Nicholas, Tsarina Alexandra, and their five children had been assassinated by the Red Army at Yekaterinburg, where they were held captive following the Tsar's abdication in March 1917.

"We don't know who to offer condolences, so we offer them to you," Nick said.

"His cousin, King George V, should have offered him asylum."

"It's wartime. Politics—"

"But Russia bowed out of the war in March."

"Remember, they were enemies. Besides, a civil war is now raging in Russia."

"I heard Watsonville is sending more boys to the war."

"Same here."

Jack's eyes moved from Nick's face to Frank's. "Any word from your sons?"

"Just a brief note from Anton that his unit is on the way to Siberia."

After he reflected a moment, Jack said, "My guess is they're fighting more than one war."

Nick and Frank proceeded to the back after each purchasing a Habana cigar. The room was so packed they had trouble getting a seat until a couple of guys tossed their cards in and retreated with their meager winnings. "Thanks," they said as they took up the vacated chairs.

After a few hands, Nick folded. "Sorry, fellas. But I just remembered an errand I have to take care of. Catch you later."

Frank followed him out.

As they hurried past Jack without a goodbye, he shouted behind them, "Don't forget about the donation for Serbian relief."

When they got outside, Frank said, "What's put a burr under your saddle?"

"What Jack said about fighting two wars. I need to find out."

"How do you intend to do that?"

"Make a trip up to the Presidio with a gift box of Newtown Pippins. A little birdie told me the officers have developed a taste for them. Want to ride along?"

Nick and Frank swung by the packinghouse and loaded as many crates of Newtowns into the trunk of the Studebaker as it could hold. Then they were off, heading north on Highway One along the coast.

First, they went by the Serbian Relief Society to deliver several crates of their best apples for the upcoming fundraiser at the Cort Theatre. The woman who took possession of their donation said, "This is shaping up to be the most elaborate fundraiser the city has ever held. We've got some big Hollywood stars coming—William Crane, Maude Adams—rumor has it she might make her appearance flying across the stage as Peter Pan."

"Now you're making me regret I don't have a ticket."

"There are still some left if you want one."

Nick looked at Frank and held up four fingers.

They drove on to the Presidio, at the northern tip of San Francisco. "Every time I glimpse the Presidio, I'm reminded of the tragedy that befell Pershing's wife and three daughters."

Frank shook his head and remained silent.

Once they were admitted through the gate, Nick drove straight ahead to the Public Affairs office. "We should be able to get some information here. If not, we can always barge into the officers' club."

"That would be bad form, and might even land us in the stockade."

"Not if I can remember the name of Dr. Vidmar's friend."

"And who is he?"

"Some big shot around here—a buddy of Pershing's."

They entered the PA office, introduced themselves, and explained their purpose. "We'd also like to ask you a question about the army's mission in Russia. My son was sent there, but I thought Russia bowed out of the war."

At that moment, the door opened, and an officer entered, his uniform shirt covered with medals and ribbons. The PA officer snapped to attention and saluted. Once he was put at ease, he said, "General, these men have a question you would best be able to answer."

After they shook hands, Nick said, "We have come bearing gifts for your officers—Newtown Pippin apples from Watsonville. We also donated a nice cache to the Serbian Relief effort."

"Serbs...they've had a hard time of it. I admire their fighting spirit. Now, what can I help you with?"

Nick repeated his question to the general.

"I guess I won't be giving away any secrets if I tell you they're en route to Vladivostok to pick up war supplies—weapons, munitions, that sort of thing. They'll also be performing a rescue mission in Siberia to free a Czech unit. Now that I've answered

your question, I have one for you. What is your interest in
Siberia?"

"It was something a friend said in passing about fighting two
wars. My son is headed there."

"Siberia does have fighting. But it's between the Reds and
Whites. Our war isn't on that godforsaken terrain now that
Russia's out of it."

"I understand. I appreciate the information. It's difficult
being stateside with a son in the thick of it."

"Don't I know it. Four of mine are fighting over there."

"You've got me beat."

"That's right. Whenever I'm stateside, my wife can't get
enough of me. Another two will be pulled in if this war goes on
much longer."

After they were back in the car, Frank said, "Did he answer
to your satisfaction?"

"Unfortunately."

"I don't follow."

"Jack was right."

CHAPTER 47

"The government is floating its fourth Liberty bond," Nick said to the members gathered at the Croatian Sokol Lodge.

"I guess we need to prepare for another parade," said Frank.

"We have to do one to get enthusiasm up. Let's set a date. How does September 28 work for everyone?" Nick waited for the response. "From what I've heard, you all agree. Then September 28 it will be. So as not to recreate the wheel, let's take up our previous tasks, unless someone objects."

On the way out, Nick and Frank noticed Dr. Vidmar at the back of the room. "I've got a present for you. Is there somewhere we can go to talk?"

"Are you staying at the Appleton again?" Frank asked.

"I'll probably drive back up to the city tonight."

"We can't let you do that, can we, Frank?" Nick said.

Nick drove the group to his house and asked Jelena to get one of the spare rooms ready for their guest. Then he ushered Frank and Dr. Vidmar into the living room and grabbed the slivovitz.

"Cheers," said Nick. "All right, now that we've all had a shot, what kind of present did you bring us?"

Dr. Vidmar had carried a flat box into the room that

measured about two feet by three feet. He bent down to the floor where it lay and opened it, trying to shield its contents until he was ready for the presentation. "This will work best if you close your eyes. And no peeking." Satisfied that both Nick and Frank had their eyes shut tight, he stood and unfurled the flag. "Okay, you can open them now."

"It's the new Jugo-Slav flag," Nick said. "Where did you get it?"

"The Southern Slav National Council office in DC. I thought I'd save them a stamp."

Nick stood and touched the flag. A tingle of pride surged through him. "We must display it in the upcoming Liberty bond parade. This will charge up all the Slavs."

"Did anything strike you about the design?" Vidmar asked.

"You mean the tricolor blue, white, and red stripes?"

"Exactly."

"Why don't you just tell us rather than keep us guessing. You can see we're ignorant."

"I apologize if I offended you. The new flag design is based on the one for the first Pan-Slavic Conference held in Prague in 1848."

"It's of historic significance," Frank said.

"The Pan-Slavic movement didn't just get pulled out of the Great War air. It's been a long-time dream."

"Soon to be a reality," Nick said.

"If all goes according to plan at the Versailles Peace Treaty. President Wilson needs to hold to his Fourteen Points. At least the one that concerns us."

"We have to win the war first," Frank said.

"We're near the end point," Vidmar said. "Now, I have some names to run by you." After he listed the names, Vidmar asked about Luka and Gabe.

"They're doing well and glad to be farmers again."

"I want to alert you to something I learned in Washington that may help them."

Nick and Frank perked up their ears. "We're listening."

"Congress passed a citizenship bill for enlistees that gives them almost instant citizenship."

"How would that help Luka and Gabe?"

"They could enlist. The rules bypass most of the other requirements. You could be their two witnesses."

"They're too old for the army."

"You're wrong. They're taking them up to age forty-five."

Nick started counting on his fingers. "I think they just might qualify."

"If not, there are ways to deal with these things." A cunning smile crossed Vidmar's face. He was an old hand at such deceptions.

Nick and Frank wasted no time talking to Luka and Gabe about the citizenship idea Dr. Vidmar had floated by them.

"We're too old to go to war. Besides, we have orchards to tend," said Luka.

"Ivan's older than you and he's soldiering." Nick let that reminder bring them down a peg. "But if we plot this right, you'll bag citizenship without having to serve."

"You can't control a war," Gabe said.

"The war is about to end. If you slip in your enlistment at the right time, the plan will work," Frank said. "Citizenship would give you protection from deportation. You don't want Canadian authorities tracking you down and sending you to prison. You did that once and didn't much like it."

Luka and Gabe moved aside to consult each other without their brothers listening in. "When do you need an answer?"

"Soon. Real soon," Nick said. "Seize the moment before it flees."

Luka and Gabe whispered between themselves again. "We'll do it. But you better not be wrong about the war."

"I'll be here in the morning to drive you to the enlistment office."

"Whew," Frank said. "They were a hard sell."

"They don't understand the consequences. Once they escaped the camp and moved here, their lives dramatically improved. But they could face stiff penalties in Canada if they're forced to go back."

"What about their farms?"

"We may have to arrange for an agent to sell them unless they've already been confiscated."

Luka and Gabe's enlistments went off without a hitch, and the next day they swore an oath of citizenship with Nick and Frank as witnesses. "Let's keep our fingers crossed that the war ends before we get called up or else," said Luka. He drew his forefinger across his neck.

"What's that supposed to mean?" Frank asked.

"It means I'll get killed and so will Gabe."

"Huh?" Nick said.

"We decided not to tell our wives."

"Line up behind the flag. Show your support for the Jugo-Slav state," Nick said to the Slavs gathered. The flag had been mounted on an oak cross bar, a symbol of Dubrovnik which is surrounded by oak groves and derives its name from them. Nick and his Liberty bond partner were chosen as flag bearers.

"Gabe and Luka," Nick said, "you march with Frank and make sure you look happy doing it." As new citizens, Nick and Frank thought this would make a great debut for their brothers and put any question of their loyalty to rest.

Spectators lined the parade route, the Croatian colony turning out in force to show support for their new flag. Along the way, marchers sang "Hey Slav," the tune that became a rallying song of the Pan-Slavic movement. Organizers had planned ahead and handed out the lyrics to supporters. By the time the group arrived at the auditorium, everyone knew the words by heart and sang out loud and proud.

Dr. Vidmar stepped out of the crowd. *What is he doing here?* Nick wondered.

"I wanted to share in the pride of seeing our new flag displayed for the first time in this Slav town. May I have the opportunity to address the group?"

Dr. Vidmar moved in front of the flag and turned around to face the crowd. "You sang beautifully, as do your brethren on the battlefield. Slav soldiers on the front lines use the song to iden- tify each other. Knowing blood joins them, they sing to not spill a single drop. They are saving each other for our great Jugo-Slav state which will be their mutual homeland."

After Dr. Vidmar made his remarks, he sidled up to Nick. "But nothing can save them from the Spanish flu. It's dropping them like flies."

Nick didn't have time to ask questions as the crowd pushed him inside the auditorium. He hoped he could catch Vidmar afterward, considering he usually stuck around to debrief.

"I can't stay over tonight," Vidmar said.

"Do you have time for one drink?"

"If we can make it quick."

They walked to the closest bar and ordered a couple shots of slivovitz. "What's this about the flu killing our boys? There's no news here about it."

"Nick, are you still so naïve? We're at war. That means news blackouts and censoring. The only reason the word is getting out at all is because of the Spanish news media. Neutral Spain has no reason to withhold the truth."

"How bad is it?"

"My sources tell me it's killing at three times the rate of the enemy."

"Is it on our shores yet?"

"It may have started here. Disease experts believe military men at a Kansas army base carried it overseas, and it spread like wildfire. War is stoking it with the movement of troops and tight conditions in the trenches."

"What are we doing here to stem the tide?"

"Little to nothing."

That night as he crawled into bed, Nick had the flu on his mind, among other things. "A bad flu may hit us this year."

"Worse than other years?" Jelena said.

"That's what I heard. Did you get your throat blessed at the St. Blaise Mass this year?"

"I try to go every year."

"Those of us from Dubrovnik swear by his powers. That's the reason he's our patron saint." Nick was about to tell Jelena about the toll the flu was taking on soldiers, but thought better of it. *No point scaring her to death. She's worried enough about her son taking a bullet from the enemy. She would be bowled over if she knew it was an invisible enemy that he had no way to fight that is the real threat.*

Instead, he asked, "Jelena, are you tired?"

"If you mean, am I in the mood, you know I never refuse you."

CHAPTER 48

An article in the paper caught Nick's eye. The Spanish flu had arrived in town. Doctors said that it was not more than the old-fashioned grippe. They cautioned people to live sensibly, avoid crowds, don't take a cold shower, and don't get scared. This too shall pass.

Nick put the paper down and headed out the door. When he arrived at the *Pajaronian*, he searched the newsroom floor for Howard Dawson. Not finding him there, he strode down to his office. He caught him at his Royal, fingers flying over the keys.

At the sound of Nick's footsteps, Howard looked up. "I can type fast because this machine doesn't jam."

"You impressed me. I'm sorry to interrupt."

"My fingers need a break. Take a seat and let's discuss what's on your mind. My instincts tell me this is not a social visit."

"I'd like to hear what you know about the Spanish flu."

Howard pulled out his pipe, packed it with tobacco and lit it. "Do you mind?"

"No, go ahead."

After taking a puff, he said, "My instincts also tell me you have some information on this pandemic that could be helpful."

"Perhaps."

"I'll give it to you straight. It's pretty bad over there on the battlefield. But with the censoring, it's difficult to know how bad. The AP is sending out some stories from Spain, but we can't judge how reliable they are. Now, your turn."

"Okay. I'll level with you. My source told me that our boys are dying more from the flu than from war. It's a veritable pandemic over there."

"We've learned much the same then. I guess AP's sources were right."

"What are we going to do about it? The doctors seem to be taking a very business-as-usual approach."

"Not more we can do."

"The hell there isn't. In Dubrovnik, they understood disease and how it spread as early as the fourteenth century. Trade was important, so they didn't stop it. Instead, they'd quarantine any newcomers to the city for forty days. That's how quarantine got its name."

"Are you suggesting a quarantine here?"

"We've got soldiers returning from all sorts of places over-seas. Before you know it, the disease will run rampant."

"Maybe I should visit our local health officer."

"The sooner the better."

A few days later, Howard Dawson stopped by the packinghouse to see Nick. "I spoke with Dr. Morton, our local health official. He said that no Spanish flu cases are known in the town, but when it is warranted, measures will be taken to ensure the disease does not become widespread. Dr. Morton said the State Board of Health has issued instructions which I will be publishing in my article. They recommend the common-sense measures we already talked about. Although he mentioned that closing of schools, churches, and theatres had been considered but were deemed unnecessary at this point."

"I'm still in favor of a quarantine of any newcomer to town. I didn't hear you say where that stands."

"If the City Health Board doesn't want to close facilities, they certainly won't quarantine people for forty days."

"It doesn't have to be forty—just whatever the incubation period is for this flu."

"When things get worse, I'll bring it up."

"The way disease spreads, it's bound to get worse and in short order."

"Thirty cases." Nick shouted out while reading the morning paper.

Jelena put down her coffee cup. "Are you talking about that flu?"

"Less than two weeks ago, Howard Dawson told me there were no cases in town. And now there are thirty. The disease is taking hold, even though they say the cases are light. Next thing, the undertaker will be digging graves by the dozens."

"You're being overly dramatic. Every season, the flu passes with little notice. Occasionally, a senior citizen in poor health passes on from pneumonia—what we affectionately call the 'old man's friend.' But the death is a welcome release from their worldly suffering."

Nick did not want to alarm Jelena about his knowledge of the Spanish flu and how it was not discriminating between the old and young. But he wanted her to take precautions. "We need to follow the guidelines, especially about avoiding crowds."

"What? And miss church?"

"If the town doesn't close the churches, we might have to exercise our common sense and avoid them. At least for now."

"We've got two problems," Nick said.

"I know of one. And if we don't get more workers in here, the fruit will go bad," Frank said.

"I'll put an ad in the paper for workers, even women. We can't be too picky now."

Frank grimaced. "As long as Helen is not one of them. I don't want my wife working among these men. She'd pick up some bad habits, like swearing, for instance."

"There are better ways for Helen and Jelena to spend their time."

"So, what is the second problem?"

"The County Health Officer is requiring citizens to wear a gauze mask. Failure to do so will result in arrest."

"Where are we supposed to get them?"

"Of course, he doesn't mention that. It's as if he thinks we keep gauze masks on reserve to use in case of emergency. Most of us have never seen a gauze mask."

"I suppose that means the workers will have to be talked into wearing them."

"Talk will not do it. Rules are what they'll respond to."

"I'll stop by the pharmacy to check if there's any in stock. If not, we could hire a few ladies to sew them."

Frank bought a few gauze masks, but not enough for all the workers.

"Until there's more, we have to use them strategically," Nick said.

"What do you mean by that?"

"We'll make sure our foremen have them and then divvy the rest out among the workers, the most dependable receiving them first."

"That makes sense. What about us?"

"Let's reserve a couple and then decide. We don't want to give the workers the idea that we're saving ourselves first. No captain of a ship would ever do that, and no captain of industry should either."

After the men had lunch, Nick called them to meet. "The health officer is requiring that everyone wear a mask. If you own one, please wear it tomorrow. We purchased a few and more are

being made. I will distribute the ones in hand according to merit
—workers putting in the longest hours given priority."

"What if we don't want to wear one?" a voice from the back
yelled out.

"Then you'll be arrested and prosecuted—not by me, but the
district attorney. Before you decide to challenge the law, I'd like
to share what researchers at the University of California discovered. While the virus lives six minutes unless it finds a host, a
virus that gets caught in gauze dies immediately. Think about it.
A mask is foolproof protection. In San Francisco, they've also
found a mask has held numbers down on some of the most
feared illnesses such as diphtheria, scarlet fever, whooping
cough...not to mention the common cold." After Nick and Frank
passed out the masks, those in possession of one put it on and
returned to their station.

It wasn't long until the health commissioner made a surprise
visit to the packinghouse, catching Nick and Frank off guard.
Nick intercepted him the minute he recognized the officer and
steered him into the office. "Is something the matter?"

"Packinghouses have been identified as breeding sources of
the Spanish flu virus. I'm inspecting every packinghouse to
determine what best practices need to be implemented."

"You can see for yourself that workers are wearing masks.
The supply in town was slim, so we are having some made for
the rest of the workers."

"Masks are only part of the answer. Some doctors even
believe their greatest benefit is not to protect against infection,
but to settle nerves among the timid. They're becoming contro-
versial."

"What do you mean?"

"When the wearer breathes, he creates a moist environment
where germs can breed. It's a perfect storm."

"I thought the virus was supposed to die upon contact with a
gauze mask."

"Perhaps. But what workers need is an environment that is

warm, dry, and clean. During my rambles, I have only found one so far that meets the gold standard—that's Cranford Brothers."

Cranford—the perpetual thorn in my side. "We're trying our best."

"Trying is not good enough. We've enacted an ordinance, using Cranford as our model. Besides a proper place, workers need regular breaks and if they're cold, they should be provided a warm brick to heat their feet. And of course, if anyone appears ill, they should be sent home, not to return until they are well again."

"We'll do our best to comply."

"And one more thing. Encourage your workers not to drink liquor, even on off hours. Doctors no longer advise whiskey to cure a cold since liquor appears to help the flu virus take hold."

Nick rolled his eyes. "I'll mention it. But trying to shut down slivovitz consumption would be akin to withholding breast milk from a baby."

"It would not be a bad thing if this flu epidemic sobers up a few drunks."

That night at dinner, the subject of the flu came up. "I hope you're wearing a mask."

"I try, but sometimes I forget. Besides, it's hard to breathe with it on."

"It can save you. Force yourself to remember."

"Now that I'll be serving as a nurse's aide, I won't have a choice. The hospital requires them."

Upon hearing this news, Nick tried to hold back his alarm. "I don't think it's a good idea for untrained people to be hanging around hospitals."

"The Red Cross has been training us because the hospital staff is getting overwhelmed. Even the Japanese Association is sending workers."

"I don't like you taking a chance."

"The hospital is counting on us women. Don't worry. I can take care of myself."

CHAPTER 49

In the early morning hours of November eleventh, church bells rang out around town while newsboys rode bicycles through the streets and stood on corners, yelling, "Extra, extra. Read all about it."

Nick jumped out of his bed and ran out to the front yard to pick up the paper—he couldn't open it fast enough. The headline read, "Great War Comes to An End. Armistice Signed."

Jelena ran down the stairs. "What's happening?"

Nick wrapped Jelena in his arms and swung her around. "The war's finally over. The Allies won. And the Jugo-Slav state is no longer a pipe dream." Then he gave her a big kiss on her lips, followed by one on each cheek.

"That means Anton will be home soon. We must have a party to celebrate his return. And AJ's, too."

Although soldiers began returning to Watsonville, Anton was not among them. Instead a letter, dated before the armistice, arrived.

Dear Ma and Pa,

I have arrived safely in Siberia where it is constantly snowing and cold with temperatures as low as minus thirty degrees. But we have the right provisions, so I'm able to keep warm.

On the way, we stopped at Vladivostok and Tokyo for brief layovers.
I felt right at home among the Japanese people after growing up with
them in town.

We are praying for the war to end so we can return home. It looks like
we will win it which will make all of our sacrifices worthwhile.

Give my regards to all the family and friends.

With all my love,

Anton

"He doesn't mention any illness. I wonder if the flu isn't such a threat in that godforsaken climate?" Jelena said.

Nick shrugged without speaking a word.

Nick picked up Frank and as they drove through town to the cigar shop, they witnessed celebrations everywhere.

Jack had a big smile on his face when they entered and handed them each a Habana. "On the house."

Nick and Frank used the knife on the counter to clip off the end, holding them for Jack to light. After Nick took a long inhale and let it out, he said, "We're calling a meeting tonight at the lodge to determine our next move. Be there."

The back room seemed more like a sewing circle than a poker hall as voices rose, spreading gossip among the group. Nick and Frank pulled up a pair of chairs and tossed their money in the pot. "Deal us in."

After a few lost hands, Nick folded and picked up his remaining cash. "I'll pass the word about the meeting tonight," he said to Frank as he stood. "You do the same when there's a break in play."

Nick and Frank arrived at Odd Fellows Hall early to set up the room. "We need to put out every chair and allow some space along the walls for guys to stand," Nick said. The men also arrived early, looking forward to a chance to celebrate the war victory and the creation of a Jugo-Slav state.

Nick slammed the gavel on the podium several times, calling

the meeting to order. "We have a lot to celebrate today and soon we will welcome our boys back from war—yet an even greater opportunity to celebrate. But we need to plan our next steps to support the Jugo-Slav state. I want to call your attention to a Talk of the Town article that appeared in the *Pajaronian* a few months ago. It discussed the jumble of nationalities that make up Southeastern Europe and their conflicting interests. They claim that Slavdom is divided against itself. And they're not entirely wrong. On that, I'm sure we can all agree, having witnessed it ourselves.

"There is no doubt Vienna, through her clever statecraft, is promoting divisions among us. Dr. Vidmar bore witness to these underhanded dealings when he served in the Austrian diplomatic corps. Consequently, there are Slavs who prefer to be under Austrian rule with more autonomy. Others would like to see Napoleon's Kingdom of Illyria restored. Let's not allow our few differences to divide us. Now is the time to stand together if we want to see our dream of a Jugo-Slav state come true. It's time to get to work."

When Nick got home, Jelena wasn't there but arrived soon afterward. "Where were you?"

"I had a shift at the hospital. But it was like no other. There was so much kissing and hugging that everyone forgot the pandemic for a while."

"Kissing and hugging? I hope you were wearing a mask?"

"We put them on once we had expressed our joy over the armistice."

"Jelena, you can't pick and choose when to protect yourself. A virus is invisible so you won't know when it's lurking nearby, just waiting to strike."

"It was just this one time. We couldn't hold back our happiness after so many depressing days among the dead and dying."

Nick grimaced. Jelena was always a bit headstrong, and he gave up trying to control her years ago.

CHAPTER 50

Jelena picked at her dinner.

"What's the matter? Aren't you hungry? You love seafood risotto."

"For some reason, I have little appetite."

"At least try to pick out a few clams, mussels, and squid. That's where most of the nutrition is."

Jelena combed through the rice with her fork until she found a clam. Nick watched her closely as she put it into her mouth and chewed. After she swallowed, she said, "I can't eat any more. It's not sitting well in my stomach."

"You need to go to bed early and try to sleep off whatever is bothering you."

"I think I will." Jelena stood and carried her plate to the kitchen.

Nick heard her coughing as she cleaned the dish. He jumped out of his chair and bolted in her direction. "How long have you had this cough?"

"I don't know. With the frenzy of the war ending, it's difficult to remember."

Nick held his hand to Jelena's forehead. He shot back, restraining his fear.

"Am I hot?"

"I won't lie. You're running a temperature, according to my touch. I'll call the doctor while you get ready for bed."

Doctors were few and far between with the number of flu cases on the rise. But Dr. Grayson promised to stop by the house as soon as he could. It was the wee hours in the morning before he showed up. By that time, Jelena was sweating profusely. After examining her, the doc stepped into the hallway to speak to Nick. "I'm sorry to tell you she has the classic symptoms of the Spanish flu. If she worsens, she must be moved to the hospital where we can better care for her."

Nick sent a telegram to Lana to alert the family in San Francisco. Without even being asked, Lana took a train to Watsonville, arriving at Jelena's bedside in less than twenty-four hours. "Let me nurse Jelena while you rest," Lana said to Nick. "As a mother, I've nursed sick children through many illnesses which taught me what to do."

Lana stayed by Jelena's bedside with only brief breaks for her own bodily needs. She made sure Jelena took in lots of liquids to keep her hydrated. But by the next day, instead of being better, she was worse. Lana left the room in search of Nick, finding him in the living room with a shot glass in his hand. When she entered the room, she said, "I fear she has pneumonia. Her breathing is ragged, and she's struggling for air."

"I'll track down Dr. Grayson and bring him here right away."

"Check the hospital first. Jelena told me he's there almost constantly."

In less than an hour, Nick returned without the doctor. "He couldn't leave his patients and insisted we take Jelena to the hospital before it's too late."

"I'll get her things together and then prepare her."

As soon as Jelena noticed Lana packing a bag, she said, "I'm not going anywhere."

"The doctor thinks it's best for you to be in the hospital."

"I'm familiar with the hospital. It's nothing more than a holding center for the dying until they're dead."

"You know that's not true. They have the means to better heal you there."

"I don't care. I'm staying right here in my own bed."

Lana didn't want to argue with her. She left the room to recount to Nick what Jelena had said.

"She's going. That's all there is to it. I don't want to have any regrets."

But Jelena's powerful resolve won out.

"We need a real nurse here. Not that you're not doing a fine job, but you require help and relief."

Even though Nick offered to pay top dollar, he could not find a nurse who was available for home duty. They were all busy at the hospital, attending to multiple patients at once. But he found a Croatian woman to lend a hand.

Meantime, Dr. Grayson stopped by from time to time but only shook his head. "She's not improving. Prepare yourself."

The best preparation Nick knew was to call a priest who came right over and performed last rites. Despite the funereal aspect of the sacrament, it seemed to offer temporary solace as Jelena took on an almost beatific glow.

A few days later, Lana ran out of the room and from the top of the stairs shouted, "Nick, come here right now."

He bounded up the steps and one look at Lana's face told him what he feared.

"She needs you now."

Nick took a deep breath as his heart clenched. He entered the room and stood on one side of Jelena's bed while Lana stood on the other. He took Jelena's hand in his and gently stroked it, saying, "I love you so much."

As she struggled for air, Jelena said, "I love you, too. And kiss Anton for me when he returns."

Tears welled up in Nick's eyes, but he tried to hold them back while Jelena continued to gasp and groan and grow weaker.

She spoke again. This time to Lana. "Take care of Nick for me."

Lana and Nick's eyes met as Jelena let out a sigh. Her breath of life surrendered. Then Nick fell onto the bed and cradled Jelena in his arms amid tears and sobs and moans of despair.

Lana moved around the bed and rubbed Nick on his back a few times before stepping out of the room so as not to intrude on their final sacred moment.

After a funeral Mass at St. Patrick's, Jelena was interred at St. Francis Cemetery next to the son she lost years ago. Mourners came to Nick's house afterward, where they ate and drank and tried to comfort him. Once they left, the house felt vacant. Yet everywhere he looked there were signs of Jelena left behind—a shawl flung over a chair, a sewing basket full of mending, a cherished keepsake staring out from the curio cabinet. Memories and reminders of loss.

What will I do without Jelena? She was my life. How am I supposed to live without her? And now the Christmas season is upon us—her favorite time of year and mine, too. This year there will be no tree decorated, no cookies baked, no presents purchased, no reason for joy. Only a wreath hung on the door, bearing a black satin ribbon tied in a bow.

CHAPTER 51

Dr. Vidmar showed up on Nick's doorstep with a pot of white daylilies in his hand, leaving no doubt the reason for his call. "I've been in Washington and just heard the news about your wife. I apologize I couldn't be at the funeral."

"Thanks for coming today. It means a lot to me." Nick took the plant and set it on a table as they took up seats in the living room.

"Someone told me it was the flu that took her."

"She spent a lot of time at the hospital, helping the doctors and nurses. There's no doubt in my mind she contracted the virus there."

"The Spanish flu has been a terrible plague on our world. And I think I mentioned before, it has claimed more soldiers than the war."

"I worry about our son. He has not yet made it home."

"There's still fighting in Siberia. But it will end soon." Vidmar recognized concern on Nick's face, mixed with anguish over the loss of Jelena, and let silence fill the room. Then he changed the subject. "I'm returning to Europe to help with the reconstruction of the Jugo-Slav state."

"What do you plan to do?"

"Try my hand again at the diplomatic corps where my skills can best be used. I'm to serve as a liaison between the new government and the US Agriculture Department. Hoover is heading the task force. That's why I've been in Washington so long. My time's been filled with bureaucrats, blunders, and boondoggles."

"What made you choose to work with the agriculture department?"

"Actually, I read a letter someone had posted in the *Jadran* that was from his nephew on the island of Brac. People are still starving over there. The young man spoke of the lack of food and the high price of goods. The flour America sent over helped bring prices down. As long as there's no bread, there'll be no democratic state. Hoover understands the importance of a full stomach."

"I've received good news from my family. They're all well and optimistic about the new state. My brother Ivan said that people are finally living in harmony."

"It warms my heart to hear that, after all they've been through. We have a lot of work ahead of us. First, we have to help farmers make the most of their land again. With the return of the men, they should have the workers necessary for a good harvest. Then, after we feed the hungry, we need to clothe the naked. Apparently, shoes are nowhere to be found, and clothes so scarce that bodies are forced to go bare."

"All this reminds me to count my blessings. Things could always be worse. Here in this land of plenty, it's easy to forget there are people without the basic necessities to sustain themselves."

"Not so plenty. America will continue Meatless Mondays and Wheatless Wednesdays. In addition, food-saving regulations just went into effect that should help us send more food overseas. The fifteen percent cutback during the war enabled the US to double its food shipments to the Allies."

"What types of cutbacks?"

"Flour but also butter, cheese, and sugar."

"Have you learned how the starving Slav children are doing? Did they get returned to their families?"

"I believe they survived. The priest who spearheaded the effort is running for parliament."

Nick's eyes widened.

"Apparently, he's become a political activist."

Nick drove up to San Francisco for one of his regular dinners with the Babiches. When he arrived at their townhouse, he was greeted by Lana.

"Mama and Papa have taken ill. We can't do a family dinner tonight, but I'm still available if you like."

Nick could barely suppress his glee. "I'd enjoy that. Grab your things and we'll find a place to dine."

The restaurant was a small, cozy cafe in Little Italy. Nick wanted to take Lana somewhere unpretentious that would also have a touch of romance to it. The restaurant was typical, with red and white checkered tablecloths and candles glowing on every table, lighting up scenes of Italy that filled the walls. A flash of Venice crossed his mind, and he banished it. He didn't want old memories to spoil the evening.

Nick and Lana laughed their way through dinner as they shared episodes from their lives. At last, Nick had to attack the elephant in the room. "We've never spoken of that day."

Lana's face grew somber as she stared straight into Nick's eyes. "It's about time, isn't it?"

They were both crying by the time they finished letting out their long-repressed deathbed emotions. "Let's get out of here," Nick said. He took Lana's hand as he led her out of the restaurant. "It's a nice evening—let's walk."

They passed several cafes, and when they came to Washington Park, Nick suggested they sit for a few moments on the nearby bench.

"Do you think it's safe?"

"You're with me, remember."

As they sat down, Nick put his arm around Lana and couldn't resist giving her a sweet kiss on the lips. When he pulled up, he saw Lana looking deeply into his eyes, as if she wanted him to kiss her again, but he refrained. "I hope I wasn't out of line. I didn't mean to offend you."

"Oh, Nick, you could never offend me." She gave him a quick kiss on his cheek to confirm it.

As they got ready to leave, Nick noticed the Church of Saints Peter and Paul standing watch, still under construction after the earthquake that left it in ashes. *And now it's rising again.* They continued walking to Lana's townhouse, where the full moon overhead cast a warm glow.

"Would you like to come in for a nightcap?"

Nick hesitated while their eyes held the moment suspended. "I'd like that." And he followed her in.

CHAPTER 52

A telegram arrived for Nick from Dr. Vidmar, inviting him to dinner before he left for Europe. They met at a restaurant on the wharf in Santa Cruz. The sun had already set, but the sound of waves lapping at the pilings could be heard in the background. After the waiter opened a bottle of wine, Dr. Vidmar handed Nick a letter.

"What is this? I don't know Dr. Michael Pupin."

"Remember, a few years ago, a representative for the Jugo-Slav cause came to Watsonville to speak?"

"Yeah, but his name wasn't Pupin."

"He was sent by Dr. Pupin and the Serbian consul in New York City."

"He's a professor at Columbia University. Correct?"

"Pupin is more than a physics professor. He's a scientist and, among his many inventions, he developed sonar to detect enemy U-boats."

"Anyone who combatted the U-boat threat has my utmost respect." Nick shook his head. "Those German subs were always a worry when we shipped apples overseas."

"He's also an honorary Serbian consul. His diplomatic efforts will interest you. He went to Canada seeking the release of Austrians from internment camps."

"I have to assume he wasn't successful."

"Let's hope his recommendations for boundary lines for Jugo-Slavia are more successful. He spent months at the Paris Peace Conference trying to work them out. President Wilson's disavowal of the London Treaty, which gave Italy parts of Dalmatia, Istria, and a few Adriatic Islands in return for their support of the war effort, should have helped."

"There'll be hell to pay if we don't keep Dalmatia. Guys in this town will be fighting mad."

"The last thing anyone wants to do is trigger another war. Pupin is aware of all that's at stake."

"Do you think he can be trusted?"

"He was cattle herder on the Serbian Frontier in his youth. There's no duplicity in him. He'll do what's right for our people."

Nick read Pupin's letter, which thanked District Attorney George Smith for his support of the Jugo-Slav movement in California.

"Now read this. It's an article that will appear later this week in all the newspapers in the county."

Nick scanned the article. Then he looked up in astonishment. "District Attorney Smith gives our town credit for starting the campaign over a decade ago."

"The plot was hatched when the managing editor of the *Jadran*, F.F. Akacich, lived there. He hadn't founded his paper yet and was just a working man. Perhaps he didn't stand out."

"Now it's coming back to me. There used to be a lot of scuttlebutt around the packinghouses. But at that time, it was just a pipe dream."

"It always starts with a dream."

"And now it's reality."

"Almost. But it will take years before Jugo-Slavia becomes the country it's destined to be. Older people will only witness a bare glimmer. And young people coming of age will miss the opportunity. That's why I want to let you know a bit of information I picked up in Washington. There's talk of establishing an immigration quota."

"Why is that?"

"Let me finish. They intend to use immigration numbers from 1890 before the big wave came in. Does that tell you anything?"

Nick grimaced, clenching his jaw. "They want to keep Eastern Europeans like me out. It's back to Balkan barbarians."

"I'm passing this on not to hurt your feelings but to give you warning to get family and friends out now before the barrier goes up. Like I told you, it will be at least a decade before Jugo-Slavia finds its footing."

When Nick returned home, he stopped by Western Union and shot off a telegram to Ivan about possible quotas and whether relatives or friends wanted to emigrate, especially their sister Ana, who already had children in America.

Then he passed word among Croatians from Cilipi and Cavtat that he would make a trip to Croatia, and anyone who wanted to come back with him was welcome.

CHAPTER 53

The front door flew open and a voice rang out, "I'm home," as a duffel hit the floor. Nick ran out of the kitchen into the hallway and at the sight of Anton's face, he could not suppress his tears and wrapped him in a bear hug to help hide them.

"I wanted to surprise you—not give you a heart attack," Anton said. "Where's Mom? Hasn't she heard all our commotion?"

At his question, Nick clung to Anton even more fiercely as a sharp pain cut through his heart.

"Dad, what's wrong? It's not like you to be so emotional."

Nick released his hold and drew back. As he stared into Anton's face, he said, "She's gone."

"Gone? Where to? When is she coming back?"

"The flu got her."

"No...not Mom." Then he ran into the kitchen and stopped in his tracks, seeing only one set of dishes on the table. He pounded his fist on the oak table. "No, no, no. I've seen so much death...enough to last a lifetime. I thought once I was home, it would all be behind me."

Nick hugged his son again and let him weep for his mother. He knew what it felt like when the heart was pierced, bursting wide open with pain. "Tomorrow we'll go out to the cemetery so you can pay your respects."

They spent most of the day reminiscing, and that night, they went to dinner at Frank's. Helen and her daughters had prepared a festive meal to celebrate Anton's return, and AJ's much earlier. After everyone had a slice of duck on their plate, Frank made a toast to the two soldiers. "You have secured freedom for the world and paved the way for the new Jugo-Slav state."

Everyone raised their glasses and drank to the sentiment expressed.

"I found out what Anton was up to in Siberia. More specifically, Archangel," Nick said. He waited until all eyes were on him. "He was fighting the Red Army. Our war ministers wanted Russia back in the war. They thought if the Reds were defeated, the White Army might jump back in. The Allies needed a distraction on the Eastern Front to move troops away from the West, where they were losing."

"But sadly, it didn't work out that way for our great Slav country," Frank said.

"On another subject, I'm moving ahead with my plans to go to Jugo-Slavia...that word sounds so strange, but it feels good to say it. I want to travel before the cold sets in so I can be home for Christmas."

"Have you heard back from Ivan yet?"

"No. But I'm going anyway, no matter what he says. Besides, some Croatians in town would like me to escort family members over."

"These two boys missed a lot when they were away. I think we should share our part in bringing about the new Slav state."

Nick pulled a letter from his jacket pocket. "This is the letter Professor Pupin sent. I've already shown it to Anton. After you read it, pass it on to AJ and Helen and the girls, too."

Frank pulled out his reading glasses and read the letter. "This does not give enough detail. I think we need to fill it in for our sons so they realize the war efforts on the home front."

"Better yet, let's give them our district attorney's overview that appeared in the *Pajaronian* last December. He covers everything from the causes of the war, the spies in our midst, and the formation of our south Slav state. He gives credit to our little town for starting the movement that ended Austrian domination...imagine that! I clipped the article out of the paper and filed it."

"I saved one, too, that I'll let AJ read. George Smith, who is half Croatian and speaks the language, made an important point that some might have overlooked—Germany was on the verge of taking over the world with trade. Every product on sale before the war was marked *Made in Germany*."

"That's right. They produced such quality items at a fair price that no one, including us, had the incentive to compete. Consequently, our people lack the skills and training."

"It should be a lesson to us to not get too dependent."

"Enough talk of war. These boys want to forget about it and get moving on with their lives. We need to find some nice Croatian girls to introduce them to. Helen, this should be right up your alley."

Anton and AJ looked at each other and rolled their eyes.

Nick had everything in order for his trip but reservations. Frank was an agent for the Cunard line, among others, so he didn't expect a problem. Then a thought struck him. *Why not bring Anton along?*

He found Anton in the living room, looking through an old picture album. When Nick walked into the room, he closed it and covered it with his jacket. But there was no doubt Nick had seen it. "We should go through the pictures together, and I can fill in the missing pieces."

"Later, maybe."

"Now is as good a time as any."

"I just can't right now."

"Your mother will always be part of you. And when you have children of your own, you'll be passing on a bit of her to them. That's the power of family." Anton nodded, but Nick noticed his lips quivering. "Should I leave you alone?"

"No, it's okay." Anton wiped his eyes. "You must want something since you followed me here."

"The timing might not be right, but I need to ask if you'd like to accompany me to Jugo-Slavia?"

"I just got home and had one long ocean voyage."

"That confirms you're seaworthy."

"Maybe so, but I'm also battle weary. This body needs a rest."

"On this trip, you'll be put up in a state-room. We can go overland to New York, where you can take in the sights before departure to Le Havre. We can also make a stopover in Paris and Venice if you like. Or we can skip the overland trip and go straight from San Francisco to Le Havre via the Panama Canal."

"You're tempting me with your carrots."

"That's my intention. What do you say?"

"Let's take the train. I need to see this country that I fought for."

Frank took Nick and Anton to the depot to catch the train to San Francisco, where they would board the transcontinental. "I hate to leave you holding the bag during the height of the season, but I want to get over and back before the cold weather sets in."

Anton chuckled. "You don't know what cold is until you've bivouacked in Siberia."

"Anyway, I want to be back for Christmas and in time to lay a wreath..."

No one said anything for a few moments, not wanting to touch a nerve, until Frank broke the silence. "I think I spotted the train's headlight. Let's get your luggage on the platform."

Nick and Anton grabbed a pair of seats next to the first

window available. "It's a beautiful day for a ride along the coast. I hope it's as beautiful in San Francisco."

When they reached the station, they had a few hours left to squander. "I'll check our luggage with the porter, then we can walk around San Francisco for a while." Nick headed on a direct course toward the Babiches' diner. He had told Lana that he would stop in to say goodbye before departing. She was there waiting tables, just like he found her all those years ago.

"I saved the corner table by the window for you," she said as she gave Nick a warm smile and leaned in to give Anton a hug. "It's good to have you home at last."

"Only Dad didn't give me much time to enjoy it. Now I'm off again."

"This time it's for pleasure. You'll have a great father-son experience."

"My goal is for him to meet the rest of my family and see the country of my birth."

"It should be a real education. Now, it's lunchtime. What can I get you?"

"Any specials today?"

"I think the chef was making seafood risotto. The fish is fresh—right off the boat."

Nick glanced at Anton. "We'll take two. And why don't you join us?"

"Unfortunately, this is our busy time. I'll sit with you when I can but won't eat. Papa's not coming in until later, so it's up to me to run the show."

"Business. It always comes first, doesn't it?"

Lana shot Nick a frown. "It's the way we earn our bread."

Lana knew Nick had a fondness for apple strudel. After lunch was finished, she cut two large pieces, plated them and set them before Nick and Anton.

"You really know how to please a man," Nick said as he watched Lana blush.

After coffee and dessert, Nick excused himself to use the

restroom, which was at the back of the diner. Once he was behind the screen, out of view, he took Lana in his arms and kissed her tenderly. "I'll be back in time for Christmas. Keep me in your thoughts until then."

Anton had been watching passersby and appeared not to notice his father's unusually long trip to the loo. When Nick was back in his seat, Lana presented the check. "I would offer it on the house, but you can afford it."

Nick laughed and leaned in toward Anton. "When I first came to the diner, I could barely afford a coffee."

"You've come a long way, Pa."

"True. But I can't sit on my laurels. There's still much to do, starting with my sister, Ana."

"Have you convinced her to emigrate?" Lana asked.

"Ivan's supposed to be working on that angle."

The transcontinental journey proved to be a remarkable one. Anton kept his eyes glued to the window except for brief periods to eat or sleep. "Every American should take this trip at least once," he said. "Then they'll better understand the treasure they have and the need to protect it."

When they arrived in New York City, Nick hired a carriage to take them to the Holland House Hotel, the same one he and Jelena had stayed in on their honeymoon. He couldn't resist a chance to reminisce, even if it would only be in his memories. "If it's all the same to you, let's dine at the hotel restaurant and call it a night after that. I'm bushed after four days on the train."

In the morning, they got an early start on sightseeing, with Nick playing guide. He first took Anton to the southern tip of Manhattan near Battery Park, where he could get a view of the Statue of Liberty. "This is what most immigrants remember greeting them upon their arrival. I say most because it wasn't here when I arrived. Frank missed it, too."

"What's the building nearby?" Anton asked.

"Ellis Island, the immigration station. I showed up before it was constructed and came through Castle Garden just around the bend."

"It still amazes me what you and other pioneers in our town went through just to get here."

"We were willing to put up with any hardship to set foot on the land of freedom and opportunity."

Once they returned to the hotel, Nick looked at his watch. "We don't have much time until our dinner reservation, so let's hustle." In less than an hour, they had both showered and dressed. "I avoided lunch in Little Italy because we're dining at Barbetta tonight—one of the oldest and best Italian restaurants in the city. It's also nearby the theater." After a classic Italian dinner of pasta, fish, and cannoli, they arrived at the New Amsterdam Theatre with only a few minutes to spare. "The hotel recommended the Ziegfeld Follies. It's supposed to be quite an extravaganza."

As they were filing out, Nick said, "That was some finale, wasn't it?"

"You can say that again."

"Did you have a favorite scene?"

"I have to admit, I got a kick out of 'I Am the Guy Who Guards the Harem.' Irving Berlin has a way with words—music, too."

Nick laughed. "I enjoyed that one as well. But 'Spanish Frolic' put me in the mood to dance the flamenco."

"Thank you for this special evening. I had none of this during the war. Siberia is more wasteland than cultural hot spot."

Nick nodded. "Fortunately, the actors' guild ended its strike in September. Otherwise, we would have missed out on this spectacular evening."

"They struck, too? I've read that strikes have popped up all over the country."

"Between inflation and a flood of workers from returning soldiers, pay is down and money doesn't go as far."

"It's always something, isn't it?"

"That's the law of cause and effect. We got lucky that the harbor strike didn't affect our trip. Things were tense back in January when marine workers struck, holding up the return of troops and supplies to Europe. The president intervened, but if he hadn't, it would have been the housewives. New York City can't survive without daily goods brought in by ship. They live hand-to-mouth, which a little disruption can turn into a tragedy."

CHAPTER 54

The next morning, the SS *Rochambeau* was waiting at the pier to take them and hundreds of other passengers to Le Havre, France. After getting settled in their state-room, Nick said, "This will be home sweet home for the next couple of weeks. Get used to it."

The first few days on the ship passed pleasantly until the morning of October two greeted them with rumors of President Wilson's health. "I have to find a newspaper to learn if the rumors are true," Nick said. When he put his hands on the *New York Daily*, the headline read—"President Wilson Gravely Ill." Nick collapsed in the nearest chair to read the article. Wilson had cancelled his League of Nations tour a few days earlier. "I wonder what this will mean for the peace? Especially Jugo-Slavia."

"Pa, we're a nation of laws. If Wilson is incapacitated, the vice president will take his place and carry on. It doesn't all hinge on one man."

"Sometimes it does, son. In between the lines, personalities rule the world." He thought of Franz Joseph, who died in the middle of the war on November 21, 1916. He had been a part of all the intrigues that led to the conflict. But his successor,

Charles I, had different ideas and tried secretly to negotiate Austria's exit from the war.

A somber mood took over the ship as people continued to speculate over Wilson's ability to handle the office of president. Although not everyone was somber. Some even seemed gleeful. Nick couldn't help speculate on who they were and what they were up to.

Gay Paris was a welcome respite after the atmosphere on the ship. Nick and Anton painted the town red—the Folies Bergère a highlight. They were more than exhausted when they boarded a train at Gare du Nord, but in a few hours, they were in Venice —the City of Love. Nick's heart fluttered as he remembered his last visit. He knew this visit would pale in comparison. "Your mother and I spent part of our honeymoon in Venice. I booked the same hotel for us—Baglioni Hotel Luna. It's a real gem near San Marco Square."

Nick was anxious that Anton learn as much about Venetian history as possible during their stay. "We Croatians were often at war with the Venetians, although they ruled us for a time. In the mid-fourteenth century, we broke away. However, the treaty limited our boats to trade in the Adriatic. We solved that problem by building bigger boats seaworthy in the Mediter- ranean, which allowed us to trade in the Levant and Egypt."

"What a crazy history Croatia has had."

"That's what happens when you're a small state surrounded by big kingdoms. Most of them dominated us—even the Ottoman Turks. Russia was the only one that left us alone— they're a nation of Slavs, too."

The next morning, a water taxi picked up the pair at the hotel dock and ferried them over to the port where they caught a sailboat to Dubrovnik. The winds were favorable on a bright day with scant clouds in the sky, allowing them to sweep through the clear blue waters of the Adriatic at top speed.

At the port of Gruz, they disembarked and grabbed a carriage to Cilipi. When they reached the Old Town, Nick asked the driver to pull over and wait. "I can't pass up Dubrovnik without giving you a chance to see it. We'll have lunch then continue on."

After they passed through the Pile Gate, Nick pointed his finger up and Anton saw St. Blaise sitting in his niche. "Our patron saint." Once inside the city, they took the stairs to the left and walked around the ramparts until they came to the corner overlooking the sea. "There it is, in full view—the Adriatic. It always takes my breath away."

"Mine, too. It must be in the blood."

They continued walking until they came to a set of stairs. "We go down here." The stairs opened to a harbor filled with boats. "There's a little cafe farther on where we can eat and watch the activity." Nick ordered a bottle of white Croatian wine, not even giving the waiter the chance to hand them menus. When he returned, Nick said, "Mussels, Croatian-style. Two orders. And lots of bread."

He turned to his son. "Tell me your first impression and be honest."

"Hands down, this is the best medieval city I've ever visited."

"Out of how many?"

"Venice is the only one. In fact, Dubrovnik reminds me of Venice."

"I hate to admit it, but Italians helped rebuild Dubrovnik after the earthquake. Civic leaders hired their finest craftsmen to create a city that would rival Venice in beauty. Another thing I hate to admit is that Ragusa modeled its form of government on Venice's."

After lunch, Anton lingered. "Don't worry. We'll be back. I haven't brought you this far to only experience a little of the Old Town. There is much more to see. And to prove it, I'll take you to the Fort of St. Lawrence."

When they arrived, Anton stopped in his tracks, casting his eyes upward in awe, the fort towering one hundred twenty-one feet above him. "This is one magnificent stone structure."

"We consider it Dubrovnik's Gibraltar. Let me recount its fabled beginning." And he shared the lore. "Now that you've heard the story, what do you think?"

"It makes me proud to be a Croatian."

"Let's climb the stairs and look inside." When they reached the entrance, Nick pointed to the inscription over the gate —*Freedom is not sold for all the gold in the world.* "Those are words imprinted on every Croatian's heart."

"And you and all the Croatians in town, as well as California and elsewhere, have helped bring about freedom once again for your country."

"Remember, it all still hinges on Wilson's Fourteen Points."

The driver woke up when they jumped back into the buggy. Startled, he gave the horses a kick as he yawned and tried to regain his presence.

Nick looked at his watch and shouted, "Let's pick it up. We don't want to miss dinner."

The driver nodded and shook the reins. That's all it took for the horses to move into a fast trot.

When they reached the Church of St. Nicola, Nick told the driver to halt. "I have to pay respects to my mother first. Do you want to come along?"

"Next time. You should have your own private time first."

There were so many Markoviches in the graveyard it took longer than expected to find the grave. When he did, the finality of it overwhelmed him and he let out a primal cry. On the way back to the carriage, he wiped his face and choked back tears. He wept not only for his mother, but Jelena, too. The two most important women in his life—gone forever.

The driver stopped at Nick's father's house, where the old man was waiting. He still had a full head of hair, but it had gone white. And he used a cane for support. Anton senior did not speak English, but Anton junior knew a few words of Croatian, which helped them communicate. Nick helped his father into the buggy and they continued on to Ana's house. After assisting his grandfather's dismount, Anton grabbed their luggage while Nick took care of the driver, who did a double take at the tip and smiled. "Americans."

Ivan opened the door, shocking Nick into silence as he regarded his brother's appearance—haggard and bone-thin. Time had taken its toll. But his handshake was still firm and his voice strong as he welcomed them.

Ana and Petra bounded out of the kitchen with outstretched arms. Nick hugged Ana first, who felt frail to the touch. Her face had aged, displaying fine wrinkles and faded blue eyes. Her hair, once honey blonde, had gone white. After he hugged Petra, Nick shot a glance at Anton who appeared overwhelmed by all the displays of affection.

Ana led them to a twin-bedded room so they could get settled before dinner. Then they heard more commotion and realized Ivan's children and their families as well as Ana's must have arrived. When they showed their faces, they were again besieged with hugs and kisses. Ana spoke to Nick in Croatian, and he translated for Anton. "They're only here to say hello but will join us tomorrow at the restaurant where there will be plenty of room for the party."

"Party?"

"It's always a party when a group of Croatians get together."

After the extended family left, Nick spoke to Ivan while the women were still in the kitchen. "Has Ana decided yet if she'll emigrate?"

"Not yet. But life is hard for her now since she lost her husband in the war. Besides, some of her children are over there. She wouldn't be too lonely."

"We have to convince her."

"I'll try my best. But you may remember how stubborn she can be."

Nick knew about stubborn.

Ana and Petra had prepared a feast for Nick and Anton's welcome dinner. It started with a hearty vegetable soup made with root vegetables and ended with a plum tart. Fish filled the courses in between because meat was scarce. "You'll have roast pig tomorrow at the restaurant, so we thought you'd appreciate fresh fish from the Adriatic tonight."

"I do," Anton said in the best Croatian he could manage.

Nick beamed with pride. "You know I've always loved fish."

"Tomorrow, we must show Anton around so he can learn about his ancestral home which, God willing, shall always be here for him," Ivan said.

"That sounds like a plan. We stopped by the Old Town on our way here, but he needs more time to explore."

"And see all the other sights. The Old Town is just one jewel in the Crown, even if it is the best one."

"I also want to visit some families here to determine who is coming back with me and get their paperwork underway. In a couple of days, I plan to make a trip to Belgrade to verify what's needed."

"How long do you plan to stay?"

"A couple weeks at most. I hope to be home in time for Christmas."

"Some people may be reluctant to leave before then—you know how tied we are to our traditions."

"They can always come later. But if they want someone to guide them, they must go on my schedule."

Ana had left the table and returned with a bottle of slivovitz and shot glasses. After pouring, she and Petra cleared the dishes and spent the next couple of hours in the kitchen while the men talked and drank.

"So," Nick said, "the war took its toll."

"We'll recover. We always do."

CHAPTER 55

Nick had ten families to contact in Cilipi and Cavtat. He borrowed a horse from Ivan and rode it from house to house while Anton explored the town. It had been years since he had been in a saddle, but some things were never forgotten. Although more than once he wished he had his Studebaker for cruising around. But the horse proved faster than walking and always got him to his destination, even if the road was unpaved.

By lunchtime, he had met with four families on the list to determine who planned to emigrate and what paperwork they already had for it. Most of them didn't even have a birth certificate. But they could get a document from the priest at St. Nicola, the only Catholic church in town, the one their families belonged to for generations.

After several hours in the saddle, Nick returned to his sister's home with saddle sores and bow legs. The party was tonight, but he didn't feel up to it.

Nick hobbled into the restaurant on Anton's arm while his relatives watched, stunned. "I was in a saddle all day and am not used to it. I drive an automobile at home." Laughter broke out as heads nodded in understanding.

Nick's father was seated at the head of the table—the seats

on either side of him reserved for Nick and Anton. The waiters opened the champagne and filled the glasses while others plated appetizers of fried fish, olives, and bruschetta with tomatoes and sardines. Ivan was about to make the toast when Anton senior struggled to stand. Nick quickly moved in to give him his arm to steady himself.

He spoke in Croatian. "Our family has stayed strong because we have transplanted ourselves, growing in new ways on fresh soil. Croatians have been doing this for generations and we have flourished. Nikola left many years ago but has not forgotten us. He gave some of us new lives in America. And he is here again to do the same for those who wish to emigrate. But while some leave, others will stay and rebuild. And we are grateful to Nikola, Francis, and their friends for helping us win our own country back again at long last. Freedom will reign once more not only in our hearts but in our lives."

"Gee, Dad. I hope you can say the same about me one day."

Tears ran down Nick's face as he wiped his nose on his sleeve. "I have no doubt you will exceed my accomplishments. Indeed, you already have. I never went to college. I never was a soldier. I never fought Reds in a hellhole like Siberia."

The next morning, Ivan had the carriage hitched with two horses. "This will be faster. Cavtat would be a half day's journey on horseback."

Nick winced at his words and rubbed his backside—it was still sore.

"Did you speak with Ana yet?"

"I'll find time today and get my wife to help me. Two are often better at convincing than one."

Ivan is a slyer dog than I gave him credit for. Maybe he learned new tricks in the army, trying to outsmart the Austrian overlords.

Once he returned, Nick said to Anton, "I told the families in Cavtat to meet me after church on Sunday with their paperwork.

I intend to pass the word to the Cilipi families as well. My body can't take much more riding on these rough roads."

After Mass, Nick waited on a corner of the square for the families to find him. In short order, he was surrounded by future immigrants, each vying for a spot in line. He took down a list of names and the paperwork they presented or still needed. There were close to twenty who applied to travel with him, but Nick knew that number would dwindle in half by departure time, which was drawing near.

Dr. Vidmar offered to help expedite the paperwork, and he came to Dubrovnik for a meeting. They arranged a dinner at a restaurant in the Old Town, overlooking the Adriatic. Nick brought Anton along.

"I was hoping to meet you in Belgrade. I've never been to the White City."

"My advice is to wait until its rebuilt."

"That probably won't happen within my lifetime."

"The city's been destroyed over forty times during more than one hundred wars. They've learned to build fast in Belgrade."

Before Nick could reply, the waiter interrupted them with the wine list. "Champagne or white wine to start?" Nick asked.

"We diplomat types have learned to stick with champagne. It's more dependable."

The waiter returned with a bottle of Moet and Chandon Brut, and filled the fluted glasses. "To world peace and prosperity," Nick said.

"Without prosperity, there'll be no peace. If the people's bellies aren't filled, the communists will take over. And then we'll be back at it."

Nick and Anton stole a glance.

The waiter briefly interrupted again while he set a plate of caviar on the table. "I thought I'd splurge," Nick said.

"There's nothing better. A good dry champagne enhances caviar's briny taste. A match made in heaven."

"Anton, we better enjoy this while we can. That blasted Volstead Act may go into effect soon."

"No more champagne?"

"No more alcohol, period."

"Don't look so glum," Vidmar said. "Americans will figure a way around it. But you have worse problems on the horizon."

"What could be worse?"

"The Red Scare."

"You mean Bolsheviks?" Anton asked.

"That's right. It's the real reason Wilson sent troops up to Siberia."

"And I was one of them."

"Your father told me. Later, you can give me an eyewitness account to circulate among my coterie of colleagues. They're still fighting up there, you know."

"They didn't tell us much, and we saw even less. Our commander, General Graves, walked a tightrope, trying to avoid an international incident."

"So far, he's kept the lid on. I hope he has a watchful eye on the Japanese, too. They were supposed to bring seven thousand troops but showed up with over seventy thousand. They could make off with territory like bandits."

"They told us our mission was to safeguard munitions in Vladivostok and help the Czechs get to the Western Front."

"That was the official line. But truth be told, the Allies wanted Germany to be concerned about its Eastern Front as well, so it would dedicate some troops there. At the time, the Allies were losing in the West."

After a dinner of grilled sardines accompanied by Swiss chard and parsleyed potatoes, talk finally got around to immigration procedures. A bottle of slivovitz sat at the center of the table while they sipped the plum brandy.

"I can help expedite the paperwork. But I won't be here much longer because I have to get back to Belgrade."

"What do you need from each person?"

"Verification of birth, photo, and reason for immigration."

"I'll be meeting the people on Sunday and bring you what I have. Where are you staying?"

"A little apartment on the Stradun. Our department keeps one since we're in and out of Dubrovnik often. It's not fancy, but the location can't be beat."

On Sunday, Nick collected the paperwork from prospective immigrants after Mass. When he got back to the house, Ana was fixing lunch. He stepped into the kitchen and waited for her to notice him. "Have you made up your mind?"

She didn't answer. Instead, she left the room and returned with an envelope, handing it to him.

Nick opened it and glanced inside. Then he gave her a hug. "You won't regret your decision."

The next day, Nick left a note for Dr. Vidmar at the apartment and sat down at the restaurant to wait.

Nearly an hour later, Dr. Vidmar appeared. "Not here. Follow me."

"Are you still worried about spies?"

"Always. You thought I was obsessed during the war. But I can now reveal your district attorney uncovered a nest of spies in Santa Cruz. Unfortunately, the Imperial one escaped to Mexico. I suspect he's back in Vienna by now, plotting their next move."

"Next move?"

"There's always another move on the great chessboard of politics."

They entered a building near the Church of St. Blaise and took the stairs down to the basement. Dr. Vidmar unlocked the door, revealing a government office. "Please make yourself comfortable."

Nick took a seat on a hard, wooden chair where he could watch Dr. Vidmar work at a war surplus desk, begging for a paint job.

He quickly scanned through the documents and counted the number of passports needed. "Your sister elected to emigrate."

CHAPTER 56

Departure day finally arrived. Nick and Anton waited with Ana while the group gathered. The immigrants numbered fourteen. Nick handed everyone a passport and a ticket for the sailboat to Venice. Once they disembarked, Nick did not let anyone dawdle except to say a quick prayer before Basilica di San Marco. Then he hurried them onto the train where he purchased tickets through to Le Havre. When they finally arrived at the SS *Rochambeau*, Nick handed everyone a ticket for steerage except Ana. She would travel first class with them.

The voyage was uneventful except for a couple of rough spots in the middle of the Atlantic. When they sailed into New York Harbor, Nick could hear the cheers from the decks below as the immigrants got their first glimpse of Lady Liberty. Since Ana was a first-class passenger, officials did her required medical checks at the ship's infirmary. It didn't take long because very few new immigrants traveled in luxury. The ship pulled up to the dock to let off the first- and second-class passengers. Then it went onto Ellis Island where the steerage passengers would have to wait for the green light.

As the trio lingered, snowflakes danced in the air, a reminder that the Christmas season had arrived. Nick worried until all thirteen cleared Ellis Island—he didn't want to leave anyone behind. But luck was with him. The entire group passed their tests and entered America. Nick looked at his pocket watch. There was no time for hugs and kisses. They barely had a minute to spare to catch the Jersey City ferry for the transcontinental. He did a quick head count as each member of his group boarded the ferry. He hadn't lost one yet.

When they reached the train station, Nick ran to the ticket office to purchase tickets. Then they made a beeline through the station to the train. Nick found a third-class car that still had seats and ushered everyone aboard. He had forgotten how uncomfortable these cars could be, but he wanted to stay with the group.

As hard as he tried, Nick could not suppress the memories that flashed through his mind. The first time he rode in one of these boxcars, his life lay ahead, filled with hopes and dreams but also doubts and fears. Yet, fate had played her part through a chance encounter with Pero Loreto, which led to his first apple job at the San Francisco fruit exchange where he met Karlo Rajkovich. After that, his life's course had been set in motion. But now, most of his years lay behind him. He couldn't complain because they had been good ones. Yet, God willing, he would have more years of life until the last grain of sand left the hourglass. Again, he was filled with hopes and dreams as well as doubts and fears. Nick banished his negative thoughts as the nuns had taught him to do by meditating on the Word of God. *Be not afraid.*

When the train reached San Francisco, Nick led the bedraggled immigrants out of the car and Anton picked up the rear. He hustled them over to the local track, the train set for departure. Once aboard, Nick breathed a sigh of relief. *Almost home.* And when they arrived, he muttered under his breath, *mission accom-*

plished. Families were waiting for their loved ones to take them home.

Frank, always dependable, was there, too. "Welcome to America," he said as he kissed Ana on both cheeks. She managed a weak smile as her eyes twinkled with love.

Frank helped Nick and Anton settle Ana before he departed. "Don't forget dinner tonight. Seven o'clock. Helen has prepared a feast and Ana's children will be joining us."

While Ana was napping, Nick slipped out to send a telegram to Lana to wish her a happy Christmas with her children and grandchildren. He also reminded her of her promise to come celebrate New Year's with him and his family. Then he went by the Morning Star Restaurant to reserve the entire place for the celebration.

Franz Joseph's look-alike took the reservation. "I will be in full regalia for the occasion."

"Just make sure you have a Croatian band booked for the evening, complete with tamburica."

Having finished his most important errands, Nick returned home to get ready for the evening. Helen had outdone herself for Ana's homecoming—leg of lamb surrounded by a variety of root vegetables the centerpiece. "I told you, didn't I," said Frank. "Helen has been planning all week for this meal."

Helen smiled, basking in the praise. "And don't forget you're invited for Feast of the Fishes on Christmas Eve."

Frank smacked his forehead. "I almost forgot. On Christmas Eve, just before sunset, the town will be having a celebration for all the children at the plaza, with its first town Christmas tree. Rumor has it St. Nick might even show up." He gave his brother a wink.

Christmas Eve arrived a few days later. After breakfast, Nick headed downtown to do some shopping, as was his custom. He wanted to buy something special for Ana's first American Christ-

mas. *Jewelry. Women always love jewelry.* Jelena had taught him
that. He made haste for Kramer's jewelers, which was already
crowded with men doing their last-minute shopping.

The wait would give him time to look around before making
a decision. Cuff links popped into view. *Anton needs a pair of gold
ones for his dress shirts.* Then he hesitated, remembering his
wedding night. *He'll have to learn the hard way, like I did.* He made a
mental note to buy a pair. *But what for Ana? Older women often
wear brooches.* He found the case containing a variety of them. An
American flag—too patriotic. A red rose—too sentimental. A
peacock—too flashy. At last, his eye was drawn to the case with
pendants. A simple capital *A* in script beckoned him. *A for Ana.
A for America. A for apple.* He stopped there, reaching three—a
trinity.

When it was finally Nick's turn, it didn't take the clerk long
to bring out his choices for closer inspection. "We can engrave
the cuff links after the holidays."

As Nick waited for the clerk to wrap up the gifts, a bauble
caught his eye. When the clerk handed Nick his presents, he
said, "I'll take that, too."

"You have exquisite taste. Let me get the—"

"Just wrap it up."

"Are you sure you don't want to examine it first? It is quite
costly."

Nick pulled a wad of bills out of his wallet. "I can pay cash."

The clerk wasted no time retrieving the item and wrapping it
in silver foil paper, placing a white satin bow on top. He
presented it to Nick for him to add to his bag. Nick took a long
look at the small, beautifully wrapped package, remembering the
old adage that the best gifts come in small packages. *Lana will
love this.*

That afternoon, when the townsfolk gathered at the plaza,
Nick surveyed the crowd. The Croatian colony had come out in
force and as he scanned each face, he could put a name to it
because most of them were relatives of one sort or another. In

less than forty years, the colony had grown from a handful of single men to dozens of families, with hundreds of members. And he was one of its patriarchs.

He wished Jelena had lived to see this. But Anton was here, and Frank and Gabe and Luka and Marija and Dora and their families, and now Ana as well. Their clan had been transplanted, and because of that, the Markoviches would survive. And those in America would most likely thrive like him. But what about the clan in the new Jugo-Slavia?

A tear trickled down Nick's cheek as the sweet voices of children sang "Silent Night." *The world is calm. The future is bright. The new year will be a fresh start for the Slav nation and its people. I wonder what the tamburica will say when she sees me again. Will she be impressed that I did more than carry Croatia with me—that I helped set my fatherland free.*

AUTHOR BIO

Barbara Anne King is the author of two historical fictional novels—*The Apple King* and *The California Immigrant*, which take place in her hometown.

Barbara was born and raised in Watsonville, California, a third-generation Croatian-American whose great, great uncles were pioneers in the town's apple industry. She holds a BA degree in political science from the University of California, Los Angeles, and is a proud member of the Slavic American Cultural Association (SACO) and Native Daughters of the Golden West.

Barbara lives in a New York City suburb with her husband in the place they've called home for over 25 years.

ACKNOWLEDGMENTS

I'd like to thank the following sources for their help and information which brought this story to life.

Blossoms into Gold by Donna F. Mekis and Kathryn Mekis Miller
Jean Johnson, first reader and reviewer
The Slav Community of Watsonville, California edited by Thomas Ninkovich
The Inside Story of Austro-German Intrigue by Josef Goricar
UCSC Regional History Project, Agricultural History Santa Cruz County
Watsonville Memories that Linger, Volumes 1 & 2, by Betty Lewis

BOOK CLUB QUESTIONS

—Xenophobia and bullying are themes woven through this novel. How do they resonant in today's political climate?

—Did your opinion of Nick change when he stole the wallet of the deceased train passenger? Did it reveal more of his character? Did it add to the story?

—Croatians in Watsonville created a world-class apple industry. What were the reasons for their success?

—Many felt Croats were clannish. Did it help them succeed? Have other nationalities practiced this?

—Immigrants still come to America from desperate situations. Do you think it is any easier for them to succeed?

—The female characters have the traditional roles of the period, but the author represents their strength of character in many ways. Discuss.

—The daring rescue of Nick's brothers was an interesting turn of events. Did this episode add a new facet to Nick's character?

—We're in a pandemic. Are there similar issues to the Spanish Flu? What can we learn from a pandemic that occurred a century ago?

—Setbacks in our lives can lead to innovation and improvements. How is this evidenced in Nick's life and business ventures?

—Croatians remained strong ties to the Fatherland and were in a position to help it achieve freedom. Do you think other immigrants here do the same?

—Croatians wanted freedom from Austria. Did they get it with the new Jugo-Slavia?

—Today Croatia is an independent country. Discuss what occurred before that was achieved.

—What are *The Apple King's* themes?

—A major theme of the book is freedom. Why do people risk everything for it?

—What are *The Apple King's* major takeaways?

Made in the USA
Las Vegas, NV
28 June 2021